Carol Marinelli recentl[y] ... for her job title. Thrilled ... her answer, she put 'wri[ting'] ... Carol did for relaxation and she put down the truth: 'writing'. The third question asked for her hobbies. Well, not wanting to look obsessed, she crossed her fingers and answered 'swimming'— but, given that the chlorine in the pool does terrible things to her highlights, I'm sure you can guess the real answer!

Karin Baine lives in Northern Ireland with her husband, two sons and her out-of-control notebook collection. Her mother and her grandmother's vast collection of books inspired her love of reading and her dream of becoming a Mills & Boon author. Now she can tell people she has a *proper* job! You can follow Karin on X, @karinbaine1, or visit her website for the latest news—karinbaine.com.

HOT NIGHTS WITH THE PARAMEDIC

CAROL MARINELLI

A NURSE, A PUP, A SECOND CHANCE

KARIN BAINE

MILLS & BOON

First published in Great Britain 2025
by Mills & Boon, an imprint of HarperCollins*Publishers* Ltd,
1 London Bridge Street, London, SE1 9GF

www.harpercollins.co.uk

HarperCollins*Publishers* Macken House, 39/40 Mayor Street Upper,
Dublin 1, D01 C9W8, Ireland

ISBN: 978-0-263-32527-0

12/25

MIX
Paper | Supporting
responsible forestry
FSC
www.fsc.org
FSC™ C007454

This book contains FSC™ certified paper
and other controlled sources to ensure responsible forest management.

For more information visit www.harpercollins.co.uk/green.

Printed and Bound in the UK using 100% Renewable Electricity
at CPI Group (UK) Ltd, Croydon, CR0 4YY

HOT NIGHTS WITH THE PARAMEDIC

CAROL MARINELLI

MILLS & BOON

For Lucinda

With love always

xxxx

CHAPTER ONE

'I WISH YOU'D bought some of that sunshine with you.' Vicky sighed as she drove the ambulance through the streets of a rainy North London afternoon. 'How do you afford all those holidays?'

'I save for them,' Luke said, then added, 'and I don't have a partner or kids to budget for.'

'True.'

'So I can wait for last-minute offers to come up and take advantage of them.'

'Michael and I want to get away…' Vicky sighed. 'Mum and Dad have promised to have the kids. Just for a weekend.'

'Can you go midweek?' Luke suggested. 'You'll save a lot'

It was the type of chatter that was common between paramedics. Long, long shifts, sometimes involving a lot of standing around and patiently waiting, other times intense situations where you relied on each other to have your back. Luke, though he could make small talk with anyone, was a private person. Vicky, on the other hand, never stopped…

'I don't get how you've got a tan,' Vicky grumbled. 'You were only there for three days, yet it looks as if you've been sunning yourself for a month. Spanish skin?'

'Argentinian.'

'Oh yes…'

They were headed back to the station, Luke happy with

silence as he caught up on some paperwork, but Vicky had more questions. 'Did you go with anyone?'

'No, just me.'

'But I thought you were seeing…' She pulled a face, trying to recall the name of his latest, but Luke didn't enlighten her. More to the point he wasn't seeing anyone right now. Vicky only knew who or when he was dating because she sometimes overheard him on the phone during their breaks—he tried not to bring his love-life, or rather his sex life to work. 'Oh, what was her name?' Vicky tutted in frustration, as if trying to recall what other films an actress on her screen had been in.

Luke chose not to enlighten her. 'You need to get with the times, Vicky.'

'Oh, you mean she's history now?' Vicky shook her head ruefully then glanced over. 'You don't put those good looks to waste, do you?'

Luke offered no comment.

'You know I'm grateful for my uncomplicated love-life—married, two children…'

That sounded complicated to Luke. He couldn't imagine devoting the rest of his life to any one woman, let alone having kids.

'And what's the fun of going on holiday on your own?'

'Why would I take someone with me, when I'm taking a break, trying to kick back.'

'But all that time on your own…'

His silence must have been telling, because Vicky laughed. 'I have no idea, do I?'

They had been on since seven this morning and would be working through to seven this evening—or when their final job ended.

Vicky was driving and Luke was treating—not because he was most senior—he was in fact Vicky's mentor, more because the shifts were long and treating tiring, so to stay fresh and on top of things they took it in turns. On this cold afternoon it was Luke's turn to treat.

Unless there was a birth.

Vicky was desperate to deliver a baby, and Luke had agreed that if a birth arose then it would be hers.

With him assisting.

Or stepping in.

Vicky must have read his mind because she briefly turned. 'Are you looking forward to tomorrow?'

'I guess,' Luke said—they had a professional development day on the maternity unit at The Primary, a hospital in North London. 'I'd rather be on the road, but a day on maternity should be interesting...' He thought for a moment. 'Helpful.'

'Helpful?' she checked. 'But you've delivered lots of babies.'

'I've delivered a few, though I'm not very up on the antenatal side,' Luke admitted. 'And I'm certainly not good at midwife speak.'

'Meaning?'

'You know—' His deep, rather steady voice took on a rare eager tone. '"Good job! You're amazing. You've got this..."'

'No,' Vicky laughed, 'I can't imagine you being Mr...' She paused. 'Mr Midwife.'

He glanced at the monitor, which was giving them information about a new job.

'Fifty-four-year-old, unable to get out of bed,' Luke relayed. 'Seen by paramedics two days ago, discharged from Barnet last week. Multiple admissions...'

Then the address dropped down and the patient lived in Crouch End. As did Luke.

'Might be one of your neighbours.' Vicky smiled as they inched through the traffic. Even allowing for the schools getting out and rush hour starting, the roads were ridiculously congested. 'God, this weather's filthy,' she added as the sky darkened.

The wipers were working overtime as the rain intensified—people were scattering, running for bus shelters and doorways. There was a loud clap of thunder and the blackening sky lit up.

Both knew the board at the ambulance control room would be lighting up too with all the incidents a sudden storm can bring.

Then another job came down.

Priority 1.

The radio relayed more information. 'Multivehicle collision, on A406…' or the North Circular—a ring-road that connected various London suburbs.

The police were the first on scene and had reported fatalities as well as multiple injuries…

Luke knew the area well—not only was his flat and ambulance station close by, but on an even more personal note, as the precise location came through, it was the same junction where ten years ago his parents had died.

He'd been to several accidents at that very spot, and if he chose to let it affect him, he'd have worked elsewhere. Even colleagues, who knew he'd lost his parents in a car crash had no idea as to the location.

Luke never gave out specifics.

He wasn't close enough to anyone.

Luke radioed back, accepting the job, but even with lights and sirens blazing the progress was slow.

'The traffic lights are down.' Vicky's voice was a touch alarmed as they approached a junction. 'Nobody's moving…'

'They will.' Luke, who was more than used to this, was calm. The traffic lights were flashing orange, and confused drivers were attempting to clear a path. As they inched forward on a crossroads, he made sure they'd been seen. 'Clear left,' he said, and they made it through.

The blue lights of their vehicle were shining in shop windows and reflecting off the wet streets, but finally they were on the gridlocked ring-road and being waved through by other emergency services.

'This is bad,' Vicky said, and Luke could hear the slight shake in her voice and knew that, though Vicky had worked on several major traumas, this was her first major incident with multiple patients involved. They were also one of the first crews on scene and, for now at least, they had minimal backup.

'Cheng's here.' Luke was relieved to see a station manager was already on scene and he came over as they were unloading their equipment onto the stretcher.

'Can't get the helicopter here,' Cheng shouted in the wind, 'but we've got a trauma team arriving from Barnet and one from The Primary…' He carried on allocating the personnel that had arrived. 'Vicky, go and assist with the minibus. Rory's in charge there. Take the stretcher and equipment.'

'You've got this,' Luke told her, but she looked a little pale and unconvinced. 'Vicky,' he said, 'I know you've got this.'

She nodded, but there was no real time for pep talks. Cheng was calling his name and signalling for him to follow.

There seemed to be two major sites—there was a minibus upturned on the slip road entrance, and on the carriageway there was a van facing the wrong direction with several cars piled into its front. 'We've got a driver trapped in the first car I want you to treat—hit head-on and then rear-ended. Female, late twenties, GCS 15, obs within the flags…' Luke took in all the information as he swiftly made his way over. A glance over his shoulder showed him that Vicky was dealing with a small child lying seriously injured on the road. From the poor angle of her body Luke guessed she'd been thrown from the vehicle, and he wondered why he was being sent to a patient who sounded relatively stable…

'She's thirty-three weeks pregnant.'

That was why.

'Pinned by steering wheel, we've got a cervical collar on,'

Cheng elaborated, 'but apart from that there's not much access. Karen's treating for now, but I want you to take over and for her to assist.'

Karen was new, just a few days out of training. While he'd prefer Vicky, with whom, though relatively new herself, Luke knew he worked well, the leader had made the decisions.

The weather event and blocked access meant there were fewer emergency staff than ideal, though the sirens in the distance heralded their desperate approach. And while usually an air ambulance would be on its way, the storm made it too treacherous.

All this he took in as he made his way to his patient, carrying his emergency satchel, assessing and fine-tuning the plans he'd been making since the job had come down.

'Hey, Karen.' He greeted the junior paramedic who was holding a bag of IV fluids. 'How is she doing?'

'Conscious...' She relayed the obs she'd been able to access—her blood pressure was on the low side of normal and her pulse was a touch raised, and her sats were in the mid-nineties. 'She's pinned by the steering wheel though. She can feel her legs,' Karen said. 'I've just got a line into her right arm, but I could only get a small one in. Her veins are difficult.'

'At least you got some access.' Luke nodded appreciatively. A trapped trauma patient needed two large lines, but at least for now there was some access.

'What's her name?'

'Jasmine.'

The vehicle was concertinaed—crushed between the minibus and several cars that had impacted from behind. Luke had one more question before he got started. 'Was there anybody else in the vehicle?'

'No.'

Lowering his head he looked in to see a blonde lady with an ashen complexion, the collar forcing her to stare ahead as he greeted her. 'Hi, Jasmine.' Her pale blue eyes were open and her teeth frantically chattering. 'I'm Luke, a paramedic. We're going to have you out of here as soon as we can.'

'I can't feel my baby move. It kicked for a moment but...'

'Jasmine,' he interrupted, 'before I take a look at you, I need you to answer a question for me. It's very important.' He glanced to the crushed rear of the car, his eyes raking the wreckage for a child seat. 'Was there anybody else in the vehicle?' Even though Karen had told him no, Luke wanted to make certain for himself.

'Just me...' Jasmine confirmed. 'The van came from nowhere... I couldn't avoid him.'

And while the airbags had been deployed and done their job, she'd then been rear-ended.

Jasmine's colour was pale, her lips a little white, and he was deeply concerned that there were some serious internal injuries.

'Her sats are 92 percent,' Karen informed him.

They had dropped lower, and that was concerning.

'Can you take a couple of deep breaths for me, Jasmine.'

'I can't. It hurts...'

'Try,' Luke said, and she did try, but the steering wheel simply didn't allow for much chest movement.

'Put some nasal prongs on her, and keep an eye on her obs for me.' Luke told Karen the drugs he wanted readied. 'And have another bag of fluids ready to go. I'm going to see if the firefighters can open up the passenger door so that I can get inside.'

He looked out at the busy scene and waved to one of the firefighters who were preparing to cut the roof of the car off. 'Any chance you can get me in the passenger side?'

'I've got someone coming to take the door off now.' The firefighter nodded. 'There's not going to be much room though.'

'I know.'

The car was seriously damaged, but the firefighters were

on to it and worked quickly. Soon, the passenger door, or what was left of it, was being peeled off and Luke attempted to fold his large six-foot-two frame into the crushed car.

'Hey.'

It was quieter in here—he still needed to speak loudly to be heard, but they could certainly talk and he could also secure the nasal prongs Karen had applied a little better around her left ear.

'Take some breaths of the oxygen,' Luke told her as he did a rapid assessment. Her airway was clear, her breathing made difficult due to the steering wheel, but there was some dark bruising on the top of her chest that boded chest injuries. There was no visible bleeding he could see, and beneath the deflated airbag he could see her pregnant stomach. 'Can you feel your legs?'

'Yes,' she said. 'Just not the baby.'

'Are you having any contractions?'

'No.'

'Do you know if your waters have broken?'

'I'm not sure… I think I wet myself when the accident happened.'

She was very stoic and factual and also, Luke guessed, petrified. Some people sobbed or screamed, and some went very quiet. 'Do you have any pains in your stomach?'

'Just my chest.'

'Okay. Jasmine, I'm going to put another needle in your arm, so we can give you some fluids and medicine before we move you.'

A firefighter peered in. 'We'll be starting soon, just need a couple more guys.'

'I want to get more fluids in her,' Luke said, because there was such a thing as 'death by rescue.' Freeing an entrapped patient with a possible crush injury was precarious and he wanted to get her as stable as possible first. He ran through crystalloids, her sats had moved up to 95 percent and her blood pressure remained normal, though he knew that in advanced pregnancy, with the increased blood volume, that finding could be deceptive.

'I'm going to give you something for the pain.'

'Will it hurt the baby?'

'No, it's to help with your pain and so that you can take deeper breaths.'

'But is the baby okay?'

The question Jasmine had been asking since he'd climbed into the wreckage of her vehicle, but the answer Luke didn't know. 'Take some nice breaths of the oxygen,' he said, deflecting the question and administering the pain medication. He knew the guidelines, but even so, checked them with Karen and hoped they would take away some of her pain and anxiety as they moved her. 'They're just dealing with another vehicle, then it's your turn...'

'I'm wearing white trousers,' Jasmine said. 'It's going to show if I've wet myself.'

'Serves you right for wearing white,' Luke lightly teased, pleased that she gave a little smile and that they were building a rapport. He leant over a little and saw Vicky was back to assist and asked her to bring around a blanket. 'I'll make sure you're covered,' he reassured Jasmine. 'No one will see.'

Only that wasn't really what was troubling her. 'Why isn't the baby moving? I felt it just after the accident, it *really* moved, but since then, nothing.'

'Jasmine,' he said, 'let me take care of you for now. Breathe. That's important for your baby. Big breath in through your nose...' He kept talking, letting her talk, just doing what he could to be there for her through this.

'The police said they're contacting my husband.'

'That's good.' He'd already found out that this was her first pregnancy. 'Is he excited to be a dad?'

'Very. Do you have children?'

It was a very frequent question in his line of work and he gave his usual response. 'I don't.' However, given the circumstances, he did elaborate more than he usually would. 'I'm going to be an uncle soon.'

'First time?'

'Yep.' As Vicky leant in and passed him a blanket and some more supplies, he had a brief word. 'Send some photos of the vehicle to the receiving hospital, try and get the cabin intrusion…' As Vicky leant over him with her iPad to capture the shots, he carried on talking. 'Kelly, my brother's girlfriend, is due in a couple of weeks.'

'Are you excited?'

'I am,' Luke said, deciding Jasmine didn't need to know he'd been less than thrilled by the news.

'Is your brother excited?'

'He can't wait.' Luke gave a wry laugh. 'We're pretty close.'

'Luke raised them,' Vicky said, uninvited. Had there been room to move, he would have turned to flash her a look—the last thing Jasmine needed was to find out his parents had been killed in a motor vehicle accident. But thankfully her mind had jumped to another snippet Vicky had revealed.

'Them?' Jasmine checked.

'Twins.'

'And you raised them?'

'Sort of,' he agreed. 'Since they were twelve.'

'How come?'

'Just family stuff,' he said, deciding he really would be speaking to Vicky later. She could be just a little too indiscreet at times. Of course, now wasn't the time or place to address it. 'Okay, Jasmine, I'm going to give you another dose of pain control before we move you…' As he slipped her the drugs, he carried on the conversation. 'I guess it means I'm more like a parent to them than a brother.'

'So, when the baby comes, you'll be more like a grandfather.'

'Careful,' he warned with a light tease.

'Hmm,' she gave a sleepy half laugh as the drugs took away the horror of her circumstances. 'You got the hard part…' Her eyes closed. 'My mum says that babies and toddlers are cute so that we love them before they turn into teenagers.'

'Here you go, Officer.' A firefighter handed him a pair of earmuffs. 'Wear these.' For OHS reasons Luke was supposed to wear them, and given there were several vehicles involved, Luke rather guessed they were in short supply.

'It's going to get very loud,' Luke told Jasmine, deciding she needed them far more than him. 'I'm going to put some earmuffs on you—you'll still hear it, but not as much.'

'You'll stay with me?'

'I shall.' He looked out, the stretcher was waiting and Cheng was there too, all ready to help for her release, but there was no trauma team. He frowned to Cheng, who understood his unvoiced concern, but shook his head, then gestured it towards the minibus.

'We'll have you out soon,' Luke told her as he slipped on the earmuffs.

'What about the baby?'

There was no answer, and even if there was, he'd already put the earmuffs on her.

Then there was no point even shouting, no words could ever reach her above the sounds of the equipment tearing through the metal… He admired the skill of the firefighters who peeled the metal, like foil off a Christmas turkey and then came the tricky part. The firefighter and his colleagues were carefully freeing Jasmine from the twisted wreckage, and he assisted the lift from the passenger side. He covered her as best he could, and the stoic Jasmine remained conscious throughout. Finally she was on the stretcher, still with full spinal precautions in place, being sped through the lashing rain to the waiting ambulance.

'Trauma team and obstetrics are waiting for her at The Primary,' Cheng told him as he was about to climb into the ambulance. 'We couldn't get them onsite.' He then had a word in Luke's ear. 'Vicky's lost her patient.'

Luke nodded, glad to have the heads-up as he climbed on board.

This really had been a major incident—there were multiple ambulances onsite now, and the hospitals would all be at full stretch. Jasmine, from what he could glean, wasn't the most seriously injured.

Vicky was putting on the monitors and a little quiet for once as Luke came in.

'That's better,' he said, looking down at Jasmine in the relative calm of the ambulance.

'I can see you now...' Jasmine smiled.

The cervical collar had meant she hadn't been able to turn her head, but now Luke was above her, and checking her over, while carefully monitoring her.

'Where are you from?' Jasmine asked, perhaps choosing to talk about anything other than her predicament.

Luke was listening to her chest, but as he removed the stethoscope from his ears, he answered. 'Crouch End,' he said and then smiled, knowing her real question, his jet-black hair and almost black eyes elicited another regular question from patients. 'Argentina.'

Even if he was chatting amicably and outwardly calm, he was on high alert—her abdomen was hard to examine for injuries with the pregnancy, and then Jasmine said she thought she might be having a contraction.

'Let me just slip down your trousers.' There were no visual signs of labour and thankfully no blood, but unseen by Jasmine, he opened up the obstetric pack just in case it would be required en route.

It wasn't a matter of just scooping her up and heading straight to the hospital. The traffic was still heavy from the storm, and Luke wanted to be sure they were prepared for any eventuality. 'I'm just going to put in another line...'

He left the one Karen had inserted, but soon had a wide bore needle in her right arm too.

'Where am I being taken?'

'The Primary.'

'I was there last week for antenatal checks.'

His brother and his brother's girlfriend had been too, though he didn't divulge that. Instead, Luke watched as she closed her eyes for a moment and perhaps thought back to far nicer times, but then she gave a small sigh. 'I waited for hours to be seen.'

'Well, there'll be no sitting in the waiting room for you today—you'll be getting the five-star treatment. They'll all be there waiting for you to arrive.'

He was pleased that Jasmine gave a small smile back.

'We're working there tomorrow,' Vicky said, chatting to Jasmine as Luke ran an ECG. 'Professional development day.'

'Hopefully I'll be home by then,' Jasmine said, and though Luke knew from her injuries that would not be the case, he didn't correct her—Jasmine was swaying between dread for her baby and absolute hope they would walk out unscathed.

'Okay,' Luke said, though more to himself, 'I think we're good to go.'

He sat to the side of Jasmine as Vicky contacted the hospital and updated their ETA.

'The hospital wants to know if her membranes have ruptured,' Vicky called.

Luke had already checked, but before responding he spoke to his patient. 'I'm pretty sure it's urine, but I'm going to get Vicky to tell the hospital there's a *possible* rupture of membranes,' he warned, and Jasmine screwed her eyes closed as he did just that.

'This is your first pregnancy?' Luke checked what he'd

gleaned in the car, preparing for handover. There was a nurse at The Primary who just loved to find fault, and it irked him. Nurse Picky he called her in his head. No matter what he or his partner did, she'd find the one thing he hadn't, and Luke was determined to be ready. 'So thirty-three weeks and how many days?'

'Two.'

'How's everything been going?'

'Well, but they said at the last visit baby's a bit small.'

He chose not to start on paperwork, instead keeping a very close eye.

Vicky drove skillfully, but the weather conditions and the heavy traffic meant it was slow going, and his alert eyes noticed when Jasmine's face grimaced a touch and her hand moved to her stomach.

'How are you doing, Jasmine?'

'The same.'

'Any new pain?'

'No.'

'Are you having a contraction?'

'No, I'm just...' Her voice caught on her breath as she cradled her stomach. 'Why isn't my baby moving...' The cervical collar prevented her head from turning but her question was direct. 'Luke, what do you think?'

Luke had reassured where he could and evaded the question at times, but they were past that now.

Jasmine wanted assurances, and they were something Luke couldn't give.

He didn't believe in false hope.

The police who had knocked at his door that night had told him his parents were critical, and he'd later found out they had been killed outright. That glimmer of hope had proved devastating. It had meant he'd dragged Josie and Daniel from bed to race to the hospital, when it would have been kinder to break it to them at home.

'Do you think the baby's dead?'

She asked the question outright.

'There could be many reasons why your baby isn't moving.' Luke chose a line he used in these times. 'The truth is, Jasmine, I'm a jack-of-all-trades, master of none.' He said it very gently, and if he was lightening the question it was with good reason. He didn't know, and hopefully the back of an ambulance was not a place they'd find out. Of course if she looked to deliver, they would pull over and deal with it, but for now… 'What I do know for sure though, is that we're getting you and your baby to experts, and they'll take the very best care of you both.'

'Yes.'

'We're almost there,' Luke said, feeling the sway as the ambulance turned off the ring-road and onto the final approach to the hospital. 'You've been great.'

There were a lot of ambulances ramped at the entrance, but as they pulled in, the doors were opened, and soon they were guiding the stretcher to the team waiting in resus.

As well as the trauma team, there were a few extra team members for Jasmine, and he looked at the labels on their theatre gowns as Jasmine was lifted over.

MIDWIFE

PAEDIATRICIAN

OBSTETRIC CONSULTANT

But for now, the trauma team were in charge, and on the team leader's instructions Jasmine was lifted off the stretcher, and then Luke gave a detailed handover.

'Twenty-nine-year-old female, driver, high impact, airbags activated, cabin intrusion. No LOC, GCS fifteen throughout…'

He went through all that had been passed on to him and all that he knew since he'd taken over her care.

'Extensive bruising to right upper chest and lower abdomen, G1 Para 1, 33 weeks, plus 2…'

He told them the IV's and drugs that had been given on scene and en route to the hospital and her obs throughout.

As the team took over and the monitors and equipment were changed over to the hospital's, there was time to step back. 'Do we have contact details?' May, the nurse unit manager, asked, and Luke nodded.

'I believe the police are contacting her husband.'

'Did you do a blood glucose?' the permanently picky nurse asked.

'Yes, it was normal.'

'What was the reading…'

Luke relayed the normal reading—he hadn't yet completed the paperwork so was going from memory.

'So, thirty-five weeks?' the nurse verified.

Incorrectly.

'No,' Luke said, taking a breath, about to correct her, but first he had to ungrit his teeth. 'Thirty-three.'

'But you said…' Nurse Picky started, but then a voice chimed in.

'The paramedic's correct.' Luke glanced up and saw it was the obstetrician speaking, and she give him a small smile. 'Thirty-three *weeks* and two *days*.'

It was a simple mistake from the nurse. For one thing she wasn't a midwife, and in fairness Luke wasn't a master in obstetric handovers. Still, it felt nice that this doctor had his back, then she asked him a question. 'Possible ruptured membranes?'

Luke walked over to her side of the treatment bed. Even if Jasmine might not be able to hear him, he wasn't about to loudly declare what had embarrassed her at the scene. 'Not sure,' he admitted. 'Jasmine thinks she wet herself. I checked in the ambulance and I think that's all it is, but I thought it best to alert just in case.'

'Absolutely.' She nodded and Luke headed back to help Vicky with all the equipment and stretcher and clear the way.

'Your husband's here,' May told Jasmine. 'As soon as we can, we'll bring him through.'

'What about the baby?' Jasmine asked, but there were so many doctors and nurses swarming around her question went unheard.

Luke wanted to know about the baby too.

The primary survey was underway, and of course the mother's health had to come first, but he wasn't moving till the secondary survey and he knew how the baby was.

The obstetrician was quietly feeling Jasmine's abdomen as the rest of the team worked on. She squirted some jelly and then placed the doppler, and Luke found he was holding his breath.

He glanced at the paediatric warmer all ready and waiting and saw the theatre packs and knew they were ready to do an emergency caesarean.

He'd never seen a caesarean, and though he would like to, Luke really didn't want it to be necessary now.

The obstetrician was elegant and very calm amidst the ordered chaos, just stepping forward and checking the baby quietly. She wore navy scrubs and there were strands of chestnut hair peeking out from a pale blue cap. Her skin was pale, and despite the activity of the emergency room, she appeared completely unflustered.

But then he watched as her eyes briefly closed, her slender shoulders dropped a touch and a slight hint of a smile spread her full lips. He knew then that she too had been deeply concerned. She looked up, straight to his eyes, and she gave him a small nod that told him she'd found the baby's heartbeat.

Luke exhaled in relief.

'Jasmine,' the obstetrician said in a clear voice, then addressed the team. 'Can we all hush a moment, please.' There was a command to her voice that did not go unnoticed, because everyone either paused activity or fell silent. 'I think Jasmine might like to hear this.' The sound of a rapid heartbeat filled the room. 'That's your baby...'

'Thank God,' Vicky said.

Indeed.

'Thank you.' The obstetrician nodded to her colleagues to continue and the hive of activity resumed.

Luke stood near the doors at the back and made a start on his notes as Vicky went to register the patient. He was just bolding the blood glucose reading for Nurse Picky's eyes when the scent of summer cut through the antiseptic hospital air.

The obstetrician was slightly to his side, reading his notes. 'I'm just checking how much fentanyl you gave. Two rounds prior to extraction?'

'Yes. Then a further dose in the ambulance.'

'Okay.' She picked up the phone on the wall, but before she made a call, added, 'Thanks for the photos of the vehicle, it was good to get a heads-up.'

'That was Vicky, my partner...' His voice trailed off. It was clearly an irrelevant detail for her as she spoke to whomever was on the phone. 'Monica here, don't stand down theatre just yet...' She listened to whatever was being said and then nodded. 'Yes, but that depends on the trauma team. I'll let you know more soon.' Then she paused and her voice was a little terse when next it came. 'Tell her I'm rather tied up right now...' Then she took a breath and added more lightly, 'It's fine, I'll call her myself when I get a chance.'

So, her name was Monica.

And her scent was a contradiction.

Light, summery and floaty, it seemed in slight contrast to the focused, assertive woman who had, just a few moments ago, held the room, and who had just snapped at whoever was on the phone.

Luke got back to his notes. The resuscitation room was not the place to notice her slender figure. Or the summery scent that he'd breathed in as she'd stood near his shoulder. Now, though, she'd ended the call but didn't dash back to the bedside. Like him, she held back, watching.

'How does it look?' Luke asked.

'Right now, I'm letting the trauma team do their job. She's dropped her blood pressure a touch. My main concern is placental abruption but the baby's heartbeat is strong—he doesn't sound in distress.'

'He?' Luke checked, and as she gave a slight eye roll, he couldn't help but notice the vivid green of her eyes.

'I don't actually know.'

'Jasmine felt a lot of movement at first, then nothing.'

'There can be lots of reasons. Most likely it startled but then went back to a sleep cycle.'

'You mean, baby heard the alarm, then hit the snooze button?'

'Something like that.' She gave a soft laugh at his portrayal of events. 'I'm going to do a detailed ultrasound just as soon as they give me any room.'

Luke nodded. There was certainly a hive of activity around Jasmine. 'I'm just glad they both made it here…' He stopped talking as her pager shrieked, and having glanced at it, she took a tense breath. 'More trouble?'

'Nothing to do with work—my mother feels the need to remind me there's a storm.'

Luke couldn't help but smile—her consultant title put her at least mid-thirties, her gorgeous features put her a few years less, but whatever the age… 'Mums worry.'

'Believe me, it's not me she's worried about. I'm to offer to be a taxi to my younger sister.'

'Oh, I know all about being a taxi driver.'

She turned and glanced at his uniform and then huffed a small laugh. 'I guess you would.'

Luke really was good at small talk, just gentle banter as they both stood watching the trauma team work. Now and then, Monica called out an order—adding the blood tests she wanted and increasing the units of blood to be crossmatched in case an emergency caesarean was required. Clearly, she wanted to get in there, but of course Jasmine had to be stabilised.

But then his attention turned to Vicky, who was back from registering, and he remembered that her young patient hadn't made it this far and so the gorgeous doctor was forgotten. And so too was Vicky's little slip-up in the wreckage—today wasn't the day to be having a word. 'How are you doing?' he asked.

'I don't know,' she admitted, and he put a hand on her shoulder. 'I just...'

'Let's get a coffee.'

As they went to walk off, May called out her thanks.

'Thanks, guys,' she said and added a light tease as she often did. 'Don't bring any more.'

Glancing into the corridor, he could see that Cheng had arrived, and there was another crew from the incident, looking both spent and drenched, and now they would debrief.

There wasn't even a chance to say goodbye to Jasmine as she was being prepped for a procedure, but there was no real need—he was one of many new faces Jasmine would meet today. The obstetrician, Monica, was talking to her, and Luke was pleased to see his patient in good hands.

And then a surprise.

'Vicky...' Monica looked up and called her over and, a touch curious, Luke went too. 'Thanks for the clear photos, it gave us a lot of information.'

As Monica took a moment to verify the importance, Luke

took the chance to wish Jasmine well. 'I told you you wouldn't have to wait. Though that was one hell of a way to get seen quickly.'

She was a very strong woman because even now she managed a smile. 'Thanks, Luke.'

Oh, neither Jasmine nor her baby were out of the woods yet, but for now they were here and safe.

CHAPTER TWO

THE SUN WAS just rising as Monica's car turned into The Primary.

She was early for work and with intention.

Indicating to turn to the maternity department, she saw a parking attendant hold up his hand and it was then she saw a large yellow sign.

TEMPORARY DIVERSION

Monica didn't want any diversions. She'd been late home last night and had crashed and now wanted a quiet hour in her office to hopefully clear her inbox and go through her presentation slides before her workday *and* night officially commenced. A blast of cold air hit her as she slid down the window to ask what was going on.

'Storm damage from yesterday,' she was informed. 'The staff car park is inaccessible—full of potholes.'

'I don't use the car park,' Monica told him. 'I've got an on-call spot at the maternity entrance.'

'It's all closed off,' he said. 'You are…'

'Dr Hamilton,' she said as he consulted a printed list that looked as if it might blow away any minute. 'Monica Hamilton,' she added.

'Obstetric Consultant?'

'That's me.'

'Found you.' He nodded. 'You've been allocated a temporary on-call spot outside Accident and Emergency.'

'Thanks.'

'Your ID should work at the barrier but if there are any problems…' His voice trailed off, and when he didn't offer any solution Monica gave a wry smile and crossed her fingers and the parking attendant did the same. 'Thanks.'

Her ID that *should* work actually did—the yellow boom gate lifted, and soon she was parking in a reserved spot close to A&E.

Stepping out of the warm car, she was icy cold, and though it was a short walk to the main entrance, it was freezing enough to pull on her coat and then gather up her computer and bag. It was then that she saw Richard.

And Richard was someone she was trying to avoid.

A few months ago, at a medical conference, she'd seen him getting into a lift with a gorgeous redhead…

It had been late at night, and…enough said.

It should be none of her business.

Except Richard's wife happened to be her best friend!

Of course it was rather more complicated than that, but on this freezing November morning she didn't have the head-space to deal with it.

Unfortunately, he'd seen her!

'Richard.' She gave him a smile and, belting up her coat, walked over. 'Are you working in A&E today?'

'I am. How are things on maternity?'

'Oh, you know…' Monica gave a tight smile. 'Lots of babies.'

Things had become awkward between them.

Not terribly so.

Just a touch.

And that saddened her—not that she ever let her feelings show. So she spoke about potholes and storms, rather than what mattered, but the difficult conversation halted when a man in green uniform caught her eye and she saw the rather gorgeous-looking paramedic from yesterday.

Richard had seen him too, and perhaps grateful for the diversion, greeted him. 'What have you brought us, Luke?'

'Nothing,' Luke said, falling into step beside her. 'I'm only just starting.'

Monica stole a look and understood Richard's assumption that it might be the end of his shift. There was a dark shadow over his jaw and his brown eyes were a touch heavy lidded… as if he'd been up all night.

Yet his scent as he joined them was morning shower fresh. Unlike yesterday, when he'd been dripping wet, his black hair was dry, though it remained dead straight and just a touch longer than the usual clean-cut look she preferred.

'I'm just waiting for my partner.'

'Oh,' Richard said, 'don't you meet up at the station?'

'We're not on the road today,' he said. 'It's a professional development day. Maternity unit…'

Monica's booted stride faltered.

Not a lot.

It probably went unnoticed by her companions, but Monica herself noticed; she was just rather unsure as to why.

'Luke!'

He turned at the sound of his name. 'Vicky,' he greeted, and then farewelled Richard. 'Good to see you.' And then those dark eyes briefly met hers, and he gave a small nod of acknowledgement. It was all that was required for the situation, but then he added—

'Doctor.'

'Monica,' she corrected and then met his eyes. Yesterday she hadn't had the headspace to take in their colour, but in the grey morning light they were almost as black as night and the eye contact wasn't actually that brief. It was Vicky who broke the odd spell, telling Luke they had to get going. As they walked off, she turned and faced Richard, a little flustered and still unsure as to why, though deciding to blame Richard.

And deciding to face things head-on. 'I'm visiting Jess at

the weekend,' she told him, 'Is there anything you want me to bring?'

'I was just there,' Richard said. 'Actually, could you do your magic with the tweezers. I don't think she'd want me messing with her eyebrows.'

'Sure.' She gave him a smile that felt too tight for her lips, and they both knew it was false.

'Monica, do you want to talk? We could get a coffee.'

'I'd love to but I simply don't have time.' She shook her head. 'I've got a packed schedule today.' And while that was true, she knew, in his very polite way, Richard was offering to address what she'd seen at the conference.

It was a relief to get away.

The Maternity Unit was never completely quiet, but it had a welcoming feel to it.

She glanced at the screens at the nurses' station. The CTG monitors, if attached, displayed the reading, and Monica checked the board and saw there were two women labouring in the delivery suite.

One of the babies in a little Perspex crib was unsettled and there were two snugly sleeping and everything was calm.

For now.

In her office she hung up her coat, then checked her appearance. Today she wore a dark suit—her dream was to make it a whole day without changing into scrubs, but it hadn't happened yet. Still, she had a presentation and was on an interview panel this morning and so had made an extra effort.

Her chestnut hair she tied back into a sleek ponytail and, while it was still early, decided that before collecting her on-call pager she'd check her emails.

Monica loathed a messy inbox.

Diligent, organised, she liked to be in control, and she was, at least professionally. She worked through them briskly but then paused on one—an updated paper on declining fertility of women in their thirties.

Monica herself was thirty-five.

And a half.

A generous half.

She moved the paper to her research folder unopened and then swallowed when she saw she had an email from The Royal.

Mr Rossi had responded.

Or rather, his secretary had.

Mr Anton Rossi was a top fertility specialist and held a monthly pre-conception clinic at The Royal for mature women. And, fertility wise anyway, Monica was all too aware that she was one.

She'd ended her last serious relationship a couple of months after Jess's accident. And really, apart from a couple of disasters, there had been no-one since.

Monica knew she was doing well professionally, but socially...

She'd always hovered on the outside, like a nervous kid on the edge of a swimming pool, scared to jump in, and then landing awkwardly when she did.

It had changed at med school; she'd fallen in with a wonderful group of friends and especially Jess.

Dating though, had always been a disaster.

Oh, she would love to do things the natural way, but with no glimpse of Mr Right on the horizon she felt as if time was running out. She wanted a baby. And now she was considering, more than considering, taking things into her own hands.

Or rather, Anton's skilled hands.

Egg retrieval, IVF, or possibly artificial insemination.

Since making the enquiry she had found out that Louise, the newly appointed unit manager, was married to Anton and naturally Monica didn't want her personal life getting out. Privacy was something she'd discuss at her first appointment.

When?

She hoped soon, before Christmas at least, but then sagged in disappointment as she read the email.

Mr Rossi liked his patients to abstain from oral, transdermal or intrauterine contraceptives for a minimum of three, preferably four months prior to the first appointment.

First appointment!

It was already November, and her birthday was in March, by then she'd be thirty-six!

And yes, she didn't have a sex life, but she liked knowing when to expect her period and also the lack of cramps.

Damn.

She just wanted to speak with him.

Frustrated, rattled and a bit irked, she headed to the kitchenette to make a hot chocolate and then became rattled and a bit irked for very different reasons.

'Hey.'

Luke was in there, sitting at the table and eating a toasted sandwich he'd presumably got from the maternity's staff and visitors coffee shop and reading a manual.

'Hi.' Monica gave him a brief smile and wondered since when had making a hot chocolate become complicated—there was more powdered chocolate on the bench than in her cup. 'So you're here for the day.'

'Yep.' He closed the manual he was reading. 'Luke Arias.' He introduced himself properly and even shook her hand, then sat back down, but didn't end the conversation. 'Can I ask how the patient I brought in yesterday is doing?'

'Of course.' She liked that he hadn't asked outside A&E, but had waited until they were on the unit. 'I'm actually about to review her.'

'She was admitted here?'

'Yes, she kept me here till ten…' She gave a wry smile that showed she'd been deeply concerned. 'I'm rather sure everyone's been kept on their toes overnight. She had a couple of rib fractures and a lot of bruising…'

'No pneumothorax?'

'Thankfully no, but she started having contractions when she arrived on the unit. No delivery according to the whiteboard! I'm interested to see how she is today too.'

'Monica…' Louise came in, all breezy and bright and raring to go. 'Just to let you know we've got two paramedics with us today.' Monica was more than well aware of the fact. Luke was sitting quietly, back to reading his manual, yet she was ridiculously aware of his presence, Louise, though, only then noticed the gorgeous hulk sitting at the table, 'Oh, there you are, Luke.'

How on earth had she missed him, Monica thought. And, how come Louise didn't suddenly start spraying chocolate powder, or rather, dropping tea bags, as she calmly made herself a brew. 'Vicky's newly qualified and hasn't yet seen a delivery, though that's about to be righted—she's already in Labour 4…'

'You didn't go in?' Monica asked him.

'The patient didn't want two of us watching,' Luke said. 'I wouldn't want an audience either.'

'I think a caesarean section is high on Luke's wish list, though we don't have any booked today.' Louise turned her bright smile to him. 'Remember what I said, if you hear the emergency buzzer, follow it. Things change pretty quickly here.'

'Got it,' he said.

'So…' Louise asked her. 'Did your mother get hold of you? I finished at five, but…'

'She did.' Monica nodded. 'It wasn't as urgent as it sounded. She just wanted me to *casually* drop in on Clara and offer her a lift…'

'I'm sure Clara wouldn't have appreciated the fuss.'

'Oh, she wouldn't have.' Monica gave a tight smile—it was

the story of her life. Her mother's attention was homed solely on Clara, her younger sister. It didn't matter that Monica might have been in resus with a potentially critical patient... Still, she didn't have time to dwell on things now. 'Have you heard how Jasmine's doing?'

'The trauma patient?' Louise checked. 'I didn't actually see her yesterday, but apparently, she had quite an uncomfortable night. They inserted an epidural...'

'Yes, I was there for that, I'll just have a read of her notes, then review her.'

'Can Luke join you?' Louise asked. 'I'll check with Jasmine, of course.'

'Oh, I'm sure she won't mind.' Monica nodded. 'Luke was with her in the vehicle.'

'Really?' Louise's blue eyes widened and she turned to Luke. 'You'll have to tell me *all* about it...'

Of course Jasmine didn't mind, in fact as Monica approached with both Louise and Luke in tow, she gave her rescuer such a nice smile.

'Luke!'

'Hey, Jasmine. We meet under better circumstances.'

'They couldn't be much worse than yesterday.' She looked to Monica and frowned. 'Do you know that Luke was in the car...'

'I do.' Monica knew Jasmine's recall of yesterday might be a bit hazy. 'So he knows the history, but I'll just bring him up to speed. Jasmine came to us with a nasty seatbelt injury... thankfully no fractured sternum, but two fractured ribs as well as lower abdominal bruising. Her membranes were intact and no regular contractions until late in the evening...' Luke took notes, writing down the findings and medications given to stop labour and also to promote the baby's lung maturity should that prove futile. 'I just want to have a listen to your chest.'

'This is gorgeous,' Louise said, helping her to sit up, adjusting a fluffy blanket.

'My husband brought it in for me,' Jasmine explained, but Monica was already listening to her chest.

'I want you to take deeper breaths.'

'It hurts.'

'I know it does. I'll get the physio to come in and see you… Let's take a look at your stomach. I'll get you to lie down.'

As Louise lowered the head of the bed, Monica noticed that, without prompting, Luke helped Jasmine to lie back. He was very at ease, rather than some who stood a little awkwardly.

'Okay,' Monica said, 'note the bruising.'

'It's more pronounced than yesterday.'

'Always try and get a visual look at the stomach,' Monica said. 'Not just in pregnancy. An abdomen can feel unremarkable…'

He nodded. 'I had a large lady the other week who'd fallen, her stomach felt soft, but when I lifted her jumper, I was taken aback by the bruising.'

'Did she end up having internal bleeding?'

'I'm not sure—they took her straight for a PAC scan.'

Monica gently examined the bruised pregnant stomach and the baby had changed position. 'Your baby's head down…'

'It wasn't last night.'

'No, but at this stage there's still room to move around. Can I just show Luke?'

'Of course.'

'Yesterday the baby was left sacrum anterior…that's possibly why she couldn't feel much movement.' She glanced up to Jasmine. 'Luke thinks your baby hit the snooze button and went back to sleep.'

'That's what I tend to do,' Luke said, making Jasmine laugh and forcing Monica to remember her para-training and not blush. Well, she hadn't ever been in the paramilitary, it was just a joke medical staff shared at times of duress…

And Luke, discussing his sleeping habits, even if he was being nothing but polite, placed her under unfamiliar duress.

He wasn't awkward, he felt the abdomen and nodded. 'Yes, that's the head…' He had another slight feel. 'And that's a foot,' he added as baby gave a deft kick. 'You could have done that for your poor mother yesterday.'

He really was, Monica noted, at ease talking with the patients, and that, in turn, relaxed them. 'How much movement?' she asked Jasmine.

'A lot this morning.'

'That's good. Right, I'm going to examine you.' She was about to ask if she minded Luke being present when he spoke.

'I'll just step out.'

'No need,' Jasmine said, and he stayed at the head end, chatted to her about the accident and how loud the jaws of life had been as Monica pulled on some gloves. 'It'll be your turn to be here soon,' Jasmine said to Luke. 'When did you say she was due?'

'Not for couple of weeks…' Luke replied. 'It could be any-time now.'

'You might be working here…'

Oh!

Luke was about to become a father?

For Monica there was a sudden feeling of relief.

If she had remotely fancied Luke, then the fact he was soon to become a father quickly killed it.

And Monica was actually glad for that.

It made it easier to be herself.

'Your cervix is a bit softer than yesterday,' Monica said when she'd finished the examination. 'I want you to stay on bed rest,' she told Jasmine. 'I'll come and check on you a bit later.' As they walked off, she added to Louise, 'Keep a close eye.'

'For sure,' Louise agreed. 'Luke, do you want to go and join Diane? She's in suite three.' As Luke walked off, Louise rolled her eyes. 'Stunning, isn't he.'

'Louise!'

'He is, and I'm going to tell Anton tonight all about him and make him a little bit jealous, keep him on his toes…' She gave a cheeky grin. 'Or elbows.'

Monica laughed, Louise was gorgeous, as well as talkative. Flirty and funny and, like a lot of the midwives, utterly happy to discuss sex and cycles and such things—Monica, while matter-of-fact with her patients, was not so prone to sharing.

Heading to the nurses' station to write up some notes, she found herself going back to the admission, not the doctors' notes; instead, she read the paramedics' case sheet.

There was a picture of the front and back of the patient where the paramedic would note injuries, and she looked at his write-up.

She looked at the times and saw he'd been in the vehicle with Jasmine for over an hour… Gosh. Imagine sitting on a wet and cold motorway. Luke would, Monica decided, be a very nice person to have by your side…that calm, but very male presence would be reassuring indeed.

Now she no longer fancied him, or rather, now she knew he was off limits, she could let herself think about him a bit. Now that she knew he was a father to be, the attraction rattled her less.

Actually, she was relieved that this fledgling fancy had been doused. She had noticed him yesterday, of course. Not just his dark good looks, but that brief eye meet when she'd found the heartbeat, had jolted her. And, as she'd waited impatiently to examine her patient, she'd been ridiculously conscious of him.

It was purely physical, she'd decided. And the physical attraction had been too intense, too instant, way more than anything she was used to.

He was attractive, that was a given, and solidly built.

She liked big men.

Her last guy had been big, until he'd discovered cycling

and macronutrients, then whittled himself away until Monica had felt like a carthorse in bed.

Cringing at the memory, she looked over to Luke, who was making a patient laugh as he stood at the end of the bed chatting, utterly at ease.

'Monica…' Louise came over, her eyes wide with concern. 'I've just had a call from May in A&E. A nurse has been assaulted… She's twelve to fourteen weeks pregnant, at least on examination. The poor thing didn't even know she was pregnant until now.'

Louise was effusive, Monica practical—'What are her injuries?'

'Upper abdomen.' Louise explained that the patient had slammed a gurney into her. 'The surgeons are going to take a look, though she doesn't want word getting out that she's expecting. I'm happier to have her brought up here to be seen…'

'No.' Shaking her head Monica explained her reasoning. 'I want the surgeons to clear her before she comes up to the unit. I'll head down to A&E now and see her.'

'Could Luke come with you?' Louise suggested. 'I'll let May know and get the patient's permission, but he's into all the trauma and stuff…' She lowered her voice. 'As well as that I don't really know what to do with him. The mothers I've asked have agreed to the female paramedic only.'

'Perhaps remind them they might not get a choice if they deliver at home; the more experience the paramedics get today the better for the patients,' Monica said and stood, then startled that Luke was there and must have heard what she'd said.

'Thanks, Monica.' He gave her a smile. 'Honestly, I don't want to make anyone uncomfortable. It's not an issue for me. I'm actually more interested in trauma…'

'And learning midwife speak,' Louise teased. 'Vicky told me.'
Luke rolled his eyes. 'Vicky talks too much.'

Monica was too busy to chat. 'I'm just going to hand my pagers over to Vince.' She did so, and Luke stood waiting for her and not impatiently. It was hard to explain, but in the way that some people, even without a word or a toe tap, can make you feel rushed, Luke was the opposite.

There was something rather patient about him.

'I just need to stop by my office,' she said.

'Sure, do you want me to wait here for you?'

'Then I'd have to come back and get you.' Monica was not one for wasting time, and gestured for him to join her as she brought Louise up to speed on her movements. 'I'm on an interview panel at nine, then I'm giving a presentation in lecture theatre one…' She sighed as they walked to her office. 'I wanted to go through my slides.'

'Is there time now?'

Monica didn't answer him, but Luke took no offence—she was clearly in demand.

Her office was bland, just as any doctor's office, but it had a lovely summery scent, and he leant on her desk as she re-tied her hair for her interview and presentation, then added a quick slick of neutral lipstick before she took her jacket off.

'Jasmine's blanket—I seem to have picked up every fibre… I was hoping not to have to change into scrubs before my presentation.'

Good grief, Luke thought, was she going to get changed here!

Of course not.

She produced a lint roller, the sticky kind, and ran it over the back of her jacket. Then over her skirt. It was a non-event. At least it was back at the station, where it was a case of *pass the lint roller* at times!

But the initial thought of the rather undemonstrative doctor suddenly stripping off, had caused a bodily chain reaction, and Luke found himself hastily looking away.

In fact, he looked at the white wall as *squeak, squeak* went the lint roller over her thighs and stomach. God, he was having lint roller fantasies and wanted to take it from her, first sort out the shoulders of her jacket, then the back of her skirt, then slowly turn her around…

'Ready!'

'Great,' Luke said as they headed out. He was startled by how much he liked her. She was a little bit prissy and then suddenly bold, and, really, he found this contrary woman as sexy as all hell.

'Thanks for this…' he said as they took the elevator down. 'It will be good to see what happens to patients after we leave them in A&E.'

'It's nice that you're interested,' she said and then added, 'And if it's any consolation, I'm not very good at midwife speak either.'

'Really?'

'It's a skill I don't possess. Louise, on the other hand, is brilliant at it. I'm sure it's her first language.'

They came to the main corridor, the central line of the hospital, at least it had been, Monica explained, before the new wing had been built. 'Now we're a considerable distance… of course it's not a problem…'

'Unless there are potholes in the new car park.'

'Unless,' Monica corrected, 'we have a critical patient in A&E.'

'Did you have to run yesterday?' Luke asked.

'I did.'

She smiled, not that he could see it, he just heard the lift in her tone.

'May's moved the patient to a quiet area,' Monica said. 'So, we'll try and not make an entrance. It must be dreadful to find out you're pregnant at work.'

'That's a problem I'll never have to face,' Luke said, and he liked how she laughed, how she got his dry humour.

A woman was walking towards them, and given she had a white cane, Luke rather thought they should step to the side, and when it seemed Monica hadn't noticed, he reached for her arm to steer her…but Monica brushed off the brief contact and actually came to a rather abrupt stand. 'Clara!'

The woman stopped and smiled. 'Hi, I'm just heading up your way. How are things on Maternity?'

'Not too bad. We've got a couple of patients waiting for you.'

'And this is?' Clara asked, her face turning towards Luke.

'Oh, forgive me.' Monica, for the first time, was a little flustered. Usually, she'd have introduced Luke straight away, but her arm was warm from the briefest of contact with his hand and she felt as gawky as a teenager. 'This is Luke.'

'Luke?' Clara frowned slightly, clearly expecting more information, and usually Monica would have been the first to give it. She knew only too well that Clara didn't have the visual clues of a uniform or name tag to glean more information, but the brief touch from Luke had unsettled her.

'I'm a paramedic.' Luke was the one who filled in the gaps, and Monica watched as the frown faded from Clara's expression and she turned to his voice. 'Here for a professional development day.'

'We're just heading down to see a patient in A&E,' Monica said, rather hoping to get away, but Clara's interest seemed piqued and she and Luke chatted for a few moments, mainly about a colleague of Clara's who counselled emergency responders.

'I know Matthew,' Luke nodded. 'Well, I haven't utilised his services, but he's a great guy.'

'He is,' Clara agreed. 'So are you just here for the day or…'

Monica, still a little flustered from Luke's light touch had no idea why Clara was being so chatty, and decided to end the conversation. 'Sorry, we really do have to get going.'

'Of course.' Clara smiled as Monica walked off.

Luke, though, refused to be summoned and answered Clara's question. 'Yes, just here for today. It was nice to meet you.'

'You too.'

He caught up with Monica in a couple of strides and, aware she'd sounded a little terse, she explained the situation to Luke as they walked on. 'Clara's my sister.'

'Oh.'

He turned and stole another glance—they could not be more different. Clara was blonde and sunny, whereas Monica was darker and more serious.

'I know,' Monica said, clearly reading his thoughts. 'We're complete opposites.'

They arrived in the accident and emergency department and were greeted by May, the nurse unit manager with a smile and a discreet word about the patient. 'Sorcha Bell, she's twenty-eight and has only been working here for a few weeks. She's Scottish, so a little far from home.'

'Okay.' Monica was taking mental notes as they walked.

'Richard's in with her now. I don't think she had a clue that she was expecting.' May gave Luke a little nudge. 'Are you playing midwife today?'

He was clearly used to May's cheeky ways. 'Didn't you know?' He nudged her back. 'I'm thinking of changing careers.'

'Where's our patient?' Monica asked a little tersely. Oh, she knew Luke and May were joking, but even a glimpse of having this ball of masculinity on the unit 24/7 was unsettling. An hour into her shift and she was already struggling. Her reaction to Luke had thrown Monica completely off kilter. She noticed him far too much. Not just his clear good looks, but his energy. How Clara had lit up, how he made Louise smile, and lightly joked with May in a way Monica never would. There was a certain magnetism to Luke and no-one seemed immune.

May opened up the cubicle, and as they stepped in, there was Richard with the patient. Sorcha had long red hair, and Monica hoped that that accounted for her very pale complexion. She was vaguely familiar, though Monica assumed it was from work; that hair was rather unforgettable. The poor thing looked both washed out and anxious and rather frail, lying on the gurney. 'Hello, Sorcha.' Monica introduced both herself and Luke, then asked a couple of questions.

'Now…' Monica glanced at the notes. 'I hear you've had two shocks this morning.' She smiled at Richard. 'You think she's around twelve weeks?'

'That was Mr Field's assessment,' Richard responded. 'Though *we* think that's right,'

Monica frowned a touch and then, out of the corner of her eye saw Richard take Sorcha's hand and give it a squeeze, and it dawned on her that Sorcha wasn't actually his patient. 'We had a contraceptive failure at the end of September,' Richard said. 'It must have been then…'

Sorcha's red hair really was unforgettable, and Monica knew then where she'd seen her before. It wasn't from work. Sorcha was the woman Richard had been with that night of the conference.

Monica was brilliant at hiding her emotions, but she almost felt her mask slip as realization dawned and she mentally fought for a moment to retrieve it, snapping on a formal businesslike smile. 'Right,' she said, knowing for Sorcha's sake she had to address this head-on. 'Richard, could you excuse us for just a moment?'

'Of course.'

'Luke, May…would you mind stepping out, too? Just briefly.'

'Of course.'

'Sorcha,' Monica said when they were alone. 'I'm not sure if you're aware that I'm a friend of Richard…'

'And Jess,' Sorcha added, perhaps so that Monica didn't have to.

'Yes.' She nodded. 'I will understand completely if you'd rather I called a colleague to take care of you.'

* * *

Oh, it was fun being a fly on the wall at times!

Luke stood outside, and he was very good at reading the room—a necessary skill in his job, and he watched Richard arch his neck as he sat at the nurses' station.

A man who'd just found out he was about to be a father, Luke understood him being tense. He, himself, would be strapped to a cardiac monitor if he'd just found out the same!

Luke had seen Monica's expression falter, then shutter and heard her professional, calm voice when she'd asked them to leave.

If that was all he'd seen, he might not have given it much thought, but he'd seen Monica and Richard earlier walking together.

Did Monica like Richard?

Had they been an item, or were they an item?

If that was the case, poor Monica.

He was soon invited to step back in. If he hadn't seen her chatting with Richard at the start of the day, he'd never have guessed that this particular patient might be proving an issue. Monica was polite and the consummate professional, patiently explaining things to Sorcha as Luke took notes, and then clarifying things a touch further as they walked back to the unit.

'The mother must always take priority,' she explained as they walked back to the maternity unit. 'It's important her injuries are assessed and treated—if the surgeons clear her, I'll get a detailed ultrasound, then admit her to the unit for observation.'

'How long for?'

'That depends on the findings and her home circumstances.'

'Her partner's a doctor here?' Luke said, glancing over as he did so and noticing her full lips press together.

'Hmm,' Monica responded evasively. She was shaken inside by the morning's events and certainly not about to confide in a stranger.

In anyone.

She'd learnt long ago to keep her feelings inside and not just at a professional level, but in her personal life too. So instead of responding, she changed the subject with a question of her own.

'So, your partner's expecting?'

'God no.' He startled. 'What made you…' He thought back and realised what Jasmine had said and how it might have sounded. 'No, no, it's my brother's partner who's expecting— Kelly.'

'Oh!'

'I told Jasmine I was about to become an uncle when we were waiting for the firefighters to start cutting. Just…' He shrugged. 'Small talk to keep her calm.'

'I see.'

'I'm not even seeing anyone,' Luke added. Needlessly? Pointedly? He wasn't sure which.

'So,' she said, instead of reciprocating with a glimpse into her love-life. 'You're about to be an uncle?' She turned her head and met black eyes that rolled.

'Indeed,' he said with a droll edge.

'I thought you were excited.'

'I said that to Jasmine.' He gave a low laugh. 'How I actually feel is another matter.'

'You don't approve?' Monica checked. 'Don't you get on with your brother?'

'Nothing like that, Daniel and I are really close,' he said. 'And his partner's great, I just think they're far too young.'

'How old are they?'

'Twenty-two.'

'Gosh.' Monica let out a burst of laughter. 'You should see how young some of the mothers I take care of are.'

'I guess,' he agreed, though he didn't sound convinced.

They made polite and pleasant conversation as if there wasn't this unspoken frisson between them. There was nothing to denote it—Monica remained her slightly icy self and Luke was his laid-back self—just two colleagues for the day walking along—except they kept stealing glances at each other. And walked just a touch further apart than two colleagues for a day otherwise might—just a little too aware of the other.

But then, as they arrived at the elevators where they would part ways, he had another question. 'Are you okay?'

'Pardon?'

'You seemed a little taken back in A&E.' When she frowned, he elaborated. 'About Richard and—'

'Excuse me!' She couldn't quite believe he was addressing what had happened, that those black eyes were now meeting hers rather than looking away.

'I've had a couple of incidents at work where I've known the patient—my sister's best friend took an overdose.'

'I'm not quite sure what you're referring to.' She flashed him a warning look, one that would shrivel most, but he didn't so much as flinch.

'You seemed surprised they were together.'

'I might happen to know the partner, but I addressed the matter with the patient.' Luke's gaze remained upon her, and it felt as if he knew she was upset about Sorcha.

Only she wasn't.

She was upset about Jess.

For Jess.

Though she wasn't about to discuss it with a stranger. Ridiculously though, she wanted to. 'There's no issue.'

'My mistake.'

'Yes,' Monica replied a little crisply, suddenly frantic to get away from those dark knowing eyes. 'I have to head over to admin now.'

'Good luck.'

She turned, a small frown between her brows, unsure what he meant.

'With your presentation.'

'Oh!' She was surprised that he'd remembered. 'Thank you.'

'I'm sure you'll kill it.' He smiled then, and her stomach seemed to fold in on itself. The presentation wasn't her concern at this moment.

A day with Luke might prove a little more than she could take.

What did this man do?

CHAPTER THREE

IT WAS ALMOST lunchtime by the time she arrived back on the unit, and there were a couple of patients awaiting discharge…

As well as Louise, there were midwifery and medical students and Beth, her resident. Vicky was still with a labouring woman, but Luke joined them and took diligent notes…

Monica was aware that such a group could be intimidating for her patients and that was why she addressed many concerns up-front.

'You can resume sex whenever you feel ready…' she told her antenatal patient. 'So long as you feel comfortable.' And for the postnatal patients she suggested resuming when they felt ready, though it might take a few weeks. 'There's no rush, take your time, but whatever you do, make sure you're using protection. I've had several patients already pregnant at their six-week postnatal check.'

It was Luke's steady expression that faltered this time. His eyes rising towards his hairline as he underscored his notes. Perhaps he'd be reiterating that fact to his younger brother, Monica thought to herself with a smile.

The final patient on the round, Monica saw alone.

In fact, she didn't just ask the staff to disperse but the partner too.

'I just need to do a quick examination,' she said to the partner.

'It's nothing I haven't seen,' he said, but then Louise stepped in.

'I need to go through the car seat with you,' Louise said in her sweet voice. 'Have you fitted one before or…'

In a moment Monica was speaking with the patient alone.

A short while later, walking into the staff room to find Luke sitting there, Monica decided to keep all topics work related, and as she heated up her food she explained why she'd asked the posse to leave.

'I wanted to speak with the patient away from the partner. I had a couple of concerns…'

'I get it.'

'You'd deal with similar?'

He nodded. 'Though when you're in their home it's a little harder to ask the partner to leave.'

'It would make things more difficult.'

'We have different strategies and ways to report our concerns. Still, if there's even a hint that abuse is occurring, I try to bring them in to hospital and make the triage staff aware of my concerns.' He seemed to reflect for a moment, perhaps about the patients he'd seen. 'It's not always so easy though.'

'No.' She waited for him to elaborate but he didn't, and with her lunch warmed up, her resolve to speak only about patients was fading. 'You'd see a lot,' Monica commented, thinking about it as she sat down. 'Does it…' She was curious and interested rather than being nosey. 'Does it get to you?'

'Depends,' he said, peering into a canteen chicken roll and wishing he had whatever Monica was eating because it smelt amazing. 'Not often though, I just block it out. I couldn't do the job otherwise.'

'What about the ones that do hit home?' She was honest. 'I didn't give it much thought until Clara mentioned about her colleague that worked with first responders. You'd see the patients that don't even make it to the hospital.'

He nodded. 'There's a psychologist available and a chaplain, follow-up calls…'

'Does it help?'

'It helps some, though it's not for me.' He shook his head. 'I like the debrief after a big job, working out what we could have done differently on a medical level, but I don't like going over things.'

'Things?' She frowned and then got what he meant. 'You mean feelings?'

'Yes, I don't see the point when it doesn't change the outcome. How do you deal with it all?'

'I don't see as much as you. There are some very difficult days—it's not all healthy babies, but there's peer support and we have a good team.'

'I can see that,' he said. 'So, what do you…' He paused.

Luke had been about to ask what she did to unwind. Actually, he'd been about to take this conversation outside the realm of work.

And that was simply not appropriate here.

'What do I?' She checked whatever he'd been about to say, but thankfully, Vicky burst in then, high with delight at the birth she'd just witnessed. 'Oh, Luke…it was incredible! I cried,' she happily admitted. 'Did you?'

'What?'

'Cry at your first delivery?'

'I did not.'

Monica found she smiled at his definite answer and then Vicky's glassy gaze was aimed at her. 'Did you cry, Doctor?'

Monica thought back. 'No! I was so shocked I just stood there. I was a medical student and I thought birth was ages away. We all did. But then the midwife came in and suddenly there this baby was…' She laughed fondly. 'It was pretty incredible.'

'My second one came quickly like that.' Vicky smiled and

Luke bit into his roll. He knew Vicky's personal birthing stories back to front as she'd told them many, many times. 'We almost didn't make it to the hospital.'

He saw Monica's polite smile and how she tapped salt onto her fabulous-smelling lunch as Vicky went into further detail…and when she'd got to the delivery of her placenta, she made a statement.

'You must love your job.'

'Most of the time.' Monica nodded.

Vicky wasn't finished though. 'Did you always want to be an obstetrician?'

'Yes.'

Monica was rather more sparse with words than she had been with him, and that quietly pleased Luke—told him he wasn't imagining the connection he felt between them.

'Do you have children?' Vicky asked.

As she always did.

'No,' Monica rather tartly said, and Luke watched the slight tension of her lips at the rather personal question and was mightily relieved he had not ventured to ask about her life outside of work.

She *fascinated* him.

And that was unusual for Luke.

To be fascinated.

As Vicky headed out to find something to eat, Luke addressed his rather verbose partner.

'Sorry about that.'

She glanced over.

'Vicky can be a bit…' He blew out a breath. 'I've been meaning to talk to her.'

'About?'

'Tact.' He put his head back. 'Her question was well meant.'

'I know it was.' She nodded. 'It just irks. I get asked more than most.'

'I'll bet.' He smiled and tilted his head to the door and lusty cries of the babies outside. 'It's Hormone City here, isn't it? I thought it was bad enough in my line of work, but here...'

'You get asked it too?' She seemed surprised.

'All the time.'

'Then you get a little odd look,' Monica said. 'As if...' Her voice trailed off.

'As if you couldn't possibly get it.'

'Yes!'

They shared a small laugh and their little child-free bond made it a touch easier to elaborate. 'Vicky cannot comprehend that I absolutely do not want to be a father.'

'Well, there's the difference,' Monica said. 'I do want to be a mother.' She gave a tight shrug. 'Honestly, don't worry about your colleague. I'm more than used to being asked.'

She was gorgeous, Luke decided.

It was as if there was an invisible wall built around her, a shield or barrier, yet every now and then she permitted a glimpse behind. For Luke it wasn't merely physical attraction, but a desire to know her more and one question he had was answered when Louise popped her head around the door. 'Ooh, that smells good. Is it moussaka week?'

'It is.'

'Moussaka *week*?' Luke checked.

'I make a huge moussaka to last the week.'

'Or cottage pie,' Louise added.

'Shepherd's pie,' Monica corrected.

'What's the difference?' Luke asked, but no-one was listening, Louise had come looking for Vicky.

'She's just gone to find something to eat.'

'Well, when she gets back, can you let her know that the twins aren't far off.' She offered an apologetic smile. 'Mum only wanted a female present.'

'No problem.'

'Oh, there she is...' Louise said, collecting Vicky before she had time to eat.

'Do you get a lot of that?' Monica asked him as Louise took a seat.

'A bit,' he said. 'There's not much of a choice when it comes to paramedics. Occasionally they ask for a female to treat them, but I'm generally the most experienced. If that's the case, I try and stay back and just direct the traffic.'

'That's a nice way of putting it.'

It was nice too to chat as they ate. 'I don't usually take such a long lunch,' Monica revealed, 'but I'm on call, so I'll take a break when I can.'

'You're here all night.'

She nodded.

'Do you get to sleep?'

'On and off.' She nodded. 'I'm only called if there's a problem but…'

'There are always problems?'

'Indeed.'

She had a few questions for him, asking about their long shifts. 'There's a lot of flexibility with shiftwork, while the long shifts don't leave time for much else, they're followed by a block of days off before the madness starts again.'

'What do you do with your days off?'

Luke's roll paused midway to his mouth, because he'd been avoiding asking that very question, wary of crossing any lines, but now those gorgeous green eyes were meeting his. 'I like to get away as often as I can, somewhere warm.'

'I noticed the tan.' She smiled. 'Where's it from?'

'Canary Islands.'

'Wow.' She sighed and put her head back a touch as if picturing it. 'I haven't been away for…' Her voice trailed off as she pondered. 'Too long.'

'I love getting away,' Luke said. 'I'm always looking out for offers, or last-minute escapes.' He stopped, realising she probably didn't need to look at last-minute deals.

'What else do you do?' she asked. 'When you're not flee-ing the country?'

Boom.

She had given him the perfect opening.

And if it were anyone else, Luke would glide in like a cob, tell her about the bar he frequented—the great music, food from home, but there was a rare hesitancy to him, unsure if he was misreading things. Usually, he'd have a woman's phone number by now. Seriously. He dated easily. Very easily. A little too easily by some standards, and he doubted her standards were as casual as his. 'Mainly catching up with family,' he settled for, rather than suggesting La Milonga!

Monica smiled, enjoying talking to him. She liked that he seemed close to his family and she was curious too. 'Are Dan-iel and his partner looking forward to being parents?'

'Very much so.' He nodded.

'So why do you think they're too young?'

'I don't know, I guess it's just so much responsibility.'

'They sound ready for it,' Monica said. 'Have they been together for long?'

'Three years now,' Luke said, and he seemed to ponder that for a brief moment then gave a huff of laughter. 'Who am I to judge? Three months would be a record for me.'

'Really?'

'Three weeks, even.'

'Hmmm.'

They'd been making eye contact easily but he fully met her gaze then, and it felt as if he was sending a warning. Those dark eyes holding hers as his words let her know he didn't do long-term while silently acknowledging the attraction between them. Monica wasn't one for blushing, and she refused to start now. She remained cool under pressure, and she put that to the test now. So instead of blushing or looking away, she carried on the conversation with a question. 'Your brother works?'

'Yes.'

'What about his partner?'

'Kelly? Yes, though she's on leave now...'

'Then stop worrying,' she told him. 'Seriously, I get such young mothers, and if they're happy and it sounds as if they are, they're going to be wonderful. With a little help from family, of course.'

'Yes,' he said, his black gaze still locked with hers. 'So, I'm going to be pretty busy.'

There was more there, she could sense it. Why would becoming an uncle make this slight wanderer so busy? Yet, a lunchtime chat in the staffroom was perhaps not the place to probe, especially as her pager was going off.

Checking it, she rolled her eyes and then reached for a phone and made a quick call. 'I have to go.'

'Of course.'

'It was nice talking to you.'

'Likewise,' he said, but as she got to the door, she heard her name. 'Monica?'

'Yes?' Turning she met his black gaze.

'Do you...'

She swallowed.

There was a slight giddy feeling—this sense of knowing he was about to ask if she wanted to resume this conversation elsewhere.

Did she?

On a day she was considering giving up on men and flushing her pills and seriously exploring motherhood for herself, the sexiest man she had ever met had crossed her path.

A man who considered a three-week relationship his norm.

'Do I?' she prompted.

Did she?

His eyes flicked away then, and he cleared his throat.

'Do you think I could be there when you admit the A&E

patient?' She was certain that wasn't the question he'd been intending to ask. 'I'd like to hear how you take a full history.'

'Of course.' She nodded. 'As long as it's okay with Sorcha.'

'Sure.'

Their paths didn't cross through the afternoon.

Sorcha arrived on the unit for observation but the curtains were pulled, and he found out from Louise they were letting her rest. 'The ultrasound looked good. Monica will probably discharge her in a few hours.'

'So she won't be admitted?'

Louise frowned. 'She has been admitted.'

'Oh.'

He watched a newborn hearing screen, and then as his stint on the Maternity Unit neared its end Luke held a baby for a mother who wanted to have a bath. 'You don't mind?' Louise checked.

'Not at all.'

He sat at the desk holding the infant as Louise did her nursing notes and in between explained all the CTG tracings on the screens in front of them. 'We're keeping a close eye on Jasmine,' she told him. 'Her contractions are becoming more uniform and regular.' She smiled as he put the baby on his shoulder. 'You're a natural.'

'Louise, this feels *so* unnatural.'

They were both laughing as Monica passed.

She was looking even more gorgeous—her hair had become loose, and now she was wearing scrubs as she'd been yesterday when he'd first seen her.

He'd liked her then.

Of course he'd been too focused on Jasmine to really register it at the time, but today, all day, had confirmed things.

He liked her.

And perhaps he ought not to let that show.

After all, she was a consultant, and he was at work.

'Luke, I'm about to discharge Sorcha. You wanted to see a full admission.'

It was Luke who frowned now. 'I thought she'd been admitted.'

'To the unit, but she'll be under my care from now on. I'll take a full obstetric history as I would if I were seeing her for the first time in outpatients.'

Louise put her arms out. 'Give the little one to me.'

Luke, aside from fancying Monica, did want to see a full obstetric history being taken, and to hear the questions that were asked. It was the type of thing that was invaluable in his line of work.

Aside from that, he was still curious as to the nature of Monica and Richard's relationship. She'd overreacted when he'd offered support earlier. The lady really had protested too much!

Now, though, she was utterly together and calm.

'Sorcha,' she greeted the woman, and told her that all her results were normal. And only when Sorcha made it clear she was keeping the baby, Monica congratulated her and told her the due date was June 10.

In fact, as Monica took down her history and told her what lay ahead, she was so utterly together that Luke second-guessed himself. Perhaps he'd been wrong about there being something between her and Richard.

The interview was thorough, and she explained things to Luke as she went. 'We do a lot of mental health screening,' she explained, and he nodded and carried on taking notes. The interview was finishing up as Monica asked about her living accommodation. 'You live alone?' Monica checked. 'Is there anyone who can keep an eye on you for the next forty-eight hours at least.'

'I think I'll be staying at Richard's.'

Luke looked up from his notes but there was absolutely no reaction from Monica, at least not on the personal front, just a nod of confirmation. 'Good.'

Yes, he decided, he'd been wrong.

'Okay,' Monica said. 'I'll sign you off work for two weeks and see you in clinic before you return.'

'I don't need that much time off—' Sorcha started, but Monica was insistent.

'These things can take a few days to catch up with you,' Monica said. 'You've had a proper fright. Still, I'm very happy with how things are—though you should bear in mind that you're going to be very tender from the bruising, so I want you to really try and rest over the next few days.' She checked her own extensive notes. 'I think that covers anything. Do you have any questions for me?'

Sorcha didn't answer and the slight flush that came to the patient's cheeks was unseen by Monica as, assuming the consultation was over, she went to walk off.

Sorcha's eyes flashed to his and Luke *knew* the question she wanted to ask.

It was the same one Monica had addressed with all other patients without prompting.

Sex.

It was a gaping omission and Luke amended his thoughts.

He was right!

'Monica?' Luke said. 'Sorry.' He scanned his notes. 'I must have missed it. When can the patient resume intercourse?'

'Oh!' Monica came back over. 'Sorcha, I'm sorry—I thought I'd mentioned that. Sex is fine. As long as you're comfortable, of course.'

She swished off and as Luke followed, she briefly turned. 'Thanks for that.'

Monica, who didn't usually blush, was starting to.

And Luke, dammit, was quietly smiling.

'No problem.' He shrugged. 'As I said before, it can be awkward when you know a patient.'

'I don't know the patient,' she retorted. 'I know Richard.'

'I see.'

'I don't think you do!' Those black eyes seemed to see right through her facade, and she flared then. 'I didn't omit to mention sex deliberately.'

By the slightest margin he raised thick dark brows and combined with that smile, it infuriated her.

'Are you suggesting I'm out to sabotage their sex life?'

Still that slight smile.

'There's nothing between Richard and I. We've been friends since medical school.' Boy, did Luke have things wrong and, with relish, she would let him know just how wrong he was. 'If you're sensing awkwardness, then perhaps it's because I happen to be best friends with his wife!'

'God!' Instead of the take-down she'd hoped for, instead of backing down with a strenuous apology, he laughed. 'Now that *is* awkward.'

The funniest part? She laughed too.

Monica didn't tell him all of it. None of it really. She didn't tell him that Jess, her dear friend, had been in a coma for the past three years. For now, she let the hurt go, and they just laughed as the wretched parts of her day all faded away.

But then the best part of this day was fading away too, because Louise called for him and said that Vicky had gone as the unit was quiet.

'There's really not much going on,' Louise said. 'You might as well go.'

There felt like unfinished business here though.

'I hope you've had a good day. I'm sorry we didn't get you in to see any births.'

'No problem at all. It's been incredible,' Luke admitted. 'I was saying to Monica how hard you guys work.' He glanced over as Monica joined them at the nurses' station. She was eating a chocolate bar, and still had fourteen or so hours to go.

Luke did not mix work and pleasure.

Ever.

Yet, this wasn't quite his usual work.

And nor was Monica his usual pleasure.

Her status, her beauty, her slight iciness all intrigued him. There was something so gorgeous about her. God knows he wished he'd found that green gaze at La Milonga. Hell, he'd have preferred they'd met at the frozen food section of the supermarket—Luke was rather certain they'd have melted the aisle down to the last frozen pea.

Instead though, they'd met at work.

'Seriously, thanks,' Luke said. 'And to you, Monica, you've been generous with your time.'

'I hope it's been helpful,' Monica said, and her eyes met his, and it felt as if they were having a separate conversation.

Are we going to take this outside?

'Monica,' Louise suddenly said.

Her name was said in a way any medical person would recognise, and Luke turned his head abruptly, flirting and fun forgotten.

'Bed 6…'

He glanced at the monitors, and CTG tracings were not his forte, but as Monica dashed off, Louise hit a buzzer, and he was given a very quick tutorial.

'Decels,' Louise said, 'And the foetal heart rate's very low,' she said before dashing off.

He stood there staring at the screen as the already busy unit suddenly became alive with activity.

People were appearing, the trolleys being pushed, phone calls made and theatre alerted, and he stood there, not wanting to break away.

It was Jasmine.

He didn't like following up on patients almost for this reason. Had he left ten minutes ago, then Jasmine and her baby would, in his head at least, both be okay.

Louise dashed over then. 'You wanted to see a caesarean?'

'Can I?'

'Absolutely.' Louise nodded. 'Better than seeing it road-side for the first time.'

They mobilised incredibly fast.

Luke wished he'd checked the time, at the time, but it must have been fifteen minutes from the first urgent push of the buzzer to Jasmine being on the operating table.

Monica was getting into her gown and she looked up as a man rushed in. 'Hi, George,' she said, then went over to Jasmine. 'George is the paediatrician; he's going to be looking after your baby.' She held her gloved hands up and in front of her, keeping them sterile. 'I know you want to wait until your husband's here, but it's very important we get this little one out.' She was firm and assertive but also very kind. 'I know it seems sudden but it needs to be born.'

'I understand.'

Jasmine was so strong, Luke thought.

For all she'd been through, he hadn't seen a single tear shed, and now she lay staring fixedly up at the theatre ceiling.

A theatre nurse came and sat by Jasmine then, reaffirming what was happening as Monica prepared to commence.

'Can you feel this, Jasmine?' Monica asked and Luke watched from a distance as she checked the epidural's effect.

'No.'

'You'll feel some tugging, but it's not going to hurt.'

Luke stood at the back wall watching the rapidly unfolding events. Just observing while playing no part. There was an odd feeling of relief in being completely supernumerary—there was nothing expected of him, nothing he had to do, no-one depending on him.

He hadn't known that for the longest time.

And not just at work.

Not since he'd had to tell twelve-year-old twins that their parents were never coming home.

He stood in the midst of an emergency and everyone present knew more than him and knew what to do and he felt privileged to simply watch.

There was the gurgle of suction as the membranes were ruptured and then Monica spoke. 'It won't be long, Jasmine.'

Jasmine was stoic, she stared up at the ceiling, just as she had stared ahead yesterday.

Monica was incredible. Absolutely steady and calm as she stood in the eye of the storm. He liked her control and seeming lack of emotion, though he'd glimpsed behind the cool facade a couple of times today.

The little reveal about how being repeatedly asked if she was a mother hurt.

The slight glare in her eyes when he'd suggested things might be awkward for her with Richard if they shared a history.

Best of all though had been the laughter that had followed—how her lips had parted and she'd thrown her head back. Real laughter, that belonged more between old friends than temporary colleagues.

There were fears and emotions and real passion there—just not readily displayed, and Luke admired that.

He couldn't believe the speed of it as he watched her deliver a limp dusky infant and immediately hand it over to the waiting team.

'You have a little boy,' Monica said.

'Is he okay?' Jasmine called for more information, as she had in the car and ambulance. Needing to know if her baby was okay. But again, there was no immediate answer.

'The paediatric team are with him,' Monica said and got back to focussing on surgery.

She'd learnt to switch her emotions off at the age of five or so.

Clara had been so delicate, and with her impairments her

mother had repeatedly asked Monica what she had to be upset about in comparison.

"Nothing."

And when she was older and studying, or the other kids at school were being mean, the same sort of words—what do you have to complain about?

"Nothing."

And switching off her emotions and never revealing her feelings had gone from being agony to her superpower.

When Jess had had her accident, she'd been able to push her own fears aside and help and offer support to Jess's parents and Richard. At first there had been rehab, and hope and she'd kept that alive as things had worsened. Focussing on Jess's grieving relatives and remembering she was just a friend.

And in her career, it certainly helped. Conditioned since childhood to ignore her own feelings and to quash them, meant that she could block out the fact the baby wasn't crying, ignore Jasmine's pleading questions and focus on the sudden haemorrhage as she delivered the rather gritty and small placenta.

If she appeared cold, it didn't matter. Right now, she was saving the mother's life.

Luke walked over to the resuscitation cot, but stayed well back, watching the little baby and the skilled team. Even before he was attached to the monitors a nurse or doctor had a stethoscope on his chest and was tapping out the heart rate with their hand, as another team member counted it out.

'What's happening?' Jasmine was calling, and he looked over. Jasmine's monitors were alarming, and the scrub nurse was looking concerned, and then he saw the bloody suction and realised that Jasmine was haemorrhaging.

There was nobody by her side. The nurse who had been there was now running through blood and preparing for a transfusion. There were now two very sick patients in the theatre suite and it was all hands on deck.

'Tell me…' Jasmine said and then her voice weakened, her voice slurring. 'I feel dizzy.' Luke glanced over to Louise and gestured his head to Jasmine and pointed to his chest, offering to sit with her.

Louise nodded.

'Here we are again, Jasmine,' he said, because he'd sat by her side as the roof of the car had been cut off.

'I don't feel right.'

'You're going to be okay.'

'He isn't crying.'

'I know.'

He looked to Monica, who had just delivered the placenta and was placing it in a silver bowl and saw that the blood was going through.

'Can you tell me what's happening?' Jasmine asked, her voice a little groggy but her question still urgent.

'There's a team with him. I don't know any more than that, Jasmine. I just know they're doing their best for him.' Then he told her the one thing he did know. 'He's very cute.'

'Has he got hair?'

'It's black, well, from what…' Luke halted, the baby was crying. Not loud lusty cries like the babies on the unit today, more little squeaks, but they sounded beautiful.

'That's him…' Jasmine said, a smile spreading on her pale face.

'Yes.' He looked over to where the baby was being treated and told her all he could see. 'He's kicking his legs.' Luke didn't add that they were now a beautiful pink rather than that awful dusky blue he'd first seen.

The cries were growing stronger, little indignant squeals and he looked at Monica, still working away, perhaps blocking out the sound, because whether the outcome was happy or sad, good or bad, she still had an operation to complete.

And Jasmine's numbers were coming up—her blood pressure was now stable, her pulse less rapid, her voice steady again.

Then he turned as the nurse whose seat he had taken returned, but then another arrived and with company. 'You have a visitor,' Luke said, happy to vacate his seat as Jasmine's husband arrived, a touch pale and breathless.

'I'm sorry I couldn't get here sooner...'

He kissed his wife and took the seat beside her. 'A boy,' Jasmine said and then Luke watched as Jasmine broke down, sobbing as her husband stroked her face.

'It's okay,' he said. 'I'm here.'

Jasmine had been scared and petrified in the times Luke had seen her, yet had somehow held it together. Now, with her husband, she felt safe to let go...

It made him sniff.

Just a small sniff, but that was a lot for Luke, who tried not to bring emotion to work. Then he felt eyes on him and turned and saw Monica watching him, or more likely she glanced at Louise, who had come to check on the mother, but for a moment her eyes met his, and Luke smiled. 'Nice job,' he said, and from behind her mask he was sure she smiled too, and then she was straight back to work.

Louise was brilliant at midwife speak! 'Well done, Mama. You've been so brave; your baby was a little bit stunned when he came out but he's picking up now.'

'Can I see him?' Jasmine begged.

'They're about to move him to another area and then up to NICU, but I've asked them to do a little drive by.'

The resuscitaire was wheeled over. Even with tubes everywhere, his limbs were flailing and he was a feisty little thing, Luke thought.

Finally, Jasmine got to see her baby, even holding his tiny hand for a short moment before he was whisked off. Luke was asked to get the doors and as the precious load was wheeled past, Louise gave him a smile.

'Well, you got to see a caesarean.' Louise was peeling off her mask and as she let the team dash by, gestured to the theatre annexe.

'I certainly did.' Luke nodded, walking out of the theatre and into an annexe with a glass window that looked out to theatre. There, he peeled off his gown and tossed it in the linen skip as Louise did the same, chatting as they did so. 'So, you work in theatre too?' he asked.

'Well, I'm unit manager, so I oversee all the staff, but in truth this was a case of all hands on deck. It really was a full emergency. Usually, I'd have the med students and midwives and such, but they'd all gone home. Thanks for sitting with mum.'

'I was just glad to be useful. What happened?'

'I think, though I've yet to speak to Monica, that she was bleeding behind the placenta.'

'Because of the car accident?'

'I honestly don't know,' Louise admitted. 'The baby's a bit small for dates, so there's a chance the placenta hasn't been doing too well for a while. I'm just so relieved she was on the unit when it happened. Monica's been all over her care, she's been worried about her all day.'

'She's pretty impressive.'

'Oh yes,' Louise agreed. 'Monica's brilliant. She got this little one out very quickly and he's picked up nicely.' She gave him a smile. 'I hope you've enjoyed your day, and if you ever decide to do midwifery...'

'Oh no.' Luke grinned. 'One day in and I'm exhausted. But thanks so much, Louise. I've seen a lot, you've all been really welcoming.'

And that was it.

No reason now to stay.

One reason to linger.

He looked through the thick glass window and there was Monica, working on...

And he would not be hanging around to ask her out.

For one thing he didn't bring his sex life to work.

Ever.

Not that this was strictly his workplace...

But as his thoughts nudged him to reconsider, reminding him of the look they'd shared, the attraction he was sure existed between them, Luke for once felt a little daunted.

Not just because Monica had told him she wanted babies.

Her status could not go unnoticed—he'd embarrass them both if he'd misread things.

So, no, the work experience guy would not be asking the consultant out!

It was, Luke decided, time for home.

CHAPTER FOUR

LUKE HAD *NOT* misread the signs!

More than a week later Monica still couldn't get him out of her mind.

'Honestly, Jess, I've never been so attracted to anyone—not even close!'

If Jess had been able to hear and respond her mouth would have gaped in surprise, because Monica never really spoke like that. Had never really felt as she had the previous week.

She hadn't intended to tell Jess about the sexy paramedic. After all there really wasn't much to tell...

After she'd finished up Jasmine's caesarean, of course he'd been gone.

There were few benefits to your best friend being in a permanent vegetative state, but she did have a captive, if not communicative audience. And, for a moment, or rather, for a few moments, it actually felt like old times.

A little like when Jess had admitted she was crazy about Richard and the excitement of their first date... And even if that had been almost two decades ago, over the years they'd still had excited chats about Jess's love-life—her engagement, their wedding, honeymoon...

In contrast, Monica's news had been a little bland over the years.

She'd dated guys who were nice enough.

Actually, she'd almost got engaged to one that had turned out to be not nice enough.

But never had there been the impact, the sheer force of attraction she'd felt that day with Luke.

'I noticed him the day before during the handover in resus,' she told Jess. 'Honestly, he is so not my type—seriously into singledom, doesn't want kids…'

Then she paused, because for a moment she could almost hear, or rather feel, her dear friend interrupt her.

'*So what!*' Jess would have howled laughing at that statement. '*Have some fun with him.*'

'Anyway,' Monica carried on, as if her thoughts hadn't interrupted. 'I doubt I'll see him again—unless we get a direct admission to maternity or I'm called to A&E, which isn't that often. There's little chance of bumping into him…' She stopped then, surprised she'd said so much, but the visits were so difficult sometimes, it had been nice to fill the long silent gaps. 'I'll do your eyebrows,' she said, going to the bedside drawer and finding the tweezers. But as she did, she saw the wedding photo by Jess's bed and her breath quickened and for a second, she closed her eyes.

She couldn't quite believe that Richard was going to be a father, and that the mother wouldn't be Jess.

She looked back to her friend, curled up in bed, so frail that it scared her. She wasn't cross with Richard. It had been three years since the accident, and of course the world moved on.

If anything, she was jealous.

Not of Sorcha, Luke had been so wrong when he'd suggested that… No, jealous that Richard could move on, jealous that he was dating again, *having a baby.*

Then she looked back to Jess, and sitting down, brushed the hair back from her forehead but didn't tackle her eyebrows as she usually would. Instead, she did what she'd been avoiding since she'd arrived for a visit. Really looked at Jess, properly. Saw the sallow skin and sunken cheeks, and as she listened to her laboured breathing, she took her friend's fragile hand in her own.

And she knew then why she was blabbering away about some sexy guy she'd met but once—it was far easier than the truth…

Jess was fading away—nearing the end of a long and difficult journey. It could be weeks, months or days, but it was coming.

'You're the best friend I've ever had,' she told Jess. 'You taught me it was okay to be sad.'

It might seem an odd gift to be grateful for, but with her sister's ailments, she'd always been told she had nothing to complain about, nothing to cry about, no right to be upset.

She thought back to the day of her graduation, how Jess had found her in tears.

'You're the only person who's ever seen me cry,' Monica admitted, and for the first time since Jess's accident, she let the tears fall.

Life moved on.

Work was busy and she felt a little disloyal to Jess when she saw Sorcha in outpatients and realised she liked her.

'Are you ready for Christmas?' Monica asked.

'Not at all.' Sorcha sighed. 'Richard disnae even have a tree I can put up.' Then she went a little red, perhaps feeling awkward at the situation, and changed the subject. 'Can I go back to work?'

Monica knew it needed to be addressed again.

'You can. We'll see you in antenatal in four weeks, after your anatomical ultrasound. Usually, you'd see a midwife, but given the accident you've been put in higher risk category so you'll have to see a consultant.'

'You?'

'Yes, though if you'd prefer, I can arrange for a colleague to take over your care.'

'Oh no.' Sorcha shook her head. 'I'd prefer to see you. Richard's told me how good you are.' She paused. 'So long as you're okay with that. I know you and Jess were close. I mean, are close.' She met Monica's eyes. 'Would it be difficult for you though?'

'Of course not.' Monica smiled, calling on her superpower.

Of course it was, Monica thought as she made her way back to the unit at the end of a long working day that had started in theatre and ended up in outpatients.

'Ready for home?' Louise smiled.

'Not yet. I've got some results I need to chase up, but I might shut myself in my office.' She hesitated. Luke had been right, it really was Hormone City here, and right now, she ached. Maybe it was time to ask Louise for a favour and see if she could sneak her in to see Anton a little earlier. It was a bit cheeky. Anton really was a renowned fertility specialist, but she was desperate to move things along. 'Louise, is it possible to have a word?'

'Of course.'

'It's a private matter…' But as was often the case on a busy unit, the conversation halted.

Louise turned her attention to a patient, or rather, a relative. 'Is everything okay, Daniel?'

Monica knew in an instant it was Luke's brother, not just from the name; he had the same dark hair and eyes, the same high cheekbones. He was a much younger version though and visibly upset. 'I'll be fine…'

'It can be a difficult time for dads too,' Louise gently said. 'Being a new father brings out so many emotions.'

'I just don't want Kelly to see I'm upset.'

Monica glanced up at the board, trying to glean what she could, but of course there was nothing she could glean. Gosh, she hoped nothing had gone wrong, and not just in a professional sense, more…

Oh, that day still danced in her heart.

'Everything okay?' She checked with Louise, when Daniel had gone.

'Fine,' Louise said.

'He seemed upset.'

'He lost his parents.' Louise gave a sad smile. 'Years ago, but he's feeling it today and doesn't want his partner to see.'

'Oh.' She swallowed. 'He's young to have lost them both.'

'Yeah.' Louise sighed. 'Car accident. I'm going to ask for a referral to Clara. Mum's a bit anxious and they don't have much support.' She shook her head. 'Don't worry, it's not one of your patients.'

Monica nodded—she did not want to find out about Luke's private life by these means.

Yet, she did want to know.

Luke had lost his parents in a car accident? How dreadful. And to think he hadn't mentioned it when they'd been discussing Jasmine. Or his brother.

There were so many questions that felt unanswered, so much that had felt unsaid…

'Your office or mine,' Louise said, and Monica blinked. 'You wanted to talk.'

'Another time,' Monica said. 'It's nothing.'

'You're sure?' Louise frowned.

'It will keep.'

'Well, if you change your mind…'

And then, just when the ache to see him was becoming completely undeniable, when the highlight of her day was parking outside A&E in the hope she might see him, suddenly there he was—the man who had been in her thoughts and even her dreams since the moment they'd first met.

Luke was walking towards her. Dressed in dark trousers and a white shirt, and holding the string of a bunch of pale blue balloons. Monica quickly realised it wasn't the man in uniform she'd found attractive. It was the man *in* the uniform.

'Hey,' he said by way of greeting.

'Luke!' She glanced at the bunch of balloons. 'I'm guessing congratulations are in order?'

'Thank you.' He smiled. 'Have you seen him?'

'No, I haven't been in the department, I had…'

Luke finished her sentence for her. 'Theatre this morning, then outpatients.'

'How do you know?'

'I asked for you at the desk,' he said and looked right at her.

'Oh.' She swallowed. 'Were you here earlier then?'

'Yes, they called me when he was born. I was working, but I managed to come in for a little hold. This is a proper visit though.'

'That's nice.'

'I was, I admit, hoping to catch you.'

'Oh.' She stood, a little flustered, then decided she knew why he'd been asking after her. 'Did you want to know about Jasmine…' She didn't get to finish. Daniel, looking a lot happier than a few moments ago, had come out.

'Luke.'

'How are they?' He smiled, and they chatted for a very brief moment as Monica hovered a little awkwardly. 'That's great,' he said to his brother. 'I'll be in in a minute.' Then, when alone, he looked at her. 'Are you on your way home?'

'Not yet. I've got some work I need to catch up on.'

'Can I speak to you once I'm done here? I doubt Kelly will want me to stay too long.'

'Of course,' Monica said. 'I'll be up at the desk or in my office. It's the room just down…'

'I know where your office is,' Luke said, and she couldn't read the look in his eyes, just that it seemed to set her on fire.

'Good.'

And those eyes were on her, she was certain, as she walked to her office, and once inside, closed the door in breathless relief.

He wanted to know about Jasmine.

Or to ask about another patient from that day.

It had to be that.

She took a seat at her desk and took out some of her endless paperwork, to at least look as if she wasn't a quivering wreck at the sight of him.

The knock on her door had her heart thumping.

'Yes.'

The door opened and there he was.

'Come in.'

But Luke didn't. Instead, he stood at the open door.

'Monica. I don't want this to be awkward. Or to cause any offence...'

Luke really didn't. She was sitting at her desk and he just did not know how to play this.

Had he got this wrong? She was incredibly hard to read, yet there was this energy between them.

'I may be wrong, and if that's the case, then I apologise in advance.'

Monica liked that this confident man was now a touch tentative. She liked that he didn't close the door and stride towards her, even if a part of her wanted him to.

She felt respected.

'There's no need to apologise,' Monica said.

'Ahh, but you don't know what I'm about to say.'

'Perhaps close the door before you do,' Monica suggested.

'Sure.'

There was a lovely click as he closed the door, and then he looked over at her, those black eyes like flint sparking a reaction.

'I've been thinking about you,' he told her.

Monica bit the side of her lower lip at the slight husk to his tone and then was honest in her response. 'I've been thinking about you too.'

She stood as if beckoned and walked over.

'A lot,' he said, slipping hands around her waist while looking right at her.

'And me.'

He didn't need to say more, he just lowered his head and she felt the brush of his lips on hers and closed her eyes as he kissed her. The tentative Luke was gone, and he claimed her mouth and devoured her. His lips, his tongue, his scratchy jaw and the hands on her waist, pulling her in. She had never known such a kiss, one that didn't end when his mouth left hers, because he pulled her even tighter in and kissed her neck, and then kissed up her jaw. 'God, you smell so good…'

Oh, so did he—the clean scent she'd caught that morning was delectable, and she was searching for his mouth, pressing her body in and wondering how it had taken so long to find this bliss.

It was a decadent, thrilling kiss, and she really should have turned the Do Not Disturb light on. One hand was pressing into her bottom the other in her hair, and she felt as if she were falling, as if his body was the only thing steady. He kissed her till she was breathless, then his head moved back and he looked down at her with hungry eyes.

'So,' he said, 'are you going to buy me a glass of champagne to celebrate being an uncle?'

Monica laughed. 'I thought you'd never ask.' But then her smile faded, and she felt just a little bemused, because she really wasn't one for casual dates, especially with guys who barely made it to three weeks. 'Luke…' She was breathless, in the very nicest of ways. 'We're very different.' She didn't know how best to put it. 'We want different things.'

'Long-term, we want different things. Right now—' he pulled her in even closer '—I'd say we want the very same.'

Yes.

She wanted him in a way she'd never wanted another, not even close.

This heavy desire combined with light-headed lust and she'd spent her life being sensible and contained.

Yes, right now, they wanted the same thing and right now was enough.

'Let's just have dinner,' Luke said. 'Just us.' Then he groaned at the pleasure. 'Without interruption.'

'Yes.' It sounded like bliss. 'I should be finished in an hour or…'

'Take your time.' He told her the name of a bar. 'La Milonga, do you know it?'

'No.'

'The food's great,' he said and told her where it was. 'We can meet there. Or I can wait here for you?'

'No, let's meet at the bar.'

'No rush.'

He would wait.

And for Monica that made finishing up work a very nice breeze.

It was a Spanish bar and very lively for so early in the week. At first it seemed all high tables and bar stools, but glancing around there was a quieter area, the dim lighting cast a glow over weathered leather couches and low rustic tables, and there was Luke.

'Hi.' He stood as she came over and they shared a light kiss and she took a seat by his side. They were tucked away just enough that the vibrant music was dulled to allow them to speak.

'I'm driving,' she reminded, 'but I'll get you that champagne.'

'No need.' He pointed to his glass of red. 'That was just a ruse to get you here.'

There were menus on the table and she picked one up, but it was mostly in Spanish and having glanced through it, she shook her head.

'I have no idea,' Monica admitted. 'I'm too hungry for tapas but…' There were so many gorgeous things she wanted to try, but Luke was ahead of her and the waiter placed down two plates, as another came over with some dishes. 'You've already ordered.'

'Just some starters,' he said, 'I didn't know what time you'd get off and I was starving. I haven't eaten today.'

'Too worried?'

'I guess. If you didn't get here in time, I was going to eat them and not tell you.'

Monica laughed and then gazed longingly at the food the waiter had placed down and was naming. But in Spanish!

'*Patatas Bravas*,' the waiter said, placing down the first dish. '*Y Gambas al Ajillo, y Empanadas Criollas—*' He smiled at Luke. '*Tan bueno como los aperitivos en Buenos Aires. ¡Que aproveche!*'

Luke nodded approvingly, picking up one of the *empanadas*. '*Seguro, gracias—pinta barbaro*,' he responded easily.

Monica frowned, intrigued by the exchange. 'Buenos Aires? Are you from Argentina?'

'I am, we came to England when I was seven or so. Most of my family are still there, I go back when I can.' He gestured to the food and translated. '*Patatas bravas*…hot chips with a kick and these are prawns in chili oil and these…' He pushed a plate forward.

'*Empanadas*,' she said. 'I know them.'

Only she knew more the frozen kind.

These though were little parcels of pastry stuffed with beef and olives with a spicy cumin edge and served with *chimichurri*, they were so hot that she had to wrap them in a napkin to eat them, and they were utterly delicious.

'What was the waiter saying?'

'That the food here is as good as home,' he translated, 'and it is.'

'Wow!'

'The music too…we can dance later.'

'Please no.' Monica laughed. 'I don't think you quite get how…'

'How what?'

'It's Monday!'

'You don't dance on Mondays,' he checked with a light tease.

'Not usually.'

Monica, who was driving and working tomorrow, was introduced to pomelo sodas—a drink served in a retro glass and poured over ice and a slice of grapefruit, dressed up enough to feel such a treat.

The company was the real treat though. They just spoke so easily. At first about the baby.

'When did you find out she was in labour?'

'Daniel called late last night, which meant I barely slept.' He tore apart another pastry. 'We're closer than most,' he explained why, and Monica was glad she hadn't probed Louise for information—it was so much better hearing it from him. 'We lost our parents a while back.'

'How long ago?'

'The twins were twelve, so ten years ago now.'

'Twins?'

'Daniel and Josie.'

'How old were you?'

'Twenty-two.'

'So who raised them?'

'Me. Well, I had a lot of help from my aunt. She lives close by.'

'Even so… I'm so sorry.' She swallowed. 'How did they die?'

'A car accident.'

'You weren't on duty?'

'No, thank God. I doubt I'd still be a paramedic if that had been the case.' He took a sip of wine. 'It was a long time ago.'

'No wonder you're close. Do you all live together?'

'Not now, I kept the family home until they were…' He gave a fond laugh. 'The plan was until they were eighteen, but I didn't want them to feel I was just waiting for them to get out. Daniel went to university and Josie went to tech, so I kept it for one year, you, know…' He waited for her to nod, but instead she waited for him to continue. 'Well, so they could come home for breaks and things, then we sold it.'

'That was nice. Not selling it from under them.'

'It was time…' He nodded. 'We're not set up for life or anything, but it gave us all a start. I'm trying to tell Josie that it won't last that long if she doesn't get a decent job.'

'What does she do?'

'Very part-time waitressing, and she makes jewellery, which she barely sells.'

Monica laughed. 'What about Daniel?'

'He studied accounting, like my father. I told you, he's more sensible than me. What about you?'

'Just one sister, Clara. You met her that morning.'

That morning…

'She's five years younger than me.'

'How is it, working at the same hospital?'

'It's fine. Our paths cross quite a bit, but we keep things professional.'

'What about your parents?'

'They're great.' Monica's hand wavered. 'Well, they're very protective.'

'Of you?'

Her eyes narrowed and she looked back at him. 'No, of Clara.'

'Because she's blind?'

'She has low vision,' Monica tersely corrected, but he rather guessed that wasn't aimed at him because she took a sharp breath and then let it out. 'She had a lot of health difficulties when she was born and into childhood. It's natural for them to be protective. The thing is Clara doesn't want it. She's incredibly independent, hates people making a fuss…'

'So, you two are similar after all.'

Monica smiled. 'I've never really thought of it like that.'

He waited, wanting more of a glimpse into her, but she denied him that with a shake of her head. 'They're great,' she added.

Luke wasn't so sure.

There was hurt in her eyes, and he was rather certain that Monica's independence wasn't quite by choice. He still wanted to know more, when usually for Luke, the music, the food and beautiful company would be enough, yet he'd chosen to sit in the alcove.

The waiter had noticed too.

As he came with some more delicious food and to top up their drinks, he had a question for Luke '*¿Cómo es que no estás en la barra? Es tu banda favorita.*' Topping up Monica's glass, the waiter translated what he had said. 'I ask him why he's not at the bar when his favourite band is playing.'

'*Eh,*' Luke said, '*algo diferente esta vez.*'

Then, alone again, Luke told her his response. 'Something different this time.'

Their eyes met and held then.

'Very different,' Monica agreed.

This wasn't what she did on weeknights, or even on the wildest of weekends, and she was not talking about the food—more where her mind was wandering.

The kiss in her office had left her breathless and wanting, and now, the sensual music seemed to be slinking towards them, the singer's husky voice almost beckoning for them to join her.

'What is this music?'

'*Tango neuvo,* I think…they mix it up a bit…'

'You come here a lot.'

'Yes, it's nice to keep up my Spanish. Daniel and Josie aren't really interested. I tell them they should learn.'

'Is this where you bring your dates, or is it where you meet them?'

She wanted more information, to know more about the rules of this man.

'Both,' he admitted, his eyes never leaving hers, 'but as the waiter said, I am generally having a seat at the bar.'

'I'm getting the special treatment.'

'You deserve the special treatment,' he said in a way that made the unflappable Monica blush from her roots to her toes. 'I wanted to ask you here the day we worked together. I didn't know if I should…'

'I like it this way,' she said. 'It could have muddied the waters. I mean, I don't…'

'Don't what?'

'I'm not sure quite what I mean,' Monica admitted, then decided to at least try and be up-front. 'I guess I don't know what I'd have said if you had asked then.'

She'd needed a few days to get her head around the attraction, to think things through, even talk things out. She thought of Jess. 'I have a confession.'

'Not yet you don't.' He smiled, and so naturally they shared a kiss that tasted of all the promise to come, then gazed at each other for a moment.

'I meant, about my friend Jess.' She moved back and took a sip of her drink. 'I wasn't being fair on Richard—the reality is Jess is in a coma, or rather a persistent vegetative state. She had a horse-riding accident three years ago. There was a chance of some recovery for the first year, but then she had a secondary bleed. Richard has just about given away his career to take care of her. She's in Wales and he visits all the time.'

'Do you visit?'

'Of course. I was there this weekend, I've been worried

about Richard for a long time. I'm a bit torn, but really, I'm happy for him. He's had the most dreadful time of things.'

'So have you.'

'It's nothing in comparison.'

'You've lost your best friend.'

'I haven't lost her yet.' She pushed out a smile, and it was Moncia's turn to shut the conversation down, but he didn't take the cue, just stared with those black eyes, awaiting more. 'I don't think she's got very long.'

'I'm sorry. Is it difficult being Sorcha's doctor?'

'Of course not.' She flashed a smile, and when he didn't return it, she felt he knew that her smile had been forced. 'I might just freshen up.'

In the ladies, there was a small queue, and as she waited, she read a noticeboard. There were cooking demonstrations, dance classes, tasting nights…it was like discovering another world.

The music was loud as she stepped out, a female singer with a smoky, gravelly voice had taken to the stage.

Luke didn't wait for her to take her seat; in fact he stood as she approached. 'Are we heading off?'

'I thought we both wanted to dance.' He laughed a deep sexy laugh and held out his hand. 'Are you saying you don't want to?'

'No,' she said and stood. 'Though I'm not sure we should.'

'Oh, we should,' he said, leading her to a small and quite crowded dance floor. 'We very much should,' he said, pulling her into his embrace.

The music was sinfully sexy. Monica rather thought the band might like Luke too, because the trio seemed to turn up the heat just for him. His hands were loosely on her hips, their foreheads close and his mouth so near it made her own ache.

'I like this music,' she admitted, and he pulled her closer and lifted her hair, and she felt his breath on her neck and then the brush of his warm lips.

It was a lot for a Monday!

A delicious lot.

Their bodies melding, they moved, his hands sliding low on her hips, as her own moved to his neck, their bodies pressed tight on the crowded dance floor. It was the sexiest she had ever felt, and that took account of her entire sexual history. Nothing came close. Their movements were sensual, their hips swaying in sync, the heat building with every step.

And it was as confusing for Monica as it was new.

'I don't do this,' she said.

'Well, you should, you're a brilliant dancer,' he said, pretending he'd misunderstood.

'Fall into bed with a guy I've just met.'

'I asked you to come for a drink,' he reminded. 'And something to eat. Who said anything about bed?'

Their bodies did.

'And the bar closes in a little while,' he told her. 'We'll be on our way home. Relax…'

Fine for him to say, but she was turned on in his arms and unfamiliar with such sensual feelings, the music seemed to have its own pulse and one that beat through them.

Yes, nothing untoward was happening.

As they stepped out into the chilly night, it would seem they were headed to their individual homes. 'Where are you parked?'

'There.' She pointed her keys and flashed her car lights.

'So, I don't need to walk you to your car,' he said, pulling her into his arms. 'We'll say goodnight here.'

'Where do you live?'

'Ten minutes on the tube.'

'I can drive you.'

'No need.'

Every need—she did not want this night to be over. 'It's no problem.'

He gave her his address and as she punched it into her

phone, they also exchanged numbers. 'Can I call you?' he asked. 'Sort out another night?'

'I'd like that.'

He really was a gentleman, even if it was Monica driving him home.

'Where do you live?'

'Hampstead.' she told him.

'So not too far to go.'

'No.'

'Thanks for the lift.'

He leant over and gave her a kiss, a lingering one, but not too deep, and then he did as a gentleman would and got out.

Damn.

'Luke.' It was Monica who called him back, and he lowered his head and peered in from the passenger side. 'Aren't you going to ask me in for a drink?'

'If I ask you in,' Luke said, 'it won't be for a drink.' He smiled a very wicked smile and took out his wallet. 'You need a permit to park here overnight.' He handed her a slip of paper.

A temporary permit for her temporary diversion.

'Kind of ruins the spontaneity,' he said, in that gravelly sexy voice that couldn't ruin a thing, 'but I'm not coming out wearing a towel at 2:00 a.m.'

'Excellent.'

'You have to be gone by eight or you risk getting towed.'

He made her laugh, he made street parking sexy, he made her forget all her worries about tomorrow and just focus on this night.

CHAPTER FIVE

IT WAS COLD and his apartment was in one of those glorious buildings with a long, curved stairwell that they climbed together.

Inside, it was very male in decor, with beautiful long windows, and just as cold as the street outside. There was no question of getting her bearings though, or taking details in—they were barely through the door, and Monica was still in her coat as he spun her around and kissed her hard.

The sort of kiss that had been missing her entire life because it was laced with passion and deep, aching desire.

It was a kiss that pressed her to the wall, and there he pushed her coat down her arms, but only for more access. As it fell to the floor, his mouth continued to claim her. And Monica reciprocated, her want so fierce, while knowing that if she paused to think it would shock her.

The hands that had been lightly suggestive on the dance floor were indecently indiscreet now, slipping under her silk top and stroking the skin with his palms, then unhooking her bra and squeezing her breasts. Only it clearly wasn't enough for Luke.

'Lift your arms,' he growled, and in a second, she was naked from the waist up.

Monica was just as impatient, eagerly undoing the buttons on his white linen shirt, tugging it out from his trousers, and then catching her breath at the beauty of him. No waxing or lasers or whatever for Luke, instead there was a gorgeous fan of dark hair, but no time to linger. Immediately, she was undoing his belt, his kiss a breath away, his rough jaw on her cheeks as she unzipped him…

It felt as if the world might be ending and there was not a second to waste, because when he hitched up her skirt, it was Monica slipping her underwear down, stepping out of it, as if scared she might die not knowing the bliss of feeling him inside.

'Please.' She was kissing his neck as he slowed things down enough to find a condom and the very sensible Monica's common sense was almost gone.

'I'm on the pill.'

'Don't be reckless,' he warned, and it felt like a little slap, just a jolt as she realised that he was the one in control here, and not her.

And as he rolled it on, she was shaken, nicely though, but shaken at her own recklessness, and liking that he held it together. Not for much longer.

'I have to be inside you.' His hands were between her thighs, feeling her intimately, moist and so turned on. When he lifted her up, and she lowered onto him, as she distributed her weight to his hips, she almost laughed at the joy of him.

Luke did *not* make her feel like a carthorse.

She was mired in sensation—the press of his hands into her buttocks, the cold of the wall against her back and the building heat between them. Her arms were over his wide shoulders, her hands balling into fists at the delicious build of tension, and she knew she was close.

Except for this, except for them, every thought in her head seemed to have disappeared. There was only room for pleasure. 'I'm going to…' She usually took forever. Or faked it just to be done. But the staccato rhythm of his thrusts, the ragged sound of his breath, *all* of it had her tipping towards the edge.

He gave a breathless shout in response, not just to her

words, but her intimate tightening. As he shot into her it felt as if every muscle in her body twitched in spasm, her orgasm the deepest, the most intense, she'd known.

'Oh God,' she said. They were ear to ear, her looking over his back to the semi dark room. Her mouth open, a little stunned.

'Yeah,' he said, as if he felt exactly the same, then he pulled his head back so he looked right into her eyes as he lowered her down.

She felt shaky standing on the wooden floor.

Different.

Better.

She'd never let herself go quite so much before, never wanted so badly, or given herself so much.

It was liberating.

Tonight had been the biggest adventure of her life.

'My apologies,' he said as he led her through to the bedroom. Switching on the light, she looked at his low, unmade bed. 'I wasn't expecting company.'

It was a very sexy, very male room. There was his uniform over a chair and a couple of belts, a heavy wooden wardrobe and wide floorboards, wonderfully understated. The scent of his cologne hung in the air. An open book lay facedown on his pillow, and it was some manual on emergency procedures.

'Odd bedtime reading.' She smiled as he took the book from the side where she would lay.

'Not when your brother's partner is in labour.'

'True.'

'I'll get another glass.'

There was a jug and glass on what must be his side of the bed, so she took off her rather rumpled clothes, or what was left of them, and slipped into presumably the guest side of his bed, trying not to think about how many guests there had been, or how normal this was for him.

It was so abnormal for her.

She took forever to get into bed with anyone, or rather to have sex.

When it came to Luke, she'd barely made it through the door let alone into the bed!

And she couldn't blame it on the wine. She'd been on sparkling grapefruit all night. Monica had been the one driving and supposedly in control.

'Here.'

He put a glass of water by her bed and turned on a side light before turning off the main one. 'I've just got to make a call.'

'Sure.'

'My brother...'

They spoke half in English and half in Spanish. Mainly in English, but there were little phrases and slices of the man she'd met in the bar tonight. And they were close, she could just tell.

'They've called him Gus.'

He took her in his arms. 'That's gorgeous.'

'After our father.'

She lay silent, not quite sure what to say.

'Are you working tomorrow?' he asked. 'Should I set an alarm?'

'I am working, but I have an alarm set. You?'

'No, I'm taking a family day,' he said. 'I have to build a cot tomorrow. That was Daniel asking me. Oh, and fit a car seat.'

'Is it superstition, or tradition?'

'What?'

'That you don't do it before the baby arrives?'

'No, it's just my lazy brother, getting me to do something he doesn't want to.' He laughed and pulled her close. 'So, yeah, tradition in my crazy family. I should get the chocolates for the midwives. I can guarantee he won't think to.' They lay together, talking sleepily. 'What about you?' he asked. 'I've already told you I don't do deep relationships. Have you been married or...'

'Gosh no.' She shook her head. 'I was close to getting engaged once, but I dodged a bullet.'

'How come?'

'He was very focused on his career.'

'I get that,' Luke said, a little surprised by her response. He lifted his head and peered down where she lay with her head on his chest, then smiled when she elaborated.

'He wanted me to focus on his career too.'

'Ah!'

'And he…' She paused, not really wanting to talk about an ex, feeling the crinkly hair of his stomach and the solid body by her side, and she did *not* feel like a carthorse. 'It just didn't work.'

It was such a nice sleep.

She woke to the scent of coffee and a cup being placed on the table and, even better, Luke slipping back into bed and spooning into her.

'Are we going to sort out when we do this again?' He was kissing her back and making the short stretch for her cup of coffee seem an impossible feat because she wanted to roll over to him. 'I'm working now till Saturday morning.'

'I'm on call this weekend.'

'*Carajo*,' he cussed, or rather it sounded like a light cuss.

His hands were pressing into her stomach, pulling her back to slowly enjoy the morning, but her alarm was singing and there was no time to indulge.

Carajo indeed!

'Look, maybe it's better.' She rolled over to look at him, deciding to just voice the truth. 'We're going nowhere. We want different things.'

'I know what I want,' he said, toying with her breast, then those black eyes lifted to hers. 'What do you want?'

'What I mean is, there's no future.' She didn't really know how best to say it. 'I told you I wanted a baby.'

He laughed. 'You're in the wrong bed for that.'

'I had gathered that much.' She smiled, but then told him the truth. 'I'm booking in to see a specialist. I'm going to go it alone.'

He said nothing.

'And I'm supposed to come off the pill for at least three months prior and…'

Surprisingly he gave her a light scold. 'Are you sure that's a good idea? You didn't give it much thought last night…'

'That was last night,' Monica said. 'I am careful.' She couldn't really tell him she'd never been so bold in her life, and still felt a little foolish suggesting they go without a condom, especially given their temporary status. 'And now it's the cold light of morning, literally. And we're going nowhere.'

'True.' He offered a regretful smile. 'You wouldn't want me. I am hard to pin down, unreliable, unless you are family, and don't worry, I never involve my dating life in that.'

'Never?'

'God no, I decided ages ago it was too confusing.' He didn't elaborate, which she wished he would, not that they had time, and he didn't lie, which she liked. He didn't make promises he couldn't keep.

She used his shower; all male scents and dark towels and she pinched his comb to sort out her hair. Wiping the steamed up mirror with her hand, she startled when she saw herself. Oh, she should look at her wild hair and smeared mascara, but instead even she could see the effect this night had had. There was no regret in her eyes, no sting of shame tightening her mouth and for a second it felt as if she was looking at a stranger. She looked carefree, happy even… As if he'd brought out a side to her she didn't even know.

'I have to get home and change.'

'Why?'

'I wore this yesterday.'

'Pinch something of mine.'

'Stop.' She laughed, as he went in his wardrobe. 'It would

be huge. And I don't have…' She paused. Actually, she did have fresh knickers, she'd been stuck at work too many times not to have the basics in her bag. And now he was coming at her with a sheer grey jumper and slipping it over her head. 'Told you,' she said. It fell to her thighs, and there was room for two of her in there, but he wasn't deterred—tucking the jumper into her waist, and then pulling it out a touch, so it fell rather nicely.

'See,' he said, coming up behind her. She watched as his hands slipped beneath her arms and he arranged the hem he'd created. 'It looks good.'

'I guess I could change into scrubs when I get there,' she said, watching as his hands spanned her stomach.

'And you'd have to return it,' he said, holding her breasts and pinching them through the fabric as she watched. 'Because I like that jumper, or do I just like what's in it?'

'Luke…' She wanted him to peel off her clothing as expertly as he'd put it on. And she wanted to go back to his bed, but to be made love to this time, slowly. To take their time, except she had to be at work and as well as that… 'I am not a casual fling person. Last night was an exception.'

'Last night was exceptional,' he seduced. 'And I haven't finished with you yet,' he said. As she inhaled sharply with indignation, he added, 'Have you finished with me?'

Then he kissed her, softly, too softly, till her tongue was chasing his for more, and her body ached for the relief he'd delivered last night.

'No,' she admitted, because she didn't feel finished yet. 'But…'

'Was last night fun?'

'It was,' she admitted.

'So, why not keep things like this for as long as it lasts? Then you can throw away your pills and I can get back to…'

'To what?'

'Not constantly thinking about the sexy doctor in maternity.' He smiled. 'I can be your final fling.'

Her first fling, actually, not that she said.

'Do not,' he warned, pulling her hips into him, 'come off the pill.'

'If we do see each other...' She set her own rules. 'And I mean this...'

'Name it.'

'No one else. When it stops being fun, we end it but, in the meantime...'

'I get it,' he said. 'Exclusive as long as it lasts.'

'Yes.'

'*Trato hecho*,' he said. 'It's a deal.'

'*Trato hecho*,' Monica said. 'One more thing...'

'Tell me.'

'Make me late for work this morning.'

Well not late exactly.

She just didn't arrive at work early.

The temporary diversion sign was still up, and this morning it made her smile.

Arriving on the unit, her long chestnut hair was damp from the morning shower, taken with him. Monica selected some scrubs from the trolley.

'Morning, Monica.' Louise beamed. 'God, I love that jumper.'

'Thanks.' She nodded and attempted to flee to her office.

'No, I seriously love that jumper,' Louise said. 'Oh, why can't I get my French tucks to sit like that?'

French tuck?

'Where did you get it?' Louise asked.

'I honestly can't remember. Erm...' Because she was surrounded by touchy-feely midwives it should come as no surprise when Louise's bony fingers dived into her back for a label.

'Facon?' Louise frowned. 'Never heard of it...'

Gosh, she'd never been happier to flee to her office, but instead of sorting out her inbox, she was reading about a Buenos Aires company and their artisanal goods inspired by the gaucho culture.

Oh, there was such a masculine, earthy vibe to Luke, and she didn't want to ever give him his jumper back. Lifting up the neck, she breathed in deeply, hoping for just a trace of the bergamot, tobacco scent of his cologne, and there it was. Monica inhaled and felt a little dizzy. For the first time, where a man was concerned, she was floating.

It was a busy morning, and at eleven, having just delivered a gorgeous large baby to a diabetic mum, she was more than ready for a hot chocolate.

'He's beautiful.' Monica spoke with the anxious mother, but as George explained, even though he was big, he was actually a touch premature. His size didn't match his dates.

'I know you told me to expect this...' the tearful mum said, 'but now I've seen him, he looks so well.'

'And he is well,' Monica assured. 'We just want to keep a closer eye on him. He needs his blood sugars to be regularly checked...'

Louise came in then. 'Are you worrying, Mum?' she said and wrapped her arms around the anxious woman in a way Monica couldn't. Louise really was brilliant at this. 'He's gorgeous and very, very cute. We really just want extra cuddles.'

She made the teary mum laugh, and as Monica left them to it, she headed to the nurses' station to update her notes and then hopefully take a break and have something to eat.

'Thanks so much.' A box of chocolates was being placed on the ledge of the nurses' station and Monica looked up and saw Daniel with his partner. He was holding a baby capsule and a little pink face was just visible and she dared not peek. She did not need to know how gorgeous Arias babies were.

'Chocolates!' Louise beamed. 'You didn't have to do that.'

Monica couldn't help but smile, knowing Luke had actually done that, as well as fitted the car seat.

'Cute baby,' Louise commented as the new parents headed for home with their precious bundle.

'You say that about all of them.'

'Of course, but little Gus has these huge navy eyes that are going to be black in a few weeks. My younger one's eyes were navy like that.' She sat at the desk. 'What was it you wanted to talk about, Monica?'

'Sorry?'

'Yesterday—you said there was something you wanted to discuss, but we never did get a moment.'

'Oh yes.' Monica shook her head. 'It's fine.' Again, Monica shook her head. 'I was just…' She truly didn't know what to say. 'I can't even remember what it was about.'

'Sure?' Louise frowned as if she didn't quite believe her. 'There's not a problem on the unit I should know about?'

'Nothing like that.' Monica knew she was being evasive and that wasn't fair. 'It was a personal matter. I'm just…'

'That's fine.' Louise patted her arm. 'If you ever do want to talk, I'm here.'

'Thanks,' Monica said.

No doubt she'd soon be asking Louise if she could get her in to see her fertility specialist husband.

For now, though, her baby plans were on hold.

Even if she was surrounded by them.

CHAPTER SIX

LUKE WAS A little surrounded by babies too.

Or rather one baby.

As December arrived, he took a phone call from Daniel, who was stressed at work. 'I did what you said and took over all the feeds last night, but Kelly could still hear him and kept coming out. She's barely getting any sleep.'

Neither was Luke…

He peered at the time and blew out a breath.

'Do you want me to bring him here for a couple of hours?'

'Could you?'

'Sure, I'll head over now.'

As well as colicky infants, the off-duty gods seemed to have it in for Monica and Luke—their carefree, fun time together took quite a lot of planning.

They made time though.

It was sex, yes, but there was so much more. Once, when Luke finished an exceptionally late shift and Monica was off the next day, he'd taken her for a drive to see the Christmas lights.

'You've got a baby capsule…'

'Yes, I bring him back to mine now and then, just so Kelly can get some sleep.'

And because, like all emergency workers, he knew the very best places to eat after midnight, she'd found herself sipping an espresso martini and eating fluffy pancakes…

They'd gone back to his and stayed not just for the remainder of the night, but the rest of the next day. Luke lightly snoring, as he squeezed in a solid eight hours before his night shift might not sound romantic or fun…

Possibly it wasn't.

For Monica it was a different kind of bliss as she wandered out to the shops near his flat and assembled a massive moussaka for her next roster and added a couple of portions to his freezer.

And it was a different kind of bliss for Luke, when after a very long shift, he went in the freezer and finally he got to taste the source of the delectable scent that had teased him that first day. 'I want you to make your cottage pie next time,' he'd said.

'Shepherd's pie,' she corrected.

'What's the difference?'

The difference was, not just that she answered his question this time, more of those little confirmations that this was still fun and there would be a next time.

And a next.

Squeezing in breakfast in bed, even if one or both hadn't been in said bed the previous night, was a favourite—this morning Luke had arrived to her little town house in Hampstead. He'd slipped in bed beside her and she'd woken to his cold, solid body and his kiss.

Now they lay eating croissants and trying to carve a full night together, preferably this year!

Their schedules clashed spectacularly, and the rare weekend in December they did share was one where she was visiting Jess.

'I'd feel terrible if I didn't see her all month.'

'I get it.'

Luke did.

He too was a bit snowed under with little Gus, or rather his brother and Kelly, who were panicked new parents. A lot of his time seemed to be spent over there, reassuring them.

'Then I'm at my family's for Christmas.' Monica sighed.

And Luke was working after that.

'We'll work something out. Right now we'd better get going, or you're going to be late…' He peeled her from his now warm body and went to haul himself out of bed, but Monica had a better idea. 'You don't have to go now—sleep here.'

'You're on call tonight,' he pointed out. 'You won't be back.'

'So…' Monica shrugged. 'You can let yourself out when you wake up, just lock up behind you—I'll leave some keys.' She headed to the shower as if what she'd said was no big deal, but they both knew it was another step forward. A step towards where they didn't quite know, because they really did want different things for the future. Yet, she'd slept at his apartment a couple of times when he'd headed off to work, and she had the keys and access code to his flat. She'd even met Mr Nicholas, his elderly neighbour who couldn't work out his television remote.

He had let her into a little more of his life.

And now she was offering the same for him.

It was no big deal, they told themselves.

On New Year's Eve, both were working of course, and as the new year approached, she sat at the nurses' station with Louise, who was doing a stint of nights.

'How's Mrs Atkins?'

'Sore,' Louise said. 'I'm going to help her get into the salt bath, I'm just running it now. She doesn't want to leave her…' She looked down at the very little grizzly girl she was holding. 'Give Mummy five minutes peace.' She looked over. 'So what did you do over Christmas?' Louise asked. 'You were working?'

'Yes, but I had Boxing Day off and a couple of days after. I spent it with family, and…' she paused '…caught up with a friend.' Monica knew damn well the midwives were gossiping. Luke wasn't easy to miss, and he had been to the unit quite a few times of late, bringing in a hot chocolate and stealing a kiss in her office.

'A friend?' Louse checked, waiting for Monica to elaborate, which she didn't. 'Nice,' Louise said. 'What are your New Year resolutions?' she asked, then promptly answered the question for herself. 'I have loads. I'm going to learn Italian. I want to actually converse with Anton's family when we visit. He's Italian…' she added.

'I had guessed.'

'Oh, and get back to Pilates. And I want to read a book every month.'

'You're going to be busy.'

'I am,' Louise agreed. 'Oh, and I want another baby…'

Monica said nothing.

'I've just got to convince Anton. As I told him, I didn't marry a fertility specialist for nothing…' There was a long pause and Monica just kept on writing. 'So, what are your resolutions?'

'I'm not sure,' Monica admitted.

'You'd better hurry up and decide—there's less than an hour to go.'

Monica smiled, but it faded as Louise popped baby Atkins back in the cot and headed off to take care of her fretful mum.

Every year she made one, and apparently, she was a rarity, because generally she kept to them.

For many years it had been vigorous study plans, and in later years it had been to find a better work-life balance. She had worked diligently, exercised regularly, caught up with friends…

After Jess's accident her resolutions had changed.

Be there for Jess.

Monica had been and would continue to be. Becoming a mother herself was becoming an increasing priority, or it had been until she'd met Luke and her plans had derailed.

Now she was seeing Luke, it was early days and yet her heart skipped a beat every time she saw him.

His touch, his kiss, the way he made her feel.

It had been six weeks—almost a record by Luke's standards, and she kept waiting for the gloss to wear off, to not feel so quite taken by that black-eyed smile and his kiss that could melt. For the pink clouds to disperse so she could get back to her baby plans…

Her reminder pinged then for her to take her pill. A slightly odd time, but she had long ago worked out that half an hour from midnight was the safest time. She was up if she was at home, and working if not…

Baby Atkins did not appreciate the lack of attention. The squawking in the cot grew a little louder. She was utterly used to the sound of a baby crying, the welcome first cry after birth, the constant background noise of hungry or unsettled little ones, was a normal part of her day.

But this little cry pulled right at her heart.

Turning, she looked at the little infant—her blanket had fallen and she was all untucked and uncosy. She went to pull it over her, but she kicked it off…flailing, and Monica was no midwife who could effortlessly settle the fussiest baby, but she did make an attempt to swaddle the little one.

'Gosh,' she said as the baby soon discarded her effort, her wails growing louder, and finally she picked her up.

Many thought this would be a common occurrence, that she spent half her time dealing with babies, yet it wasn't. Monica took care of them in utero and then delivered them. From there their care came under the midwives and paediatricians… Yet she was surrounded by babies every minute of her working day. And there was no real solace in her office. Her inbox was filled with articles flashing her declining fertility, or the outpatients' appointments were filled with incredible, determined woman who had chosen to go it alone.

As had she.

But now all plans had been placed on hold, for a guy who had said from the start that this would never last, and she'd put motherhood off for the pursuit of fun. She went into her pocket and slipped the pill onto her tongue, then checked off the reminder.

No accidents for Monica—she was too diligent for that.

God, but she wanted a baby.

They were everywhere. No longer was it confined to work. Luke had a baby seat in his car, and his gorgeous jumpers—she was still holding on to the grey one—had a slight baby scent at times.

Just no baby for Monica.

And at fifteen minutes to midnight she sat in the semi darkness of a fading year and held a hot angry infant and felt her soothe, the cries fading, and she ran a finger over her eyebrow, watching her eyelids closing.

She didn't know when the assumption she'd one day have a baby had turned into a want, and lately it felt like a need.

Jess hadn't been able to have children. She wasn't sure if Richard knew that she knew. It had been years ago that Jess had cried when she'd told her.

Richard didn't mind at all, Jess had told her.

Jess had minded though.

It stuck in her craw a little that in June, Richard would be a father.

'Thanks, Monica.' Louise snapped her out of introspection as she returned. 'Mum could hear her crying and was getting stressed.'

'No problem.'

The only problem was that she was very, very close to tears and lowered her head so as not to let anyone see as she placed the little one into its crib.

She looked over to Louise and was so desperate to ask about Anton, to call in that favour, just to find out her options *without* going off the pill, that she decided it might be safer to leave the unit for a little while.

'I might head up to the party and watch the fireworks…'

They couldn't see the main London fireworks, but there were local displays, and it was a nice annual get-together for staff, or at least those who could get away from their posts for a little while. The party room was in fact an old ward now used for teaching, the beds and equipment had been pushed aside and trestle tables were spread out, the catering done by those present and Monica placed down her offering—several bags of chocolate sweets she'd bought from the vending machine. Then she chatted to a couple of colleagues. George was there and they'd been friends for a long time too, but as midnight struck, she drifted from the group and watched the sky light up and the fireworks fizz...

And her thoughts were no longer on babies or even a sexy Argentinian paramedic, but the best friend she'd ever had.

Oh, Jess.

Monica knew in her heart this had been Jess's last Christmas. And, while she didn't want to miss her time with Luke, she wasn't about to give up on her best friend now.

Then a low voice had her heart soaring like one of the rockets that shot into the sky, then burst into a pink peony, showering light into the night sky. 'Happy New Year.'

'Luke...' She turned. 'How come you're here?'

'We all try and get up if we can. May gave us her pass. I'm doing my paperwork up here. Vicky's never worked a New Year's Eve before.'

Vicky wasn't even looking at the fireworks, she was filling up her plate and enjoying the food.

It was so nice to snatch a few moments and welcome in the New Year together, though she ached to turn around and really welcome it in with a kiss. But of course, they were at work, and now Vicky had joined them.

'Busy night?' Monica asked.

'It's about to be.' Vicky nodded. 'I'll go and make up the stretcher. I'll meet you down there.'

'Sure.' Luke nodded. 'I'll just finish up the paperwork and let them know we've cleared.'

But first.

They went to the stairwell. 'Happy New Year,' Luke said. It suddenly was.

This night was made better by a few moments alone, and it almost scared her that this man was stealing her heart with each and every touch.

He kissed her as they'd ached to inside.

'So have you made any resolutions?' Monica asked, hoping for a deeper glimpse.

'I have,' he told her. 'Dance lessons.'

'Dance lessons?' She started to laugh, because from anyone else, it wouldn't sound sexy, but then, until lately, she'd never danced with anyone like him!

'I've booked them. We can just rock up whenever we can make it. They're on a Wednesday.'

'Hold on,' Monica said. '*We?*'

'Well, they do say it takes two to tango!'

'When?'

'We have to work that one out. We can just rock up, it's all paid for.'

'I can't wait,' Monica admitted. 'Hey, why don't we go there tonight?'

'They're only on a Wednesday.'

'Just for something to eat.'

'I can't tonight. I've got something on.'

'Luke…' She didn't try to hide her exasperation. They had barely seen each other over Christmas, and now, when they finally shared a night off, it would seem he had other plans. 'I get you're not into commitments, but if this is casual dating, then it's a bit too casual for me…'

He had the audacity to smile. 'You miss me?'

'I don't like being slotted in,' she retorted.

'I get it,' he said, and pushed back her hair and kissed her tense mouth.

For Luke there was quite a conundrum. He missed her too, yet family had always come first. And certainly, he'd always kept his dating life separate.

'I'm babysitting Gus tonight. I know I've had him a few times to help Kelly get some sleep, but this is official babysitting.'

'Why didn't you just say?'

'It sounds like a bit of a lame excuse, but it isn't one. Kelly's barely left the flat since she had him. They're going to bring him over to mine and go to a movie.' Then he smiled. 'It's helps that Gus is cute.'

'You like being an uncle?'

'Actually, yes. All the fun, no responsibility…' he said, but then stopped joking. 'I feel responsible though.'

'I get it.' More than that, it melted her. She adored how he took care of his family. 'I don't mind keeping you company,' she offered.

Luke was about to decline; it didn't seem fair to lumber her with his commitments.

That wasn't what they were about.

He wanted to see her though.

And Monica wanted to see him more than she dared to admit.

His apartment felt different.

There was that gorgeous baby smell, and all the paraphernalia that accompanied a six-week-old when they ventured out. There was a bottle of milk on the coffee table, little blankets with bunnies on them and in the corner a portable cot.

'Is he asleep?' she asked.

'For now.'

'Gosh.' She peered into the cot as Luke served up dinner. 'He's so big…' Then she clarified, 'I am so used to teeny newborns.'

He had black hair and long dark lashes, and his mouth was making little sucking motions. 'How was Kelly leaving him?'

'A bit nervous. I've had him over a few times but usually during the day,' Luke explained, carrying two plates over to the table. 'She's a bit low, he's quite demanding.'

'Is she seeing someone about that?'

'Yes, she spoke to her GP at the six-week check. She was the one who suggested they have an evening out together. Kelly doesn't get on well with her parents, and I'm the only person they were okay leaving Gus with. Josie's great but she's had nothing to do with babies.'

'They trust you.'

'I would hope so.'

There was a little cry then from the corner of the room and Luke glanced at his dinner as if farewelling it.

'I can get him.'

'Relax,' Luke said. 'I've got it.'

He picked up the fretful baby, and Gus startled in surprise when he perhaps saw that it wasn't his father or mother, because his cries stopped abruptly and Monica watched as he stared up at his uncle.

'It's good they've got you,' she commented, though felt a little guilty tucking into steak and a buttery jacket potato as Luke walked the floor with Gus.

He was certainly competent, warming up a bottle and then settling down on a couch and carrying on the conversation as he fed the baby. Really, he was as adept at carrying on a conversation as Louise was while feeding a little one, only it wasn't work.

And for the first time Monica realised it might not have been such a sensible idea to insist it was no problem to join him in babysitting.

It was a problem because this was somehow the life she wanted.

Not just a baby.

This.

A lazy evening together with nowhere to go but here.

The constant fun was at times a little tiring.

'I'm going to make some time for us,' Luke said, standing from the couch and placing Gus high on his shoulder, so that those gorgeous Arias eyes peered back at her, even as Luke faced the other way. 'I'm working on something.'

'What?'

He laughed, and then Luke turned and little Gus's eyes were replaced by the adult version. 'Just an idea…'

'Tell me.'

'No. When's your birthday?'

'March.'

'Oh.' He sounded a bit disappointed.

'Is that too far off for you?' she teased.

'Meaning?'

'Well, you time your love-life in dog years…'

'I'm not with you.'

'One month in Luke time equals seven for most,' Monica said, popping the last piece of steak in her mouth. 'We're temporary and March is a long way off.'

'It will be here before you know it and, given the state of our schedules, we haven't had time to get sick of each other…' He gave her a flash of that sexy smile. 'My fault for dating a busy woman.'

'Yes.'

She sat on the couch with Gus as Luke ate his dinner.

He was podgy, with huge dark eyes that stared up at her, and the Arias genes must be strong, because she could certainly see Luke and Daniel in him. 'He's gorgeous.' Monica smiled at the baby, taking his little feet and playfully tapping them together.

'I was joking about you being too busy.'

'I know that. We're both busy.'

'Yes, but usually my time is more my own. I just know if my parents were here…' His dinner done, he came over, and taking Gus from her, placed him in his lap, his head at Luke's knees, and being too cute for words. 'They would have been there for them.'

'You're here.'

'Yes,' he said, and looked down at little Gus. 'I am.'

Gosh, the gap his parents had left was as long as it was painful, right into the next generation, and she admired how he stepped up and did what he could to fill it. Being the person his brother could turn to.

'They'd be proud of you,' she said.

'I don't know about that. I don't think they got the childhood my parents wanted for them.'

'Of course they didn't,' Monica said. 'They would have wanted to be there for their children.' She looked at him. 'And I'm sure they didn't want this for you either.' He looked over as if her words had hit him. 'Nobody wanted this, but from everything I've seen, you've done a brilliant job.'

'You haven't met Josie.' He rolled his eyes, then he smiled. 'She's doing better. I'm trying to explain to her that yes, she's got some money from them, but it's not going to fund her for life. She'll get there…'

It sounded as if he'd told himself that a lot.

'What was it like? You were twenty-two?'

'It was hard work,' he admitted. 'I couldn't show them how upset I was, and there was much to sort out, their estate, coroner's court…'

'Twelve-year-old twins.'

'Yes, then they hit their teenage years, and they were hellish. They were grieving of course, but there was all the usual stuff—homework, dreadful friends, parties…'

'Were you seeing anyone?'

'I was when the accident happened. Actually, I'd been seeing Siobhan for almost a year.'

She felt her lips tighten when she heard the slight affection in his voice.

'It wasn't for her though.'

'What?'

'Being a stepmother of sorts. She was young, wanted to go out not stay in and I don't blame her a bit.'

Little Gus was kicking his legs, and Luke held his feet and cycled his chunky legs, smiling down at him. 'The twins were more upset when we broke up than I was. It was a relief to end it really. It was just all too much, trying to keep three people happy. I made the decision that I'd keep any relationships away from the twins. Well, not that I had any serious relationships after that, but I didn't bring anyone home.'

'You stopped dating.'

'No.' Then he smiled down at Gus. 'Once a month my aunt would take over for a weekend. Freedom. Sometimes I'd get a longer stretch and head overseas. I still do…'

'Is that why you weren't thrilled…?' Monica asked and then halted, wondering if it was too deep of a question, but he answered.

'I just thought they were a bit young for such a commitment, but yes, maybe, a bit, I knew more would fall on me.' He was honest. 'I didn't know I was going to fall in love with him too.'

'Funny that.' Monica smiled.

'Even if he does smell!'

Nappies and bottles and tears.

Gus didn't sleep.

Not once!

'Thank God,' he said a few hours later when the intercom buzzed and the parents returned.

Both Kelly and Daniel smiled and said hi, but there were more than a few curious glances in Monica's direction.

'How was the film?'

'Long.' Kelly sighed, but having scooped up little Gus, she

was smiling as she carried on the conversation. 'Actually, it was really good. It felt odd being without him...'

'If there was a problem I'd have called.'

They didn't stay long. Soon Gus was bundled up for his trip to the car.

'Thanks for that,' Daniel said. 'It's appreciated. I would offer to return the favour, but...'

'You'll never have to return the favour,' Luke said, and it was a joke, clearly a running joke between brothers—but it rammed home again that it wasn't a vague *I don't want children*, it was a known.

The door closed on them, and Luke peered around his rather untidy living room.

'You've been baby-bombed.'

Indeed, he had been.

'I'm exhausted,' he admitted as they lay on the bed, totally wiped from four hours with one tiny little person. 'I'm not doing that every week.'

'Oh, you will.'

'Nope, Daniel was talking the other day about not wanting him to go to child care when Kelly goes back to work. Hint, hint...' He looked over. 'I'm not that soft.'

'I think you might be.'

'Oh, I'm not.' He rolled into her and proved it. 'I like this life...' He stared down at her with black eyes on fire and kissed her with intent and made love to her in a way she'd come to crave.

But getting up in the night for water, there was another craving, and one he would never fill. She saw the baby's bottle and the cot in the corner and on the very first day of the New Year, she still wasn't quite sure as to her resolutions?

Fun, which meant Luke.

Or go it alone.

Which meant ending them.

CHAPTER SEVEN

LUKE WAS RIGHT.

March was there before they knew it.

Monica's birthday dawned and Luke woke in his own bed alone, not quite ready to face the dreaded 6:00 a.m. till 6:00 p.m. shift.

He went to the snooze button but then remembered he had to get away bang on time today.

No matter what!

He'd told Cheng that he would be leaving on time and that they would have to send backup if he was stuck on a job.

So, best not to be late.

He showered quickly and pulled on his uniform then tied on his boots and decided to leave his shave for tonight.

But the table was booked for seven.

No time.

He arrived bleary-eyed, whereas Vicky must have had her batteries on charge overnight because she was chat-chat-chat as they checked the ambulance and signed for drugs.

'Have you texted Monica yet?'

Vicky knew what was going on of course—and yes, usually he kept his sex life out of things, but it was clearly more than just that. And, as an absolute unromantic, he'd needed a little help with things.

'She won't be up yet.'

'Yes, but it will be nice to wake up to a text.'

Luke rolled his eyes and took out his phone.

Happy Birthday… he typed and told her he was looking forward to tonight.

'Love Luke,' Vicky nudged, peering over his shoulder.

'I don't do all that,' he said, hitting Send.

'Have you told the restaurant it's her birthday?' she asked.

'Why would I?'

'So they can do a little cake, write Happy Birthday on the plate and sing to her.'

'It's dinner,' he said, deciding not to tell Vicky he had a little cake in the fridge at home, 'not a kid's birthday party.'

'So, what did you get her?' Vicky asked. 'Please tell me you got her a present.'

'Earrings from Josie's jewellery collection. She hasn't sold much…' He explained as Vicky pulled a slight face. 'What?'

'I'm sure her jewellery is lovely, but if it's not even selling at the market…' She glanced over. 'Monica is a consultant. Are you sure those little beady earrings are going to cut it?'

Luke gave a begrudging half laugh. 'It was all I could think of.'

That wasn't quite true, he'd been giving Monica's birthday a lot of thought. But, just as he hadn't given the restaurant personal details about tonight, neither would he be sharing everything with Vicky.

Karen and Andrew were called away to a job then, and he and Vicky headed to their vehicle. Their first job of the day, an ankle injury… 'Four days ago,' Luke sighed as he read out the details to Vicky, who was driving today.

Honestly, he tried not to judge, but he'd broken his ankle once and had got a taxi to the hospital. Still, he looked on the bright side. 'Hopefully we'll get lots of simple jobs. I don't mind being a taxi today if it means that we get off on time…'

His voice trailed off as Ambulance Control came over the airwaves.

'Category one, twelve-week-old, found unresponsive…'

He heard Karen's response over the radio—that they were on their way.

'*La pucha…*' His mind flew to Gus but then he consoled himself that he was a little older, though his jaw clamped closed as he awaited the address.

'It isn't him,' Vicky said when the address came through.

'I know,' he nodded as Ambulance Control asked them to provide back up. 'Confirmed. On our way.'

It was the worst of calls, and they drove lights and sirens despite the relatively empty streets.

As Vicky pulled in, Luke jumped out of the ambulance. The front door was open, and as he entered the house he saw a man, sitting at the top of the stairs, wearing boxers, with his head in his hands.

He briefly looked up and implored, 'Do something.'

Luke moved past him, and on the landing there was a woman slumped in the hallway, a towel around her and she didn't even glance in his direction. Luke had never seen anyone look so alone.

Entering the nursery, he saw the baby was on the floor and resuscitation was underway.

'Wait there,' he said to Vicky, who was coming up the stairs with the equipment. It was a wretched sight and they really did try to limit unnecessary exposure from the many dreadful things they saw. 'Stay with the parents.'

Possibly that was the more difficult option, Luke briefly reflected as he walked back into the bedroom.

There was a night-light delivering patterns to the wall and a stuffed elephant on the floor, but they were just peripheral things. On the floor they were working on the little baby.

Andrew was on the airway, delivering little puffs of air as he brought Luke up to speed.

'Dad was doing compressions when we arrived… Asystole on the monitor, though no rigor mortis or lividity…'

Luke got in an IV line, and as they worked on their tiny patient, the father came to the door. 'She was fed at four…'

'Has she been unwell?' Luke asked.

'No, maybe a cold, but…she was fed at four…' he said again. 'She was fine…' He knelt down. 'Come on, Mia…'

Luke glanced over to Karen, who was giving chest compressions and turning bright red in an effort not to cry.

'Do you want me to take over?' he offered, and when she nodded, he did so, delivering compressions with two fingers to the tiny baby. The father started pacing.

'What's your name?' Luke said and the father frowned. 'What's your name?'

'Paul.'

'Paul, go and get dressed, we'll be taking Mia to hospital soon…'

They made the decision to transfer.

'Should I bring the stretcher to the bottom of the stairs?' Karen asked.

'I'll carry her to the ambulance,' Luke said, 'I can give compressions and Andrew can bag her…'

The father returned then, half dressed and half crazed.

'How is she?'

There was nothing.

'We're taking Mia to the hospital.'

Cheng arrived then, and he was a very officious man, but also very kind, and suggested that Vicky and Karen remain with the parents and drive them in the second ambulance to the hospital.

'Luke are you okay to drive to The Primary? I'll assist in the back.'

'Sure.'

The mother was still sitting on the landing. Vicky was trying to feed her arms into a jumper but that was all Luke really saw.

He carried the little bundle down the stairs and back out onto the street.

The neighbours were out, standing in their coats and dressing-gowns and watching the early morning show as he carefully carried the tiny infant. And as he placed her on the stretcher, he felt as if a ribbon of fire constricted his throat, because she was so utterly perfect, apart from the dreadful colour of her skin and vacant eyes.

Little got to Luke.

He simply would not allow it.

This wasn't his first sudden infant death, but this one… As he moved in the driver's seat and turned on the engine he saw the police arrive. The mother was being led out with her husband, wretched sobs shaking her body, Paul steadying her, his gaze stoic and resolute. But then he looked to the ambulance that carried his precious baby and then, for the first time he met Luke's eyes…just briefly.

His expression Luke did not want to read.

And for a moment he saw, not the father, it was as if he was looking at himself.

He looked away, started up the ambulance and drove lights and sirens to the hospital, as Andrew and Cheng continued the resuscitation. There was a hum of activity in the back, and Luke's eyes were on the road…

The team were all waiting as they arrived. Andrew gave his handover as the primary team took over.

George was the paediatrician and completely wonderful and compassionate. He examined the little baby as the resuscitation continued…

'Did the parents come with you, Luke?' May asked, her voice a little gruff, but practical all the same.

'They're on their way,' Cheng responded, when Luke didn't.

And when it was clear that nothing could be done, George put a hand out to stop the resuscitation.

'Should we wait for the parents?' May asked, but George shook his head.

'I'll go and speak with them.'

Luke admired him—he would not offer false hope or prolong the agony of not knowing.

'Time of death, seven twenty-six.' George said then looked over as Vicky and Karen arrived.

'Mum and Dad are in the interview room.' Vicky's voice was a touch trembly, her gaze falling to the silent bed.

'May, would you come with me, please…' George asked then he turned. 'Clara, thank you for coming down.'

'Of course.'

Monica's sister was here, Luke realised, and he watched as May went over to fill her in.

'Thank you.' George addressed the paramedics. 'For your efforts.' He looked over to the vast resuscitation bed and the tiny little infant. 'Such a beautiful baby.'

'Yes,' Luke went to say, only his voice didn't work.

'Perhaps we should pause for a moment,' May said.

The pause was used at The Primary, especially when there was the death of a child. It was a practise spreading globally and could be requested by anyone.

It was a moment where the staff, who chose to, stood as gentle words were said, acknowledging the life that had passed and taking a moment of silent reflection… It wasn't compulsory but Luke always partook.

This time though, staring at the bed, for the first time he wanted to leave rather than pause and reflect.

He looked over to Andrew whose eyes were closed, to Vicky who had her arm around Karen, to May who was blowing her nose…to George and Clara, and it seemed to Luke that everyone knew how to be.

For the first time he didn't.

He wanted to turn and walk away, but of course he remained and quietly stood there.

'Thank you,' May concluded, and Cheng came over then. 'May's given us the staffroom. We'll do a debriefing there.'

He was used to debriefings and the pastoral care and the support call that would come through tomorrow, and tried to carry on as he usually would. He put his arm around Vicky. 'Come on.'

'That was awful,' Vicky said. 'I feel dreadful, but I'm just relieved we weren't first on scene.'

She would be one day, and he was glad that she'd had a gentler entrance to something so tragic.

Karen, who was newer to the job, was already in there, crying, and he sat down beside her and listened as she questioned if she was really cut out for this work. 'I almost ran.'

'You didn't though. You saw it through,' Luke reminded her.

Andrew spoke then, but Luke couldn't really hear what was said, he just went through the motions…

'How are you doing, Luke?' Cheng asked.

It was odd because usually he nodded or went through the technical part of the event rather than the emotional side. But this morning he did neither.

He could still feel the weight of the baby in his arms. Still see the mottled face and he just couldn't shake it as he usually did.

'Why don't we head back to the station?' Cheng suggested.

Of course it was more complicated than that. Luke and Vicky had to drive Cheng back to the scene, so that he could collect the vehicle he'd first arrived in.

There were still a couple of neighbours outside in the freezing cold, and there were police cars there now…the sky dreich and grey as if the low clouds might never lift, no matter how long the day.

Back at the station, Cheng was there with his answers. 'We'll have some coffee, perhaps something to eat, and…' To Luke, Cheng's voice sounded as if it was coming from underwater, all distant and distorted.

And Luke didn't want to debrief; he'd done it many, many times before and knew it wasn't going to help today.

'I'm going home.' He abruptly stood.

'Luke, let's talk it through.'

'I don't want to talk,' Luke said. 'I just…' He shook his head. 'I'll sign out the drugs.' He did so, and then he went and checked in on Vicky. 'You okay?'

'I am.' She nodded. 'I mean, I just dealt with the parents…'

'There's no *just* about it.' He was about to say, *who'd be a parent*, but knew that wasn't the right thing to say when Vicky had two little ones at home.

And Andrew had one on the way.

Karen? He didn't know.

Luke just knew that whatever he said now could well be the wrong thing, because his filter was coming undone and he was angry with the world, and he didn't want a patient with a sprained ankle using him as a taxi to be the one to take the brunt of it.

'You're upset,' Vicky said. 'I know you thought for a moment it might be Gus…'

'It's not that.' He shook his head.

It was that though.

The sudden panic when he'd heard there was an unresponsive baby, and now the dreadful thought of it happening to his brother. Losing Gus…

But it was more than that too.

It was the father's eyes, the way Paul had held up his wife, somehow pulled himself together when everything was falling apart.

It felt as if Luke had been looking at himself for a moment.

And he was not opening up to Vicky!

To anyone.

Luke, for a very long time, had dealt with his emotions alone.

'Luke, I know you don't have a baby, but…' He closed his eyes, Vicky really wasn't helping…

'I'll be fine,' he interrupted and signed off the drugs. 'Hey, I must look like hell because Cheng's offered to drive me home.'

'Good,' Vicky said. 'I'll see you tomorrow?'

'You will.'

'I hope you have a nice night.'

It would be a night with pizza and maybe whisky, except he was working tomorrow, so that ruled the latter out. But it would not be a nice night.

Cheng was a good egg and didn't try to make small talk as he drove him home, just as they pulled up at his flats and before he got out, he turned. 'Luke, reach out if you need to.'

'I shall.'

'You never do though.'

'I just need a day to myself.'

'Fair enough. I'll call you this afternoon.'

'I'll hopefully be asleep.'

'Before I finish my shift,' Cheng said. 'And if you don't answer, I'll do a welfare check.'

'I'm okay, Cheng,' he said, 'I just can't today…'

God, he'd never walked out on a shift; sometimes, after a particularly gruesome job they'd been stood down, but he'd never just thrown in the towel and walked off.

He lay on the couch and stared at daytime TV and perhaps fell asleep because it was four when his phone woke him.

'Cheng,' he said, 'I'm fine, I just needed…' He didn't know what he needed. Certainly, a day spent lying on the couch, either blankly staring at the television or dozing hadn't helped. He could still feel the weight of the baby in his arms, though he wasn't going to tell Cheng that.

'You're working an early shift tomorrow?'

'Yes.'

'Well, make sure that you don't oversleep.'

Luke even managed a slight laugh—he knew what Cheng

meant. There really would be a welfare check if he didn't turn up for his shift tomorrow, especially with all that had happened today.

He rang off, wondering if he should ring Vicky and check if she was okay, then frowning as he recalled her words...

'I hope you have a nice night.'

Damn, Luke suddenly remembered, it was Monica's birthday and they were meeting at her favourite Greek restaurant.

Cancel.

It was the obvious answer. Certainly, he wasn't going to be the best company and it wasn't a milestone birthday or anything...

Monica had woken to Luke's text and smiled, then got on with her busy day.

It was a nice day though.

Louise, who kept on top of birthdays and such, arranged a cake for her at morning coffee. She caught up with Clara for lunch, and her sister handed her a beautifully wrapped present.

'What's this?' she started, then caught a gorgeous waft of lavender. 'A sleep mask.' It was beautiful, luxurious velvet and as she looked at it, Clara's hands came across the table and she touched it too. 'I got it in violet, I know you like that colour.'

'I do.' Monica nodded. 'It will be perfect for on calls. Thanks so much...' She smiled over at Clara, who looked a little pale. 'How have you been?'

'Okay.' She nodded.

They got on.

Sort of.

Their parents though had forced a bit of a wedge between them—insisting Monica look out for her sister, which annoyed Clara whenever she did.

And as for problems—Monica had never been allowed to admit she had any, let alone share them. It felt too late to start now.

They bumped along, loving each other, liking each other, but there had been many hurts along the way.

When it was just the two of them though, they were okay.

'You've been quite busy of late.'

'Yes.' Monica took a breath, she wanted to tell Clara, hell she wanted to tell the world that she was dating a guy who made her heart soar. Except how did she explain the temporary nature of them—how? It was getting increasingly impossible to carve out enough time, and she knew that Luke, or even she, might give up soon.

As it turned out she didn't have to tell Clara.

'How's that gorgeous paramedic?'

'Pardon?'

'Luke,' Clara said with a satisfied smile. 'What's happening between you two?'

'What are you talking about?' Her mouth gaped. 'Have people been talking?'

'Not that I've heard…'

'Then how do you know?'

'I met the two of you, remember?'

'We weren't seeing each other then.'

'You were laughing, Monica.' Clara smiled. 'In a way I haven't heard in a very long time…'

'Seriously? You knew then? I didn't even know.'

'I could feel the sparks flying off the two of you,' Clara teased. 'Were you ever going to tell me?'

'I don't know what to tell,' Monica admitted. 'It isn't serious, we're just enjoying each other for as long as it lasts.'

'But you don't do casual relationships.'

'I didn't,' Monica corrected. 'Until I met him.' She did not want Clara analysing this. Monica didn't want to analyse it herself. She was scared at how close she was getting to Luke. She had to keep things light, and not just with Luke. 'It's just a temporary thing…'

'Why?'

'Because...' Monica said evasively and quickly changed the subject. 'What have you been up to? How's the herb garden?'

'Don't!' Clara snapped, then instantly regretted it. 'Sorry, it's just...'

'What?'

'You know how I was going to go to the garden centre this weekend...'

'Yes.'

'Mum and Dad are now coming...oh, and Dad's building it.'

'Tell them you want to do this yourself.'

'I have to tell them that for everything.' Clara's voice sounded strangled, and Monica was appalled to see tears pool in her eyes. 'I'm being unfair...' She collected herself.

'No, you're not.' She took a breath. 'They interfere.'

'It's a herb garden, I should be grateful they want to help.'

'No.'

'I'm just upset. It's been a bad day. There was a SIDS in this morning.'

'Oh no.'

'I've spent the morning with the parents. I'm heading back down to A&E now. They're spending time with her.'

'I'll walk with you,' Monica said. 'Not because you need me to, I'm not being Mum or Dad.'

'I know you're not.'

'Do you want me to come over tonight?' Monica offered.

'Haven't you got better things to do on your birthday?'

'Not if you're upset.'

'I'm okay, I'll be working late. I haven't got much else done today.'

They arrived at A&E and Monica found her eyes scanning the ambulances all ramped up.

'Is he here?' Clara said, and Monica laughed.

'No.' Then she turned and looked at her sister. 'Let me talk to Mum and Dad.'

'Please don't.' Clara shook her head. 'It will just make it worse.'

God, she wished she knew what to do.

Instead, she headed to outpatients, and it was actually a very smooth clinic, with no dramas, and no nasty surprises on any of the tests that had been run.

Just one tricky bit.

'Perfect size.' She smiled as she examined Sorcha's growing bump. She was now twenty-four weeks along, and after the scary start it was going beautifully well. With the examination over, Sorcha joined her at the desk. 'How have you been?'

'Really well.' Sorcha nodded.

'You're still working full-time?'

'For now.' Sorcha nodded. 'I'm hoping to keep going for as long as I can.'

Monica went through all her test results, which were spot-on, and then all the usual questions.

Then a tougher one. 'How are things at home?'

'They're great. Just…'

A tiny pause, and Monica rather knew why. Oh, this was so difficult and she could not let it show.

'Jess isn't doing so well. You'd know that, of course.'

'Yes.'

'Richard's there with her now…'

'That must be hard.'

'No, I want him to be there for her, it's just…' She started to cry and then nodded. 'It is hard. He's losing his wife and trying not to upset me with it.'

'Sorcha, it's such a difficult situation, but have you spoken to him about it?'

'Yes, we've talked, and I told him that I might go to my parents for a couple of weeks.'

Monica inwardly frowned, not that she showed it, but she didn't want to have rose-coloured Richard glasses on when it came to her friend. 'Are things difficult at home?'

'No… I didn't mean like that, I'm not leaving him.' She blew her nose and gave a little laugh at the misinterpretation, but it soon faded, because the subject was too sad. 'When she dies, I think, it would be easier on Jess's family…easier on me maybe…he'll need time to grieve her.' She looked over to Monica then. 'Sorry, this must be hard for you too. She's your friend.'

And this was her job.

She'd looked after patients in similar situations, and in truth admired how Sorcha and Richard were dealing with things.

It *was* hard though.

Still, she had a week's leave coming up and consoled herself that the break would help.

She finished up in outpatients for once on schedule and made her way back to the unit to change.

'That's me for the day,' Monica said.

'Woohoo.' Louise smiled. 'So, where are you off to?'

'Dinner…' Monica said without elaborating, not that it stopped Louise.

'With?' her colleague asked with a little smirk and a lot of sparkle in her blue eyes.

'Just a quiet dinner.'

And she was so looking forward to it!

Knowing there would be little chance of making it home to change, she had brought her clothes and shoes to work. Having freshened up, she put on a pretty dress, dotted with flowers—as opposed to the dark suits veered towards work—and some nice espadrilles that would look better with a tan, but it was early March, so a tan would have to wait.

'*Just* dinner!' Louise laughed. 'Oh my, you look gorgeous.'

'Thanks.'

'So where is the sexy paramedic taking you?'

'What do you…' She gave up denying them.

It was supposed to be temporary, and yet here she was four

months later—still heady at the thought of seeing him and excited to share her birthday with Luke.

'To my favourite Greek restaurant.' Monica smiled, 'If he gets off on time.'

'Well, have a wonderful night.'

Oh, she hoped to.

Walking down the corridor towards A&E, she told herself she must stop parking there. Sooner, rather than later, her access would be revoked and she was going to find herself stuck at the boom gate. Usually Monica was a stickler for rules, but it was worth going a teeny bit rogue for the occasional glimpses of Luke.

And Vicky!

'Hi, Monica.'

'Are you guys just finishing up?' she asked, perhaps a little hopefully, given that there was an elderly gentleman sitting up on the stretcher.

'No chance.' Vicky shook her head. 'I think we're going to be stuck here for a couple of hours.' She smiled to her patient. 'Aren't we, Ted?'

Ted didn't seem to mind. He was tucking into sandwiches and slurping tea.

'So no chance of finishing on time…' Monica checked, wondering if it might be better to change their reservation for later but deciding to check first with Luke. 'Is Luke in admissions?'

'No, he went home early.'

'Oh.' At first she smiled, secretly pleased that he'd made such an effort to be on time this evening, but then the smile faded from her face as Vicky spoke on.

'We had a dreadful job first thing this morning…'

'Is he okay?'

'He wasn't hurt or anything…' Vicky moved a little away from the stretcher and the patient and in low tones told her.

'I'm so sorry, Vicky. I actually heard about it from Clara. I didn't know you two had attended.'

'There were two crews,' Vicky explained. 'We were backup.'

'How are you doing?'

'I'm okay, I think. We went back to the station for a debrief and I wanted to just keep working. I'd rather be busy, but Luke just wanted to go home. I think it really got to him.' She gave a helpless shrug. 'I've never seen him like that, but I'm sure he'll be fine. You're going out tonight?'

Monica nodded.

'He probably just needed a day to himself.'

'Of course. And you take care of yourself tonight,' Monica said. 'And in the days and weeks ahead if you need someone to talk to, outside of the usual support, I'm here.' She meant it. The death of a baby hit everyone in different ways and not always immediately. 'Anytime.'

'Thanks.'

Vicky got back to her cheerful patient and Monica was soon seated in her car.

Luke had left work this morning?

She scrolled through her phone, wondering if she'd perhaps missed a message, but then he was hardly going to message her about it—Luke didn't talk about the darker side of his job.

They were about fun.

He could cancel—she'd understand.

Then she sat there, recalling her slight petulance at the limited time they spent together and maybe he hadn't felt able to.

Perhaps he just wasn't going to show up?

There was a worse scenario than that she could think of though—Luke arriving all smiling and happy, pretending everything was okay.

CHAPTER EIGHT

THIS WAS WHY he preferred to stay single, Luke thought as he dragged himself to the shower. He wanted no company, and certainly not smiling waiters and champagne. He wanted to lie in the dark rather than force a smile and celebrate.

'Snap out of it,' Luke told himself, except he couldn't.

He kept washing his arms as if to bring back the warmth, yet he could still feel the weight of lifelessness on them.

He very rarely cried, in fact he hadn't in years, but this late afternoon, edging into the evening, alone in the shower he did. The images of this morning flashed before his closed eyes, and the sounds too—the anguished sobs of the father, and the lack of sounds too—the stupefied look on the mother's face, as if she herself had just died, and the silence of the baby.

Crying didn't clear his head nor erase what he'd seen. He gave himself a shake, turned off the water and came out. Slinging a towel round his waist he cleared the misty mirror telling himself to shave.

He'd barely soaped his jaw when the doorbell rang.

Luke chose to ignore it.

Then it rang more loudly and he guessed it was Mr Nicholas who still hadn't worked out his television remote.

'Monica.' He frowned. 'I thought we were meeting at the restaurant.'

'I cancelled.' She held up a brown paper bag. 'Or rather I asked them to give me takeaway.'

'Takeaway?'

'I saw Vicky as I was leaving work. She said you'd gone home after a difficult job.'

'Vicky talks too much.'

'Maybe she does, but I figured you wouldn't feel like eating out.' She stepped in. 'I can just leave this here.' She placed the bag on his rather untidy table. 'If you're not up to company.'

'It's your birthday though.'

'Come off it, Luke.' She looked at him, his jaw half soapy, his eyes red, and despite his height and strength, just somehow, defeated. As if she could push him over, and as if to prove it, she tapped his chest and he sat down on the couch behind him.

'I get it,' she said, and he nodded. 'Honestly, I do.' She told him about her parents' fortieth. 'I'd lost a mother, I was just beside myself, but I had to go to their party.'

'Couldn't you tell them?'

'I didn't want to ruin it. Anyway, they're not exactly understanding.'

'Unlike you,' he said and pulled her onto his knee and breathed in the scent of summer.

'I'm not being very fair on them. Gosh, I sound like Clara, making excuse for them. But in this case, it wasn't their fault. Sometimes you just have to paint on a smile, but you don't for me, and certainly not about something like this.'

'Thanks.' He took a breath. 'I'm not much company.'

'I'm okay with that,' she said, 'I honestly don't mind if you want to be alone.'

And usually he did, yet not tonight.

'You won't get birthday sex if you stay,' he warned as they lay down together on the couch.

'I don't want it.' She poked his naked chest and they laughed a small laugh and then lay silent. They lay like that for a long time.

'Clara was there,' he told her, stroking her hair.

'We had lunch, she told me about it.'

'Do you two get on?'

'Yes.' She hesitated. 'Most of the time.' She gave in. 'Not really. It's my mother, both our parents…'

'Tell me.'

'Not tonight.'

'Yes, tonight.'

Perhaps he needed the distraction, so she told him how her parents had changed. 'I don't really remember much before Clara was born, just that it was different after. She was in hospital for months. Lots of doctors' appointments after. They were so…' She paused. 'Scared for her. And really, Clara was the most confident out of all of us. She was always bold. I guess all the attention went to her.' He gave her shoulder a squeeze. 'And I didn't mind, well, sometimes I did. But mostly, I understood. It was just sometimes…'

'Sometimes?'

'They were never there for me,' she admitted. 'I was a bit bullied at school.' She thought back. 'And as they liked to point out, it was nothing compared to what Clara was dealing with. Even my achievements…' Luke was the first person she'd really spoken about it with. Not even Clara fully knew. 'Clara was very premature. The labour wasn't handled well. I guess that's what drove me—still does.'

'Are they proud of you?'

'I don't know. On the day I graduated, my mother said that if Clara didn't have a vision problem she could have been a doctor.'

'God.'

'She's right, but the thing is, Clara could be anything she wanted to be. She *chose* to be a psychologist.'

'They couldn't give you your moment.' He was still stroking her hair. 'God, you should see some of the crap Josie makes, and I tell her it's wonderful and how proud I am.'

She gave a half laugh, but then as she thought back to that

day, it died on her lips. 'Jess found me crying,' she sighed. 'She's the only person who's ever seen me cry.'

'You're going to miss her?'

She wanted to nod, to turn and weep on his chest, but that would hardly be fair, given the day he'd had. As well as that, she daren't cave in now. She thought of Sorcha, how she had to hold it together for her, and Richard, how she had to be strong for her friend.

'I've missed her for a long time,' she said, instead of revealing the agony. 'She got how difficult my parents could be. It's hard on Clara too, they don't leave her alone. That storm that day, they wanted me to give her a lift. And this weekend she's building a herb box. She wants to do it herself, pick her own scents...'

'Can you tell them that?'

'Clara doesn't want me to, and they'll just accuse me of being the jealous big sister.'

'No.' He shook his head. 'Not jealous.'

Just never put first.

'Tell them,' he said. 'And if they accuse you of being jealous...' He shrugged, and her head moved on his chest. 'I'll still...' Luke paused, because he'd been about to say the most ridiculous thing and deciding it was the awful day muddying his head, he hastily settled for something far less. 'I'll still be your friend.'

'Thanks.'

'You're not going to tell them, are you?'

'No.'

He gave a soft laugh and they lay quietly for a while longer before he addressed the morning, but in a roundabout way.

'Vicky thinks it got to me because of Gus.'

'Did it?'

'I don't know,' he said. 'In part. It was the father who upset me though,' he admitted. 'I met his eyes, just as I was about to drive off with the baby.'

She nodded, and he liked that she didn't ask him to explain more, because it allowed him to do just that.

'I think he knew his baby was gone, and I knew she was too. There was no hope in his eyes and I don't think there was any in mine.' He stroked her arm, sort of idly, but tenderly. 'I hate false hope, but I felt I'd just told him that there was none.'

'Maybe you prepared him a bit.'

'Maybe.' He hadn't thought of it like that, and he told her about his parents, how they'd rushed to the hospital in the middle of the night. 'I sort of knew how he felt.'

She lifted her head. 'From when you lost your parents?'

'It doesn't really compare, I mean I haven't lost a baby or anything, but the police arriving, having to be strong…' He stopped then. 'It just got to me.'

'Of course, we're not robots.'

'Not today.'

It couldn't be described as a nice night, more a gentle night, and they had a gorgeous dinner heated in his microwave.

They sat at the table, Luke still wrapped in a towel, Monica in her pretty dress. They ate lamb souvlaki, wrapped in soft white flatbreads and an oily delicious salad washed down with sparkling water, chatting about not much, or chatting not at all.

He brought it up again when they lay in bed.

'It just got to me. More than most.'

'Some do,' she agreed. Her job was terribly good a lot of the time, and deeply sad on more than the odd occasion. Telling parents bad news, or delivering a child that wasn't healthy or alive. But Luke saw dreadful things on regular occasions, things that didn't even get to hospital, and this little one had touched that hardened core. Her tales were not needed tonight.

She was though.

For the first time she felt it, this closeness, this joint need, as if she was the only person he'd allow in tonight.

'What time are you working tomorrow?' she asked, setting the alarm.

'Seven till seven,' he said. 'You?'

'I'm on at eight, then on call...'

'Well, I'm glad I got to see you tonight.'

He kissed the top of her head and soon he was asleep, and the oddest thing was, even if her birthday had gone practically unacknowledged, she felt closer to him than ever. As if they were truly together, perhaps for the first time.

Monica fell asleep, knowing she wanted more...

Of this.

And she awoke wanting more of the same...

'Happy Birthday to you...'

More of Luke's deep singing and the sight of him back in a towel, still unshaven and carrying a cake lit by candles...

'Luke!'

'I bought this for after the restaurant,' he said as she held her hair back and blew the candles out. 'Vicky wanted the waiters to sing to you.'

'I'd have died of embarrassment,' Monica told him.

Instead of cringing as waiters sang, she feasted on rich chocolate cake and strong coffee, and he looked more himself than yesterday. 'Sorry for the crappiest birthday. I intend to make it up to you.'

'I like that we don't have to pretend. I don't want false smiles and promises.'

'Yeah, but the deal was fun.'

Monica felt uncomfortable—yes, she wanted fun, but she wanted the other sides of him. Wanted more than they had agreed to. Still, he seemed to have shaken off yesterday's events and was back to his slow smile.

'Are you going to open your card and present?'

She went straight for the little parcel. 'Tut, tut,' Luke said, 'I thought Miss Manners opened the card first.'

'Not me.' She smiled. Though in truth the present was the easy part. She wasn't sure she was ready for a Luke card.

As she opened her present, she tried to hazard a guess what his card would say.

Dear Monica.

Best wishes.

Or *Monica, hope you have a lovely day.*

From Luke.

Or

Love Luke, and then she'd wonder if he wrote that for everyone.

Gosh, she was a dreadful temporary girlfriend, and she knew it; she'd been crazy about him from the start, even if they were going nowhere.

'Wow!' She held up the dangly silver post amber earrings.

'Josie—made them,' he said. 'Though I did buy them…'

'They're lovely,' Monica said—a teeny bit disappointed that his sister's unsellable jewellery was his gift to her. 'I'll wear them today…' Then she groaned. 'I have to go home and get changed or I'm going to be rocking up to work in last night's dress. Again!'

'You've got a spare one here.'

'Crumpled.'

'I washed it.' He smiled. 'It's hanging in the wardrobe. It will go nicely with the earrings.'

'Yes.'

She was grateful for the gift, thrilled really, even if he was helping out his sister. She gave him a kiss, and then with time marching on went to move from the bed.

'Thank you for my cake and lovely earrings…'

'Card.'

'Oh yes.'

She opened the white envelope and it was a very Luke card. From the newsagents, she was sure. Funny and noncommittal. Not a glittered heart on the front, nor a 'someone special' she could see.

'It's an ambulance with a naked woman running after it…'

She frowned and then got it. 'Ambulance chaser.' She groaned, and it was too cheesy to be irked. 'Do you think I'm chasing you, Luke?'

'I hope so,' he said, and she felt his eyes as she opened the card.

Dear Monica,
We leave on Monday.
Luke

No kisses, no declarations and she frowned as she re-read it.

'Leave for where?'

'Cyprus.'

She blinked. 'Cyprus?'

'Before the school holidays so it will be nice and quiet. You've got leave. It's a boutique hotel with no kids, mild weather, heated pool...'

'I can't just...' Her voice trailed off. 'I'm supposed to be reading George's paper and Jess is so...' Her voice faded for a moment. 'It could be anytime now.'

'I know.'

'Would you just take off if, say, Kelly was eight months pregnant?'

'I did *exactly* this when Kelly was eight months pregnant. The day we met I'd just got back from a trip.' He looked right at her. 'Let's take these days. I promise you if someone needs you, really needs you, then they'll find you.'

'And if I can't go?'

'I'll send you a postcard.'

She sucked in her breath and somehow knew he damn well would. She couldn't believe he'd organise something like this without consulting with her.

Leaving on Monday?

For someone as meticulous and as organised as Monica, there was no such thing as in impromptu holiday...it was an impossible ask, surely...

'Yes?'

'Good.' He gave her a quick kiss. 'Now I have to go or believe me, I'll have Cheng or the police at my door for a welfare check.'

'Seriously?'

'They do look after us really...' he said and was soon out of the door.

He made it to work, just in time to meet Cheng's raised eyebrows. 'Cutting it fine, Arias.'

'Sorry about that.'

'How are you?'

'Fine, I just needed a day.' Cheng didn't look convinced. 'Seriously, I'm fine, and I'm going away for a few days next week.'

He felt fine.

Well, not completely.

Checking supplies in the ambulance with Vicky, he checked the paediatric equipment and thought of yesterday, fighting this sudden urge to call Daniel, check in.

'How was your night?' Vicky asked.

'It was good.'

'Did Monica like her earrings?'

'She loved them,' he said.

'She was being polite.'

He laughed and was almost back to himself, but not quite; he kept thinking of the father...all the hellish things he'd be doing today.

'You're quiet,' Vicky observed as they cleared from the first job.

'You don't give me a chance to get a word in,' Luke shot back, but yes, he was aware he wasn't his usual self. Still, the thought of blue skies and some uninterrupted time with Monica would help...

'What are you doing?' Vicky asked as his fingers moved

over his phone on their morning coffee break. 'Messaging Monica?'

'Nope,' Luke said and got back to his messages. 'Just confirming things with the hotel…'

Oh, and also checking a box he wouldn't have bothered with if he was travelling alone.

Upgrade me!

'*Carajo…*' he cussed as another five boxes popped up.

He was about to swipe No Thank You, but then one of the boxes caught his eyes.

Romantic Getaway for Two!

Well, it wouldn't be for three, Luke thought, glancing over and making sure Vicky wasn't peeking.

Yes Please!

Done.

Not quite.

Add On.

Romantic evening boat trip?

'No thank you,' he muttered, wondering what on earth he'd started, but excited by the upgrade all the same.

Monica deserved it. Hell, so did he…he just couldn't shake off yesterday.

Some jobs took a while longer, he told himself.

Of course they did.

They deserved this…

Needed it even?

CHAPTER NINE

STANSTED AIPORT AT four in the morning wasn't a sight to behold.

'Like the A&E on a Saturday,' Luke said as they stood in a long line under bright fluorescent lights, watching passengers argue with a tiny female worker who was doing her best to direct the endless caravan of people.

Monica, whose occasional holidays and business trips were rather more planned and started in the business lounge was jostled and tense, but of course Luke was eternally calm.

'We'll get coffee on the other side,' he said.

Coffee for Luke and a tepid hot chocolate did nothing to lift the ambience. Then followed a four-hour flight surrounded by guys heading for a stag do.

'Are there going to be lots of stag dos?'

'I'm not sure.' Luke shrugged. 'Maybe,' he said, smiling to himself at the slight face she pulled.

He knew full well that the lads hadn't been able to get a flight to Larnaca, so they'd be transferring onto a coach… and he'd made sure that the hotel he'd booked was a quiet one. But she was so easy to wind up.

To the lovely sound of the revellers, Monica fell asleep, so deeply she wasn't even aware that they'd landed.

'Are we here…?' She startled. 'Already?'

'We're here.'

The bright blue of the sky made her blink as she stepped out of the plane, a breeze catching the skirt of her dress.

'Here,' Luke said and took her bag so she could hold down the skirt of her dress with one hand and hold the rail with the other.

It really felt like another world. The airport was small and such a contrast to the business of Stansted and with only hand luggage they were soon outside and getting into a taxi.

Monica gazed out at unfamiliar terrain. She'd been too rushed to get properly excited, and a little nervous about their sudden adventure too. She wasn't a last-minute person like Luke. Any holiday or trip was usually meticulously researched and planned, but glimpsing Coral Bay for the first time had her breath catch in her throat. The aqua sea, the bay nestled between cliffs, the stunning resorts and shops—it was beyond anything she had imagined. There was a bubble of excitement that she hadn't expected, a desire almost to dash out of the taxi and simply explore, though of course they paid and thanked the driver and then wandered into a beautiful foyer and were greeted warmly by the manager.

'*Yiass, kalos irthate tze...*' He beamed. 'Welcome.'

They were indeed made to feel welcome, Geo, the manager, was warm and informal as he went through things with Luke.'

'A little extra *anaváthmisi*.' He smiled.

'Pardon?'

'Upgrade, you requested the...'

Possibly he saw the urgent widening of Luke's eyes because he halted.

'Why don't you relax?' the manager suggested to Monica. 'Take a seat by the pool. Agyro will bring you a drink...' He smiled when he had Luke alone. 'Are you going to propose?'

'No!'

'So why the secrecy?'

'Because...' Luke said to smiling eyes, 'I don't want her to know it's the romantic package.'

'I'm confused.'

'I just want Monica to think we got an upgrade.'

'Ah, so you want it to be romantic, without telling her you're being romantic?'

Luke grinned at the savvy manager. 'Something like that.'

'Well, luckily for you,' he said as Monica wandered back over, 'we have an ocean view that has become available.'

'How lovely.' Monica smiled.

It wasn't just lovely.

It was divine.

'Oh, Luke…' They stepped into a large suite, and Monica gasped. The floor-to-ceiling glass doors were open, a breeze catching the voiles on the windows that had been pushed back too, to reveal a stunning vista of a sapphire sea, glittering in the midday sun. 'It's stunning.'

There were cushioned seats on the balcony and a teal table, and on it, a silver bucket with champagne and two flutes. 'For us?'

'Must be the upgrade.'

'Wow!'

She wanted to stand and take in the view but for now she turned to explore. The living area was bathed in soft whites and muted blues, echoing the sea beyond. And wandering into the bedroom she found a huge king-size bed angled to take in every drop of the ocean view.

'It's stunning!' She could actually feel the tension of the previous weeks, no make that years, slipping away, as she wandered the suite. 'There are even flowers.' Tiny wild orchids on the coffee table, beside a basket of fresh figs. 'Luke, I thought it was a quick getaway. Please tell me how much this cost.'

'Stop right there,' Luke said. 'I booked a nicer hotel than I would if it was just for me and they gave me an upgrade. Do not offer to pay for your poor paramedic.'

'Are you sure?'

He nodded. 'We just got lucky.'

So lucky.

They showered in a beautiful bathroom—a retreat on its own—the walls and benches a creamy travertine with gorgeous citrus-scented toiletries that they took in turns to soap into each other.

'Beach, pool or bed?' Luke said, lathering her breasts.

'Bed,' Monica said, as they sensually kissed, and as he lifted her, and she felt the cool stone on her back, it was Monica who was sensible.

'I don't think showers and condoms are a good mix.'

'True.' He regretfully lowered her, and they stared at each other for a long, assessing moment. 'You are still on the pill?'

'Luke?' she checked.

'Do you really have to ask?'

'Of course not.'

'Because I want you…'

'I know,' she said, stroking him beneath the rain showerhead, 'but we're not risking it.' And then she dropped to her knees and tasted him, citrus and soapy, and Luke was smoothing her hair. Pushing it behind her ears, and this was perfect, he told himself, because her mouth knew him so well, and there was nothing better than good head.

Except he wanted to be unsheathed and inside her and was coming to that very thought.

'Oh.' She fell back onto her heels as he turned the water off, a little dizzy from her own orgasm, and looking up, she gave a half laugh. 'I was worried…' she admitted.

'About what?' he asked, helping her up and then wrapping her in a towel.

'I don't holiday with others easily. I was worried you'd get bored or…'

'Oh no.' He shook his head. 'Let's go to the beach…just a walk. It's too cool for a swim. One rule though.'

'What?'

He located the hotel safe. 'Phones stay in here.'

'I really can't.'

'Monica…' He wasn't having it. 'We're going for a walk. Just us.'

Their first day was a long wander on the beach.

The intention had been to have dinner at the hotel's cliffside restaurant, but their short wander had turned into quite a long one. Walking hand in hand along the beach, standing in the softly lapping waves at times…

It was almost deserted, just a few local fishermen and a dog bounding along, chasing seagulls who squawked as they rose into the air, then landed seconds later, just for the happy dog to chase them all over again.

She took a deep breath, filling her lungs with salty sea air and unwinding, feeling the wind whipping her hair. 'This feels good,' she admitted. 'I haven't been away for ages.'

'When was the last time?'

'It's been far too long.' She thought back. 'I tend to go to Wales and see Jess if I've got a decent stretch of time off. I went to Barcelona a couple of years ago,' she said, 'for a conference, I had a couple of days sightseeing and that was incredible. I saw the cathedral.'

'I haven't been,' Luke said. 'It's on my list.'

'Do you do this a lot?' she asked. 'I mean…before Gus was born?'

'I try to,' he said. 'Well, I don't generally do romantic walks on the beach.'

'Is this a romantic walk?'

'It's about to be,' he said, turning her to face him.

The sun was dipping on the horizon, the sky gold and pink, and this wasn't a part of the upgrade. This was just a couple on the beach, staring at each other, a little lost in each other. Kissing each other in a way neither had before.

And he was stealing her heart, Monica knew.

She just didn't know how to get it back.

It was so romantic, the whole thing, and it wasn't because of the upgrade.

There was breakfast in bed and days spent walking, exploring the Tomb of Kings or the tourist shops and cafés and getting to know each other in a way neither had with another.

No phones, no interruptions and it flew by all too fast.

On their last full day, they hit the heated pool, the early spring sun not quite warm on her shoulders, but she didn't need a fierce sun when with Luke. They had the pool almost to themselves, apart from an elderly couple Luke had chatted with and found out they were enjoying every minute of their retirement.

'Have you done a wine tour?'

'We didn't have time,' Luke said. 'We go home tomorrow. How long are you here for?'

'A couple of months.'

'Nice,' Luke said, and with friends so easily made he got into the pool.

'Lucky them,' Luke said.

'I don't want to think about going back…' Except they soon were. 'I should get something for Clara,' she said, floating on her back.

'Get something at the airport.'

'Maybe something for Jess.' She stood up in the water. 'That sounds ridiculous.'

'No, it doesn't.' He shook his head, then went for a lazy swim of a couple of lengths of the pool.

He returned, and beneath the water, he caught her leg and then came up to kiss her, guiding her to the edge of the pool.

'Get her one of those giant shells.'

Luke could pick up a conversation better than anyone she

knew, and she liked how he'd given it some thought. How thoughtful he could be. How sexy he was.

'You look like the day I first saw you,' Monica said, running her hand through his thick wet hair.

'Did you want me then?'

'I was a bit busy.'

'Did you want me then?' He persisted and kissed her neck, 'because I know that I…'

He halted and looked up.

A family had entered the pool area, a young couple with a little baby, and he felt that odd band of fire around his throat, the one he had felt that morning. 'I thought it was a no-kids hotel…'

'Luke?' She frowned. 'It's Geo's grandchild.'

'I know.' He corrected himself, but he could hear the splashing and laughter of the little family, and when usually it wouldn't bother him—if anything he'd smile and chat—today, it reminded him of a week ago. That dreich, grey day, and he looked up as if half expecting clouds to have gathered. 'Why don't we get ready for dinner? We still haven't tried the hotel restaurant. Geo will never forgive us if we don't.'

It was a blip.

One tiny blip in four days and it was forgotten.

Almost.

Monica had splurged in one of the local shops and bought a lilac dress that was all floaty and summery, and instead of the espadrilles, she had on a pair of pale leather sandals, she'd splurged on too.

And when he saw the effect, Monica looking utterly beautiful, he realised he'd never wanted anyone more. Hell, it was just as well they were leaving tomorrow or he might make Geo's wishes come true and propose.

She was that beautiful.

The restaurant was set on the cliff edge, and as they were led through, Luke couldn't believe they'd almost missed it.

'We really saved the best to last.'

The tables were dressed in white cloths, and the sun was a fiery orange and about to descend into the water it had turned into molten lava.

'You're wearing your earrings.'

'I love them,' she said, because she really did now.

'Vicky told me off for getting them.'

'Vicky really does talk too much.' Monica smiled.

'Yeah, I've got to address that.'

'Why?' Monica said, sipping dessert wine, all velvety sweet with a caramel tinge. 'Surely your job's tough enough without being told to keep quiet or police your words?'

'Well, I have to say something.'

'I'm sure you'll find a nice way.'

Their first course was served. *Avgolemono* soup, a silky lemon egg soup served in small bowls, and perfect to take off the first chill of the night. 'This has been perfect,' Monica said. 'I just need you to come up with a gift for Clara now. If she ever talks to me again…' She flashed him a smile. 'Last time I take your advice.'

She'd taken his advice regarding the herb garden and told her parents that Clara was upset.

It hadn't gone well.

'Sorry about that.' He smiled. 'So you need a present to make up for it?'

'She's almost trickier than Jess.'

'One of those snow globes. The ones with the pelicans and sand instead of snow, you could get her name on it.'

'Aside from the fact she wouldn't be able to see it. They're dreadful.'

'You're a snob, Monica.'

'A bit,' she admitted. 'Actually, it might make her laugh— they are fun.'

She was coming to hate that word.

The whole four days had been wonderful, and yet they'd

been more than fun. She'd been herself and told him things that she wouldn't share with some casual fling. Well, not that she'd ever had a casual fling—the only one she'd ever had was sitting opposite her four months later and they had to untwine their hands as the main course was served.

Lamb *kleftiko*, slow cooked to perfection...

'I love lamb.'

'I had noticed.' Luke smiled. 'With your shepherd's pies and moussakas.' He glanced over and saw Geo at the bar, watching, waiting...

Then dessert—*loukam*, honey-drenched balls of dough, dusted with cinnamon, and the simple dessert was perfection... or was it the company? He holidayed often, but had never come close to this.

'Sorry about back at the pool. I just...'

'No, I get it,' Monica said. 'You booked a child-free hotel, and with Gus and everything, you deserve a few child-free days.' She laughed, clearly thinking of the constant noise on the maternity unit. 'I do too...the quiet has been bliss.'

And he nodded and chose not to say any more.

Not just because he didn't want to ruin the holiday, or for things to get dark, more he didn't even know what he could say. Couldn't quite pin down if something was even wrong.

He certainly didn't want there to be.

And so, instead of ruining the moment, he pinched her last *loukoumades* and laughed at her protest. Then they did what they did very well when they had time.

Danced.

'We haven't had our dance lessons yet,' she reminded him as they swayed on the dance floor.

'The first Wednesday we both get off,' he agreed, breathing in her summery scent and so pleased he hadn't said anything, because right now everything was back to okay.

A perfect last night and they were back in their lovely hotel suite, and there were little wrapped sweets on their pillows.

And she never wanted to leave.

'You taste of honey,' he told her as they shared sticky kisses, and then he said the same as he kissed her elsewhere, and she held on to the sheets in deep pleasure.

And, when she came to his mouth it took a Herculean effort to reach bedside for a condom when he really wanted to just take her.

It was getting harder to be sensible now.

For both of them.

She huffed in tense frustration and wanted to remind him again that she was on protection.

Except an accident would be a disaster for them.

'Oh...' she moaned as he squeezed inside and then went back to honey-tasting kisses as he took her.

It made her dizzy, this affection, this want, this tenderness, and it felt like everything. It felt so good, not just in body, but in her heart, that it almost made her want to cry.

'It's okay,' he said, and he wiped her cheek and she realised that she was crying, just a bit. It was almost too much pleasure. He was looking right at her, taking her and consuming her, and it felt as if they knew the other's soul.

Not the parts they showed, not the smiles and the laughs, but somewhere beyond that, somewhere she was scared to admit existed, because she could only be there with him.

'Luke.' She said his name, but it was more a sob, the deepest orgasm of her life, easier to give in to than reveal her heart.

And it must be the same relief for him, because he came to her body's urgent demand and, for a while at least, they were sated.

Only it felt as if they'd peeked into each other's hearts.

They lay on their back, side by side and together, but both deep in their own thoughts.

The breeze came through the open doors, blowing the drapes and gently cooling, but it carried with it the sound of a baby. Probably Geo's little grandchild, and it was sweet rather than invasive, yet it felt as if their one big issue was chasing them, even tonight.

Luke closed his eyes and wished it was so easy to close his ears on the baby's crying. He couldn't stop thinking about the silence last week.

She knew Luke could hear the baby because she'd felt him tense.

And she would ask just once.

But she had to ask.

'Could you see yourself changing your mind?'

Luke was silent when a few short months ago he'd have jumped straight in with a hard no, or never, or not a chance, but knowing how much it meant to her, he considered the question.

Could he see himself ever changing his mind?

It would be too easy to lie in a post sex rosy glow, closer to a woman than he'd ever been, but he didn't believe in false hope.

And right now, with the events of last week making odd appearances in his mind, there wasn't even a sliver of hope that his stance might change.

'No,' Luke said, perhaps a little too harshly, but he could not see himself changing.

Not now.

It was Monica's turn to be silent.

To consider his word.

He liked that she didn't move to dissuade him, or nudge him to reconsider, or put impossible scenarios into play.

Instead, she turned her head on the pillow and looked right at him. 'Then we have a problem.'

'Not tonight, we don't.'

CHAPTER TEN

IT WAS RAINING at Stansted.

And raining in Hampstead when, close to midnight, he dropped her home.

'Are you coming in?'

It was already late, and while Monica still had a few days of leave, she knew he started at six in the morning. 'Better not. I've got an early start tomorrow.'

'Well, thank you for such a lovely time. It was wonderful, every moment.' Well, except for those two tiny baby-shaped blips.

'It really was,' he agreed. 'Oh, I almost forgot.' He reached into the boot and pulled out a small bag, one he'd been carrying since the airport. 'I got you a present.'

'Really?' She went to peel open the bag, but he put a hand over hers.

'Wait till I'm gone.'

He saw her inside with all her luggage and things, and then gave her a very nice kiss, the sort of kiss that didn't want to end, or rather, one that wanted them to end in bed.

'Stay,' she suggested again, and he breathed in hard as he held her, and she could feel him wrestle within.

'I *have* to sort out my uniforms,' he sighed, very reluctantly letting her go. 'It might be a bit depressing after such a nice break to watch me doing laundry.'

'Just a bit,' she suitably laughed, but deep down Monica knew she was lying.

She wanted that bit too.

The unpacking, getting sorted for the workdays ahead.

Not just the holiday and fun parts but all the normal stuff.

'Thanks,' she said again, in case she blew their carefree holiday with baby questions or confessing she wanted to try living with him. 'I had a wonderful time.'

'And me.'

She closed the door and, of course, the second he was gone opened the bag he'd handed her.

As she peeled open the tissue paper she started to laugh.

Both Monica and Jess had giant seashells, but Luke had bought her one of the snow globes they had laughed about. A little bit of coral and a lady on a sun lounger with a cocktail. Instead of snow it was sand...there was even a flamingo.

It was tacky and utterly glorious, and it was the first thing she laid eyes on the next morning.

She missed him already.

'How pathetic is that?' she asked the happy lady in the snow globe. 'If Luke knew the real misery I was.'

The lady just smiled back.

Of course, life wasn't a permanent holiday, and Monica was soon sorting out her own laundry when her phone buzzed.

And the second she saw that it was Richard, she knew.

Oh, thank God for phones that tell you who's calling, because she was able to steady herself before answering.

'Hi, Richard...'

'Things are close.' She could hear the shake in his voice. 'Very.'

'I'll come now.'

'Thank you,' he said and then added, 'Drive carefully.'

'Yes.'

'Monica, I wouldn't stop for coffee.' He let her know how close it was. 'Can you call George?'

'I'll sort out all that,' she told him.

There had been many frantic trips to Wales over the years. The day of Jess's accident, her second big bleed, pneumonias… This drive, though, was different. It was the end.

She didn't want to share the news on the Jess update group—that circle was a little too wide. As well as that, what a dreadful way to find out.

So, she called George from the car, and he was at work, but would do his best to get away. 'And can you call Ravi?'

'Sure.'

Jess had held on, and Bronwyn, Jess's mother, gave Monica a hug when she arrived. 'She waited for you, Monica.'

'That's good,' Monica said, 'because I bought her a present.'

They were such a lovely family, and they even gave her some time alone with her most wonderful friend. And she held the shell to Jess's ear and hoped she could hear the sea…

Somewhere.

'I love you,' Monica told her. 'And you're not to worry about a single thing.'

And then Richard and Jess's parents came in, and Monica sat in the pretty gardens outside, with Ravi and George, and an hour or so later Bronwyn came out and her friend was gone.

She was sitting alone in the garden a while later when Luke called.

'Hi.' She took a breath, doing her best to keep her voice steady. 'I'm in Wales.'

'Oh, I didn't realise you were.' He paused and must have worked out this wasn't a scheduled visit. 'Is Jess worse?'

'She passed away an hour ago.'

'I'm so sorry.'

'Richard rang this morning and said things seemed close.'

'Why didn't you call me? I'd have driven you.'

'It's not my first frantic dash to Wales. Anyway, you had work.'

'I know, but…' He was silent for a moment. 'How are you?'

'I'm okay.' She looked out at all the trees and the pretty flowers waving in the breeze, and it all looked so lush and vibrant and in contrast to what had happened. 'It wasn't unexpected.'

'Can I do anything?'

'No.'

'I can head over, stay in a hotel?'

'Why?'

'Because it's hard losing someone you care for, and you don't have to be on your own.'

'We're not about all that,' she reminded him. 'We're about fun.'

She heard him inhale; knew he was containing himself from snapping back. 'Anyway,' she said, 'I'm heading back tonight. I've got work tomorrow.'

'But I thought you were on leave?'

'I've had to do some swaps, so I can take a couple of days for the funeral. Best friends don't count with HR.'

His suggestions annoyed her. All of them. Especially the next one—

'Do you want to come and sleep here?'

'No, I need sort some things out at home.'

'Well, I can come over and bring dinner.'

'No!'

And Monica knew then why his suggestions annoyed her. It was because she wanted him here, or wanted him there, wanted to fold over and cry, and to lie with him tonight and get through this hellish feeling, but she was too scared of breaking down.

And so, she avoided him.

Fired back one-liners to his messages, or a quick thumbs up. And it was actually a crazily busy week, because on several of the occasions he did call, she was mid-delivery, or in the middle of clinic, or theatre.

Not all the times, of course…

Luke gave her space, but refusing to be completely blanked, he turned up on the ward a couple of days later. He came onto the unit and his dark green uniform caught her eyes, as well as a cup of hot chocolate from her favourite café, which he handed to her.

'You'll need to warm it up.'

'Thanks…' They headed to the kitchen, and she was back to all fingers and thumbs as she pressed the buttons on the microwave. Wanted to flee, rather than let him glimpse the agony.

'How are you doing?'

'I'm okay.' She took out her drink and then turned and gave him a smile. 'Just snowed under.'

'You're avoiding me.'

'I'm honestly not,' she said.

'You honestly are.'

'I'm busy here, and when I'm not here I'm sorting out photos for the service.'

'What day is the funeral?' Luke said, 'I can change around my shifts.'

'There's no need for that.'

He frowned.

'I'm driving Clara and all the old crowd are going to be there.'

'Monica, let me be there for you. You were there for me the other week.'

'You were upset for one night,' she pointed out, then saw his eyes shutter and tried to check her tone. 'I just need a bit of space.'

'Sure.'

Even at the funeral she dared not cry.

She sat with Clara behind Richard and Jess's parents.

Sorcha, as they'd discussed, had gone to Scotland for a few days to allow Richard to properly say goodbye to his wife. And to grieve and cry…

She couldn't.

Then the drive back to London with a pensive Clara.

'I can't believe it's over,' Clara said. 'I mean—' she turned her head to Monica '—I remember their wedding.'

'Yes.'

'And it seems wrong that Richard's going to be a father in a couple of months and it won't be with Jess.'

Monica could feel her hands gripping the steering wheel and was relieved that Clara couldn't see. She forced her voice to stay light. 'It's been three years, Clara.'

'I know, but I just…' Her voice was soft and sad. 'I bet he asks you to be Godmother.'

'I don't think so.'

'I do,' Clara said, 'you've been there for him, for Jess, for the family.'

'It wasn't a chore,' Monica snapped, and then fought to correct it. 'I did it for Jess.'

'I was always a bit jealous of Jess,' Clara admitted. 'You were so close. More like sisters than we are.'

'Because we were the same age.'

'Maybe, but you spoke to her in a way you don't talk to me. I bet you told Jess about Luke.'

Monica felt a stab of guilt, because she actually had. 'You and I are close,' she attempted, but then took a breath. 'I want to be closer, it's just every time I try, Mum and Dad seem to get in the way. Like the herb garden…'

'I asked you not to tell them, and you had to dive in and fix it.'

'I know.' She took a breath. 'I'm blaming Luke for that one.'

'How are things going there?' Clara asked. 'I thought he might be here today.'

'He offered, but I said no.'

'Why?'

'Because we're not about all that. We're just keeping things light.'

'Life isn't always like that.'

'I know.'

'And if he offered to be there…'

'He doesn't want children.' She almost barked it out, but ridiculously, it didn't matter. They were, in that moment, as close as they'd ever been.

'Oh, Monica…'

'And, no, he isn't going to change his mind, and I'm thirty-six, and I can either keep having fun with Luke, or get on with the life I want. The baby I want.'

'On your own?'

'Yes, well, unless there's another Luke out there who wants to make babies with me. I can't see that happening.'

Clara laughed, and even Monica did.

They even stopped for ice cream as they filled up with petrol and were pondering the issue when he texted.

'That's him now, asking how the funeral went,' she said, firing back a reply.

'That's nice.'

'Yes.'

Only it wasn't quite as nice as Luke had been in recent weeks because Monica was the recipient of a thumbs up now.

No offer to come over.

Or for dinner tonight.

Perhaps her misery of late had been too much, when she'd tried so hard not to show it.

But whatever standoff they were in had a brief respite late that night, when he called her.

'How are you doing?'

'I'm okay,' she said. 'I'm just…' She was actually honest. 'So tired.'

'Of course you are.'

'Are you at work?' she asked.

'No.'

'Babysitting Gus?' she asked, still confident enough in them to think that might be why he hadn't offered to come over, but no, he wasn't babysitting his nephew.

'They asked me to, but…' He was silent for a beat, then didn't really answer. 'I just called to make sure you were okay.'

'I am.'

'How was Clara?'

'Still seething about the herb box.' But she smiled then. 'Actually, we got on really well. She liked her shell.'

It was a nice conversation, but just that. Nice. It led nowhere, and she couldn't quite define it, because even if she'd shut him out, she'd expected a little more of a knock at the door of her heart.

It felt as if he were walking away…

Perhaps he was too kind to call time on the night of her friend's funeral?

And then she woke to her snow globe and the lady still smiling with her cocktails, and no text from Luke.

Things had changed and she pinpointed when.

Since she'd asked if he might ever consider changing his mind about a baby.

It had to have been then.

Life went on, even without her best friend, and even without her sexy paramedic. He still called, but things had changed.

Their schedules had always been disasters, but a week after the funeral, heading home from work, she felt ridiculous relief at the sight of a green uniform.

'Vicky…' She smiled as they caught up in the corridor outside A&E. Of course, Monica was still parking there. 'Busy shift?'

'Just finishing.' Vicky smiled. 'Luke's in the ambulance doing his paperwork.'

Indeed, he was.

Sitting on one of the seats typing into a tablet, but he looked up and gave her a smile. 'Hey...'

'What are you up to?'

'Not much,' he said, 'unless dispatch tries to squeeze in another job.'

He looked tired and there were dark rings under those gorgeous dark eyes, and she knew that in an attempt to spare him her grief, she'd rather pushed him away.

'I was thinking,' Monica said and took a seat beside him. 'It's Wednesday.'

'It is.'

'We still haven't been dancing.'

He gave a half laugh and looked at her. 'You don't want to go dancing.'

'I actually do.' Monica nodded. 'I've been a bit...' She shrugged.

'You're allowed to be,' he said. 'You lost your best friend.'

'I know, but...' She thought for a moment. 'We haven't had much fun lately, maybe a night at La Milonga...'

He seemed to think about it for a moment, and she had the dreadful feeling she'd let misery be company for too long, and that her sexy paramedic was about to dump her, and if she knew where they were, she might turn on the lights and sirens, so urgent was this moment...but then he nodded. 'Sounds good.'

'What do I wear?' she asked.

'A tight skirt, black stockings and stilettoes.'

'Really?'

'No.' He laughed and for a second they were back to being

them. 'Whatever you want to wear.' He paused and put his hand up to her cheek. 'Maybe a night out is a good idea.'

'I think so.'

'I know I've been—' he paused and she felt her heart constrict '—a bit off.'

'No, I get it. I'm sorry I was rude when you offered to come to the funeral.'

'It's fine.'

She gave him a smile. 'I'll come by at six.'

She wasn't actually in the mood for dancing. She would like to fall in his arms and cry, or sleep for a week, but instead she pulled on a dark skirt and stockings to make him laugh, and clattered up the stairs.

'Whoa,' he said, pulling her in for a kiss. 'Let's not go dancing…' He paused as his phone rang. '*Carajo*.'

She frowned at his slight cuss when the phone announced it was his brother calling.

'It's Daniel.'

'Yeah,' he said, 'and I can guess what he wants.'

'What?' she checked. 'Luke, if he wants you to babysit, I'm fine with that.'

'No, we're going out…'

He spoke to his brother and he wasn't exactly abrupt…

Well, a bit.

'I can't, Daniel. Monica and I are going out tonight.'

She made a frantic sign, but he turned his back.

'No, I'm working at the weekend. Sorry, Daniel, I can't…' He ended the call. 'Sorry about that.'

'Call him back. Tell him you'll babysit.'

'I don't want to babysit,' Luke snapped.

He did not want to babysit, only it had nothing to do with dancing. He could still feel the baby in his arms, could still see the agony in the father's eyes as he'd looked to the ambulance.

Something was wrong and he didn't want to admit it, because then it was real. And surely, she had enough to deal with now?

'Look, I told Daniel I'd help when I could, but—' he shook his head '—he's taking advantage.'

'You really don't want anything to do with babies, do you?' She thought of him in the pool in Cyprus, turning his back, and how he'd tensed on their final night when the little baby had cried. And now he was turning his back on his brother and nephew for a dance class they could take anytime.

And they were two very different people Monica realised.

She wanted the cosy family nights.

Luke didn't.

And as wonderful as it had been, they were going nowhere.

'I'm going to go.' She didn't want it to end on a fight, but it did have to end. 'We want different things.' She took a breath. 'And, frankly, I don't have time to spend months or years in a relationship that isn't headed in the direction I want.'

'Wow!' He let out a low, slightly incredulous laugh. 'The baby thing, again.'

'I've never tried to hide it.'

'You'd throw away something this good, for something that might never happen?'

Monica frowned.

'What if I can't have children?' he asked. 'What if you can't? What then—do we end it because we can't have a baby? Do I dump you because you can't give me a child?'

'I'm allowed to want a baby.'

'For sure,' Luke said. 'And I'm allowed not to.'

'I get that, but, Luke, you don't even want to be around your nephew. You've changed,' she said. 'Or maybe you haven't, but the guy I met, or thought I met, would do anything for his family.'

He stood there as she let herself out.

Listened to the clip of her heels as she raced down the stairs.

And yes, some might think Monica a bit cold, a touch closed off, but he liked that about her.

Admired it.

Because when she opened up, when she spoke from the heart…

He listened.

You've changed…

The guy I met…or I thought I met…

She was right.

And it was time to sort things out.

CHAPTER ELEVEN

'HEY, LUKE.' VICKY SMILED. 'You're early. Do you want a coffee?'

'Sure,' he said. 'I'm just going to have a quick word with Cheng.'

It was difficult to knock on the door and go in.

'How are you, Luke?'

'Fine,' Luke said, even if he didn't feel it.

Everything was mixed-up and merged into a cloud instead of one neat problem, and though usually he would push through things, for Monica's sake, for his family's sake, for himself, he retracted his response.

'Not so fine.'

'Close the door.'

He walked over and took a seat at Cheng's desk.

'I'm not good at all this,' Luke said, 'saying what's on my mind.'

'I know.'

'You remember the SIDS the other week…' He looked over and Cheng nodded. 'I can't get past it. It's not the first one though, and I've dealt with kids before…'

'Luke,' Cheng said, 'we never know which job will be the one that fells us. What's been happening?'

'I don't want to babysit Gus.'

'Your little nephew?'

Luke nodded. 'And Monica and I broke up.'

'She was always out of your league,' Cheng teased, but then he was serious. 'Have you told her?'

'No. She's just lost her best friend.'

'And now she thinks she's lost you. Why can't you tell her?'

'Because I want to sort this out properly, not just land it all on her. She wants…' He stopped himself. 'I'm not going to tell you everything.'

'Will you talk to Matthew?'

For ten years, more, he'd refused to, or rather, hadn't felt he needed to, but Monica was right, he had changed.

And it would seem everyone, including himself, preferred the old Luke and so he nodded.

'Yes.'

She couldn't cry.

Monica didn't dare.

The moment she got home she'd punched every last pill down the sink and flushed them away…

And weeks later, she still hadn't cried.

But she missed him so.

This morning, she woke up to the smiling lady with her cocktail, and of course she checked her phone.

No Luke.

'Well what did you expect?' she told herself and headed into work.

It had been two months since their row, and she'd seen him in passing a couple of times, but really, just in passing.

The back of his shoulders one night, leaving work.

And then another time she'd looked into A&E as she'd passed, and he was talking with a patient.

He hadn't seen her.

The barrier didn't rise the first time she swiped her lanyard.

'Because it's over,' Monica told herself. 'Because you shouldn't still be parking by A&E.'

But then the barrier rose, and she parked her car and maybe

there was a God because there were Luke and Vicky loading an empty stretcher into the ambulance.

'Monica.'

'Hi.' She waved and decided it would look petty if she didn't go over. 'Are you starting or finishing?'

'Just starting.' Vicky smiled. 'I've got my six-month assessment coming up…' She looked over to Luke. 'Hopefully he'll be nice.'

'Be nice,' Monica said, proud she could summon her superpower and look him in the eyes.

'I always am.' He gave her a smile.

That smile that had faded in the final weeks of them, and it was bittersweet to see it back.

He looked gorgeous—his hair was cut and the dark rings had gone from under his eyes.

She wished the weeks apart had treated her so kindly, because she knew she'd lost weight and the May version of Monica wasn't quite as together as the woman he'd met in November.

'How are you?' she asked.

'I'm good.' He nodded. 'You?'

'I'm well.' She nodded. 'How's Gus?'

'Getting bigger every minute. I'm babysitting tonight.'

'That's nice.' She gave him her smile and then a quick eye roll. 'I'd better get on.'

'Monica…' he called and caught up with her. 'I'll walk up with you. I'm sorry how things ended.'

'It's fine, I was a bit…'

'A bit what?'

'I know I'm tricky, and what with Jess…'

'It wasn't that.' They walked across the ambulance bay and into the main corridor. 'I was going to give you a call in a couple of weeks. I actually wanted to say thank you.'

'I do too.' She gave a soft laugh. 'We did have some fun.'

'No, I meant for what you said that night. You were right, I had changed.'

Frowning, her stride halted and she turned around.

'I'd been struggling,' he admitted. 'Since that SIDS.' Her mouth parted in a silent shocked gasp. 'I just didn't want to be alone with Gus. I was worried about getting called out to a paediatric arrest. That baby in the pool...'

She felt ill.

Truly, embarrassed that she'd never seen it.

God, she'd told Vicky she could talk to her anytime, offered to go over to Clara. All her colleagues got the same treatment, her door was open, but in this, the person that mattered the most, she'd missed it.

'Luke, why didn't you say?' And she could have kicked herself, because she should have asked. 'I had no idea. I should have...'

'Stop,' he said. 'I had no idea what was going on either. I'm better now, well, getting there.' He gave her that smile that melted her heart. 'I'm seeing Matthew once a week. I'm babysitting tonight, first time...'

'I can come.'

'It's more about being on my own. I need to do it.'

He paused.

'Matthew was trying to tie it to my parents, or the twins and responsibility or Gus...' He looked right at her then. 'You wanting a baby.'

She winced. 'I'm so sorry.'

'Don't be. I think it brought a lot of things to a head, but as well as that—' he breathed in sharply '—it was sad enough on its own.'

'Yes.'

'I'm working things out now.'

'I'm pleased.' She wanted to linger, to know more, but it was so much safer to move to practical. 'I've got some things of yours, your jumper, a couple of jackets.'

'It's fine.'

He didn't take up the chance to meet again, and that hurt so much she dared not show it. 'I really do have to go. I've got theatre.' She walked off, but feeling his eyes on her, summoned those powers for the last time and turned and smiled. 'Be nice to Vicky!'

'Got it.'

He wanted to go after her, wanted to properly see her again and not in some draughty corridor.

He wanted to tell her the work he was doing on himself, but not yet...

He didn't believe in false hope.

And tonight was a big test.

'Hey.' Daniel came in with less baggage than a few months ago, but a much bigger baby. 'Thanks for this.'

'It's no problem.'

Only that wasn't true, there had been a problem.

'Luke, I'm sorry if Kelly and I took advantage.'

'You didn't, Daniel.' He didn't want to burden his brother with the horrors he'd seen, but he did need to address this. 'I'm sorry if I've been a bit off. I've been having a couple of problems at work.'

'What sort of problems?'

'Just, stuff.' He looked at his chunky nephew. 'It's not you and it's not him.' He took Gus in his arms. 'It's all me.'

'Why didn't you say anything?'

Because he didn't.

Like Monica.

They were too used to being the oldest and just getting on.

'Have a great night.'

The door closed and he took a gurgling Gus to the couch, and it would be so much easier with Monica here, but he needed to get past this, get back to being a devoted uncle.

'How could I be scared of you?' Luke asked, and then Gus

looked up from his lap and gave him a big gummy smile, a smile that didn't end, because he started to coo and laugh. Luke scooped him up and held him, and for the first time in weeks, his arms felt warm with that precious baby weight.

'Not scared of you,' he corrected, not wanting to land all this on the little guy. 'Just scared of…'

What?

Loving someone so much and the possibility of losing them.

He'd done everything he could to shield his heart, sworn he didn't want the drama of it or the responsibility.

Then the gorgeous icy Monica had come along.

'And you…' he said, to little Gus. 'And I wouldn't miss this for the world.'

CHAPTER TWELVE

'ARE YOU GOING to tell me I talk to much?' Vicky asked as, between jobs, Luke decided it was time for her assessment. 'Because I know Cheng and a few others…' Her voice trailed off as Luke got up from the passenger seat—he was treating today—and went into the back of the ambulance to get his tablet. 'I'm nervous,' she added as Luke returned to the passenger seat.

'Pardon?'

'I know I can be a bit indiscreet…'

'Pardon?'

She turned and started to laugh when she saw Luke had two cotton wool balls sticking out of his ears. 'You bastard.'

They laughed, really laughed, and he told her that no, she didn't talk too much, and then he smiled when he thought of something Monica had said. 'God knows we're not robots. Just keep being you.'

They were people doing their best, often in the hardest of times.

And, sometimes, in the best of times.

'Can I treat…' Vicky asked as the second the job came through—a twenty-eight-year-old in active labour, full-term pregnancy. 'If she's going to deliver, can it be me?'

'Yes,' Luke agreed looking out at the traffic to ensure they were safe. 'Clear left.'

Their patient lived in a huge high-rise in busy Canary

Wharf, but the sight of blue lights cleared the way and they parked outside.

'Nineteenth floor,' Luke said as they gathered up their equipment. As they entered the foyer he was scouting for a goods lift should he need to retrieve the stretcher, as certainly the lift they stepped into was too small to accommodate it.

They located the apartment easily, and the front door had been left open. Vicky called out, 'Ambulance.'

'In here,' came a female voice.

She was standing by huge floor-to-ceiling windows, her head on her forearm and clearly having a contraction, but as she turned her head slightly, Luke realised that he recognised her.

'Sorcha…'

It was the nurse from The Primary, the one who'd been assaulted by a patient.

'You know each other?' Vicky checked.

'We met on our professional development day,' Luke said as, along with Vicky, he helped Sorcha to the couch to be examined. 'You were busy delivering babies…'

As Vicky treated—taking obs and then checking to see if birth was imminent, Luke was chatting with Sorcha.

'Richard's got an exam today. An important one. I didn't want him to miss that, but now he's going to miss seeing our baby be born.'

'Let's just wait and see,' Vicky said. 'Let's get you to hospital.'

Poor Vicky wouldn't be getting her first delivery today!

There was no need to get the stretcher, or even the chair. Sorcha was actually a touch affronted when she was told she could walk. 'Seriously?'

'Walking's good,' Luke said. 'Where's your bag?' It was in a gorgeous nursery, with a waiting cot, and instead of that band of fire in his throat, it made Luke smile.

'I'm booked in at The Primary.'

'Because we're an emergency ambulance, we'll have to go where we're told,' Vicky explained, 'but we'll let control know where you're booked.'

Luke saw her disappointment. 'It depends how busy the departments are.'

'I know.' Sorcha sighed. She worked in A&E after all, but by the time they'd got her into the ambulance and strapped her in and Luke was sitting in the driver's seat, Control got back to them. 'Direct to labour ward at The Primary,' he called to his colleague and patient.

'Yay!' Vicky said.

It was quite a distance in the midday traffic, and if the situation changed Luke would pull over and the baby would be delivered, but her contractions were still quite irregular and far apart.

He could hear Vicky reassuring and chatting to Sorcha, and he kept an ear open for any changes, as well as both eyes on the traffic, yet he could feel the slight tension in his jaw…

Would Monica be there?

He hoped so because he wanted to see her.

But then he hoped not, because he knew this was going to be hard on her.

She was there.

Wearing a navy dress and looking very elegant and poised. Her smile wasn't forced as she greeted Sorcha, and she clearly was in the loop with things, because she knew about Richard's exam.

'He'll be finished soon,' she reassured Sorcha. 'The second he comes out he'll turn on his phone. I'm sure he'll be here on time.'

He and Vicky transferred Sorcha through to L&D and wished her well, and given Vicky was treating, he left her to her paperwork and looked for Monica.

He found her in her office.

'Hey.'

She looked up and gave him a very polite smile.

'How are you?'

'I'm well,' she responded.

'What time do you finish?'

'I'm not sure now,' she said, and when he frowned, clarified. 'I was supposed to finish up at four, but I'll stay for this little one.'

'Because she's your patient?' he asked. 'Or as a professional courtesy?'

'In part, and also Richard's a close friend. The same way I'd want him if...' She paused. 'If it were a family member.'

'Is it going to be hard, what with Jess...'

'I'm past all that,' she quickly said. 'I'm thrilled for them.'

'It is possible to be thrilled for them and to find it difficult.'

'Well, I'm just thrilled.' She gave him a thin smile. 'I ought to go and check on Sorcha.'

'Sure.' He watched her turn to walk off. 'Monica?'

'Yes.'

He watched her shoulders tense, and when she turned, he saw that she didn't quite meet his eyes. And he knew that despite her words, and the smile, that today really was difficult for her, yet she refused to reveal.

He admired that.

Wished it could be different and she could lower her guard just a touch, but this was work, and they didn't have a personal life together anymore.

'I hope it goes well.'

She nodded. 'I'm sure it will.'

'Do you think Richard will get here?'

'Richard could be taking a slow boat from China, and he'd still make it.' She gave him a roll of green eyes and a smile.

'A late night for you then?'

'I think so.'

And he understood her a little better then.

She couldn't fall apart today.

Not even a little bit.

She was, he realised, a lot like him.

'Right,' he said, and knew it would be kinder for now to leave her alone, and just let her be brave. 'I'll let you get on with things then.'

'Thanks.'

She'd lost him.

Monica knew.

He was talking to Vicky by the lifts, and she wanted to call him back, to break down, to tell him she wanted him, baby or no baby...

Instead, she headed into delivery room 3, where Sorcha was teary and tense. 'I should have told him I was having contractions.'

'Sorcha, today's going to be a good day,' Monica told her. 'It is,' she said, and even if she wasn't good at midwife speak, she was good with her patients, and Louise stayed quiet as Monica spoke. 'I happen to think it was a lovely thing you did, for both of you. He's waited a long time to take this exam.'

'Yes.'

His life had been on hold since Jess's accident, and she smiled at the woman who had turned the light back on in her friend.

'You're three centimetres dilated...' she said, having examined her.

'Is that all?'

'That's perfect,' Monica said. 'He's going to be here for the...' She was about to say the 'hard part' but she saw Louise's lips pinch a touch. Her favourite midwife liked positive words and so Monica modified her response. 'He'll be here for the birth, I'm sure.'

She went to write up her notes and Louise came to the desk. 'Nice save, Monica,' she smiled. 'You're going to have a late night, aren't you?'

'It will be worth it.' Monica nodded.

She meant it,

Yet Luke was right, of course.

It was possible to be thrilled and upset at the same time. To be both happy and sad.

Not just about Jess and Richard.

About missing Luke and wishing things could be different.

But she couldn't go there today.

A good while later Louise brought her in a hot chocolate. 'Are you okay, Monica?'

'Of course.'

'Are you sure?'

'Yes,' Monica said.

'We still haven't had that word...'

Louise knew, she was sure. Midwifes have a sixth sense, or maybe Louise had simply seen her ears pricking up when she'd spoken about Anton.

And she'd been gently inviting her to speak, but still she hadn't called in that favour.

She still hadn't made an appointment to see Anton.

'Another time,' Monica said.

'Anytime,' Louise offered.

As she quietly left the office, instead of putting her head in her hands, Monica took a sip of hot chocolate. Relishing the sweet taste on her tongue and the warmth and focussing on that rather than the jumble of her own life.

Babies come when they're ready.

Not when Mum or Dad are ready.

Certainly they don't wait for the doctor to have her life in order before they arrive. At midnight she sat in her office, and when her pager sounded, Monica went to the sink and splashed her face and headed out.

'Fetal distress,' Diane told her.

Time to invoke that superpower.

'Hey, Sorcha.' She could see Richard's tense expression as he held his wife, and there was a moment of internal panic, but then she snapped back and told herself she'd got this.

'I can't do this.' Sorcha was tiring, and though the baby did have mild distress, it was recovering well after each contraction.

And birth really was the most beautiful thing in the world. She'd hid her inner conflict, even from herself.

But, delivering the tiny little baby onto her mother, watching Richard break down as he saw his son, she struggled to contain her emotion.

Richard wasn't just a dear friend, he was a first-time father, utterly in love with the mother of his little baby.

As well as grieving.

Monica did not cry.

She truly didn't dare.

'Congratulations,' she said to the proud parents.

'Thanks for being here, Monica,' Richard said. 'For everything.'

She nodded, not quite trusting herself to speak.

Leaving the little family in the darkened labour suite to have some precious new family time, she took off her gown and threw it into the laundry skip.

It was almost one as she passed A&E, and the paramedics outside weren't the ones she needed tonight. Or perhaps didn't need, because she was about to cry.

''Night, Monica,' someone called.

''Night.'

Three years' worth of tears, some happy, some sad, all she'd kept in check seemed to be bubbling up like a shaken soda can. Climbing into her car, she put on her seat belt and reversed out, waving to one of the security guards as she passed.

And then it happened.

She swiped her lanyard and the barrier didn't lift.

So she swiped again.

'Shit,' she said, which she rarely did, and then started promising the boom gate gods that if they just let her out tonight, she would never park by A&E again.

Her temporary diversion was well and truly over!

She went to press the intercom, but the button was too far to reach, so she turned off the car and got out. 'It's Doctor Hamilton, I parked near A&E and I can't...'

'Try now,' came a bland voice.

It would seem the boom gate gods were very cross indeed, because not only didn't they lift, but now her car wouldn't start.

'Not now,' she said, turning the key again as the engine coughed and then, it didn't even do that.

Swallowing down a sob and breathing in, she called out to the security guard. 'Gerry.'

'Yes, Doc?'

It was great fun.

For them.

'Battery's dead.'

'Oh. But it started.'

'It's dead.'

She stood, in a dress not quite suitable for a chilly night, as Gerry summoned a porter, and of course it was made all the more complicated as the boom gate had again closed.

'Swipe your card,' Gerry said.

'It doesn't work,' Monica said, 'I'm not supposed to be parking here.'

It was minor, really.

The bland voice was back on the intercom, the boom gate lifting and the guys were pushing her dead car towards a car park.

And did she call out someone tonight, or just get a taxi or...

There were many choices, yet she truly felt she couldn't take another step.

Not a single one.

And it was then she did something she never thought she would.

She called him.

Knowing she might well be blocked or sent straight to voicemail if he had his Do Not Disturb on.

'Monica?'

Oh! 'Hi, Luke, sorry if I've woken you. I wasn't sure…'

'You haven't.'

'Are you working by any chance?'

'No, I finished at four.'

'Are you in bed with someone?'

'No.' He had the audacity to laugh. 'I'm actually walking towards you.'

She looked over, and sure enough there he was…

Luke, in his Cuban heels and dark jeans and a very crisp white shirt.

'What happened?'

'My car…' Actually, she might have lightly or even somewhat strongly cussed between those two words.

And not in Spanish!

'It's fine.'

'It's not though.'

'It's a car.'

It wasn't the car, but she didn't know how to tell him that.

'Why don't I take you home and we can sort out the car in the morning?'

We?

He was being nice, she decided.

For old times' sake.

And so, she nodded.

Embarrassed at being the woman who couldn't deal with a broken-down car…

He was very practical, talking with security and thanking them, then locking up her vehicle. And she didn't get how come he was here and not in uniform. Or that he didn't seem remotely surprised that she'd called him past midnight from the staff car park.

'Come on,' he said. 'We've got a bit of a walk.'

'To where?'

'The normal people's car park,' he said, making her laugh a little bit.

'How come you're here?' she asked. 'Is Gus okay?'

'Of course he is. I've been hanging around A&E, chatting to May…oh, and George. They were all waiting for news on the baby.' They reached the pay station. 'I assume, given you've finished work, that the baby's here.'

'Yes.' She nodded. 'It went well, I shouldn't really say anything, it's not my news to break, but…' She smiled and reminded herself this was Luke. 'A little boy—James. He's beau…' Her voice sort of faded when she saw the price for his parking flash up. 'How much!'

'Worse than an airport,' he said.

'No wonder the patients complain. How long have you been here?'

'Since the end of my shift. Well, I went home and got changed.'

'Oh.'

They took the lift to his car and then stepped out, and there it was, his familiar car with the baby seat and a stuffed giraffe and a work manual he cleared before she took her seat.

He didn't start the engine, just sat as she put on her seat belt.

'Thanks for this. Sorry to…'

'To what?'

'Call you.' She was a touch embarrassed that she had now. 'I didn't think you'd pick up.'

'Why wouldn't I?'

'If you were on a job, or had your Do Not Disturb on…'

'You're on my special list,' he said. 'I pick up for you.' He looked over then. 'Why do you think I'm here, Monica?'

'I don't know.' She didn't. 'Work party?' He frowned. 'Or...' her mind darted to a place she didn't want it to go. 'A friend in A&E?' There was a little sting in her voice. 'Dropping her off a hot chocolate?'

'Did I ever drop in on you when we were seeing each other?'

'No.'

'I only did that when I was working.'

'Yes.' She gave a soft laugh and it sort of strangled as she thought of happier times. 'You did.'

'So,' he said, still not starting the engine. 'Why do you think I'm hanging around A&E like a loser?'

'A loser?' She didn't know what he meant.

'I'm sure that's what all my colleagues who've seen me tonight think. They all know you dumped me.'

'I didn't.' She shook her head. 'Well, I suppose I did, but...' She wished he would start the engine, yet he just sat there. Patient. And she liked that about him, usually, but tonight she wished he'd just start the engine and get her home, not sit there waiting for her to speak.

She didn't trust what she might say.

Yet, his silence allowed her to say it. 'I think I made a mistake.' She looked out to the neon-lit car park and watched an elderly couple walking toward their car. Watched how he opened the door for her, the same way Luke just had. 'Ending things, just because I wanted a baby.'

'You're allowed to want a baby.'

'I know.'

'It's a good thing to sort out before things get too serious.'

'Yes.' She nodded, very dangerously close to crying. Oh, she already was, but they were just trickly tears she could blame on being tired and her car dying and the boom gate not moving. But if she spoke, it might turn into an ugly cry.

'The thing is, I don't know if...' She was quivering inside, all the churned-up thoughts desperate to escape, to spill out. 'You made me happy.'

'You *make* me happy,' Luke replied, causing a boiling tear to splash out. 'Even when times are tough.'

'And I threw it all away.' She hated so much that she had. 'I don't even know when having a baby became a mission. I mean, I always wanted one, but...' She halted herself and gave her head a little shake, but that damn patience of his knew no bounds, because he just waited for her to elaborate. 'After Jess's accident it became...' She thought back, because it hadn't been an obsession, more... 'Something to focus on.'

'I can get that.'

'Tonight was hard,' she admitted. 'I'm so happy for them, I really am. And I know Jess would be too. She'd want this for Richard, but just, taking care of Sorcha...' She blew her nose on a way overused tissue. 'It's been difficult.'

'Yes.'

'I wanted to take care of her.' She told him her confliction. 'I'm good at my job and I wanted her to have the best care.' She closed her eyes. 'That sounds arrogant.'

'Or accurate?'

'It just hurt,' she admitted. 'And you're right, you can be happy and sad at the same time.'

'You miss Jess.'

'So much.' She looked over. 'I tried to keep hope going that first year, and of course be positive for her parents and for Richard, and I knew that, compared to their grief...'

'Yours didn't count?'

'No, I just didn't feel it was my place. I mean, given what they were going through.'

'You discounted how you felt,' he said, and his voice had a slight edge that made her frown, 'because your bloody parents trained you to.'

She breathed in sharply, his words too true and just a little too sharp for her fragile state.

'Please don't have a go about them.' She wiped her cheeks, looked him right in the eyes and warned him not to go there. 'I don't need it now.'

'Fine,' he agreed, 'and I'm not "having a go" at them, I'm just pointing something out. Look, I did it to myself. When my parents died, I knew I had to be the tough one. I didn't get to…' He put his palms up. 'I had to be there for the twins.'

'Yes.'

'When I saw that dad…' He paused. 'Mia's dad.' He said her name. 'The police, his poor wife, the way he was trying to control things, be the strong one.' He looked over, and she caught her breath as he gave her a piece of his private heart. 'I felt like I was looking at myself ten years ago. I knew a little of what lay ahead. And that's why I couldn't look at him.'

'I wish you could have told me.'

'I didn't know,' he admitted. 'I didn't realise how it had affected me. I thought I'd get through it.'

He started the engine, and now she wished he wouldn't, because his admission was a deep one, and she knew that his sharp words hadn't been to hurt her, but to help, to reveal what he knew. But they were driving off.

'Damn,' he said, and even laughed when the boom gate didn't lift. And unlike her, he calmly pushed the intercom and flirted a little with the voice on the end. He had the gift, and instead of being charged for going fifteen minutes over, the boom gate lifted.

'Why were you in A&E?'

'Because I knew tonight would be a tough one for you,' he admitted as he drove through the dark streets. 'I was hanging around in the ambulance bay, but then went in to get another coffee. I almost missed you.'

'What were you going to say?'

'Ask if you were okay.' He glanced over. 'Offer sex.'

She laughed, a rather feeble laugh, but it was a laugh all the same. 'How would that help?'

'Helps me.' He grinned.

'Well, we can't,' she told him. 'Even if it would be a lovely distraction.' She sniffed, because even if she so desperately wanted him, saying goodbye in the morning might just shatter what was left of her heart. 'I've stopped taking the pill.'

'Oh.'

'And I don't have any condoms.'

'I don't trust them anyway. Not with an ovulating woman who desperately wants a baby.'

He did make her laugh.

Truly, he did.

He made her so happy, even with a broken heart.

'We could just talk?' he offered.

And there was no *just* when it came to Luke. Talking to him, at any time, was an utter treat. 'I'd like that.' She nodded.

They ended up at his, because it was closer, and because they sort of both needed to just be away from the hospital and car parks and streetlights and finally alone.

And it was there she finally broke down.

'I'm sorry.' She had never cried so openly, so deeply. Even on graduation day, she hadn't properly broken down, but now, at the end of the road with Luke, saying goodbye nicely, was the hardest thing in the world. 'I don't need a baby, we could just…'

'You shouldn't have to compromise.'

'I want to compromise,' she told him. 'I want…' She took the glass of water he had poured. 'You.'

'Drink that.'

'I do,' she said, gulping cool water and seeing Gus's bottle sterilizer and the little outfits folded over the back of the chair, and Luke had been right.

What if they couldn't have a baby, why would she end something that felt, in every other way, perfect.

Her tears didn't daunt him.

He felt quietly pleased that this very closed-off woman could break down to him. He thought of Jasmine, how she'd held on until the man she trusted was there.

And Monica could trust him.

In everything.

'Let's go to bed.'

'I thought we were talking.'

'We have lovely talks in bed,' Luke reminded, 'I'm wiped and I'm sure you are too.'

Monica wasn't though.

She was all wired with emotion, and it felt so wonderful to be back in his bedroom and to sit on the edge of the bed and watch him undress. He was still messy, still kicked off his boots in different directions and left his jeans in a denim puddle on the floor.

And still so sexy that even this upset she was turned on and a little daunted at the thought of being back in his bed and back in his arms and not...

'What's wrong?' he asked, fully stripped off.

'Nothing.'

Except she undressed with her back to him. Not shy, just a little concerned that her body might somehow reveal she was aching in places he clearly wasn't.

Well, possibly he was a bit, because his hand moved beneath the dark covers, and he arranged himself as she rather gingerly climbed in.

'So,' he said as she lay there, her heart hammering. 'How are you doing?'

'A bit better,' she said.

'I mean, with Jess and everything?'

'I'm sad, but it's also a relief,' she admitted, and honestly she hadn't even told herself that until now. 'I hated seeing her fade away.'

'I get that.'

'And I know she'd be happy for Richard.'

'What would she want for you?'

'To be happy.'

'Yeah.'

And she was, lying with her head on his chest, with his arm over her.

'How are you?' she asked, because she wanted to know. Not just the happy bits, but all the bits, the good and the bad and the sad.

'I'm okay,' he said. 'Matthew's been great, Cheng too.'

'I wish I could have helped.'

'You did,' he told her. 'You pulled me up. I had to sort out a lot of things.'

'Like?'

'Losing them. Being a parent at twenty-two.' He was quiet for a moment. 'I think we suffer from oldest child syndrome.'

'What's that?'

'Dunno, but I think that's what it is. We're the good ones, the responsible ones, even when we don't want to be.'

'Yes.' She thought back. 'I love Clara.'

'I know that.'

'We're getting on so much better now, and I do love my parents, but…' She thought for a moment. 'What you said in the car was true.'

'It's made you a brilliant doctor.' He squeezed her arm. 'If I didn't love you, I wouldn't have known you were upset that day.'

She froze in the warmth of his arms, sure she'd misheard, or that he'd got it wrong, and he had to have got it wrong because… 'We'd barely met that day.' She tried to make light. 'A bit early for love.'

'Maybe,' he quietly mused as her heart thumped like a jack-hammer in her chest, 'I was infatuated then.'

'I was infatuated too,' she agreed, and decided to let the little love thing go. Because if it was love, if what he'd said wasn't a slip, she wasn't sure she could bear to have thrown something so precious away…

His chest was heaven, and her hand was on his stomach, feeling the lovely crinkly hair and trying not to stroke it, while aching to.

'Are we allowed to kiss?' he asked, and she lifted her head for that bliss—the sheer relief of lips that knew hers and chased all the problems of the world away. He pulled her a little more on top of him and stroked her waist and then up to her rib cage as their tongues mingled.

'I missed you,' he told her.

'I've missed you too,' she admitted.

'I've missed this,' he said, taking her hand and moving it down until she felt him hard and warm. 'A lot,' he added as she stroked him.

And she knew he wasn't reckless, and wished to God she hadn't flushed away her pills. They were both so hot and turned on, and both had to complete, and so she wriggled down, kissed his chest and, tasting his skin and the slight salt of his nipples, worked her way down that gorgeous big body, wishing this wasn't goodbye.

It didn't have to be, did it?

'Luke…'

'Shh,' he told her, clearly wanting something other than conversation as his hand stroked her shoulder.

Or did he? Because instead of pushing her down, he was pulling her up, and in a deft motion laying her down and coming over her, so that he pinned her with that big body.

'So, no comment?' he checked.

'To what?'

'I just told you I love you.'

'Infatuated…' she corrected.

'Maybe at the start,' he said. 'I don't know exactly when it changed, but I do know I love you.'

It took her breath away, not just the weight of him pinning

her, but the glint in black eyes and to be stared at and told you were loved, even with her own puffy eyes and swollen lips, even when you'd been mean and not there when he'd needed her most.

'I let you down.'

'You didn't,' he said. 'I didn't even know something was wrong. I had to work that out myself. In the future, we'll talk.'

Now she really couldn't breathe. She was scared to exhale lest she blow away the delicious thought of a future...

With Luke.

'We're going to be happy and have fun and have shitty sad days too.' He kissed her cheeks and her ears and her neck and he was so ridiculously sexy, and, yes, reckless, because he was parting her and stroking her and playing dangerous games when so close to the edge.

'So,' he said. 'Still no comment.'

'I love you too,' she told him. 'I really do, and I want everything you said.' She wanted to make some big declaration, say something really deep and meaningful, except his fingers were so expert, and she was arching to him, then he removed those intimate beats of pleasure and took hold of himself. 'Luke...' She did not want to stop him, the thought of him unsheathed and deep inside had her on the edge of coming, but one of them had to think straight.

And tonight, it wasn't Luke.

'Put something on.' She went to roll over, but he was quite heavy. 'Luke, I've...'

'I heard you, you're ovulating.' He was just a little way in. 'I don't care.'

'That's not very romantic.'

'Oh, it's very romantic,' he said, 'when I'm telling you I want babies with you.' Then he closed his eyes and sighed in relief as he slid in. 'God, you feel good.'

'We should talk,' she attempted, but it was a pathetic attempt because she was moving with him.

'You're thirty-six,' he reminded her, making her laugh as he groaned with pleasure at her, oily and tight and so ripe for him. 'We shouldn't waste time.'

'I do love you,' she told him, coming undone, crying and aching and mired in pleasure, just awake and somehow sedated in his arms. Giving in and letting him take her, lifting her arms as he pinned her. They would talk later, have more wonderful conversations, deal with the madness they'd just made, but for now the only focus was deep sensual pleasure. He moved rapidly, urgently, a polite warning, if there was such a thing, that he was about to come, yet her own orgasm felt unhurried. An unabridged sensation, like velvet dominoes falling inside, collapsing her defenses as she contracted, every intimate pulse she gave unashamedly to him, and his harsh breath as he shot inside making her weak, and his collapse after, just lying there, locked together, was the closest she had felt to whole.

'Do you...' She checked, because men said stupid things when they wanted sex.

Not Luke.

'I love you.'

'The other bit,' she said as he rolled off of her. 'I don't want to force you into anything.'

'Force me?' He laughed at the very thought and pulled her back into the nest of his arms. 'You got me thinking...a future with Monica, or one without?'

'We have a future.' She could say it confidently now, relish it for a moment, even as she offered him an out. 'Baby or no baby.'

'I know,' he said to the dark and seemed to think for a moment. 'I always said I couldn't imagine being tied to one person, or having kids or...' He stroked her arm and spoke in a sleepy voice. 'But that was before I met you.'

EPILOGUE

'I'M NERVOUS,' MONICA ADMITTED.

'Would it help if I told you so am I.'

She looked over to Luke and smiled.

They were sitting in a waiting room at The Royal, waiting to see Anton Rossi.

Not for the reasons she had thought she'd be there. Certainly, Monica wasn't going it alone. They'd been trying for a year, married six months and still nothing had happened.

She was thirty-seven and certain she'd left it too late.

'It's probably my fault that you can't get pregnant.' Luke sighed.

'It's not about fault.'

They'd had a lot of tests this morning.

Both of them.

Bloods, urine and an extra bonus test for Luke.

A one-stop shop Luke had said when he'd seen all the slips, and found out they had to do a sperm count and motility test that same morning. Now, with all the tests taken care of, they sat outside Anton Rossi's office waiting to be called.

'It's like sitting outside the headmaster's office, knowing you've done something wrong.'

'What?' Monica checked.

'My wicked past is going to catch up with me.'

He did make her laugh, even when she was more nervous

than she dared to admit. 'I knew all about your wicked past when I took you on,' she responded with a light tease.

'Monica Arias.' Her name was called by the receptionist. 'This way, please.'

They were led through a couple of corridors to a rather dark room, which she didn't think was the esteemed Doctor Rossi's regular office. 'I apologize,' he said. 'I am a little between patients.' He was reading through notes, and his welcome really wasn't the one you wanted to hear when you'd been holding your breath for weeks for this moment. But then he looked up and gave her a lovely smile. 'Monica, it is good to see you. Luke.'

They'd seen him socially and he'd been at their wedding, but this was all very professional now.

He went through her history first.

'So, no previous pregnancies?'

'None.'

'And you have a very irregular cycle. Six to eight weeks. How long has it been like that?'

'Well, it was always six weeks or so, and then when I came off the pill last year, it's around eight.'

'How long were you on it for?'

'Since medical school.'

'I see.'

'Could that cause problems?'

'I don't think so.' He was reading through her results on the screen. 'I suggest my patients take a break now and then to see where they are at. Luke, you had a test a little earlier I see.'

'Yes.' He cleared his throat. 'I did. Are there any results?'

'I'll just ask my assistant to chase them up.'

Monica closed her eyes in mild frustration, wishing Anton had all the information back before calling them in.

'So,' he asked, 'when was your LMP?'

'Eight weeks now. I'm due any day,' Monica said. 'Does that change anything?'

'Hmm,' he said.

Gosh, he was vague, and Monica was about to get her asser-tive doctor hat on and ask for more specifics, but Luke seemed to sense her sudden tension and she felt his hand on her knee.

It was awkward, and difficult, and then he suggested they do an ultrasound so he could see where they were at.

'External and transvaginal.'

She'd known this would happen and got up on the very high bed.

'Do you want me to go out?' Luke offered, but Anton shook his head.

'Take a seat, Luke.'

Anton was very polite but not very talkative, and as he went out for a moment Luke rolled his eyes.

'He probably doesn't get a word in edgeways with Lou-ise,' he suggested, making Monica smile, but she was teary all of a sudden.

'I think there's bad news,' she said, but then Anton was back.

He did a quick ultrasound, but decided to go transvaginally.

'A bit cold,' he said.

Indeed, it was.

'Okay,' he said.

'Is it?' Monica snapped, and Luke squeezed her hand to tell her not to lose it here.

'We will have Luke's results back soon, but it would seem there is no problem there.' He turned the monitor. 'Can you see this?'

Her heart felt as if it had stopped, she could see a little flicker on the screen, like tiny flashes of blinking light, and yes, there was the foetal sac and the tiny, tiny beginnings of life. 'Oh my.'

'And here,' Anton said.

Monica frowned and stared at the screen. She read ultra-sounds as easily as most people read the daily news, yet her brain couldn't seem to take this in. Because there was another foetal sac, and more flickering.

'I'm trying to get a better view,' Anton said. 'Baby one, is to your left…'

Monica's breath hitched.

She wanted to see Luke's reaction but she couldn't take her eyes from the screen.

'Baby two,' Anton said, 'is just here.'

'Twins?' Luke checked.

'I'm just checking for more…' Anton said, and then the austere doctor laughed. 'I'm kidding, there are just two.'

'*Qué loco!*' Luke said. How crazy!

Then his head came down beside hers and together they laughed and sort of took in the incredible news together as Anton finished up.

It was a rather shaky Monica who came to his desk. 'Is that why you're seeing us here?'

'Correct.' Anton nodded. 'Your results, of course, told me you were pregnant… your B hCG is so high I wanted to rule out other possibilities.'

Her mind went everywhere then, to molar pregnancies and other problems that she would have jumped to, but Luke spoke again then.

'Twins?'

'Yes,' Anton affirmed. 'I can only see one placenta, which suggests identical twins, though I'll do a more definitive scan in a few weeks.'

'Twins,' Luke said again.

On repeat.

'Correct. I wanted to be sure of course before I said anything. You're six weeks, about four weeks since conception.'

Monica nodded.

'So still very early.'

'We know you can get pregnant,' Anton said, almost warning her not to get too excited just yet.

It was too late for that.

She was pregnant.

Now she just had to hold on to it.

To them.

'You've got this,' Luke said, 'Come on, Monica…'

As it turned out, Luke was very good at midwife speak, but only when it came to Monica.

And she was back in her superpower and certainly not about to lose it in front of Louise and co.

'One more,' Louise said. 'Come on, Monica.'

It wasn't really…

When twin one was out, she'd be doing this all over again, but her baby was almost here.

'Listen to Louise,' Luke said. 'Come on, Monica.'

And then she was here.

Dark hair and so pink and perfect and tiny that it took Monica by complete surprise. She'd seen more than a thousand babies, but it felt like this was the first.

'Oh…' She was shaking and her tiny girl was on her stomach and Luke was cutting the cord, and she ached so much to hold her. Scooping her up and inhaling that new baby scent and just marvelling at perfection.

'She's…' How to describe the tiny mewing baby she held in her arms and who lay on her chest as Diane rubbed her back and then whisked her away. 'Is she okay?'

'Perfect,' Luke said.

'George is just having a little look, mama,' Louise said, and Luke gave a tiny eye roll to Monica at midwife speak, but Monica smiled.

She was finally a mama.

'Monica,' Vince said, 'a little more work to do…'

'No rest with twins.' Luke smiled.

There was actually quite a lot more work, but then their

second miracle arrived, tiny and pink and a little jittery in her arms, but all fears faded.

'We're just checking her glucose,' Louise said, and the world felt like a carousel, all bleeps and bells and little cries and she saw Luke holding their firstborn as her second born was brought to her arms.

And then they were placed on her chest together.

Two perfect peas in a pod, and together they admired them, adored them.

'Do you have names?' Louise checked, but they didn't just yet.

They'd played with names, of course. Sophia after his mum, or even Jessica after her dear friend.

But none of them worked.

They'd ached for so long; it was time for new.

'We haven't decided,' Monica said, gazing down on little navy eyes that would soon turn black, then up to Luke's, whose were a little glassy.

They didn't need to know their names just yet.

'It's enough that they're here and safe,' Luke said and then looked at her.

It was everything.

* * * * *

A NURSE, A PUP, A SECOND CHANCE

KARIN BAINE

MILLS & BOON

This is for all the real heroes who volunteer their time
and expertise to help those in need xx

CHAPTER ONE

'IF YOU DON'T sit down, Mr Hinchcliffe, I can't do my job.' Billie was using her firm, no-nonsense tone with her patient so he wouldn't think he could mess her about despite her small stature.

As much as she loved her job as a nurse, Saturday nights working in the A and E department could be challenging to say the least.

'You think you're so much better than me, don't you?' The ruddy-faced, middle-aged man was swaying as he slurred his words, the stench of alcohol emanating from every pore.

'No. You came here for help, and I'm doing my best to help you. Now, if you'd care to sit down, I need to clean that wound and see how deep it is.' There was always an influx of inebriated patients with nasty cuts at this time, and the most challenging part was getting them to co-operate. Thankfully, Billie had a lot of experience and patience.

She folded her arms and waited until he acquiesced, albeit with a grumble. Then she set to work cleaning the bloody gash on his arm.

'Is everything all right in here, Nurse Wade? I thought I heard raised voices.' Patrick, her friend and colleague, poked his head around the cubicle curtain, his brow furrowed into a frown.

'Everything's fine, Dr James. Mr Hinchcliffe here will be on his way soon enough.' She smiled, letting Patrick know that she had this when he was obviously concerned for her welfare. It was nice that he always had her back. She'd needed that this last six months since finding out her partner, Thom, had been cheating on her. It had felt like the end of the world. Another reminder that she wasn't enough for anyone. Just like she hadn't been enough for her parents.

Even though she'd been the firstborn, her parents had never seemed particularly fond of her. As though she was a disappointment to them in some way, simply by having been born. Although she'd been well provided for, there had been a distinct lack of love. At times she thought she might as well have been a lodger in the house for all the attention they'd given her. It meant she'd tried so desperately hard to be a model child for them in the hope that they'd love her, but never feeling as though they were totally invested in her. Only that they were fulfilling an obligation by being there.

She could have put it down to them not being particularly warm people, and parenthood hadn't come easy to them. Except when her brother, Jaxon, had come along two years later, they'd seemed to instantly fall in love with him. They couldn't make enough fuss over him, and Billie realised it was just she that they couldn't love. Although she still stayed in contact with her family, they weren't close. It was the feeling of being inferior that hurt the most, and she didn't like to be reminded of it when she was with them. And when Thom had left her for another woman, the pain was even worse. Reinforcing the notion that she was lacking in some way that made it impossible for anyone to truly love her.

If it hadn't been for Patrick, she didn't think she would ever have dragged herself out of bed, never mind the darkness which had threatened to consume her after the break-up. He'd been there for her, just as she had for him when his wife, Sinead, had died two years ago. They were lucky they had each other for support, even though their group of four had now been reduced to a duo.

Her patient muttered his displeasure at being told what to do, bringing her mind back to the current battle in the cubicle, although her patient put up no further resistance.

'Okay, I don't think it's too deep, Mr Hinchcliffe. A couple of paper stitches should suffice.' Patrick worked quickly to shut the wound on the man's arm, with Billie helping to dress the area with some gauze and tape.

'Make sure you keep the wound clean and dry to give it a chance to heal. We wouldn't want it to get infected.' Neither would Billie look forward to seeing him back here any time soon. Belligerent patients often took valuable time away from others who needed medical attention.

The patient grumbled before getting up and leaving without a word of thanks or acknowledgement.

Billie sighed. 'I suppose we should be grateful it wasn't anything more serious. I dread to think how we would have manoeuvred him down to get an X-ray or get a cast on him.'

'The joys of working in A and E.' Patrick grinned, looking as relieved as she was. Like every weekend, it had been busy to the point of exhaustion. Thank goodness it was the end of shift for them both.

'Pizza or Chinese tonight?' she asked as they grabbed their things on the way out of Mourne Hospital. As had become routine these past months, on the evenings they'd been working together, they often shared a takeaway at her place to help wind down.

'Um, Chinese for a change. Can you order it, and we'll collect it on the way home?' Patrick led her towards his car and focused on navigating the dark, rain-soaked roads, leaving her to make the call for their usual order.

It hadn't escaped her notice that he'd called her place home. They'd become so used to doing things together, it had become second nature, and she appreciated the company. She looked forward to the nights they got to spend together. Otherwise she suspected she'd lead a lonely existence with only her dog, Fliss, to save her sanity. Patrick James had become a very important part of her life.

The takeaway restaurant was at the end of Billie's street, so it wasn't long before they were pulling up outside her house, the anticipation of finally getting to eat making her mouth water.

'Hello, pup,' she said, ruffling the fur of her beloved black-and-white border collie, who'd come to greet them at the front door.

Fliss's excitement was doubled when she saw that Patrick was present too, her tail in danger of wagging itself right off.

'Where's my gorgeous girl?' Patrick, and their dinner, almost ended up on the floor as Fliss launched herself at him, seeking his affection. Which, of course, he provided in plentiful supply. He handed the bag full of food to Billie so he could fuss over her dog, kneeling down to scratch her ears and rub her belly. Billie was almost jealous of the attention.

Patrick would be the perfect man if she was looking for any sort of romantic relationship. He was handsome, successful and caring. As well as a softie where dogs were concerned. Except not even a hot dark-haired, brown-eyed doctor would be enough for her to risk her heart on another man. Even though Patrick would never see her as anything other than a friend and colleague when he was still mourning his wife. They were both simply two lonely souls who'd found comfort in one another.

He tilted his head as he looked up at her, as though wondering where her thoughts were headed. She had to walk away before he realised.

Billie set the dining table with plates, cutlery and glasses before decanting the plastic containers. The aroma of their dinner soon became too much for Patrick to resist, and he came to join her, leaving a disgruntled Fliss to slouch back to her bed.

'Well, this beats grabbing a sandwich on the go,' he said, digging in to heap a sample of everything onto his plate.

'Mmm, probably not the healthiest option, though.'

Patrick slurped a noodle into his mouth, leaving a spot of soy sauce clinging to his bottom lip. 'Don't spoil it. I look forward to this.'

Billie did too. Sometimes it was easy to forget all of the heartache they'd both been through when they were so comfortable together. As though they'd always been a couple. She supposed it was because with their partners, they'd all been close for quite some time. They knew each other inside and out. Just as she knew he'd barely cooked a meal in his own house since losing Sinead. In fact, he seemed to spend as little time as possible there. When he wasn't at the hospital, he was working as part of the crew on the air ambulance. With Billie and Fliss volunteering with the search and rescue team in her spare time, her path often crossed with Patrick's even when they were off duty. They saw more of each other than anyone else.

'Maybe I'll actually cook for you some night. I might even christen that new kitchen of yours.' Patrick had renovated since Sinead's death in the hope that it would encourage him to be at home more. It hadn't.

Billie could understand that. Her place was littered with memories of Thom. Both positive and painful. Perhaps it would be a good idea for them to move, but their lives had been too disrupted recently to go through that. In the meantime, she wanted to help him in some way. Even if it was only to have a friendly face around his house to make him feel more at home there. The trouble was, the more time he spent here, the more she got used to having him. The more comfortable she felt here herself.

'I'm not sure if that's a promise or a threat.' Patrick ducked his head as he tossed the light-hearted insult.

'Ouch. In case you've forgotten, I make a mean fry-up.' In the good old days, after a late night with Patrick and Sinead, Billie would have made them all a hearty cooked breakfast. Hangover food. That was back in the days when they used to stay over at each other's houses and enjoyed a drink and a laugh together. These days it was more about consoling and looking out for one another to make sure neither starved or drowned in their self-pity.

She saw the flicker of pain in Patrick's brown eyes and

could have kicked herself. Clearly her good memories were still painful for him. Where she liked to remember the best times they'd all had together, it seemed he did his utmost to forget. As though it was easier for him to pretend it had never happened than remember how happy he'd been with Sinead on those occasions. Sometimes it seemed to Billie that he was never going to be able to move on from the loss of his wife. Though it had naturally devastated him, she knew Sinead wouldn't have wanted him to wallow for the rest of his life without her.

'More healthy food,' he eventually grumbled.

'Comfort food, and goodness knows we both need some of that.' She held up her glass, and he clinked it to hers with a sigh.

'I'm glad I have you, Billie.' It was an out-of-the-blue comment that seemed to take them both by surprise given how his eyes widened the second he said it.

She tried to lessen the impact of it by reaching across the table and giving his arm a squeeze. 'Ditto.'

That raised a small smile. She hated to see him without the great big toothy grin he used to be famed for. Since Sinead's death, he'd become more introspective, though still thoughtful when it came to making sure Billie was okay. Sometimes it seemed as if when his wife died, that fun, spontaneous side of him had died too and been replaced with a more sombre person. Understandable, of course, but she missed that side of her friend. As close as they were, she didn't think she could ever make him as happy as Sinead had.

'You don't have to do that. I'll sort the dishes out later,' Billie told Patrick as he scraped the plates and began loading them into the dishwasher.

'It's fine. There's only the two of us anyway. Besides, you hosted dinner.'

Billie snort-laughed. 'You make it sound like some fancy dinner party, not a takeaway.'

He shrugged. 'I'm just saying it's the least I can do.'

'You paid.'

Frustrated, Patrick took her by the shoulders and gave her a playful shake. 'Just let me do something for you.'

Billie fixed him with her big baby-blue eyes. 'You've done plenty for me these past months. I don't know where I'd be without you. Probably still languishing in bed, de-hydrated from all the crying.'

'Just returning the favour.' Patrick hated Thom for what he'd done to her. She didn't deserve to feel this way. At least neither he nor Sinead had any choice in her leaving. Thom had. He could have been honest and told Billie their relationship was over instead of cheating on her and making her think it was all her fault. Too many times she'd cried on Patrick's shoulder, wonder-ing what she'd done wrong, when it was entirely down to Thom that he'd decided to cheat. Despite being friends with him for years, Patrick would never forgive him for the way he'd treated Billie. Not that he'd heard a word from him since his lies were discovered. Since Billie had found him texting lewd, incriminating messages to one of his co-workers. At first, Thom had tried to make out that she was paranoid, that it was just a bit of banter. Let-ting Billie believe it had been all in her head. Until she'd seen them together with her own eyes canoodling in a bar when he'd told her he was working. She had bravely confronted him there and then. Leaving him no choice but to finally come clean and break her heart.

Patrick had been doing his best to prop Billie up in the aftermath of their split, the way she'd been there for him when Sinead had died and he'd thought his life was over too. These past months, they'd clung to each other to get through the grief and loss of their relationships. Though sometimes he couldn't help but think they were in danger of becoming too dependent on one another.

Like now, as she immediately sought comfort in him. His arms opening to welcome her to his chest. These days their automatic response in low moments was to reach for one another. Something he'd needed for a long time to help him crawl out of the darkness too. Except his feelings towards Billie had begun to change recently, and he found himself, his body, responding to her differently. More as a hot-blooded man than a friend.

Even when he was doing his best to provide her a safe haven, he was having to fight against those new feelings.

He'd suddenly become aware of the sweet perfume she wore, how soft she was against him, and how warm. After over a decade of knowing each other, it seemed she'd become more than a friend to him. Without even knowing it.

The realisation that he was seeing Billie romantically had hit him several weeks earlier. It happened one night when they'd got caught in the rain as they came out of the hospital and had to make a run for shelter. Suddenly, huddled together in a porchway, laughing and watching the rain pelt down, he'd been struck by how beautiful she was. With her damp hair curling around her face, make-up washed off in the rain, and droplets pearled on her long, dark eyelashes, the sight of her had momentarily rendered him speechless. As well as incapable of any thought other than Billie in that moment.

He already knew what a wonderful person she was, having worked alongside her and seen a lot of her in a personal capacity. This new development in how he viewed her had been disturbing. He'd felt it was almost a betrayal, not only to her but to Sinead, to see her as an attractive woman instead of just his mate.

He'd done his best to put it behind him, to carry on as they always had, but every day he saw more reasons to appreciate this woman. Making it harder to fight his growing attraction towards her. He didn't want to feel this way about her when it could mean a change in their dynamic. She was a friend he couldn't afford to lose.

Perhaps it was simply a sign he was finally able to move on. He hadn't even looked at another woman since Sinead's death, but he didn't want to be on his own forever, and he couldn't expect Billie to provide emotional support for the rest of his days. She deserved to find someone else too. Patrick figured this new reaction to physical contact with her was a reminder that he still had needs and desires. Apparently his libido hadn't died along with his wife.

Despite the inappropriate thoughts about his friend, Billie was right. Sinead wouldn't want him to be in mourning for the rest of his days. The truth was that they had drifted apart in the last years of their marriage, even though no one else was aware of it. A matter that caused him even more guilt at being tempted by Billie. Making him feel as though he couldn't have loved his wife enough in the first place. It was simply too painful to even contemplate getting close to someone else and losing them too.

A cold, wet nose nudged against his hand, reminding them both that there was another needy soul to be attended to.

'Okay, Fliss, I'm going to give you your dinner now.' Billie slowly extricated herself from Patrick's arms, leaving him feeling empty without her.

At the mention of food, Fliss began her ritual of running full pelt around the room. Her zoomies were always a source of amusement for Patrick because it was the one time Billie wasn't in full control of her canine companion. This was evidence that the collie was still very much in her puppy phase, despite her professional appearance out in the field.

'It's dinner time, Fliss! Who's a good girl?' He encouraged the dog's crazy antics, along with Billie's side-eye for doing so.

'You're not getting fed until you calm down.' An exasperated Billie tried to reason with the excited pup, but it only seemed to fuel her shenanigans.

'I don't think she's listening.' Patrick grinned as Fliss began jumping on and off the furniture before suddenly using Billie as a springboard. 'It's like puppy parkour. I think someone needs a walk to work off that excess energy.'

'You think?' Billie let out an *oof* sound as strong collie legs pushed against her. She struggled to stay upright and couldn't quite keep her balance.

Patrick grabbed hold of her, but another Fliss launch sent him and Billie both tumbling to the ground. He took the brunt of the fall, with Billie landing on top of him.

Their bodies were pressed intimately together, their faces only millimetres from one another. The waves of her chestnut hair provided a curtain around them, cutting them off from the outside world.

For a second, time appeared to stand still. Even Fliss seemed to have stopped her antics and gone quiet. In that moment, only he and Billie existed. His heart was thumping so hard against his rib cage he was sure she could feel it too when her chest was pressed so tantalisingly close against his. As he looked deep into her sky-coloured eyes, his breath hitched, certain he could see the same desire he was feeling reflected there. It seemed natural to simply press his lips against hers, giving in to this sudden need to kiss her. Her mouth was soft and yielding, and it would be easy to lose himself in the feel of her, but somewhere in the back of his mind, alarm bells were shrieking a warning.

Continuing this could change everything between them. Billie was the only person he had in his life, and he didn't want to mess things up with one wrong move. He'd surprised himself, likely as much as he had her, by succumbing to his desire to kiss her. However, a simple kiss became so much more when it was between two friends. It would complicate things if one of them wanted something more than the other, and he valued her companionship and support too much to jeopardise that simply because he couldn't control his urges. He was an adult, not a horny adolescent, and should have known better than to act on impulse like this. At least if he put a stop to things now before they went any further, there might be a chance to get back to their usual status quo.

The hands, which were holding her close, reluctantly

moved her off his body. Patrick knew they'd crossed the line, and no matter how much he'd wanted it or enjoyed it, he had to fight this attraction to his best friend. 'I should probably go and let you sort Fliss out for the night. I can see me being here is getting her over-excited.'

Patrick got to his feet, barely able to make eye contact with Billie now, knowing where his thoughts had strayed.

'Oh. Okay. If you're sure?' Billie dusted herself down as she stood to see him to the door, uncertainty written in her tense body language.

'I'm sure. Thanks for dinner.' Patrick grabbed his coat and dashed out into the night, inhaling great lungfuls of the cold night air, trying to steady himself again.

He hated that he'd already made things awkward between them, but tonight had proved one thing. They'd become too close for his comfort. Blurring the line between friendship and something more intimate would be a mistake. They were both hurting, in no frame of mind for a relationship. It would be a disaster at the cost of the bond they already had. Apart from anything else, he was already close to Billie. She meant the world to him and had claimed a little piece of his heart. Giving her any more would leave him vulnerable to more hurt, and he didn't think he could stand that after the loss he'd already suffered.

As much as it would pain him, he was going to have to make some changes. It was time he learned to stand on his own two feet again. Without Billie. Or anyone.

CHAPTER TWO

'OKAY, DO WE have an item of clothing belonging to Mr Hill that we can use?' Billie and Fliss were eagerly waiting with the operational crew at the rendezvous point in the Mourne Mountains, where they'd been called out to help locate a missing, vulnerable person.

Being part of the dog search and rescue team in the County Down area meant that any spare time she had wasn't always guaranteed to be free. Not that she minded. She was much more useful and productive out here in the wilds of Northern Ireland, hopefully helping someone in need than lounging around at home overthinking everything in her life as usual.

At present it was Patrick who was on her mind, or the lack of him in her life lately. She'd become so used to having him there with her for company, she was missing him these past few days. Of course, she knew why when things between them had suddenly become awkward at her place the other night after dinner.

She couldn't explain what had happened. One minute they were cordially tidying up after their takeaway. The next, Fliss had managed to send them tumbling to the ground. There was something in that moment, that intimate position, which appeared to have changed things.

For her, at least. She'd never been so aware of Patrick as a man until she was up close and very personal with him.

Obviously she knew he was a handsome man. With his dark, wavy hair and deep brown eyes, he was just her type. Tall and lean, fit and successful, he'd turned more than a few heads in his time. Not that he'd shown an interest in anyone other than the wife he'd lost. Billie respected the deep love he'd had for Sinead and had never seen him as anything other than a very dear friend. Yet there had been something in the moment that made her want to kiss him.

Even now, the memory of that intense urge made her shiver. She'd tried to resist at first, but all too quickly she'd found herself kissing him. So lost in the feel of him that she hadn't even stopped to consider if Patrick wanted it to happen. Obviously not, by the way he'd left pretty sharpish and they hadn't seen much of one another at work. They hadn't spoken since the kiss, though he'd sent texts with several excuses as to why he couldn't come over to her place. Their usual dog walks and takeaways together were on hold because he'd needed an early night or had other vague commitments. The underlying message that he was no longer comfortable being alone with her outside work was abundantly clear, and she could have kicked herself for it. She didn't want him to disappear out of her life altogether over one misjudged kiss.

It would be interesting if their paths crossed today to see how he'd react. Though she didn't know how she should approach him. Apologise, or hope they could forget it ever happened? She did know this: She didn't want to lose him. He'd been such a lifeline for her after Thom broke her heart. She couldn't bear it if she lost him too. It was possible that she'd leaned on him a little too much, perhaps become a tad too attached. She made the decision to take her lead from Patrick, see how he wanted to proceed with their friendship. If there was any sight of him today.

It was good she had something to focus her mind on in the meantime.

'We have a jacket his girlfriend gave us.' The police officer, part of the team who'd called in for their assistance, handed over a sealed bag containing a navy waterproof jacket.

'That's good. Fliss can hopefully get the scent if it's been worn recently by the man we're looking for.' Billie's dog had been trained to air scent. If she picked up the scent from the jacket, she could follow in the general direction of the wearer, ruling out huge swathes of forestry and scrub in the process. Otherwise, they could find themselves searching for days in the wrong area, and it could be too late to locate someone who'd been reported as suffering from a mental health breakdown.

Billie opened the bag and let Fliss take a good sniff so she knew what they were looking for.

'Mr Hill's mother said he was wearing a red hoodie and cargo shorts, so hopefully that will help us spot him. If you can get us started on the right path, we can get the drones up to take a look too.' The police officer spread the map across the bonnet of his car so everyone could see the area where the man had last been spotted. Although, given the time it took to get the team co-ordinated, it was possible he could be anywhere in the mountains.

'Come on, Fliss, let's go.' Billie set off with her clever pup, who was keen to find what they were looking for so she could be rewarded with her cherished tennis ball. It was a highly motivating tool for the playful hound.

They were both dressed in their high-visibility jackets, and Billie was carrying her rucksack with her essentials like water and a blanket in case she found the missing man first. She had her phone, and all of the team had walkie-talkies to stay in communication. They would be able to relay any relevant information, and keep track of one another, too, so no one else got lost or injured on the unstable terrain.

Terry, the lead worker on the team, and his dog Bilbo, a bloodhound, had gone on ahead. Thankfully both dogs had picked up the scent on the same pathway, though Bilbo was a trailing dog, scent-specific. He'd set a steady pace first for the rest of the dog team to follow. Sometimes they even had cadaver dogs in the party who were able to track down dead bodies, but Billie was hoping that wouldn't be needed today and that they would have a positive outcome.

'Good girl, Fliss.'

At least the dogs were telling them the man they were looking for had definitely come this way. She relayed the information to the team and soon after heard the whirr overhead as they launched the drone up into the air.

Out here in the wide-open space, narrowing down the route a missing person might have taken made her feel useful. Although her job as a nurse was rewarding too, working with Fliss was a blessing. They were providing a service to people that, although not widely recognised, was important. Having Thom cheat on her had left her feeling worthless, surplus to requirements. Just the way her parents had made her feel growing up because they had obviously favoured Jaxon, making her wonder what was wrong with her, and why they couldn't love her the same way. If Patrick had decided he didn't want to be in

her life anymore too, it was only going to validate the
notion that she wasn't any use to anyone. At least, not
in her personal life. That was probably what fuelled her
desire to help with the search and rescue team in her
spare time. It was a group that had a place for her, always
thankful for her help whatever the outcome, and invaluable to those family members waiting for news on their
loved ones in trouble.

Her walkie-talkie crackled into life, making her jump.
'This is Terry. We've tracked to the waterfall, but Bilbo's
lead's gone slack. I'm not sure if Mr Hill crossed here,
but we've lost the scent.'

'No problem. Thanks, Terry. We'll see if we can pick
it up from here.' This was Fliss's time to shine. The difference between the two types of tracking dog meant that
Bilbo kept his nose to the ground for the scent, with the
water thus proving problematic. Hopefully Fliss would
be able to pick up the scent in the air past that point.

They passed Terry and Bilbo, whose job was over for
now. The duo was on their way back for a break. They
were more likely to stick around on a day like today,
which, although not overly warm, was at least dry. Sometimes the weather conditions made the job next to impossible. The rain not only washed away the scent but made
the terrain slippery and difficult to navigate. She'd had
a few falls and scrapes these past months herself since
Fliss had qualified for the team.

The camera on the drone mustn't have picked up anything either. After a few circles around the area, it was
brought back to base.

'Looks like it's up to us now, Fliss. No pressure.'
Though the dog would not have any notion of how seri-

ous the situation was. This was a game for her, fun, with a reward at the end if she managed to find her target.

Fliss sniffed the air and led Billie up the steep, stony track until they came to the base of the gentle waterfall. She let the dog sniff away from the beaten path, careful not to get too caught up in what the others were doing. Fliss had to do things in her own way, in her own time, ruling out other areas before settling on the direction she wanted to go. It meant the search team could discount these sections of land and cut the rescue time, hopefully improving the chances of a successful outcome.

Eventually, when she came back to Billie, she indicated that they needed to cross the water.

Billie pulled on her waterproof footwear and trousers to wade through the river. By all accounts, he'd walked up here with nothing but the clothes he was wearing, which would provide scant protection against the elements if he was left up here for any length of time. There were many hikers who had to be rescued up here when they set off without knowing the conditions they would face. The team were often called to help locate school groups and tourists who'd got lost in the fog, or who were dressed completely inappropriately for the weather, which could turn at any given second. With Mr Hill apparently also suffering some sort of mental health crisis, he was doubly at risk and might not even realise he was endangering his own life out here.

It wasn't long before a circling Fliss picked up the trail again, sniffing the air and pulling Billie along behind her.

'Good girl, Fliss. You find him.' Billie's heart was pounding, that adrenaline pumping through her body not just from the exertion of climbing the mountain. There was no way of knowing what she was about to stumble upon, and she wouldn't have been human if she didn't worry about what she might see.

In her line of work, and especially in the emergency department, she was used to dealing with life-and-death situations. It was never easy, but a lot of the time Patrick was there too. Sometimes it was good to talk to someone who understood the pressures and stresses of saving lives. Especially when it didn't always go the way anyone wanted. She supposed he'd become something of an emotional crutch for her, and it was no wonder he'd appeared to have backed off. It didn't mean she wasn't missing him or the comforting hug he was always ready with in case she needed it. And she needed it. The kiss was something she hadn't managed to put from her mind, but she was beginning to wonder if it had been worth it at the cost of their friendship.

Billie was more than capable of looking after herself—she'd been doing it most of her life—but Thom's behaviour had dented her confidence, and Patrick had always been there to bolster it. Until now.

Fliss barked, reminding her they had a job to do, and currently, the four-legged volunteer was doing hers better than the human. She pulled Billie to the edge of a rocky outcrop and barked again, sitting down to signal she'd found her target. Billie carefully made her way to the edge, careful not to get too close in case she slipped or there was any erosion beneath her feet. She knew that in addition to a sheer drop, the landing would not be a soft one.

Sure enough, as she peered down, she could see the angular boulders below and could just make out a flash of red lying far below.

'Good girl.' Billie gave Fliss a head scratch and rewarded her with her prized tennis ball.

'Mr Hill? Can you hear me?' she yelled down over the mountainside, listening as her voice carried across the vast open space. The dull green and brown grasses on the hills were interspersed with vivid purple and pink heather, with bright yellow and white wildflowers Billie was at a loss to name. A beautiful sight she hoped wasn't about to become the scene of a tragedy.

'Hello. Mr Hill?' She tried again to find signs of life, with her finger on the button of the walkie-talkie to report their worst scenario. A wave of nausea threatened to engulf her as she looked down at the prone figure.

She took a deep, shaky breath, ready to call it in when she swore she heard a groan.

'Mr Hill? Mr Hill?' It was urgent she got to him to check on his condition, though at this point she was supposed to radio it in and let the paramedics take over. But she was a nurse, and more than qualified. Besides, time was of the essence. In the minutes it took for help to arrive, he could have deteriorated.

Making the decision to climb down herself, she quickly poured the bottle of water from her rucksack into the bowl she'd brought for Fliss, giving her instruction to stay.

To make sure she didn't slip on any of the rocks, Billie took off the wet wear she'd donned. Then she carefully lowered herself onto the ledge below. Pain sliced through her body as the ragged rocks scratched her skin, but she carried on climbing down regardless. Adrenaline was carrying her through for now, though she was sure it would hurt like hell later. She wasn't a skilled climber, but she did her best not to break her own neck, testing each stone with her foot before putting any weight on it. The sharp rocks managed to penetrate the gloves she was wearing as she scrabbled for purchase. By the time she made it onto the flat where Mr Hill lay, her fingers were scratched and bloody.

Billie knelt down beside him. 'Mr Hill? I'm with the dog search and rescue team. I'm also a nurse. Can you tell me where it hurts?'

It was clear he'd fallen over the ledge, but as he was lying face down, it wasn't immediately obvious how, or where, he'd been injured.

The young man rolled over onto his back with a groan. 'Everywhere.'

'Careful not to move too much until we can establish what injuries you've sustained.' Her heart rate was beginning to return to normal now with the knowledge that Mr Hill was very much alive and breathing.

Billie called in her location and told the team they were going to need medical assistance. It looked as though Patrick might be joining them today after all. She knew his shift pattern as well as her own and was aware he'd be on call for the air ambulance. It was going to be needed to access the patient up here where there were no roads for an ordinary ambulance to get through. Until help got here, it was up to her to keep him stable, and safe.

'You've a few scratches and grazes on your head, nothing serious, but it's best we don't move you in case you sustained any neck injuries in the fall. What about your arms and legs? Any pain there?'

Mr Hill groaned, mumbling incoherently. He'd likely sustained a head injury, possibly a concussion. Billie hoped she could keep him conscious until help arrived. She gave him a preliminary exam to see if there was anything she needed to relay to the paramedics who would make sure to stabilise him so as not to exacerbate any injuries before moving him.

She felt carefully along his arms, noting the same cuts on his hands that she'd sustained on her way down.

'I'm just going to check your legs, too. Let me know where it might be tender.' She explained what she was doing every step of the way whilst trying to keep him responsive.

His shorts had proved scant protection for the terrain, ripped and shredded like the skin on his legs. As Billie removed an alcohol wipe from her first aid kit and began to clean away the blood on his left leg, the man let out a yell. It could be a possible fracture, but there was no bone poking through the skin. It wasn't a compound fracture, a break that could prove more problematic and need surgery.

All she could do for now was clean his injuries and cover the open wound to prevent infection. She took a blanket from her backpack to keep him warm and try to prevent shock from setting in.

Thankfully it wasn't long before she heard the whirr of the helicopter up ahead. As it came to land as close as it could, the wind whipped loose stones and debris all around. Billie used her body to shield Mr Hill whilst doing her best not to get too close to him in case she hurt him any further.

Eventually she saw the telltale flash of red uniforms as the paramedics headed their direction. Relief flooded through her body not only because she was no longer dealing with this on her own and Mr Hill would get to hospital soon but also because she could see Patrick striding towards her. She couldn't help but smile, and the stern look he'd had on his face as he approached gradually softened.

'I suppose I don't need to tell you, Billie, that you should have waited for us before trying to break your neck climbing down here.' He strode towards her, already swinging the medical bag from his back.

Billie tilted her chin in the air, refusing to admit she'd been wrong for endangering her life to save someone else's, knowing Patrick would have done exactly the same. 'No, you don't. I made the decision, and I take full responsibility for it.'

Her tone was a little more combative than she'd expected. Probably due to the embarrassment of facing him again after what had happened at her place, and his subsequent disappearance. She was feeling a little emotionally fragile already and didn't need a public scolding for doing what she thought was right in the circumstances.

'Mr Hill, I'm Dr James. I'm with the air ambulance crew. We're going to get you stabilised and transfer you to the hospital in the helicopter.' Patrick knelt down to do his own primary survey of the patient as Billie relayed the information about the suspected leg fracture.

'Do you have a pins and needles sensation in the leg, Mr Hill?' Patrick asked the patient, no doubt trying to ascertain if any nerve damage had occurred.

Mr Hill shook his head.

'What about numbness?'

'It just hurts.' Sometimes that was better. It meant it was likely a straightforward break, easily set without complications.

'Where's Fliss?' Patrick asked Billie once he'd ascertained the patient wasn't in immediate danger.

'At the top of the ledge. She won't move until I tell her

to.' Billie hoped. She was sure if Fliss had tired of being good and having her precious ball, she would bark to let her missing mistress know she wasn't happy.

'Okay, well, we need to keep Mr Hill stable until we can get to the helicopter. It's not going to be easy given the uneven ground.' Patrick produced a neck brace to hold the patient's head in place. If he had an unseen neck or spine injury, a jolt could end up leaving him paralysed.

'I can help,' Billie reminded him. Patrick could be as stubborn as she was, insisting on doing everything himself. When Sinead died, he'd tried to lock himself away from the world. It had been Billie who'd fought against that spiky defence he'd put up until he let her in, let her help him.

'In that case, we need to stabilise the leg, too.' He passed her the brace. She carefully secured the patient's leg, doing her best not to cause him any further pain.

This is what she'd missed these past couple of days. Working together, knowing she and Patrick could rely on one another. Always in synch. She hoped they could put what had happened behind them and get back to where they were most comfortable. Together, as friends, with any notions of anything romantic firmly out of her head. Though Billie knew to get there, she was going to have to address the matter at some point with him so he didn't think that she was trying to force him into a relationship he didn't want.

'I think that's the best we can do. We'll just have to be careful getting him back to the helicopter.' Billie got to her feet and brushed herself down.

Patrick glanced up at her. 'There is no "we". You've already gone above and beyond, Billie. The rest of the crew are on their way with a stretcher. We'll manage between us. Thanks for your help, but you should get back to Fliss and the rest of the dog team.'

He was carefully and deliberately putting her back in her place, and it wasn't with him. She couldn't help but think that was meant to extend to their personal relationship, too.

'Okay. I know where I'm not wanted.' Billie made her way back up to Fliss, who was sitting waiting patiently, tail wagging. At least someone loved her, and Patrick had made it very clear it wasn't him.

Although she was wary of crossing that line with him, and that he'd clearly only wanted to be friends, having him assert the boundary still hurt. As good as they were as a team, it was a further reminder that she wasn't good enough for anything more. Just as she had proved inadequate as a daughter, and she must have lacked in some way because her boyfriend had cheated on her. For Patrick to move on from Sinead, it would take a special woman, and clearly that wasn't her.

Patrick knew he'd messed up with Billie. They were lucky they'd had her out there in the Mournes with Fliss. Otherwise the search would have gone on a lot longer and might not have had such a good outcome. In the same circumstances, he would likely have broken protocol, too, and climbed down to treat the patient. It was their job, after all, and that caring nature didn't stop at the end of a shift.

That didn't mean he wasn't upset with her for putting herself in danger. He'd already lost too many people close to him, and it would devastate him if he lost her. The very thought of it reinforced the idea that he shouldn't cross the line with her again.

It was difficult enough on these call-outs, each one a

reminder of his loss. He was aware some family member was waiting at home for news of their loved one like he had been. It was down to him to do his best for a better outcome than he and Sinead had had. He hadn't been able to do anything for her, or his father. But each person he was able to save, each life that was able to continue because of his intervention, helped to heal him a little more. It was recompense for the times he hadn't been there for those who'd needed him most.

Kissing Billie was out for the foreseeable future, because he already cared so strongly for her. Anything more than that meant risking his heart completely on someone willing to put her life in jeopardy. Increasing the chances of losing her, and destroying him.

He and Billie were very similar. That was half the problem. Theirs was a close bond, and he worried he'd mistaken it for something else.

He'd tried to create a little distance between them to see if things settled down and they could get back to normal. But he missed their chats, and even their walks with Fliss. It was beginning to seem like a big sacrifice for a small problem that might all be in his head.

Working with her to patch up Mr Hill had reminded him that she had become a big part of his life. Always there when he needed a helping hand or a shoulder to cry on. Just as he had been for her. He hadn't meant to be so short with Billie. Along with his irritation that she'd taken such a risk, he was annoyed at himself, too, because the moment he'd seen her again, those feelings he'd been trying to deny had instantly come back.

He'd pushed her away to stop from making another mistake. Except he couldn't get the look she'd given him out of his head. Of utter confusion. Her eyes had been full of pain, which he'd caused by dismissing her as soon as he could. And no wonder she was confused. She didn't know what had gone on in his head. Didn't realise that she hadn't done anything wrong. The fault was entirely his, and he had to find some way of rectifying it. He couldn't avoid her forever. Especially when they worked in the same department.

They were both on shift tonight, had seen each other in passing as they were kept busy with a steady influx of patients as usual. At some point he was going to have to make time to build some bridges, or life was going to be very lonely, if these past days without her had been anything to go by.

'Okay, everyone, we have an ambulance coming in with a family involved in a road traffic accident. Two adults and two young children seriously injured. We need all hands on deck.' As the senior nurse announced the incoming emergency, the team assembled, ready to treat the patients the second they came through the doors. Waiting was always a nerve-wracking time, but once they launched into assessing and treating the injuries, experience kicked in and kicked the nerves out. There was no room for anything but action, and despite everything else going on between them, he knew Billie and he worked well together.

As proven when the first child was wheeled in and they both immediately went to her side to get details of her status.

'This is Holly Geddes. A ten-year-old girl involved in an RTA. She was belted in the back seat but was unresponsive at the scene. Suspected head and neck injuries with possible internal damage. She has a petechial rash and suffusion over her upper chest, neck and face. Bruising on the abdomen. Airway was clear, but breathing was shallow. We applied an oxygen face mask to maintain normal oxygen saturation.' The paramedic reeled off the treatment delivered so far, but it was clear that they were going to need X-rays to discover the extent of the damage the young girl had suffered in the accident.

'Thanks. Billie, can you help me transfer her to the bed? On three. One, two, three.' Between the hospital team and the ambulance crew, they managed to move the patient onto the hospital bed so they could start assessing and treating her themselves. They were careful not to jolt her too much in the transfer.

'I'll get the X-rays and CT scan sorted.' As usual, Billie's thinking was in line with his, knowing exactly what they needed to do.

'We'll need bloods, too.' Hopefully that would give them some indication of what was going on.

'On it.' Billie set to work getting the tests organised. It wasn't long before they could see the problem.

'The CT scan is showing some bruising to the lungs, superficial lacerations to the liver, and a tear in the spleen. I'll phone ahead to get her transferred to the intensive care ward, and in the meantime, we'll get her hooked up to some pain meds and antibiotics.' He would prefer to have her conscious and out of the woods, but all he could do here for now was keep her stable and begin treatment. With time, and a lot of care from the medical team, she should make a full recovery.

'Poor mite. I hope the rest of the family are going to be okay too.' Billie gently brushed the girl's bloodied blond hair from her face. She'd sustained some superficial cuts to her face, probably from the broken glass that was still in her hair in places, too. The little girl had clearly been thrown around in the impact, but he knew he and Billie would do their best to make her as comfortable as they could in the circumstances. It was their job, after all, and he'd worked with Billie long enough to know that she gave extra care to the little ones who came in. Especially those who'd been involved in such traumatic events.

She was sympathetic to her patients. That's what made her an excellent nurse. She was composed and kind no matter the circumstances in the busy ward. It was a mark of the person she was. As much as he'd loved Sinead, she hadn't always been the most patient woman in the world. A busy project manager for the health board, she'd always had her phone attached to her ear, issuing instructions to the team she managed. Her dedication made her good at her job but had sometimes caused friction between them at home. She never seemed to fully clock out of work.

It was no wonder Patrick had spent so much time with Billie when she always seemed to be there for him. Another issue that had caused arguments on occasion. Sometimes he and Sinead had felt like ships passing in the night with their busy schedules. When they'd married, they'd talked about having children together. However, the more successful she became in her career, and the more time she spent away from home, the less likely that had seemed.

That's what they'd rowed about that night she'd had the accident. It was hard not to feel guilty when they'd parted on bad terms. Sinead had gone for a walk to clear her head and had apparently fallen in the fast-flowing river along her route. Something that would haunt him forever. Not only because it had taken two days for her body to be found, but also because it was the second loved one he'd lost after a row.

His father's heart attack had happened almost immediately after Patrick had accused him of being controlling, and telling him he was leaving to go to university in Scotland. Not staying at home in Northern Ireland with his parents, remaining a prisoner into his adulthood. Ironic that his father's death had meant he'd had to do just that. Stay home, going to university in Belfast so he could look after his mother. But she'd blamed him for his father's death, too. It hadn't been an easy time, but he'd made it as a doctor and ensured his mother had whatever she'd needed until she passed away.

When he met Sinead, he'd thought it was the start of his life. His chance to have a family again after losing his parents. He supposed that even though he'd loved her deeply, their life together had been very much based on what she'd wanted. Billie always left room for his opinions, or asked what he wanted. That was probably part of the reason he enjoyed being around her so much. She treated him with respect, as well as being an emotional support for him during the hard times. Though he supposed that was a two-way street. They had a lot in common, whereas he and Sinead had been very different people.

At first he'd thought that was what had attracted him to Sinead. Her strength and bloody-mindedness. Qualities he'd admired in her, of course, but there had been times in their marriage where she'd simply refused to compromise at all. The opposite was true in Billie's relationship with Thom, from what he'd seen. She'd bent over backwards to make him happy. Perhaps that was what had made their little group work. They were all such diverse characters with no personality clashes. In theory, Sinead and Billie would have been too different to ever get along, and though he hated what Thom had done, Patrick had considered him a friend. They'd had some good nights together on double dates when they'd all found the time, and he missed their little group. It would be a shame for him and Billie to drift apart after all they'd been through, over a moment of…he didn't know what. They managed to work together without him letting his primal urges get the better of him. Perhaps that natural attraction to a beautiful woman had simply caught him in a vulnerable moment, and he'd temporarily forgotten she had a more important role in his life as a friend than a passing fancy. If he knew Billie as well as he thought, she wouldn't hold a grudge against him for too long. With any luck, they could get back to normal.

Even now, she was acting as though nothing had happened. Of course, they were at work, and she was a professional, but he hadn't sensed any real feelings of animosity. Billie was simply getting on with what needed to be done.

She had already hooked Holly up to the monitors to keep a check on her vital signs and was in the process of doing another blood reading as Patrick went to make the call to intensive care.

Suddenly, the alarm on the monitor began to blare. When he looked over, the screen showed that Holly had gone into cardiac arrest.

'Dr James…' Billie called over to him, clearly as surprised and concerned by their patient's sudden decline.

Patrick called for the crash team as he rushed over to the cubicle. Although it was rare for cardiac arrest to happen in children, the chest trauma could have been a contributing factor. It was also possible there was an underlying heart problem they weren't aware of.

'Starting CPR,' he announced, and once he made sure the child's airway was clear, he began chest compressions.

Billie brought the defibrillator over and attached the sticky pads to the girl's chest. They had no choice but to shock the child's heart back into a rhythm.

'Stand clear.' Patrick made sure the rest of the team stood well back whilst he delivered the first shock, then watched the monitor, praying for signs of life.

Holly was a child, with so much ahead of her, and she deserved to be given a second chance. It made him think about what he was throwing away with Billie. A friendship wasn't something easily gained or thrown away. He needed to give himself a second chance and stop beating himself up over something so small. It would be a huge sacrifice to give up on their relationship simply because of one kiss. Something he was sure he would forget about. Eventually.

'No response.' Billie stood on the other side of the bed, her eyes trained on the screen, and Patrick knew she was praying just as hard as he was for a positive outcome.

He started CPR again, and Billie recharged the defibrillator.

'Delivering a second shock. Stand clear.' Patrick reapplied the paddles to the girl's chest.

It wasn't easy to watch such a small, fragile body jolted at his hand, but he knew it was the only way of hopefully bringing her back.

Patrick held his breath as he watched the screen. All other sounds in the department went silent for him as he waited for that blip on the screen. And then it came. That longed-for sign of life that immediately brought a sigh of relief before the team sprang into action again to make sure the heartbeat stabilised.

Once they were sure Holly was out of immediate danger and she was taken through to the ward, ending Patrick and Billie's responsibility for now, they breathed more easily. Even though it wouldn't stop them thinking about her, or replaying events in their heads to make sure they'd done everything they possibly could have for their patient.

The rest of the shift was busy and went quickly, though thankfully there were no more major emergencies. Patrick finished before Billie but waited around to speak to her. Despite the late hour, he was very much awake, and aware more than ever of how much he would miss her if she disappeared out of his life outside the hospital.

It was times like this that they would chat, dissect what had happened, and generally reassure one another that they had done everything they could. He relished those shifts they were on together as it felt like a wind-down after a very stressful workout session. Bringing his blood pressure back down, restoring his heart rate, and generally helping him to process whatever events had occurred. Billie had told him in the past it helped her, too. With partners who didn't fully understand what they went through in their line of work, it helped to have one another to chat with on occasion to get advice and ultimately aid a night's sleep. As far as he knew, they both got something from having a chat after a shared shift. He saw no reason why they should stop now just because his libido had momentarily taken control of his brain. As long as Billie wasn't happier without him in her life.

That thought was even more depressing than the ones he'd had about seeing out the rest of his days without her.

'Hey, Billie. Wait up.' He'd caught sight of her heading towards the exit with her coat over her arm. Since she didn't drive, and he hadn't offered her a lift as usual, she'd probably been prepared to walk the short distance home.

Another reason for him to be annoyed at himself. He didn't like the thought of her walking on her own late at night in the dark. Billie could look after herself, but he should never have put her in the position. Thankfully she stopped at the sound of his voice.

'Is everything okay?' Patrick loved that her first thought was for him. Proving that perhaps she didn't hate him after all.

'Yes. Sorry. I just wanted to see if you wanted a lift home?' He didn't know what he'd do if she said no, and it was too late to make things up after all the soul-searching he'd done tonight.

Billie yawned. 'That would be lovely. I wasn't looking forward to schlepping home. It's been a long shift.'

The smile she gave him under the orange glow of the streetlight was filled with so much warmth, Patrick knew he'd been given a second chance. This time he was determined not to mess it up. Billie was the best thing that had ever happened to him, and he wasn't going to let her disappear out of his life again without a fight.

CHAPTER THREE

BILLIE WAS RELIEVED to find that Patrick wasn't holding her faux pas the other night against her. At least, not tonight. Perhaps dealing with a life-and-death emergency involving a child had made him see a kiss wasn't that important in the scheme of things. Maybe he'd realised she wasn't such a threat after all when she'd managed an entire shift together without trying to plant the lips on him again. Whatever had caused the shift between them again, she was just thankful for it. It had been a long, difficult night, and she needed the comfort of the familiar. She needed Patrick.

It was always difficult dealing with children in such circumstances. She tended to give them special attention anyway. Especially the ones whose admission seemed nothing more than an inconvenience to their parents. She remembered what it was like to be ignored, to be treated as a nuisance. She went out of her way to ensure they felt cared for. At least once in their lives. Holly would probably never know about the treatment she'd received, and that was a blessing in a lot of ways, but Billie knew she'd given her all for her patient tonight. That always gave her a little boost.

Patrick still seemed on edge as they walked to the

car in silence. Without directly addressing the fact she'd kissed him, she didn't know how to reassure him she wasn't about to jump his bones in the confines of the car. And right now, she didn't want to examine why it had happened in the first place. There'd been enough emotional trauma for one evening.

She got into the passenger seat of the car and let out a long sigh.

Patrick gave a shaky laugh. 'It was a rough one, wasn't it?'

'Yeah, but we got her. I'm just thankful for that.' She hadn't realised how much until now. It was easy to go home without understanding how much of the job she carried with her until it hit all at once. Knowing that Holly had survived and was hopefully on the way to recovery was likely the only thing stopping the tears for now. It wouldn't be the first time she'd cried on Patrick's shoulder over a patient.

'Yeah. Me too.' They fell back into an awkward silence. Like two teens on a first date who didn't know how to act.

'I suppose we should head home.'

'Do you want to go and get a cup of coffee somewhere?'

They talked over one another, but she liked Patrick's proposal better. It meant she wouldn't have to go home just yet. As tired as she was, she wasn't looking forward to another night lying in bed, overanalysing everything that had happened over the course of the evening.

'Maybe a tea instead. I'll probably have enough trouble sleeping. Although I'm not sure we'll find anywhere open.' At this time of the night, there were probably only bars and clubs open, and goodness knew neither of them had the energy for that.

'There might be a twenty-four-hour fast food place doing drive-through, or failing that, an all-night garage with a self-service machine.' Although neither option he was offering was particularly appetising, Billie thought he was suggesting neutral ground so there wasn't a re-peat of last night. Sometimes they shared a cuppa at her place, but he probably didn't trust her to be alone with him again.

She was grateful he was even still talking to her. Billie knew how much he loved Sinead. It was likely even the thought of kissing another woman would have felt like a betrayal. So forcing him into that situation could have destroyed their friendship completely. She hated herself for doing that and betraying both of her friends. He was Sinead's husband, and Billie should not think about him that way simply because Sinead wasn't here anymore.

'Anything will do. Can we just get away from here for a while?' She needed to clear her head. Though the fact that he hadn't settled for a cup of coffee from the vend-ing machine suggested that he might want to have a chat with her, and that was enough to upset her stomach.

They managed to get a tea and coffee from a local drive-through. They parked up at the side of the road to drink it away from the bright lights and the drunks stum-bling about in the town.

Before she'd even managed to fish out the tea bag from the cardboard cup and take a sip of the now stewed tea, Patrick was clearing his throat, clearly about to broach the difficult subject she'd been dreading.

'Listen, Billie, about the other night…'

She closed her eyes and gulped down the swell of

sickness suddenly rising. 'I know, I know. Things got a bit…awkward.'

Patrick dipped his head. 'I'm sorry. I don't know what happened. Call it a moment of weakness, madness, anything you want, but can we just forget it?'

He glanced up at her, his eyes pleading with her for… forgiveness? She didn't understand it when she was the one in the wrong. Unless…

'You kissed me?' Her head was spinning. Did this mean he'd leaned in for the kiss at the same time too? That it hadn't all been in her head? That they had shared a moment after all? Although she supposed it didn't matter since it let her off the hook. Plus the outcome was the same, wasn't it? He didn't want anything romantic with her, and she was lucky that he even still wanted her as a friend.

'I don't know what came over me. I'm sorry.'

'But…but, you were the one who disappeared after. I thought I'd done something wrong.' She stopped short of admitting that she'd wanted the kiss too. Would it really make a difference? Or just make things worse? More awkward?

Patrick took his time sipping at his tea, as though carefully considering the next words about to come out of his mouth. 'I did think perhaps we were beginning to spend too much time together. That seeing each other at work, on call-outs and in our personal lives was colouring my judgement. We're friends. I don't want to change that. I thought if I stepped back and gave us some space, it would help us both to move on from what has happened in our relationships. Although I'm not ready for another romantic relationship, and I'm not sure I ever will be, it's possible that being as close as we are is beginning to muddy things.'

'Okay.' Billie understood where he was coming from. They'd both been leaning heavily on one another, to the point of excluding everyone else in their lives. That's probably why she'd leaned in to that moment too. Confusing their close bond for something romantic because she hadn't opened herself up to anyone other than Patrick since Thom.

'So, where do you want to go from here?' It was beginning to feel a lot like the breakup talk she should have had with Thom. If they'd been more mature as a couple, able to communicate how they were feeling and what they wanted from the relationship, they might have parted on better terms. He mightn't have felt the need to cheat on her and doubly break her heart.

Though even now, waiting for Patrick to decide whether or not he still wanted her in his life felt just as tough for her. She'd been pushed away her whole life by those who were supposed to love her. If Patrick did the same, she wasn't sure she would bounce back. He was her place of solace.

Heart pumping, breath held, she thought she might spontaneously combust before he put her out of her misery. Or chucked her right into the deep end of it, depending on what he decided. Billie supposed she shouldn't base her worth, or her life, on the say-so of one person when she'd been burned once too often that way. However, it had never occurred to her that she would be in this position with Patrick. She hadn't imagined a life without him in it. Didn't want to. She realized it was a problem.

Someday he would likely find someone who would fill the hole Sinead's death had left inside him.

The thought of that did nothing to make her feel any better.

'I just want things to go back to the way they were, Billie. I need a friend more than anything, and you've been my rock since Sinead died. Perhaps we both need to move on in terms of romantic relationships, and one day we won't rely on each other as much. But for now, I need our chats after work, our walks with Fliss and our takeaways together. If you can forgive me?' The beseeching puppy dog look he gave her squeezed her heart. Not least because she felt she was deceiving him in some way, not being honest about the fact she thought she was the one almost kissing him.

'There's nothing to forgive you for, Patrick. Except perhaps not explaining to me what was wrong, or how you were feeling. It's easier for me if people are just honest with me. I have trust issues these days.'

They both knew why.

'I promise to be more open with you in future.'

'Good. Fliss misses you.'

'I miss her, too.'

Billie got the distinct impression neither of them was talking about the dog, but she wasn't going to overanalyse it when Patrick had made it clear where they stood. As friends.

What prevented her from fessing up was the thought that perhaps she had read even more into that moment than Patrick had. He'd obviously examined what had happened and come to the conclusion that it hadn't meant anything to him. Nothing between them had changed, and it had simply been a by-product of spending too much time together. Billie wasn't sure the same could be said for her. She'd wanted to kiss him, and the more she thought about it, the more she realised she definitely had feelings for him that went beyond friendship.

A problem for her when he was obviously another totally unsuitable man for her. Not only was he grieving, definitely not in the headspace for a relationship with anyone, but he clearly didn't see Billie as a prospective partner either. Since one kiss had sent him running, it didn't bode well for a future together. Another rejection was waiting to happen if she continued to hold a candle for him.

If all he was offering was the same emotional support he'd given her these past years, then she'd have to take it. She'd lived a couple of days without him around in any capacity, and she didn't want to do it again. When it came to having Patrick James in her life, she'd take him any way she could.

'There are an awful lot of cars pulling up around us.' Billie noticed the car headlights coming in beside them, followed by an immediate blackout. It was a strange place to park when the quiet country lane wasn't near any of the local sights. They'd only pulled in here to have a very private conversation. She doubted the other drivers and their passengers were doing the same.

'Er, Billie, I think we've stumbled onto the local make-out spot.' Patrick directed her attention to the cars closest to them. Teenagers were either eyeing them up or mashing the faces off one another in the front seats.

'Oh my goodness!' She was horrified, though apparently Patrick had found the whole thing hilarious as they drove off. No doubt the relieved teens cheered them away. It probably looked as though they were having some sort of clandestine meeting in lovers' lane.

Chance would have been a fine thing.

At least it lightened the mood, and it felt as though they'd both been able to put the matter behind them. In theory. Putting it into practice might prove a tad difficult now Billie knew he'd wanted that kiss to happen too.

Patrick was able to breathe a little easier now everything was out in the open. It seemed he'd got himself into a tizz for no reason when Billie didn't seem fazed by his admission. The only thing which had apparently annoyed her was the fact that he'd kept his distance for a few days without proper explanation. He understood, and in hindsight, he realized they should have had the conversation sooner. Before he'd decided it would be better to back off out of her life. After everything Thom had put her through, of course it would hurt her more when he wasn't honest with her. From now on, he was going to do his best to be a better friend, because he'd tried the alternative and hadn't liked it at all.

Now they'd cleared the air, hopefully they could carry on as normal. Although finding themselves unwittingly on lovers' lane could have proved even more embarrassing if they hadn't got over that initial awkwardness.

'Do you want to find a nudist beach or go somewhere else equally embarrassing?' Making a joke out of it succeeded in getting Billie to smile again. She'd looked mortified to have been seen in such a spot with him.

'I think it's probably safer if I just head home, thanks, Patrick. Maybe tomorrow we can try booking into a hotel, only to find out there's only one bed.' Hands on her cheeks, she mocked a fake scream.

Patrick knew she was only messing about, coming up with more absurd scenarios where they found themselves thrown together in some sort of illicit misunderstanding. Yet he couldn't help but wonder what that might be like. He hadn't been with anyone since Sinead's death, and naturally, he hadn't been able to get the reminder of having Billie pressed so tightly against him out of his head. Her softness, her sweet scent, her parted lips…

He swerved the car to the right, his thoughts distracting him from the road so much that he nearly hadn't seen the turn-off towards Billie's road. Clearly exhaustion was kicking in and letting in those wayward thoughts again. He was going to have to keep his wits about him if they were ever going to get back on an even keel as just friends.

'Home, sweet home.' Patrick swung the car up outside Billie's house, pretending nothing had happened.

She unclipped her seat belt but hesitated in getting out of the vehicle. 'Do you want to come in and see Fliss?'

It was a simple gesture, but it held so much meaning. She trusted him. She was letting him back into her world, and he'd better not stuff it up again.

'Are you sure?' His question prompted an eye-roll.

'Yes, I'm sure, Patrick. You can see the dog. It's not a custody battle, you know.' She got out and let them both into the house he spent more free time in than his own.

They were immediately greeted by an excited Fliss.

'Hello, gorgeous.' Patrick bent down and buried his head in her fur. He had missed this. In some ways, they'd become a little dysfunctional family of their own. Life would have been simpler if they were. If they weren't so burdened by their emotional baggage that neither of them could commit to anything other than friendship, they might have been able to have this on a regular basis. Instead it was simply a glimpse every now and then into an alternate universe, where he and Billie and Fliss could live happily ever after. Together.

He was so caught up in his own musings he barely registered the fact that Billie was going through her post. Until the tear of an envelope was followed by a squeal.

'What? What is it?' Bouncing back up, he was desperate to find out what had caused her such distress. Or was it delight? Although her eyes were full of tears and her hand was over her mouth, he was sure he could see a grin hiding behind it.

'Look.' She thrust the contents of the envelope at him. A thick champagne-coloured card edged with gold. It certainly didn't look like a harbinger of bad news, unless someone had a very sick sense of humour.

Patrick flicked his gaze over the gold embossed cursive contents. Each word made his heart soar higher. 'You've been nominated for an award?'

'Mmm-hmm.' Billie nodded so enthusiastically she might just give herself whiplash.

'That's...that's amazing.' He read the card again. For her selfless and courageous act with the dog search and rescue team, and saving Mr Hill's life, she'd been recommended for the prestigious Northern Ireland Heroes Award.

Pride overrode every other emotion, including common sense, as he grabbed her into a full bear hug. He only realised his mistake when she hugged him back, their bodies packed tightly together, and he responded as something more than a mere friend. He closed his eyes and remembered all too well how good it had felt to kiss her, to have her in his arms. Even when the hug went on longer than was probably necessary, Billie didn't pull away, apparently content to be there too.

These physical touches between them, which had once been a means of comfort, now seemed to crackle and spark with something more. As though they were both waiting for the other to make a move. To replay that kiss and give in to this chemistry which had begun to simmer between them. Heaven knew that was all he wanted to do right now, but they'd only just got back onto an even keel, and it wasn't going to do their friendship any good if he ended up having the same doubts in the long run. He had to resist temptation this time for the sake of their friendship.

Patrick reluctantly let go, knowing he couldn't make the same mistake again. No matter how much his body yearned for it.

Billie stepped back, her cheeks a little pink as though she knew about the battle he'd fought in his head. He couldn't help but wonder if she'd felt the same, or if he had succeeded in simply making things awkward between them again.

Thankfully she didn't ask him to leave, or stop touching her, so he guessed that he hadn't stepped too far over the mark. As she glanced at the invitation again, Patrick hoped she was so consumed by thoughts of her nomination, she hadn't noticed he might have held her a little too long.

'Does it seem selfish to you if I accept the nomination? We're a team out there. Everyone was looking for Mr Hill that day. It's what we do. And you and the rest of the air ambulance crew were the ones who got him to hospital.' That smile slowly eroded from her face, beginning to look more like guilt.

Patrick didn't want her to talk her way out of the honour when she deserved it so much. Not only was it hers by rights, but she needed the confidence boost. It was about time something nice happened to her.

'Yes, but you were the one taking all the risks that day, remember?' He'd scolded her for doing so. More out of concern for her own well-being, knowing if anything had happened to her on that mountain, he would have been devastated. That moment was the beginning of the end of his isolation away from her, when he'd been faced with the idea it could have happened permanently if things had gone differently out there in the wild.

'I remember that you weren't happy with me.' She raised an eyebrow at him, but he could tell she was in too much of a good mood to hold it against him forever.

'With reason. I don't want you to get hurt, Billie. What if you'd fallen, too, and ended up in worse condition than your patient?'

'I'm not going to apologise for my actions, Patrick. You know who I am. Besides, I already had Terry reading me the riot act for not sticking to the rules. I'd barely got off the mountain that day before he tore strips off me. I don't need to hear it from you, too.' She was in battle mode, lips pursed, arms folded. Those defences firmly back in place.

He didn't want to get into an argument about it. They never ended well for those closest to him. He usually did his best to agree to disagree with people lest things got too heated. Though on this matter, he couldn't help but get passionate about it because he cared too much to stand by and let her get hurt.

She was right, though. He knew who Billie was. A woman who would never walk away from someone in need. A woman who would risk her own life to climb down and rescue an injured man without a second thought. The very reason he shouldn't get any closer to her than he already was. She was a risk-taker, and if he ever decided to be with someone else, it needed to be someone safe. Someone who would never dream of climbing mountains alone.

'You could have died.' The words exploded from his lips with a surge of anxiety as he remembered the incident. Relived the fear that something could have happened to her. Might still happen to her.

'But I didn't, and both I and Mr Hill are alive and well. So can we just celebrate that fact?' She waved the invitation in his face. There was no arguing with her, and all he could do was say his piece on the matter in the hope that the next time she would think twice about any more heroics.

'I'm very proud of you. Always. You deserve this, Billie.' It was undoubtedly a brave thing she'd done, and she had saved a life in the process, but the fact that she'd put her own in danger wasn't something he could easily dismiss. Though Patrick decided to let the matter drop for now. He didn't want to ruin her special moment. Billie needed to be celebrated, treated like the hero she was. It didn't matter if she didn't win when seeing her this happy was the ultimate prize.

'I just don't know what I've done to deserve this, or who on earth would have nominated me. It's obvious it wasn't you or Terry.' She took the invitation from him again, staring at it in disbelief. Looking for all the world like a child who'd just won a ticket to a chocolate factory.

'You're brave, selfless and just amazing. You so do deserve this.' He also might know a little about who had nominated her. That day she had both frustrated and impressed him in equal measure. Aside from his own personal feelings about her, it had also been a stunning act by a volunteer whose actions had undoubtedly saved the life of Mr Hill. His family had known it, too. They'd been the ones who had come to him with the idea, and he'd provided them with her name and an account of how she'd helped.

Not that it had been a done deal. It had been up to the committee to short-list her for the award. Obviously they had seen her for the extraordinary woman she was, too.

'I'm going to have to get a dress, and a dog sitter for the evening. Oh…' She scanned the card again, her brow furrowing into an expression of concern.

'What's wrong?'

'It mentions a plus-one.'

'So? You don't have to take anyone. Don't let that put you off.' He knew it might feel a little intimidating to turn up to such an event alone, but she'd been through much worse. Besides, this was supposed to be a good thing for her. A celebration of who she was and what she had achieved.

She screwed her nose up. 'Ordinarily I would have asked you to come with me. But I don't know if that will make things weird again between us?'

Patrick huffed out a breath. So much for getting back to normal, if she was still afraid of spending time with him, even in public. He supposed taking her to a make-out spot in the dead of night hadn't helped his case.

'If I hadn't kissed you the other night, what would you do now?' he asked. 'Don't think about it. You have a plus-one. Who would you ask to go with you?'

'You. I need your support, your company, and the way you're able to calm me down when I spiral.' She was smiling again, and he hoped that was the doubt creeping its way back out again.

Patrick didn't want her to keep thinking differently about him. He wanted her to think of him as old, reliable Patrick who could be her arm candy when she needed it because he was safe. There was no threat of messy emotions and complicated relationships. He was just there for her.

Even if his feelings for her had apparently changed.

'Well, we can't have you spiralling when you're going to be mingling with the great and powerful from Northern Ireland. So I guess Cinderella will be going to the ball with her bestie after all.' It was going to be a very public event, so he didn't think he could get in too much trouble by simply accompanying her.

'Thanks, Patrick. I guess it's nice to be recognised, and I don't know the last time I was out anywhere that had a dress code.'

'It's something to look forward to, for sure.' He couldn't remember the last time he'd been to anything like that, either. With Sinead, it had been a whirlwind of corporate dinners and galas because she liked to network. The same couldn't be said for him. He would always rate a dog walk or a takeaway on the sofa over a pretentious dinner with people who tended to look straight through him.

'Seriously, though, what am I going to wear? It says black tie, but what does that mean for me?' The anxiety for the event was apparently already ramping up, and he understood why. She was going to be on display, and that was a big deal for someone who'd had a real knock to her confidence from her cheating ex.

'Don't worry. I've been to enough of these things to point you in the right direction. There was a particular boutique Sinead favoured, and I'm sure they'll have something suitable for you.' It was expensive, but he could afford to buy something for her. He wasn't one for spending money on himself, and it would be nice to treat her. Perhaps by way of apology for ghosting her the way he had.

'Will you come with me?' Her brow was knitted together in a hopeful plea for his assistance.

There was no way he could say no. 'Of course. We'll find a day and time when our schedules match up, and we'll have ourselves a fashion parade.'

Her side-eye said they were very much back on normal terms. 'I don't know about that, but I will likely want your opinion. I'm a bit out of practice when it comes to wearing anything other than my comfy clothes.'

'I can't say I'm looking forward to being trussed up in a tux again, but it will be worth it to see you have your time in the spotlight.'

'Thanks, Patrick. I'm looking forward to it now.' Billie stopped short of hugging him the way she would usually do. His fault, but until he was able to rein himself in, it was probably for the best.

'Good. I'll let you get your beauty sleep. Not that you need it.' Before he realised what he was doing, he'd reached out to brush an errant strand of hair from her face. That simple touch sent his heart pounding and the blood rushing in his veins.

The way Billie was looking at him said that she wanted him to give in to these urges, too. They were standing so close he felt her breath hot on his face, heard the hitch in it as she gazed up at him longingly. And that was the only permission he needed to close the small gap between them. He sealed his lips over hers in a soft meet he had hoped they could pass off as a good-night kiss. Except it only seemed to ignite a passion between them that obliterated everything but need. Tongues teasing, mouths clashing, they couldn't seem to get enough of one another.

This time he knew it wasn't a one-sided event. Billie was kissing him back. Her arms wrapped around his neck, her body molten against his, she was as invested in this moment as he was. There was nothing he wanted more than to scoop her up and carry her to bed, but he was still trying to come to terms with the last time he'd kissed her. He knew taking that next step was something they would find impossible to put behind them. No matter how tempting it might be, this had to stop here. He pulled away, the dazed look in her eyes no doubt matching his own.

'We have to stop doing this.' He tried to make light of it. Acknowledging the kiss, but also the fact they couldn't let it happen again.

Billie gave a forced laugh. 'Yes. Definitely. I think we're just overtired and emotional after everything that's gone on tonight.'

'That's it, right? Anyway, I, er, guess I should go. I'll probably see you at work. Night, Billie.'

For a brief moment he thought he saw a flicker of disappointment cross her face. Then she smiled, making him think it had simply been wishful thinking on his part. They'd both had another lapse in judgement, but it didn't have to mean anything. It was clear neither of them wanted to take it any further.

'Night, Patrick,' she said, walking him to the door.

It was a wrench as he left her standing in the doorway, looking flushed and thoroughly kissed. He hadn't planned for it to happen again, but now that it had, he didn't know how to stop it occurring regularly. Because he felt at peace when he was kissing her. It was just a shame pursuing anything more would ruin the friendship he cherished so much. Patrick almost wished he hadn't kissed her that first night. Then maybe he wouldn't crave her so much.

He could feel her and Fliss watching him until he got to his car. It took every ounce of his willpower not to turn back.

After tonight's events, he wasn't sure how he felt about going with her to the awards ceremony. Of course he wanted Billie to be celebrated and enjoy her moment in the spotlight. However, if he couldn't keep his feelings platonic towards her at the end of a late work shift, he had no idea how much havoc it was going to wreak when they were all dressed up and enjoying a proper night out together.

CHAPTER FOUR

'I KNOW IT isn't easy today, Fliss, but there should be plenty of lovely scents for you to pick up.' Billie was spending her Sunday morning looking for a family who'd apparently gone missing after a camping trip. They were supposed to have returned last night, and family alerted the emergency services first thing when they didn't come home.

Given the fog last night, it wasn't unreasonable to imagine they'd got lost somewhere in the hills along the coastal path. Even now the drizzle and mist were making it difficult to get around, and the team were equipped with trackers, high-visibility kits, and everything else they needed to hopefully locate the young family. However, the rain meant it was harder for Fliss to pick up the scents. So far they'd worked the grid the search team put together and managed to rule out a whole section of it. Terry and Bilbo had located the missing family's tent, which had been battered in the bad weather last night, so hopefully they weren't too far away. Even though it was possible they'd been exposed to the elements and could be suffering from hypothermia, leaving them even more disoriented.

Despite all the pats on the back for her nomination, Billie wouldn't feel like a hero if she didn't find these people soon. She trudged through the mud, her hair plastered to her face and any trace of make-up washed off in the rain. There certainly wasn't anything glamorous about this role. Apart from the normal worries about being seen at such a public event, she was beginning to look forward to the awards dinner. Especially now that Patrick had agreed to accompany her.

She shivered, not because of the cold but the memory of that kiss. His touch. The moment had surprised them both, again. As though they suddenly couldn't control that lustful urge for one another. Billie was hoping this new attraction would disappear as quickly as it had arrived. The consequences of going any further than a kiss would endanger what they already had together.

It was clear they'd both regretted it straightaway. Their friendship more important than an ill-advised romantic liaison. With all the wounds they were still carrying from the past, there was no way they'd be able to make a relationship work.

As excited as she was about the awards ceremony, if a little nervous, she was worried how she was going to survive a night out with Patrick trying to forget the passion they'd shared. What they might have together if circumstances were different. That didn't mean she wasn't looking forward to seeing him dressed in his finest. Though she'd have to remember to keep some sort of distance if they were going to prioritise their friendship over everything else. She didn't want to swoon at his feet at the sight of him and ruin everything. It would also be a lie if she said she didn't want to dress up for him, too. She would like to see that flare of attraction back in his eyes for her, even if they couldn't act on it.

Thom's infidelity had given her confidence such a

knock she hardly thought of herself as attractive any-more. That's why the hungry look she saw in Patrick's eyes sometimes was so addictive. It was an ego boost she desperately needed. Last night's kiss had proved to her that the previous one hadn't been a fluke. That he wanted her.

They were both such a mess of contradictions when it came to their relationship, and their feelings, it wouldn't take much to upset the balance again. Something she didn't want when things at work were back to usual, and he was back to giving her lifts home. It was the most she could hope for. Even if her imagination tended to run away with her at times.

Billie had caught herself daydreaming when she caught sight of him during a rare lull in the hospital. It was only natural to wonder what could happen if they let things take their own course. Other than ruin the companion-ship they already shared. The safe place they found in each other that they both desperately needed.

It was likely she'd see him today once they located the family, with the air ambulance no doubt making the transfer to the hospital. Not that he'd have any inappro-priate thoughts about her when she probably looked like a drowned rat.

'Wait, Fliss.' Billie suddenly halted her dog's progress as she thought she heard a sound carried on the wind. Fliss stopped sniffing and came to stand beside her.

Sometimes a good pair of ears was just as important as a trained nose. At least she thought she knew what direction the noise had travelled from. Though it could have been an animal, the wind itself or even her imagi-nation, she knew if she was stuck up here, she'd be hol-lering for a rescue, too.

She stood still and waited to see if she could hear the sound again, making sure it hadn't been the echo of her own footsteps she'd heard.

After a quiet minute, she was sure she hadn't been imagining things. There was a definite purpose to the sound, as though someone was calling out.

'Hello? Is there someone out there? I'm with the dog search and rescue team. If you can hear my voice, can you shout again so I can follow the sound?' She yelled out into the grey mist, waiting, straining her ears, her whole body on alert, ready to fire into action. Fliss, too, was on her toes, raring to go. She knew if she found who they were looking for, she'd get her reward, and their work would be done for the day. Billie was sure her dog was looking forward to getting into the warm again as much as she was. They were both homebodies when they weren't out in the wilds searching for lost and injured souls.

'We're over here. Help us!' It was a man's voice. He sounded desperate and weak.

'I'm coming.' Billie prayed that the children were okay, or at least could be treated at the hospital. It was rare for her to deal with younger children. Usually it was teenagers camping who needed rescuing after getting lost or not coming prepared properly for the terrain. Or, unfortunately, men in their twenties and over who were suffering from depression. Those were the difficult cases when simply finding them didn't seem enough. And that was on the occasions when they weren't already too late to save them.

Billie and Fliss set off towards the source of the voice, asking him to call out every now and then so she didn't get turned around on herself. In this instance, the drone wasn't going to be a whole lot of help to find the lost party when it was practically a greyout up here in the hills. This was one occasion when good old-fashioned training won out over modern technology.

Although she would be relieved if and when the air ambulance turned up in case there were serious casualties to deal with once she reached the family. She could treat injuries, shock and whatever else this job threw at her, but she couldn't physically get everyone down to safety by herself.

As always, she was happier when she had Patrick by her side to give that extra bit of support.

'Hello!' she called again, trying to pinpoint the man's voice.

They went back and forth answering one another's call until she eventually saw a group of dark shapes in the distance. Fliss barked and ran on ahead until the lead was taut, still keen to get the credit, along with her prize.

'Good girl.' Billie rewarded her anyway to keep her busy with her ball whilst she tended to the family group huddled together.

'Are we glad to see you.' The woman she assumed was the mother to the two young girls with them was shivering like mad, tears streaming down her face.

'Is everyone okay?' Billie swung her backpack onto the ground to get her medical supplies.

'Lynette has twisted her ankle, and Maggie can't seem to stop shivering.' The mum had her daughters wedged to her chest in an attempt to get some body heat into them, but the whole family was soaked through their flimsy waterproof jackets.

'It'll be the cold. Could be a mild case of hypothermia, and maybe some shock setting in. I'll call in our position and get the air ambulance to transfer everyone to the hospital to get checked out.' Billie pulled some foil blankets out of her bag to wrap around the children, who looked half frozen, then made the call to the rest of the team.

'I'm so sorry, Izzy. I never should have brought us out here.' The man was scrubbing his hands over his head, clearly distraught at what had happened.

His wife tried to placate him. 'You weren't to know there was going to be a storm.'

'I should have checked the weather forecast, made sure my phone got signal up here and that we had the proper gear with us.' Clearly he was putting all the blame on himself. Something Billie was prone to do, too. Especially when it came to relationships, believing any difficulties were entirely down to how she'd failed in some way.

'There's no point in blaming yourself. We see this all the time. People just aren't experienced enough sometimes to be out here.' Billie provided the girls with bottles of water and cereal bars.

'Thanks. We haven't eaten since yesterday. When the storm got bad, we tried to make our way back down, but we got lost. Couldn't find our way back to the tent, either. We tried to take shelter behind the rocks, but we just got soaked to the skin.' Izzy explained what had happened, but Billie was honest about it happening all the time. Hills and mountains were a different animal in the dark, especially during a storm.

'I think I've some protein bars here, too.' She handed the rest of the supplies over for a little energy boost.

'Give mine to the girls. I can survive without them.' The dad was determined to punish himself over events, but if he was well enough to feel sorry for himself, Billie knew she didn't have to worry too much about him. It was the girls who would need help more, especially when they were so quiet and lethargic. She didn't want them to get to the point of shock setting in and did her best to keep them talking and alert.

'You're going to go for a ride in a helicopter, and we'll get you some nice warm clothes. Help is on the way.' Billie turned back to the parents. 'I'm afraid the tent didn't survive the night, so I doubt it would have provided sufficient cover anyway. For future adventures, I would recommend reading up on the local guides, which will advise you on what equipment you'll need to stay safe.'

'Oh, we won't be doing this again. From now on, I can assure you it will be luxury hotels and room service.' From the look on Izzy's face, Billie knew she meant business. She might have forgiven her husband for making a mistake since she'd gone along with their plans, too, but it was clear she wouldn't be camping again under any circumstances.

'I don't blame you.' It brought Billie's thoughts back to the awards dinner, which was being held in Belfast. An hour's drive at least from home, and she and Patrick might want to have a drink with dinner. She'd certainly need one for some Dutch courage. It would be too late to get a bus back in their finery, and too expensive by taxi. A room in the hotel where it was being held seemed the sensible option, but it also raised the question of sleeping arrangements. Friends would just share a room, in separate beds of course, but she imagined that was a step too far for a couple who'd been straying beyond those boundaries recently.

'Can I pet your dog?' The oldest of the girls had taken a liking to Fliss, and Billie was keen to let her fuss over the dog if it meant keeping her alert. Fliss would certainly enjoy it, too.

'Of course. This is Fliss. She helped me find you. She's a very special trained rescue dog who is able to sniff out people who are lost.'

'And she could smell us?' The little girl was wide-eyed with admiration.

'I'm not surprised,' the father said. 'We all stink of smoke. I couldn't even manage to get the fire going properly.'

'Well, it was probably too damp for it to catch light, but you're all safe now.' Billie was doing her best to distract the man from last night's events to focus on the positives. They were all still alive, and help was on the way. There would be time for recriminations later, but for now it was more important to get them to safety. The girls especially didn't need to keep rehashing everything and reliving the trauma they'd undoubtedly suffered being exposed to the elements out here last night. They were bound to have been terrified, and she needed them to feel safe again so they could begin to relax and relieve some of the strain and tension in their bodies.

It struck Billie that that was what Patrick had done for her. When Thom had cheated on her, he left her in a constant state of fear. Being abandoned, rejected, betrayed had taken its toll on her mental health. She was unable to stop replaying the intricacies of their relationship and wondering what had been real, happy times together and what had obviously been a lie. It had shaken her to her core. As though she didn't know which parts of her life were real. Apart from Patrick. He was her one constant. The person who'd kept her grounded, reassured her that things were going to be all right and they'd get through everything together. She knew she'd done the same for him after Sinead had died. It was a natural reaction to want to help someone you cared about very deeply. She supposed their vocation to assist people in need was simply something ingrained in them, and she was happy she had Patrick, who would always come searching for her when she needed rescuing. And vice versa.

Since the family weren't in any immediate medical danger, she conducted initial checks and left a more thorough examination for Patrick to do. She didn't want to overstep her boundaries when she was supposed to be here in a search capacity. It was only in emergencies that she would deign to intervene in a medical fashion. It might upset not only her team but the air ambulance crew, too, if she started interfering. She was lucky the last rescue hadn't come back to bite her on the backside when she'd put herself in danger to help Mr Hill. It was frowned upon, and she'd had to sit through a lecture on looking after her own safety first.

The familiar, welcome sound of the helicopter could be heard in the distance. Billie turned on the light on her head torch so they could better pinpoint their location in the mid-morning gloom.

'That's the air ambulance now. It means the team can get you to hospital as soon as possible for some checks. There's nothing to be scared of. They're here to help you. But as they come in to land, it's going to get noisy and windy. It's best we all huddle in until they've landed.' Billie wanted to explain to the young girls what was going to happen so they wouldn't be too frightened. They'd been through enough, and a helicopter landing close by could be a startling event. Although in her case, it was the moment she was able to take her foot off the pedal and relax, knowing she'd done her part of the job in locating the family.

'It's noisy, isn't it?' The dad yelled over the deafening sound of the helicopter blades as the wind whipped all around them, threatening to knock a few of them off their feet.

Fliss barked. She still got excited at this part, too. Probably in anticipation of seeing her favourite person, Patrick, again.

Heads dipped, hair whipping around their faces, the group waited until the blades stopped whirring before they broke apart. The sight of Patrick striding towards her dressed in his bright red flight suit always sent her heart into a flutter. Not only did his presence mean that help had arrived, but he also looked very handsome. A real man in action.

'Hi. I'm Dr James.' Patrick reassured the family as he came and knelt down beside the group on the rocky terrain. 'I know Billie will probably have explained to you what happens next, but I'm going to do a quick check to make sure everything's okay with you all before we get you transferred into the helicopter.'

'This little one has twisted her ankle. It's swollen, but I don't think it's broken. Both girls are a little subdued. Not unexpected in the circumstances, but I'm worried about hypothermia and possible shock. The adults are okay, right?' Billie checked with the parents, but apart from a little wounded pride and the need for a good night's sleep and some food, she didn't think there were any serious issues in that department.

'Okay. We'll get a look.' Patrick took out his torch and checked the girls' pupils, used his ear thermometer to take their temperature, and did all of the necessary prerequisite checks before they boarded the helicopter.

'Do you need a hand strapping that ankle?' Billie offered.

'Yes. Thanks. Can you just hold that cold pack on it for a moment to take the swelling down a bit?' He broke the disc inside the pack to activate it as Billie removed the child's sodden shoe and sock. It was a bad sprain, the skin bruised and scraped where she'd knocked it, and she yelped when it was touched.

'I know it's tender, but this bandage will help strengthen it enough for you to be able to stand on it. Okay?' Patrick's voice was soothing, almost a whisper, as he undid the bandage.

There'd been several occasions when he'd used that very tone with her. When she'd refused to get out of bed, crying herself hoarse into a sea of tissues. He'd come and lain beside her, murmuring about what a good person she was and what an idiot Thom was for not appreciating what he had in her. Although a lot of the sweet gestures he'd made to try and cheer her up had been lost on her fog of depression at the time, Billie was beginning to remember everything he'd done for her. He'd made dinner to ensure she was eating properly. The flowers and chocolates her boyfriend had never bothered to buy her were suddenly in abundance in Patrick's effort to cheer her up. He was simply a lovely, caring man, and it was no wonder she couldn't quite get her feelings towards him back in check.

Once Thom had left the scene, and she was beginning to move on from the grief of losing her relationship and everything she'd known, it was obvious things between them were never going to be the same again. There was no denying the attraction was there between them when they'd both been tempted into kissing. Twice. For anything more to happen between them, they would have to fully let go of the past and learn to live with the scars instead of letting the scars make the decisions for them. Patrick was a catch, and if he ever showed an interest in something more between them, Billie knew she would be tempted again. Despite all the reasons she shouldn't get romantically involved with her grieving friend, that physical desire she felt for him seemed to be growing day by day. Her head and her body were telling her different things, but she knew she couldn't have it both ways. As much as she was attracted to him, she needed him as a friend more.

Billie removed the cold pack from the child's ankle and let Patrick bind it with the bandage, helping him to secure it in place. When she glanced up, he was watching her with a smile playing on his lips. As if to say, *We're a great team*.

Everything they would need in another relationship, if they weren't so afraid of losing their friendship to pursue the change in the dynamic between them.

They got the family into the helicopter, and Billie stood to one side with Fliss. Unfortunately, they would be left to make their own way back down. Something Patrick obviously realised as he hesitated at the door of the helicopter.

'I have to go with them…' He gestured to the family huddled inside. 'Otherwise I would see you safely down, too.'

'I know that. I'm a big girl. I can find my way back. It's more important that you're on board in case they need any further medical treatment.' It wasn't anything new. The only difference today was the terrible weather, and Patrick's obvious guilt about leaving her to walk back alone. She knew he would switch places if he could. He was always willing to put her comfort above his own, but nothing trumped taking care of patients, and she was aware of that. Billie had done her part. Now it was time for Patrick to shine.

'What are your plans for the rest of the afternoon?' he asked, reluctant to leave her just yet.

'A shower, my PJs and a bite to eat. Then Fliss and I will probably cuddle up on the sofa with a good film.' As long as there wasn't another emergency call-out. It would be a nice wind-down before starting work again tomorrow at the hospital.

'Oh? I thought you might want to have some retail therapy and see about getting that dress for the awards ceremony. It's only a week away.' He looked almost disappointed that she'd made other plans.

'Well, I still need to shower and change...'

'You do that, and I'll pick you up once I get the family settled at the hospital. Maybe we can go for lunch somewhere.' He looked so hopeful, Billie didn't want to let him down. She knew he found it difficult to be in the house on his own and was likely looking for an excuse to get out. And she did need to get her outfit sorted or it would end up a last-minute panic buy, which never worked out well.

'Sounds good. I'll let you go, and I'll make my way back home.'

'I'll pick you up as soon as I'm done here.' The smile on his face said she'd made his day, and Billie found herself looking forward to an afternoon out after all.

Patrick rushed home to get a shower himself to wash off the grime of the rescue up in the hills. He wanted to look, and smell, his best for dress shopping with Billie. Once he was sure the family were getting the treatment they needed and the hospital staff were taking over, he couldn't wait to leave. Usually he delayed that moment for as long as possible. He didn't like rattling around the house on his own. When he'd married Sinead, he didn't think he'd ever be on his own again. Certainly not so soon.

Since he'd lost Sinead, he'd felt lonelier than ever. It had been difficult enough losing both of his parents, especially when he hadn't been on particularly good terms with either of them before they'd died. His mother had never been able to forgive him for arguing with his father before his heart attack, and as a result, their relationship had been strained. It hadn't helped that they'd had to sell the farm, too. Although his father had wanted him to carry on with it, being powerless to save his father had only spurred his dream of becoming a doctor so he could make a difference to others. His one concession had been to stay in Belfast for his studies, but his mother couldn't see past her own loss to ever forgive him.

It had been a lonely existence until he'd met Sinead. So to lose her in similar circumstances, angry with him, leaving no chance to make amends, was devastating. It was a pain he didn't think he could ever overcome when there was no way to turn back time. He'd take back every argument or cross word spoken to his loved ones if it meant he could change what had happened. But he couldn't.

Now he was left with only his guilt for company.

He needed Billie to give him something to look forward to other than work. Although going clothes shopping wasn't something he enjoyed, he did like the idea of spoiling her. Of seeing her happy. Being that friend she needed.

He stripped off his clothes on the way to the bathroom. One of the joys of being alone, he supposed. The warm spray of the shower on his naked body was a welcome relief. Even if it was no substitute for a warm body pressed against his.

His bed was even emptier than the house, and he was beginning to feel it more and more lately. It was a sad indictment of his situation when the highlight of his days had been comforting Billie in her bed when she'd been distraught over Thom. He hated himself for it when she'd been so low, and he'd genuinely wanted to offer her some comfort, but he'd be lying if he said he hadn't got some from it. To just hold someone in his arms and have someone hold him, too, was one of life's pleasures. More so when it was Billie.

As he lathered his body with zesty lime-scented shower gel, he thought about what it had been like lying there in bed with her. Like a normal couple. With no indication of their personal struggles, or life beyond their cuddle. He missed that intimacy with another person. With Billie. He wasn't sure given their current circumstances if they'd ever get to have that closeness again without worrying it would spill into something disastrous for them.

Suddenly Patrick froze, the pressure from the water flattening his hair to his head as he got lost in his thoughts. Since when was it Billie missing from his bed, and not Sinead, his wife? For a moment, that guilt was back. Not only because of the row they'd had before the accident, but also due to the betrayal now of her memory. He knew Billie would tell him it was natural for him to move on. That Sinead would have wanted him to find someone else. Except Billie probably wouldn't realise she was the one who seemed to dominate his thoughts these days.

Even today when the emergency call had come in, as well as actioning the plan to extract the family, his brain had instantly gone to Billie already out there, waiting for him. Although she'd been the first one on the scene, finding and treating them, and doing quite well without him.

He scrubbed some shampoo into his hair as though he could wash away the thoughts that were decidedly not platonic. Instead, more images of her came to mind. How fresh-faced she'd looked up there on the hill. Like one of the Brontë sisters' windswept heroines. Her lashes beaded with diamond raindrops, her wet clothes clinging to every curve of her body. Reminding him, if he'd needed it, that she was all woman.

Patrick groaned. He was torturing himself, knowing she was out of bounds. Yet his body was responding to her simply as a beautiful, strong, courageous woman. That fragile, vulnerable side she only exposed to him brought out that need to protect her. To hold her close and forget about the rest of the world. Easy to do when his senses were filled completely with her.

He could almost imagine her sweet scent, like vanilla ice cream. Almost feel her full breasts pressed against his chest now. He wanted to kiss her, desire taking over and leaving them both slaves to passion. The thoughts made dormant parts of him suddenly spring uncomfortably to life. His libido had all but disappeared these past few years. It had been all he could do just to survive. But now he was being reminded he was still a hot-blooded male.

Patrick took his erection in hand. Eyes closed, he thought of Billie. Of her touch, her lips parted, and not stopping at a kiss. His primal urges were all-important now that he was alone, inhibitions given a temporary reprieve. He slid his hand up and down his shaft, enjoying the sensation and wishing it was Billie touching him there. His orgasm was fast and frantic, spilling into the swirling water and leaving no trace of his indiscretion save for his heavy breathing and a throat raw from his roar of relief.

Legs shaking, conscience pricked, but other parts of him satisfied, Patrick rinsed away his sin. He hoped that now he'd given that animal part of him what it wanted, he would be able to move past it. Clearly he was in need of some sort of physical relationship, and though it could only be Billie in his imagination, it was time to move on from Sinead. If he had someone else in his life, he mightn't be thinking of his friend in this way at all.

He shut off the water, stepped out of the shower, and grabbed a towel. Hopefully now that he'd had some relief, he might not be so wrapped up in thoughts of Billie anymore, and he'd be satisfied with some shopping and some lunch this afternoon. Although a welcome return in the grand scheme, his libido had decided to manifest in the most ill-timed and complicated direction.

A problem which might not be solved so easily, or swiftly, when it was directed towards his best friend.

CHAPTER FIVE

ONCE THE SEARCH and rescue team had been debriefed and stood down, Billie had gone straight home. She'd fed Fliss, then nipped into the shower, keen to get ready for the afternoon with Patrick. It wasn't often that they ventured out in public together. Not that either was ashamed to be seen with the other. Rather that their time together was usually spent in one another's houses. This was something different, and she found herself reinvigorated by the thought of doing something so normal together. Lounging around watching TV didn't hold quite the same appeal all of a sudden.

She'd dried and styled her hair, put some make-up on. However, before she'd had the chance to pick out something to wear, the doorbell sounded Patrick's arrival. Wearing only a towel, she made a barefoot dash downstairs to let him in.

'Slowcoach. I've been home and showered already,' he said, acknowledging her state of undress with a tut. Though he made a thorough enough assessment of her near nakedness that Billie's skin flushed with heat.

'I had to go over everything with the team first. Besides, I have more hair than you to dry.' She noted that his was still damp and curling up at the ends. It took a lot of willpower not to start picturing him naked in the shower, and her inner naughty wanton was trying to insist that they could have saved water by showering together.

'True, but may I say you've done a spectacular job of it.' He was teasing her, mischief bright in his eyes, but she was still going to take the compliment. It was a rare thing in her life.

'You may.' Billie spun around and led him into the living room. 'You can keep Fliss company until I get dressed.'

'Yes, ma'am.' Patrick saluted her before going to have another love-in with the dog. He was clearly in a good mood, and much preferable to the introspective version of him who thought he should keep his distance from her.

Billie looked at the clothes she'd strewn on her bed. Obviously she wanted her best underwear in case it was one of those places with the intrusive shop assistants who insisted on helping to dress the customer. She picked out an ivory silk set edged with lace. There wasn't much occasion for her to wear nice lingerie, but she hoped it would help make her feel less inferior in a high-end boutique. The outfit she chose was important, too. It needed to be semi-dressy but comfortable, and for some reason, she wanted it to be something Patrick liked. Perhaps she was getting too used to the idea of him complimenting her already. She was so needy.

In the end she donned a teal pencil dress she'd bought for Christmas and had never worn because Thom had bought her some cheap red Lycra thing he insisted she wear. The deep V-neck front wrap was flattering, she thought, studying herself in the full-length mirror on the inside door of her wardrobe. It was nipped in at the waist with a ruched front panel, showing off her figure without revealing too much skin. Most importantly, she felt good in it.

And Patrick's 'Wow!' when she walked in sealed her decision.

'It's not too much, is it?' Her cheeks were already burning from his attention, and she didn't want to look too out of place and have people staring at her.

'Not at all. It's perfect. Very Hollywood glamour meets '40s elegance. You look great, Billie.' His eyes were practically out on stalks, and she had to admit to herself it was the reaction she'd hoped for.

It wasn't a shock to realise how much she was craving not only his approval but his want for her. Since she couldn't seem to get those snatched kisses out of her head, there was something inside her pushing for him to see her as more than a friend. If only to satisfy her craving to kiss him again. Anything more than that could spoil what they had, but each time he gave in to that apparent urge to kiss her, Billie got a confidence boost knowing she had that effect on him. Even if he always backed away afterwards. Something she tried not to take personally when they both knew what was at stake. Still, after being dumped for someone else, it was nice to realise someone found her attractive. She just had to make sure she didn't get carried away by the flattery. No doubt Patrick had planned this shopping excursion to remind her they were friends. Thom certainly would never have dreamed of taking her to buy clothes.

'Thank you. Maybe if we can't find anything today, I'll just wear this,' she said, grabbing her coat and bag and heading out to the car with Patrick following behind.

It was a lie. There was no way she was wearing this. Every compliment he paid her only made her want more. There had been a severe lack of appreciation in her relationship with Thom, and she found herself craving the praise Patrick was so generous with. Billie wanted to outdo the effect this dress had on him. Today's shopping expedition had become a mission to find something even more impressive. An outfit which would leave him speechless and her feeling a million dollars.

'This is it.' Patrick pulled up at the boutique just outside the city centre pedestrianised area, making it accessible for the moneyed clientele it no doubt attracted.

'Are you sure this isn't one of those places you have to make an appointment to visit? I don't want to be left standing out in the street like an eejit.' Billie eyed up the front door as though afraid to approach it in case she was denied entry. Sinead had never had such qualms. This was simply an insight into the inferiority complex Thom had left her with when he'd decided Billie wasn't enough for him. Making it her problem, when he'd been the one lacking all along.

Patrick had never thought he deserved her. She went out of her way to make him happy, but it had never seemed like a two-way street. A bit like his own relationship with Sinead, he supposed. He always got the impression that she'd regretted settling down with him. Once her career had really kicked off, there was no time for them as a couple, and she seemed happy with that. All Patrick had wanted was to be at home with her after a busy shift. He would have compromised, been a stay-at-home husband and father, if she'd wanted that. In the end, though, it was only her career which seemed to have mattered. And dressing to impress was very much part of it when it came to schmoozing at corporate events.

Billie had never been one to crave attention. She just got on with her job, finding satisfaction in the patients she helped. That was why she deserved to be spoiled for once. Besides, he was sure that dress would get her access to any venue. She looked stunning. Unfortunately, it hadn't helped him to remember theirs was supposed to be a platonic relationship when he was lusting after her more than ever.

'I'm sure they will be rolling out the red carpet once they see you in that get-up,' he said. Her tense forehead smoothed out into a smile.

'I'll settle for being allowed into the store to just look. I remember being in London once in one of those fancy department stores and flicking through rails of expensive dresses. The sales assistant actually tutted and started brushing the dresses down when I walked away. As if I'd contaminated them with my working-class hands.' Billie laughed, but he understood why that would make her a little nervous now. She didn't want to be humiliated again. Though she would probably have walked away without a word if someone challenged her. She was that sort of person. Strong and brave in her career path, but never quite believing in herself in her personal life, when she deserved to be treated with so much more respect.

It made him think of the clashes he and Sinead had in the last few years of their marriage. If he'd just let things drop on the last night they'd been together, she might still be alive. Instead, he'd argued fiercely until she'd stormed out of the house in a rage. Her mood obviously impaired her judgement when it came to her personal safety.

Patrick wondered if their marriage would have lasted even if she hadn't had the accident. Probably not. They'd become too different, almost living separate lives. Though grief had clouded his judgement in the intervening years. Looking at everything through rose-tinted glasses, convinced they'd been living a fairy tale. In reality, it had been far from that. Neither of them had been happy. And if he hadn't been weighed down with such guilt, if she hadn't died, they might have moved on from one another in the end anyway. He might have found another partner and lived the contented family life with someone else.

He tried to ignore the picture in his head of Billie. Of raising a family with her, knowing how better suited they were as a couple, but too damaged to try it.

'At the end of the day, we're all just people. No one is better than anyone else, no matter what goes on in their head, and you deserve the best, Billie.' Whatever happened inside, he was going to make sure they treated her like the queen she was.

She made no further protest as they got out of the car and headed towards the shop.

It was funny, he used to dread coming in here with Sinead, waiting as she searched for the perfect dress. Today he was looking forward to doing the same with Billie. Seeing her eyes light up as she spied the rails of dresses was priceless.

'I don't know where to start.' It was clear Billie was out of her comfort zone, but Patrick was determined to make this an enjoyable experience for her. At least that might help erase her last experience from memory.

'Excuse me. My friend has been nominated for a

Northern Ireland Heroes Award. Can you help her pick out something suitable to wear?' Patrick approached one of the elegant assistants, with Billie standing behind him looking mortified.

'Of course. Congratulations. Hello, I'm Kiki. Now, let's see…you've got a beautiful figure, so it shouldn't be too hard to find something. Is there a style or colour you prefer?' The perfectly coiffed blonde gave Billie her full attention, clapping her hands together and showing off her immaculate French manicure.

'Um, nothing too short or revealing. I'm not sure. It's black tie, so what would you usually wear to that sort of thing?' Billie seemed a bit more relaxed now that 'Kiki' was giving her the time of day. So Patrick, who seemed surplus to requirements for now, sat down in a nearby seat.

'Ah, so we want a little glamour. We have some lovely gold numbers.' Kiki pulled out a gaudy gown with a split up the side and a neckline which seemed to come right down to the navel.

Patrick refrained from interjecting and saying it wasn't Billie's style at all, because she was already shaking her head.

'Something a little more subtle, perhaps?' Billie asked.

Kiki nodded and led her over to the far side of the room, plastic covers rustling as she pulled out an armful of dresses. 'Silver or champagne might suit you better. Would you like to try some on?'

'Yes, please.' Billie shot Patrick a look as though to tell him not to escape anywhere. If she had to go through this, then so did he.

As Billie disappeared into the changing cubicle, a young woman and her mother came into the shop ask-

ing about suitable wedding dresses and something for
the mother of the bride. They were taken to a different
corner of the store. Obviously they catered for all sorts
of events in here.

Legs crossed, foot tapping to the easy listening music
playing in the background, he waited for the great reveal.
It wasn't long before he heard a 'Psst!' sound, and Billie
poked her head around the changing room door.

'Well, let's see, then.'

Reluctantly she stepped out so he had a full-length
view of the dress she'd tried on first. Patrick's mouth
went dry. He was going to be in serious trouble at this
awards night.

'I'm not sure it's really me.' She was self-consciously
covering her midriff with her arms, but there was absolutely no need for her to feel inadequate when she was
absolutely stunning.

Though she was right. It didn't suit her. He was used
to seeing her in her uniform, in her high-visibility jacket
in the mountains, or in her comfy clothes at home. Right
now she looked like a movie star. Silver sequins glittered
right down to the ground, the cowl neckline fell low between her breasts, and the fabric draped around her body
like it was meant for her. But she didn't look comfortable wearing it.

'You look beautiful, but you don't want to be fidgeting
and pulling at it all night.' Patrick wanted her to know
she looked stunning wearing it, but there were others she
might like better.

'Your husband's right. You have to find what's right
for you.' Kiki returned to give her appraisal. Thought it
was on the tip of his tongue to correct her about the na-

ture of their relationship, he didn't. Clearly Billie hadn't felt the need to, and he didn't want to embarrass Kiki simply because she'd assumed they were a couple. An understandable assumption given that they'd arrived together and that they were obviously close.

Billie looked conflicted. 'Perhaps I'll try the others on and see if they suit me any better.'

She disappeared back inside for another quick change, leaving Patrick to people-watch as he waited. The bride-to-be and her mother seemed to be having a whale of a time trying on dresses and swirling around in front of the full-length mirrors.

'You look beautiful, Anna.' The mother dabbed at her eyes with the handkerchief.

'Do you think so?' The young bride-to-be bit her lip as she studied the corseted, beaded ivory gown in the mirror.

'I know so, and Gavin will know so, too.'

'But it's so expensive. I can't justify spending this on a dress when we're going to struggle to pay our rent.'

'I will pay for it. Stop worrying. You're doing everything else on a budget, but your wedding dress isn't something you should have to compromise on. We'll find a way to make it work. Just pick the dress you want.' The talk between the bride and her mother sounded a lot like the conversation he imagined he and Billie were going to have over whatever outfit she decided on when he'd already said he'd pay for it.

His attention was returned back to his own shopping partner as she stood before him in another amazing dress. It was a strapless champagne lace maxi dress adorned with swathes of beads and a pearl waistband. The fabric was moulded to her body and fishtailed out at the bottom, making her look like a mermaid bride. Breathtaking.

'Wow!' seemed to be the only appropriate response. In his head, all he could see was a cartoon version of himself with love heart eyes bulging out of their sockets and an 'awooga!' siren going off in the background.

'You like it, then?' she asked bashfully, her cheeks pink from his reaction.

'I like it, then.'

'It suits your colouring, and you know we have the matching shoes and handbag.' Kiki's upselling managed to stop him babbling like a tongue-tied eejit.

'Oh no, that won't be necessary. I'm sure I'll have something at home that will do.' Billie shook her head, no doubt thinking about the extra expense.

Kiki gasped as though she'd said something blasphemous. 'You can't defile such a gown with inferior accessories. It will ruin the whole aesthetic.'

Patrick wasn't sure the idea was such a disaster, and Kiki was likely just trying to squeeze as much money as she could from the sale. Nevertheless, he wanted Billie to feel like a princess at the ball. Not a pretender.

'I think you should at least see what they look like together,' he said, knowing full well he was going to buy them for her.

Billie narrowed her lips and glared at him, but Kiki was already hustling over with the accessories and attaching them to her as though she were her very own life-sized dolly. 'What size are you, a four? Try these.'

'Yes, I'm a four.' Billie reluctantly cooperated, sliding her feet into the Cinderella-like heels.

Kiki stood back to admire her handiwork. 'See? It just completes the look.'

Patrick had to agree that the shoes, along with the pearl-and-bead clutch bag, did have quite the impact along with the dress.

'And one last thing.' Kiki carried over a pearl-encrusted hair comb, lifted up one side of Billie's hair and pushed it into place.

For a moment, it made Patrick think about how Billie would look on her wedding day. It wasn't too dissimilar to a wedding dress. All she needed was a veil, a bouquet and a husband. The thought of another man taking her arm suddenly and irrationally made him feel jealous. Despite the fact that he'd been the one to put firm boundaries in place so they could never be anything romantic, the thought of her marrying someone else was simply devastating. As much as he wanted her to move on from Thom and be happy, he knew that when she did inevitably meet someone else, he'd be pushed out of her life. He doubted any future partner would want him hanging around, lusting over his wife. Patrick simply didn't want to entertain the idea because it was too painful to contemplate. Instead he would have to just focus on the present and make the most of the time they had together. He would enjoy the one night they'd be able to play dress-up and get out of the house for a while.

'How do you feel about the ensemble?' he asked Billie as she adjusted the bodice. It was more daring than she'd been intending to go, and as stunning as it might look on her, she still had to be comfortable in wearing it.

'I like it,' she said with a smile, smoothing her hands

down the sides of the dress as though appreciating the tactile nature and fit.

Of course, that sent Kiki into raptures about what an excellent choice it was, saying she was going to make an impact at the dinner.

'Shall I ring everything up for you, sir?' She cleverly addressed Patrick about the sale, knowing that Billie would protest about the additional cost.

Predictably, Billie attempted to intervene in the transaction. 'Just the dress, thanks.'

'Yes, ring up everything, please, Kiki.' He smiled at the shop assistant who rushed away to get the card reader. Neither waited for Billie's response. It wasn't that he didn't respect her input. He just wanted to do something nice for her.

'Patrick…' Hands on hips, she glared at him to let him see her displeasure with his decision.

'I said I would pay, so end of discussion. You heard Kiki. The overall aesthetic would be ruined if we don't take her advice.' As he exaggerated her words, he at least made Billie laugh.

Seeing he wasn't going to take no for an answer, she eventually capitulated. 'Well, in that case, thank you very much. It's a lovely gesture and very much appreciated.'

Before he had time to prepare himself, she leaned down and hugged him, giving him an up close and personal view down the front of her dress. The fitted bodice pushed her breasts together, the swells of the soft globes sitting tantalisingly close to his face. He cleared his throat and got to his feet.

'No problem. I, er, should go and pay. Why don't you get changed out of that so Kiki can wrap it for you?' Hot and bothered suddenly, he moved towards the cash register for a little breathing room. It would be a wonder if he survived this awards night in one piece, and they hadn't even discussed the sleeping arrangements yet.

They went in opposite directions, leaving Kiki looking as though her head was spinning trying to decide which of them to follow. In the end, she went to the mother and daughter who were already waiting at the till.

'Is everything all right?' she asked sweetly, though Patrick was sure she would much rather get Billie's purchases rung up before she changed her mind.

'Anna wants this one, but it's a little loose around the waist and shoulders. Is there a chance we can get this altered?' The mother pulled at the dress her daughter was still wearing to show where it needed some attention for it to be the perfect fit.

'Of course. Our seamstress can do that for you. I'll get her now, and she can take some measurements.' Kiki rang a bell, and the couple stepped to one side, leaving space for Patrick to approach the counter.

'How long will that take?' Anna inquired.

'It all depends on her diary. I'm sure she can advise you.' Kiki seemed very keen to pass on the responsibility, ringing in the tally for Patrick and Billie's purchases and presenting him with the total on the card reader.

He quickly paid the bill before Billie had a chance to see it and made him cancel the whole thing. She returned with the dress hung over her arm just as Kiki handed him the receipt, which he hastily shoved into his pocket.

'I'm afraid I couldn't carry everything back myself. I'll go back and get the shoes and bag.'

'That's not a problem, madam. I will see to that and

make sure everything is parcelled up for you.' Now that the dress was paid for, Kiki seemed much more relaxed. There was less urgency in her step as she walked back to the changing room, leaving the two couples hovering near the till.

'What if we can't get it done in time?' Anna was clearly fretting about the timeline, and Patrick wondered how soon the wedding day was supposed to be.

'We will.' Her mother tried to reassure her with a pat on the arm, but it appeared that Anna was spiralling.

'I knew I shouldn't have left it so late, but with everything else going on, I didn't think we'd have the money. I know we don't have the money, and you don't have it either, Mum. Oh my goodness, I'm finding it hard to breathe all of a sudden.' Anna's mother caught her as she wobbled. Patrick and Billie immediately rushed to offer their assistance.

Patrick brought a chair over for her to sit down, and Billie poured a glass of water from the silver tray housing refreshments for the visiting clientele.

'My chest is so tight.' The young woman was clutching her chest, eyes wide with fear, shoulders lifting and falling as she fought to breathe.

'Anna, is it? My name's Patrick. I'm a doctor, okay?'

She nodded as he knelt down beside her. 'Am I having a heart attack?'

He smiled. It was a natural assumption when the symptoms were so scary and not unlike those experienced by cardiac patients. 'I don't think so. I think it's a panic attack you're experiencing.'

Patrick checked her pulse, which was racing beneath his fingertips.

'You're clearly under a lot of stress. Sometimes that can cause your heart rate to speed up and make it difficult for you to catch a breath. I think you just need to take a moment to calm down. Take a couple of deep, steadying breaths. In…and out.' Billie was there next to him, helping to regulate Anna's breathing. The distraction would help take her mind off whatever had clearly sent her into a spin.

'That's it. Breathe with me. In…and out.' Billie was such a calm presence in these sorts of incidents. It made her such a valuable part of the A and E team as well as the search and rescue team. They came across all sorts of vulnerable people who needed a reassuring presence to bring them back from the worst-case scenarios likely running through their heads at the time. Patients at the hospital had benefitted from her empathetic nature. He knew there had been some very vulnerable individuals in the midst of a mental health crisis she'd literally managed to talk down from the ledge. Billie was someone who didn't need a blinged-out dress to shine, even if it looked stunning on.

'She's been so stressed out lately. The wedding's in a couple of days, and we weren't sure it would go ahead at all, but Anna and Gavin want to make a commitment to one another. I thought dress shopping would be a treat. They lost everything in the house fire, you see. Everyone's okay, but they lost everything, including the wedding outfits they'd already bought. No insurance, you see, but everything will be fine, sweetheart. I promise.' Anna's mother stroked her hair, tears in her eyes, clearly concerned about her daughter.

'I'm so sorry. But yes, things like that will have a

physical toll. It's your body's way of telling you to take time out. That constant state of worry wreaks havoc on a person. All I can do is tell you to look at the positives. You're still here, and you clearly have a mother and partner who love you dearly. That's more than a lot of people have.' His voice caught at the end, almost giving away the train of his own thoughts. Thinking about the things he'd lost. The people whose lives he'd destroyed.

Now that Anna's breathing had slowed a little, Billie handed her the glass of water and told her to sip at it.

Patrick did his best to pull himself together. 'Okay, your heart rate is beginning to get back to normal. I think once you've discussed what you need with the seamstress, you should put your feet up and have a nice strong cup of tea.'

'Well, if the doctor says so…' Anna's mother looked more than happy with the suggestion.

'But we were supposed to get you a dress, too,' Anna cried.

'Don't worry about it. I probably can't afford anything in here anyway. I'm sure I have something at home that'll do.' The older woman's sacrifice made him think of Billie and her insistence that she could go without rather than take advantage of his kind nature. Patrick found himself wanting to do something to help her, too. To make her life a little brighter, and easier, as well as her daughter's.

He discreetly called Kiki over to one side and handed her his credit card. 'Put whatever the ladies want on my card. I'll be back in thirty minutes to pick it up again. Please don't tell them until I've left the premises.'

He could feel Billie's eyes glaring into him but did his best to ignore her.

'Are you sure, sir? That's very generous of you.' Kiki was uncharacteristically hesitant to take his money this time.

'I'm sure.' He gave her a curt nod of the head and walked briskly towards the door before Billie could give him a telling off.

'What on earth are you doing, Patrick? Do you have some sort of damsel in distress fetish?' She was rushing to keep up with him as he headed towards the nearest coffee shop.

'Call it a random act of kindness. There aren't enough of those these days. Speaking of which, can you shout the coffees?'

Billie rummaged in her bag and produced her card whilst muttering to herself about what a soft touch he could be sometimes.

'Two Americanos, please. Do you want anything to eat?' he asked her as the barista waited for their order.

'I thought we were going out for lunch,' she said drolly.

'Yes, of course. This is just a coffee break. It's exhausting dress shopping, you know.' He was poking the bear, but Billie held her tongue until they got their coffees and found a seat in the corner of the café.

'You're going to make yourself bankrupt, you know, if you keep riding in on your white horse to buy expensive dresses,' Billie lectured as she collapsed into one of the faded red velvet bucket chairs.

'Why are you so annoyed about it? They'd clearly been having a rough time, and I wanted to do something nice for them.' He poured the little jug of milk between their coffees and added the sugar he knew Billie liked. It was a habit. They both knew how the other liked their hot drinks and were always making one another teas and coffees. For some reason, he caught himself looking at what he was doing and thought about how much they probably looked like a married couple. Though it wasn't often he and Sinead ventured for a coffee together in those later days of their marriage. It didn't seem like an important thing to make time for then, yet he looked forward to every chance he got to sit down with Billie.

'I know that. It's just…well…people don't tend to think like you, Patrick. They might feel sorry, but they'll move on without getting involved. Although you could say stepping in to stop a panic attack was enough to make a difference.' Billie was right, but he didn't know how to explain he lived in a constant state of guilt. Always wondering how he could fix a problem, when he'd been the cause many a time in the past. If he could help someone feel a little better, then he acted. Buying someone a dress, or two, didn't feel like such a big deal. Not when it could prevent someone spiralling into a state of despair.

'Well, it's done now. I'll probably never see them again, and they'll have a nice story to tell people at the wedding.' It wasn't about making himself out to be a hero or trying to impress anyone. He supposed no one could really understand what went on in his head because he kept it to himself. He was ashamed of things he'd done in the past and trying to atone in some way.

'You never cease to amaze me, Patrick James.' She shook her head, and he hoped that was going to be the end of the matter. Except it wasn't.

'I just worry you're the sort of person that will leave yourself broken to help others.' Her concern only increased his guilt, because he knew the real reason behind it. How could he tell her he'd killed his wife, and he couldn't live with the feeling he'd been financially rewarded for it?

'You don't have to worry on that score, okay? Sinead had a life insurance policy, and the house was paid off when she died. I donated the money to the air ambulance and search and rescue team because I don't want to feel as if I've profited from her death. But it means I don't have a mortgage, which relieves a lot of financial pressure. So if I can help a beautiful woman buy a dress, I will. Okay?' It wasn't the full truth, but a version of it, which would hopefully explain his actions in some way and let them get on with their afternoon. Without Billie thinking he hung about in dress shops waiting to pay women's bills as some sort of new fetish.

'Okay,' she said softly. 'For the record, though, Sinead took that policy out to make sure you would have financial security if anything happened to her. The same way you probably did for her. To secure a future without one another. There's no need for you to feel guilty about it.'

Billie reached out and touched his hand. It was all he could do not to snatch it away. He didn't deserve her sympathy and understanding. It was better when she was mad at him. That was how it should be for someone that had caused the death of not one but two of his loved ones.

'You don't understand.' He couldn't have her feeling sorry for him when she didn't know what had happened that night.

'Then tell me.' Billie's insistence that he share his dark secret, probably so she could fix things, made him want to tell her. Then she'd realise the sort of person he really was.

'It's my fault she's dead. Okay?' He waited for the look of horror on her face, but her silence reminded him that wasn't the sort of person *she* was. Billie would save her reaction until he told her all the gory details. Wait until he was ready to tell her.

The longer the silence went on, the harder it became to keep the words inside. Until they came surging up and tumbled from his lips. 'We argued that night, and she stormed off. I knew she'd been drinking and should have gone after her, but I didn't. It's my fault she had the accident. If we hadn't rowed, if I'd gone after her, she might still be here.'

He didn't know if they'd still be together, but he was sure she'd at least still be alive. Perhaps if he wasn't so hot-headed at times, his father would still be here, too, but he'd never know. The angry words he'd exchanged with both of his loved ones had led directly to their deaths. The guilt over his father's death had driven him to succeed as a doctor. Doing his best to save lives in the vain hope it would make up for that life-changing argument. Hoping that in some way, his son's vocation would have made him happy, even if he hadn't taken over the family business.

Only to make the same mistake with Sinead and undo all the work he'd done to be a better person. How could he ever have taken a payout knowing it was his fault she was gone? His conscience would never have let him rest.

'It was an accident,' Billie said softly. 'We all argue. We all storm off, and eventually cool down and get over it. Sinead's accident meant you never got that closure, but she would never have blamed you.'

It was sweet of Billie to defend him, but she didn't know

what had gone on in their relationship. They'd always been careful not to let their problems spill out in public.

'Honestly, things hadn't been great between us for a while. We'd started to argue a lot. Perhaps if we'd tried counselling or a trial separation, we might have been able to work things out, but I'd been too proud to let anyone know we were struggling.' His fault again. He'd wanted to hold on to the fairy tale that they were happily married. Sinead was the only family he had left, and he couldn't face up to the fact that he was losing her. A cruel irony that she'd been taken anyway without them ever having the opportunity to patch things up.

'I didn't know you two were having problems.' Billie seemed almost more surprised at that fact than by his confession.

Patrick shrugged. 'We'd started to drift apart. Wanted different things. But we were very good at putting on a show, apparently. I feel guilty that we weren't in a good place when she died, guilty over the row we had, and guilty to even think about moving on. I clearly wasn't a good husband to Sinead.'

'Deep down, you know that's not true. You were good together, but everyone has their struggles. It doesn't mean you didn't love one another. I'm sorry you've been holding on to all of that, because Sinead's death was just a tragic accident. No one was to blame. Especially you. And you deserve to move on with your life.'

Patrick knew nothing was going to change her mind on that, but if they carried on this conversation, he'd end up telling her about his father, too. Something he wasn't ready to talk about yet.

'Anyway, I just want you to understand why I like to

help where I can. Right or wrong, I'm not happy about accepting money because my wife died. So if I can do something for others, I will. I thought I was doing a good thing for Anna and her mother.' He was getting tetchy because the more they talked about it, the more he was reminded of what had happened.

'You were. You have. I didn't mean to upset you. Sorry. And thank you for my dress, too. I should have said that first. Especially when you got those lovely shoes and bag.' Billie sounded despondent. Not the atmosphere he'd hoped to cultivate on today's outing. Especially when she hadn't done anything wrong.

'Don't forget about the hair comb.' He pointed out the pearl accessory still embedded in her hair.

Billie's hand flew to her mouth. 'I forgot all about it. Oh my goodness. Did I inadvertently shoplift a hair accessory? I'm mortified. We'll have to go back to the shop before I get arrested.'

Patrick grinned. Although he was glad they'd changed the subject, he didn't want her to freak out on him. 'Relax. It's paid for. I just thought you'd grown attached to it.'

Billie carefully released her chestnut tresses and put the hair comb in the box her shoes were nestled in. 'Patrick James, you're incorrigible.'

He was just thankful that they'd moved past the talk about Sinead's death. The subject never sat well. It was something he tried not to think about on a daily basis. Every now and then when he did something like donate the insurance money to special causes, or buy a dress, it was tinged with something dark. As though using his guilt money to benefit others was going to feel dirty, no matter how good his intentions were.

He finished his coffee, the bitter taste in his mouth not just coming from the special roast in house blend. 'Right, I've got to nip back and get my credit card. Then we'll find somewhere nice for lunch.'

'Sounds good to me.' Billie collected her bags and followed him, but the day already felt as though it had been ruined. Making Billie, or anyone, happy could never erase his guilty conscience.

They paused at the car for her to deposit her purchases into the boot before returning to the shop. Billie wouldn't have been surprised if they'd planned a parade in his honour given the amount of money he'd just dropped in the store. It was just like Patrick to step in like that with an offer of help. After all, he'd done his fair share for her, and not just today. There weren't many men out there who would take any notice of a woman upset about not being able to afford a dress, never mind get involved. Unsurprising also that he hadn't waited around for their reaction or praise. He'd simply slipped his credit card to Kiki and left. These days people only tended to be generous if they were filming it to show others how virtuous they were, often making themselves into internet stars. Patrick wasn't one for the spotlight, and it proved there was no ulterior motive other than being kind.

Even if he didn't believe he was entitled to any of the benefits Sinead's will had bestowed upon him, making these acts of kindness possible. Billie had known Sinead well enough to understand her intentions. Although she apparently hadn't known her and Patrick enough to realise there'd been problems in their marriage. Theirs had seemed a closer relationship than the one Billie had with

Thom. On the evenings they'd spent together socialising, Patrick and Sinead had always been checking each other were okay. Billie had seen the little physical touches between them, noticeable because Thom barely paid any attention to her in the same way.

Perhaps she'd viewed it through rose-tinted glasses. Only seeing what was going on at the surface, never looking beyond that to spoil the fantasy of a relationship she'd believed was possible. The one she'd tried to replicate with Thom by being the woman she'd thought he wanted.

It was a pity Patrick had never been able to confide in her before today. Spending all these years blaming himself unnecessarily. Feeling guilty that he hadn't been the perfect husband in his eyes. Causing himself more pain on top of the huge loss of his wife. No wonder he'd struggled to move on when he was carrying that burden. Secrets which he should have been able to share with her. Perhaps Billie hadn't been as good a friend as she'd thought. All she could do now was continue to reassure him that he hadn't caused Sinead's death in the hope one day he would start to believe it.

No matter how far they might have drifted apart in the last years of their marriage, Billie knew they'd loved each other once. She was still sure Sinead didn't want her husband to suffer any more than possible should something happen to her, or worry about money or a mortgage without her income.

Billie wished anyone in her life had been as considerate for her. It wasn't as though her family couldn't have afforded to set her up for life if they'd wanted to. But they hadn't, nor would she have let them. Not when they'd made it so obvious when she was growing up that she had been a mistake at best, a disappointment and a nuisance at worst. Not the son they'd cherished, and who'd ultimately rendered her completely invisible. Just like when Thom had apparently found someone better too. It seemed she was simply a convenient placeholder until a superior version of her arrived, apparently more deserving of love.

Perhaps that was why she found Patrick such an important part of her life. He'd never made her feel second best. And she couldn't begrudge anyone receiving the same treatment. That moment of joy, of being seen, of being on the receiving end of Patrick's kindness and generosity.

She only wished he knew how much this simple gesture would mean to Anna and her mother.

As suspected, Kiki went into raptures at seeing him enter the store again. 'Mr James, I can't tell you how much we've appreciated your custom today. Your unbelievable generosity. Anna couldn't stop crying when I told her what you'd done. You made her and her mother very happy. I can't believe you just walked in here and bought someone a dress.'

'It's his thing, you know?' Billie's remark earned her a raised eyebrow from Patrick.

The cynic in her couldn't help but wonder if Kiki's commission had some bearing on her fawning over Patrick as much as she was now.

'Can I just get my card and the invoice, please?' Of course, he did his best to brush the whole thing away. To keep it low-key to avoid anyone making a fuss and drawing attention to him.

'They'll be sorry they missed you. They really wanted to say thank you and left you an invitation for the wedding. I can pass on your details if you'd like?' Kiki reluctantly handed over his card along with the wedding invitation, seemingly trying to delay the end of their interaction for the day as much as possible.

'No, that's okay. Thanks.' Patrick did his best to end the conversation and get out of the shop as quickly as he could. He left Billie trailing after him and Kiki shouting her goodbyes and repeated thanks.

Out on the street, Billie decided to join in with the love-in, throwing her arms around him and hugging him tight. 'You're a good man, Patrick James.'

She felt him stiffen in her arms, and she hated that he couldn't see in himself what everyone else saw in him.

'Anyway, about that lunch…' She decided it was better to change the subject completely and put him at ease when he'd gone so far out of his way to do the same for others.

'Don't worry, I haven't forgotten. Though I think you deserve somewhere better than a greasy spoon when you're dressed to impress. Why don't I take you somewhere a little more salubrious? It'll be good practice for the awards dinner. Speaking of which, I booked us a room at the hotel to save us both having to make our way back from Belfast at that time of night.'

'Okay…' Billie couldn't help but sound a little apprehensive when it seemed as though he'd booked only one room. She didn't relish the thought of spending the whole night fantasising about the man next to her when nothing was going to happen. Their friendship had got them both through the toughest times of their lives, and she wasn't going to jeopardise it by trying to force him to feel more for her. That was simply courting disaster when it was clear he had a lot of emotional trauma to work through. Patrick needed a friend more than anything.

'Twin beds, of course. There's no point paying for two rooms when we're doing everything else together.'

Patrick made it sound so logical, yet Billie couldn't help but think money had been no object in the boutique. Why was he more concerned with saving a few pennies than keeping them at a safe distance now?

It was likely his way of asserting boundaries once and for all. His way of letting her down gently, reminding her that they were friends, and as such, there should be nothing to fear in sharing a room. By imagining that as something more romantic, she ran the risk of alienating him altogether.

This awards dinner was going to be a huge deal in her life in more than one way. She just hoped it would be for the right reasons, and not something she'd come to regret.

CHAPTER SIX

BILLIE WAS BUOYED up about the upcoming awards and looking forward to a night out in general. Patrick, too, had seemed in good spirits on the car journey to the hotel. He'd picked her up after he had finished his shift at the hospital, and they'd checked into the hotel about an hour ago. That's when things had started to become a little… intense. As though when confined into one small hotel room, all of those feelings they'd been trying to keep at bay had suddenly returned with a vengeance. At least, that was true in her case. She had no idea what went on in Patrick's head anymore.

He'd showered and changed first, at her insistence. She'd had her pampering in the morning, getting her nails and hair done specially for the occasion. It wasn't often she got to glam up, and she was going to make the most of it.

The only problem was having to watch him strut around the room in just a towel, collecting his clothes after his shower. His hair was wet and clinging to the nape of his neck. Those broad shoulders tapering to a vee into the terry towelling, not to mention the smooth contours of his chest, begged for her attention. That's when she realised the night was going to be torturous.

She didn't imagine Patrick as a pyjamas type of guy, and the thought of him lying so close only in his boxers would keep her awake all night. Unless, of course, he slept in the buff...

It didn't even help when he'd dressed in his tuxedo, his body covered up but looking no less handsome. If it wasn't for her carefully styled hair, she would have had herself a cold shower. In fact, he looked very handsome, like an action hero, but she wasn't about to tell him that. Things still felt a little tense between them as it was. Awkward even. She got the impression he regretted telling her about the problems he and Sinead had been having in their marriage and the row leading up to her accident. She never would have guessed, but she supposed that had been the point. Patrick and Sinead hadn't wanted anyone to know their relationship was less than perfect. It was sad to think they'd perhaps been as miserable as she and Thom after all. More so knowing Patrick had been carrying such an unnecessary burden of guilt over it all, on top of his grief. It was no wonder his head was in such turmoil.

The last thing he needed was his friend crushing on him and confusing him about the nature of their relationship. He needed to cut loose for a while, too, and hopefully tonight would prove the perfect opportunity for them both to forget their problems.

'Will I do?' he asked, trying to tie his bow tie.

'I think you'll pass muster.' Billie kept her voice steady even as she helped straighten his tie. They were so close, she could smell the clean scent of soap on his body and feel his eyes watching her intently.

Sharing a room was going to make it difficult for her

to keep her growing feelings for Patrick in check when he had such an effect on her. When every touch or look had her pulse racing and her imagination running away with her.

She swallowed hard. 'There. I think that's you all ready to go. Just let me throw my dress on, and we can get some welcome drinks.'

She was going to need them.

Armed with new underwear, her dress and her make-up bag, she hurried into the bathroom and closed the door behind her. She sat on the edge of the bath and took deep breaths, trying desperately to compose herself. They had a long night together ahead of them, and she couldn't spend the whole time lusting after Patrick. It would be exhausting, and she was already going to be emotionally drained with all of the socialising which would be expected of her, too.

That old, familiar inferiority complex tended to raise its head on these kinds of occasions. Where she couldn't help but feel like an imposter. Tonight would be full of the country's rich and famous, as well as heroes who'd performed more courageous acts than she had. It was hard not to think of herself as less than worthy of a place here when her parents and Thom had made her feel as though she didn't deserve anyone's praise or recognition. The only person who had ever managed to convince her she was as good as everyone else was Patrick, and that's why she needed him by her side tonight. Reminding her that she was special in her own way, too.

Even if he wasn't happy about what she'd done to earn her place in the nominations, putting her own life in jeopardy in the process. Or that he couldn't feel about her the way she wanted him to. Still, she was a grown-up, and she would simply have to get over whatever these new feelings for him were and accept he saw her only as a friend. Something she needed right now.

Once she managed to pull herself together, she put on her dress, freshened her make-up and faced herself in the mirror. Billie hardly recognised the woman looking back. She spent her whole life dressing for comfort and practicality. Being a nurse was about taking care of others, and there wasn't any room for being vain. The same went for her role on the search and rescue team. More so when she was usually soaked through, and caked in mud. Now, though, she'd never felt so glamorous. If she couldn't get Patrick to take notice of her tonight, she never would.

She wriggled and stretched, and did her best to reach the zipper on her dress, but had to admit defeat. It wouldn't do to start struggling and sweating in her fabulous gown, surely ruining the aesthetic Kiki had been aiming for.

In the end she was forced to emerge from the bathroom to seek assistance. 'Can you help me with the zip?'

'No problem.' Patrick crossed the hotel room floor to lend a hand, brushing her hair over her shoulder so he could pull the zipper up. Every brush of his fingers along her spine was electric, charging her body with so much energy she thought she was going to combust. It was just as well they were going to be in a very public forum where there would be plenty of people to keep them apart.

'You look amazing,' he said softly.

'Thanks.' Billie sprang away from his touch and grabbed up her bag, eager to escape this stifling tension and get some fresh air. And she was going to need a drink.

* * *

'Thanks.' Patrick helped himself to a glass of cheap champagne from the tray of a passing waiter. Billie had been whisked away for an introduction to the VIPs in attendance for a photo shoot. Rather than feel abandoned, he was glad of the space, even though his eyes kept straying towards the corner of the room where she was being celebrated. That dress, the way the soft waves of her hair were tumbling over her bare shoulders, and the sound of her laughter all kept catching his attention.

He'd known he'd made a mistake in booking that room the moment she stepped out of the bathroom and asked him to zip up her dress. In another world, they would have just been a couple getting ready for a night out, but in this situation, it felt very much like torture. Seeing her, touching her, yet doing his best to pretend it wasn't affecting him.

Booking one room had been his way of saying he was in control, that he wasn't going to let his feelings get in the way of their friendship. A way of saying that despite kissing her a couple of times, nothing had changed between them, and sharing a room wasn't a big deal. That plan had massively backfired. All it had done was intensify the feelings he already had towards her. Not least the attraction.

He downed his drink just as she made her way back over to him.

'I think I need one of those, too, to settle my nerves.' Her nervous energy was as clear as her excitement about being here as she kept touching her hair and pulling at the front of her dress.

Patrick grabbed another glass of champagne and put it in her hands to keep them busy. 'You're doing great.'

He knew how far out of her comfort zone tonight was, not only because it was such a public event but because of the knock she'd taken to her confidence thanks to Thom. The man had chosen someone else over Billie, and he knew how much that had affected her. He'd been there when she'd cried, asking what was wrong with her. Why she hadn't been enough for Thom. Questions Patrick couldn't answer because he didn't know. As far as he was concerned, she was perfect. Though she'd never accepted it when he'd told her and accused him of being biased.

Tonight was all about being judged. Her heroics would be compared to the others in her category, and there would inevitably be some element of critique from other attendees on how she looked and what she was wearing.

'Thanks for coming with me. The thought of walking in here alone was a terrifying prospect.'

As she drained the last of her drink, an announcement was made for all the attendees to take their seats.

'I'm here for you,' Patrick said and slipped his hand into hers.

She gave him a grateful smile and squeezed his hand, walking a little taller as they made their way to their table. It gave him a warm, tingly feeling inside knowing that he was able to do something to make her feel better. To make her feel safe. Even if it was just reassuring her she wasn't here alone.

Her face was flushed as she glanced around the room. 'I can't believe I'm hobnobbing with the rich and famous.'

'You deserve it. As long as you're not disappointed about being stuck with me for dinner.' Despite the fact that he was upset she'd acted recklessly in earning her nomination, Patrick wanted her to have a good time. Hopefully it would give her that confidence boost she needed, a reminder that she was someone special.

'Not at all. I need some time out. You help me keep my feet on the ground.' She leaned her head against his shoulder, and he automatically put his arm around her and squeezed her tight.

'I'm glad you're enjoying yourself. Personally, I'm just here for the free dinner.' At least the food might take his mind off Billie momentarily. The comment earned him a slap on the arm. 'Oh, and you, of course.'

'I should think so, too. You're supposed to be my cheerleader for the evening.'

'Don't worry, I've got my pompoms at the ready.' Patrick pulled out the mini sparkly pompoms he'd hidden in his pockets. He had meant to whip them out when she was mentioned during the ceremony, but apparently he couldn't wait that long.

The sight brought a hearty laugh from Billie, her eyes sparkling with merriment and her chest rising and falling perilously from the bodice of her dress. Thankfully the starter arrived, proving a temporary distraction in the nick of time as he popped the pompoms back in his pockets.

'I can't believe you did that.' Billie was still laughing as she supped her soup.

'Be careful you don't spill that down your dress. I don't want the blame for ruining your big moment if you have to go on stage with soup all over you.'

Billie snorted. 'That's a big assumption. There are a lot of people here who deserve an award more than I do.'

Patrick put his serious face on again. 'You're here for a reason, Billie. You're an amazing woman.'

He made her blush, but she would have to get used to people complimenting her tonight when this was a celebration of the woman she was. It was a recognition of everything Patrick already knew about her.

Instead of the way she usually brushed a compliment away, this time she simply said, 'Thank you.'

They carried on with their next course, making small talk with the other guests beside them. Along with the local news anchor and his young girlfriend, they were sitting with an eight-year-old boy and his parents. Elijah was one of the young people up for an award for phoning an ambulance when his mother had an epileptic fit.

'He saved my life,' the proud mum said over the chocolate fondants when they came out. 'I had an epileptic seizure, fell and banged my head. Elijah phoned for an ambulance and kept me comfortable and safe until the paramedics got to the house.'

'It's hard enough for an adult to stay calm in a situation like that. Well done, Elijah.' Patrick toasted his champagne glass to the boy's glass of cola.

'And what about you two? What did you do to get nominated?' Elijah's father politely asked.

'Oh, I'm not nominated for anything. I'm just here to support Billie.' Far from being embarrassed that he hadn't done anything worthy of an award, he was proud of Billie and the recognition she was finally getting.

'He's being too modest. Patrick was part of the air ambulance crew that helped with the rescue of a man missing up in the Mourne Mountains.' Of course, Billie wouldn't let him go uncelebrated, but this was her moment, not his.

'So you're part of a search and rescue team, then?' The news anchor whose face Patrick recognised but couldn't quite put a name to seemed very interested in their story. No doubt he was looking for content for the next feel-good bulletin.

'Dog search and rescue. Our team located the man who'd fallen and injured himself, and the air ambulance got him to hospital. All part of the job, really.' Billie tried to dismiss the incident as a run-of-the-mill story that happened every day, but Patrick knew better.

'What Billie is neglecting to tell you is that she climbed down the mountain to administer first aid to the patient before we got there. Putting herself in some danger, might I add.' He fixed Billie with a look which said he'd never forget it and would have asked her to swear never to do it again if he hadn't known her better.

'Oh.' Cue impressed looks from the local celeb and everyone else at the table.

'And was the man okay? Did he recover?' The glamorous young woman accompanying her older date seemed engrossed in the story.

'Yes. He made a full recovery,' Billie quickly updated her.

'It could have been a very different story if he'd been left there much longer, though. Exposure and hypothermia are a risk, aren't they? I've reported on lots of cases over the years of people getting lost that haven't had quite the same happy outcome.' The news guy seemed keen to be involved, too, and Patrick could see how much every question and show of interest was bolstering Billie's confidence.

'Well, yes. They can be very serious conditions if not treated in time.' Billie was very good at holding court even though Patrick knew she didn't enjoy the attention usually. At least this was an area she was passionate about and had no trouble conversing in.

'The man was very lucky to have you in his corner.' The celeb held his glass aloft in toast to Billie, and she blushed a little at the praise. Though Patrick was sure she was sitting a little taller in her chair as her success was celebrated.

'What kind of dog do you have?' Now it was young Elijah's turn to show an interest.

'A border collie.'

'What's her name?'

'Fliss.'

'Do you have any pictures?'

Billie smiled, producing her phone, which Patrick knew held dozens of photos of Fliss at home and in action with the search and rescue team. Eventually the conversation was interrupted as the MC arrived on stage to start the awards ceremony. Of course, the sponsors got their due recognition before the real celebration of guests began.

The stories behind the nominations were both heart-warming and inspiring of people going above and beyond what was expected of any mere mortal to help someone in need. Making Billie an ideal nominee.

Patrick found himself watching her reactions to the recipients on stage as they collected their awards. The wide smiles as she clapped for the achievements, and the tears she had to dab away when emotions got the better of her. Her heart was too big for her to disguise how she felt at any given time. Just one of the things he admired about her.

And when Elijah won the award he was nominated for, she was on her feet clapping and cheering with his parents. Celebrating the win as if he was part of her family, too. She'd been through a whole range of emotions before it came to her turn.

'And now, the nominations for our heroes at work...' As Billie's category was announced, she grabbed Patrick's hand.

He was nervous for her, even though he knew she'd be fine if she didn't win. It was the recognition which was important, and in his eyes, she was always going to be a winner regardless of the outcome.

Her eyes were trained on the stage as the regional weatherman read out the rest of the nominees and the stories which had earned them their places here tonight.

'And the winner is... Billie Wade.'

Patrick was on his feet before Billie, who seemed too stunned to move.

'I can't believe it.' Hand covering her mouth, she looked at Patrick as though she didn't know how to process what was happening.

'You won. Go get your award, Billie. You deserve it.' He helped her to her feet and clapped with everyone else as she made her way to the stage.

She accepted the glass award and shook hands with the presenter before stepping forward to the microphone. Patrick could see how nervous she was and knew her well enough to imagine she probably hadn't even prepared a speech for this moment.

'Thank you so much for this award. I can't believe I was even nominated when I was just doing my job, but thank you for the honour. I, er, have a lot of people to thank as I couldn't do what I do on my own. Firstly, my amazing dog, Fliss. The rest of the search and rescue team who put themselves out there whatever the weather. The air ambulance crew who are there whenever we need them and make all the difference when it comes to saving lives. Lastly, but most importantly, Dr Patrick James, who has always been there to rescue me, too. Thank you very much.' Billie locked eyes with him across the room as she held the award aloft, and his heart swelled with pride.

As she made her way back to the table, the smile never left her face. Her eyes shone with unshed tears and happiness. Patrick wished he could bottle this moment for her forever so she could always feel this way. Without thinking, he rushed to hug her, squeezing her close.

'Well done. I'm so proud of you, Billie.'

'Thanks,' she said a little breathlessly once he let go so she could sit down, accepting the congratulations from everyone else around them.

'I didn't really do anything to deserve a mention, but thank you.' It had been a touching moment for him to have her acknowledge him. They worked pretty well as a team inside and outside of work.

Billie sipped at her champagne. 'I'm still on a high. I don't think I'll come back to earth anytime soon.'

'Enjoy it.' He clinked his glass to hers, his heart full to see her so happy.

Billie was fit to burst with pride and excitement over her win. She was glad Patrick had been here to be part of it all when he was very much her partner in crime. He was the closest thing she had to family, cheering her on the way her parents had never done. It was a shame that they weren't here tonight, even though she hadn't expected it. Contact with them was minimum these days, but she had told them of the nomination. All she'd received in return was a text message saying, Well done, darling. If it had been Jaxon, there would have been a full-page ad in the national newspapers to celebrate him, but she was used to it. Unfortunately. Jaxon had eventually replied with, That's great, sis x. As much as she could hope for from her brother, who knew nothing, really, about her life, and vice versa. They'd never been close. Probably because of their parents and the great divide they seemed to have placed between them.

That's why Patrick being here to support her meant so much. She could always rely on him.

Once the awards ceremony was over, the staff cleared away the tables and set the scene for some music and dancing. Elijah and his family had gone on home, and the news anchor and his young date were too engrossed in one another to notice anyone else, leaving Patrick and Billie with only each other for company.

'Would you like to dance?' he asked, breaking the sudden silence and surprising her.

'I don't know. I'm not much of a dancer.' Billie couldn't remember the last time she'd danced with anyone in public. Probably at college.

'Come on. We're making memories tonight.' Patrick took her by the hand, apparently not taking no for an answer. Though the thought of slow dancing with him did have its appeal, it meant letting go of her award temporarily. Ultimately, holding on to him was a temptation she couldn't resist.

He was right. There was never going to be another chance for them to dance together. They were dressed to impress, and adrenaline raced through her veins. Tonight was everything she could have hoped for.

They joined the other couples dancing on the floor, and Patrick slid his hand around her waist, pulling her closer to him. She draped her arms around his neck and almost sighed her contentment to be there. He'd taken his jacket off now, and unbuttoned the first few buttons of his shirt, with his tie lying loosely around his neck. Looking relaxed and just as happy to be there with her.

'It's been a lovely night. Thank you,' she said as they swayed together to the love songs playing in the background.

'I didn't do anything. Thank you for inviting me.' His grin told her he'd enjoyed every moment, too, and Billie didn't want the night to end. She didn't want to go up to that hotel room with both of them retreating to their separate corners. It would be nice to carry on with this intimate connection and simply see where it took them. Tonight had emboldened her. She might never again feel as confident as she did right now, looking her best and buoyed by all the compliments and praise she'd received.

Long-term, she didn't know what it would mean for them, but tonight she wanted to be with Patrick without worrying about anything else.

Just as she was working up the courage to proposition him, there was a huge crash and the sound of breaking glass nearby. A shriek and a collective gasp made her aware that something serious had happened. Almost at once, the music was abruptly stopped, and the lights came up.

One of the young waiting staff was lying on the edge of the dance floor, her white blouse stained red with blood, glass and drinks spilled all around her.

Patrick didn't wait for the call for a doctor in the house before he was rushing to her aid with Billie following close behind.

'Can we give her some space, please? And can someone phone for an ambulance?' Patrick commanded the crowd before crouching down beside the terrified waitress.

'I… I slipped.'

'My name's Patrick. I'm a doctor. And this is Billie. She's a nurse. You might have seen her win an award tonight, so you know you're in good hands.' His grin was as reassuring to Billie as it was meant to be for the young girl.

'Paisley, is it?' Billie checked her name badge. 'Patrick's just going to check you over and see what's causing the bleeding. Can you tell us where it hurts?'

'My back.'

Billie could see the spilled drink on the floor, which she'd obviously slipped on, dropping the tray of glasses she was carrying. 'I'm sure the fall must have winded you.'

'I'm going to feel around your neck, Paisley. Is there any pain there?' Patrick was making sure there were no head or neck injuries before they attempted to move her.

'No, just my back.'

'Okay, we're going to roll you onto your side, Paisley, to see what's happening. If it causes you any more pain at all, let us know and we'll stop.' Patrick gave Billie that look which said he needed her help to move the girl, and between them, they gently rolled her onto her side.

'That's good, Paisley. We've got you.' Billie was holding her hand, leaving Patrick to examine her, but it became apparent at once what had happened. There was a shard of glass embedded in her back.

Thankfully the hotel manager arrived and handed them the meagre first aid kit they had. He stood anxiously to one side, watching them work and probably praying with everyone else that Paisley was going to be okay.

'I'm going to have to cut your shirt, Paisley, so we can treat your injury,' Billie let her know before she took the scissors out of the box and cut away the shirt to give Patrick better access.

'What is it? What's happened?' Paisley tensed, squeezing her hand and understandably distressed about what was happening.

'You've got some cuts from the broken glass. I'm going to clean up the wound, and Patrick will make sure there are no shards left.' Billie removed the alcohol wipes and began cleaning the site whilst Patrick used tweezers to remove the rest of the glass until there was just one large shard which had been embedded deep into the tissue.

'I think it's going to need stitches, but if we can get it patched up for now, it should hold until we get you to the hospital, Paisley. There's one piece of glass. It's quite deep, so it might hurt a bit until I've got it out.'

Paisley whimpered as Patrick warned her what was coming next. The poor girl was clearly frightened as well as in pain.

'Just take nice deep breaths for me, Paisley,' Billie counselled, watching as Patrick got hold of the shard.

He mouthed the countdown from three, and on one, he tugged on the glass. Paisley cried out, and Billie moved quickly to push down on the wound. Patrick cleaned the wound and applied a sterile dressing.

'All done for now. Sorry about that last bit, but you must have fallen hard onto it. The staff at the hospital will make sure there's no more glass in there. Then they'll stitch the wound up properly for you.' Patrick sat back on his heels, clearly relieved that he'd got that last piece out without too much trouble.

Someone handed Billie a blanket. Once she'd dressed Paisley's wound with some gauze, she covered her with it. As the drama was over, people began to mill away, clearing a path for the ambulance crew once they arrived. Patrick gave them a rundown of what had happened and the treatment they'd given Paisley in the interim. Billie moved aside to let the other medics take over and was soon joined by Patrick.

'She's going to be all right. I know it's not the end to the evening we had planned, but I'm glad we were here for her.' Patrick put his arm around Billie, and she found herself relaxing again. He had that magic touch, able to put her at ease when she needed it.

They watched as Paisley left with the ambulance crew, waving her thanks to them. The manager who had been watching the proceedings came over to offer his thanks, too.

'I can't thank you enough. If I had another award to give you, I would, but this will have to do.' He handed Patrick a bottle of champagne and shook both of their hands.

'No problem. I'm just glad she's going to be all right.

Now, if you'll excuse us, we've had a long night. I think we're going to retire to our room before there are any more medical emergencies.' Patrick took Billie's hand and was about to leave when she remembered her award was still sitting on the table.

'I'm not going without this.' She reached back and grabbed it, clutching it tight, determined to get it home in one piece. The one thing she had in her life to be truly proud of.

When they got into the lift to take them to their room and the doors closed, Billie let out a sigh of relief. 'I can't wait to take this dress off and get back to being me.'

Patrick raised an eyebrow at her, making her tut.

'You know what I mean. I've enjoyed the night, but it's draining, isn't it, having to be "on" all of the time.' It was a reminder that she was always able to be herself around Patrick. She didn't feel the same emotional exhaustion after being in his company.

It hadn't been the same with Thom. She'd always felt as though she had to be someone more for him because it didn't seem enough to simply be herself. So she wasn't always honest with him if she was feeling low or if she had worries. She tried to be the perfect girlfriend in an attempt to get him to love her. Probably as a hangover from her childhood when she'd tried to please her parents the same way. Ironic when she still hadn't been enough for them and they'd all found a replacement, leaving her feeling like a failure.

Patrick had seen her at her lowest and was still around, supporting her like no one else ever had in her life.

'Well, I think you were fabulous tonight, and you can relax now.' Patrick held up the bottle of champagne, but the best way she could relax would be to get out of this dress and into her comfy clothes again.

As amazing as the dress looked and felt, she was more at home in casual wear.

Just as they left the lift and Patrick opened the room door, Billie caught sight of a red stain on the hem of her dress. 'Oh no. I've got blood on my dress.'

'Come into the bathroom and we'll see if we can get the stain out.' He turned the light on and lifted the bottom of her dress to run it under the tap. Although some of the blood swirled away, the outline of the stain remained.

'It's ruined,' she cried, more distraught at how much it had cost Patrick, and she'd only worn it once. Absurdly, it made her feel as though she'd failed him in some way. At the very least, the discovery spoiled the night.

'Take it off.' He held his hand out and said it with such authority that Billie didn't have time to think about it.

Until she was suddenly standing in the small bathroom beside him clad only in her underwear. She supposed she should be thankful she'd treated herself to some new lingerie for the evening. A strapless champagne silk bra with matching French knickers. She handed over her dress before grabbing a bath-robe from the back of the door, though she hadn't missed the appreciative look Patrick had shot her. The thought of it made her too hot under the terry towelling.

'I, er, I'll try a little bit of soap and water and leave it to dry. We'll get it to the dry cleaners first thing in the morning.' He gently dabbed at the stain, then hung the dress up in the wardrobe, the spot unfortunately still noticeable.

'I'm sorry I ruined the dress.'

'Don't be daft. I'm sure we can get it sorted. Besides, it's hardly your fault. A patient is more important than a dress.' There wasn't a trace of temper regardless of how much he'd spent on a gown which might well be ruined. Billie was sure Thom would have gone through the roof, blaming her for being so careless. She never could do anything right, it seemed. Something she'd been used to growing up when her parents had never been happy with anything she did, either. Always criticising her whilst praising every move her brother made. Patrick was the only person in her life who'd never done that. Just one more reason for her to like him, to enjoy having him in her life. As well as increasing her want for something more. Even if just for one night.

'Thanks, Patrick.'

'It's not a problem.' He flashed her a reassuring smile, which simply cemented the realisation that she was falling for her best friend.

Patrick popped the cork from the champagne and poured it into two coffee mugs. 'Sorry, it's the best I can do.'

He handed one to Billie, who was perched on the end of one of the beds, thankfully covered up in a bath-robe now. It hadn't occurred to him when dealing with the bloodstain that he'd be knocked sideways by the sight of her in her underwear. At the time, all he'd been thinking about was trying to save the dress. It would have been a pity for Billie if she never got to wear it again.

However, the sight of her wearing next to nothing almost sent him into meltdown. He'd always known how beautiful Billie was, but there was no mistaking how sexy she was now, either. He needed a drink to take his mind off the fact all she was wearing under that robe was a few scraps of silk clinging to her curves.

'Thanks. It's been a hell of a night, hasn't it?' Her smile was as disarming as her attire, though he detected a little bit of something in it which wasn't entirely joyous.

'Is everything all right, Billie? I know it didn't go quite the way we planned, but you won. You should be very proud of yourself.'

She sighed, set her glass on the bedside table and lay back. Her dressing gown parted to expose the smooth white skin of her thighs.

Patrick sat down on the bed opposite and did his best to focus on her face.

She rolled over onto one side. 'I am. It's just… I know I'm being silly, but I wish my parents had been here, or shown any interest at all.'

He was surprised at the mention of her parents, or her apparent upset that they hadn't witnessed the event, knowing that her relationship was somewhat strained with them. 'Did they know about it?'

'I texted to tell them. Mother congratulated me, but that's as far as it went.'

'I'm sorry. Perhaps it was too short notice for them to attend?' He was grappling for an excuse why her parents couldn't see what an amazing daughter they had, but nothing seemed adequate to cover for them. They should have been here championing their daughter's success and the woman she was.

Billie shook her head. 'No, that's just typical of my parents. I thought by reaching out, we might bridge that gap that's opened up between us, but I'll have to admit defeat. We're never going to be close.'

'You never talk about your family much.' It occurred to him that in all the years he'd known her, he'd never met her parents or her brother. In fact, neither of them really talked about their pasts before coming to the hospital where they'd met. As though life hadn't really begun until then. For two people who were so close, it was surprising that they'd never discussed their families. Perhaps she was hiding a guilty secret as big as his.

Billie shrugged, but the pain was obvious in her eyes when she spoke of her family. 'There's not a whole lot to tell. Financially, I had no worries growing up. My father inherited land and money from his parents and made a good few property investments himself. I was well provided for in that way. Less so when it came to them showing me any affection. They saved that for Jaxon when he came along two years later. I guess I just wasn't enough for them any more than I was for Thom. The dynamic has never really changed over the years. Jaxon is my parents' favourite, and they've never shown much interest in anything I do. We're in contact but not close. I just don't think I'm someone they want in their lives.'

'I'm sorry, Billie. You should never have been made to feel that way. It's their loss.' He was angry that anyone would treat her as if she didn't matter when she was such an amazing person who gave so much to others.

She gave a sad sort of half smile. 'It is what it is, I guess. I moved out and made a life of my own. I don't harbour any grudges or jealousy towards Jaxon, but I guess we'll never be close. It's sad, but that's the way it is.'

Patrick wondered if that was why they'd been so drawn to one another. Two lost souls looking to fill that space in their lives where their parents should have been. Although in his case, it was his fault that he'd lost his. As far as he could see, Billie had done nothing wrong except being born.

'I'm sorry they can't see the amazing person you are, but you know you've done nothing wrong. When it comes to parents, I'm afraid I can't say the same.' He hadn't meant to make the admission, but he supposed the alcohol and this unburdening of souls had made it inevitable. If there was one person he could spill his dark secret to without fear of judgement, he knew it was Billie. He'd already told her about Sinead, and the world hadn't ended. Billie was still here supporting him. Perhaps it would do him good to get it off his chest once and for all. Then she could see what a bad child really was and maybe forgive herself.

'Both of your parents have passed, haven't they?'

He nodded. 'Dad passed just before I went to university, and Mum a few years later.'

'I'm sorry.' Billie didn't follow up on what he'd meant about doing something wrong, but he could see she was waiting expectantly for him to tell her in his own time.

Patrick imitated her movements, setting down his champagne and lying on his bed so he was facing her. 'It's my fault my Dad died, too.'

He didn't sugar-coat it, and waited to see the horror on Billie's face. Instead she simply asked, 'How?'

Patrick swallowed hard, the unexpected emotion of reliving that time suddenly threatening to overwhelm him. 'We'd had an argument that day. He was a farmer, and the farm had been in our family for generations, but I wanted to be a doctor. I'd been accepted to medical school in Scotland, but he was angry that I wasn't going to carry on the family tradition. I guess you weren't the only one who was a disappointment.'

He tried to bring some levity to the moment, but it fell flat. Billie remained silent, waiting for him to finish the sordid tale. 'Anyway, the row got heated. I told him I was going to live my own life and stormed out of the house. That night he had a massive heart attack and died. The stress killed him. I killed him just like I killed Sinead.'

'No, you didn't. I can understand that having that happen twice in your life to loved ones was distressing, but you are not responsible, Patrick. You have to believe that. You're a medical professional. You know this sort of thing happens all the time, and no one is to blame. Could there have been a history of heart problems that triggered it?' Lovely Billie was trying hard to absolve him of blame, but Patrick knew he'd been the trigger. He could still remember how red his father's face had been, his blood pressure at the boiling point as he'd raged about the legacy his son had just trashed for his own selfish dreams. If Patrick had stayed instead of walking away, he might have been able to save him.

'Nothing that we knew of, but he didn't go to the doctor if he could help it. He didn't trust them. Probably part of the reason he was against me going to medical school, too.' His father liked a drink and a smoke, but that didn't change the fact that Patrick had likely triggered the fatal heart attack with his plans for the future which didn't include the family farm.

After his father's death, Patrick couldn't bear to stay at the farm at all and be reminded of that horrible time. Eventually he'd got his mother to agree to selling up when there was no one else to run the place.

'I know the type,' Billie said with a half grin. They'd both met their fair share of older men who were suspicious of young medical staff and fought no matter how hard they were trying to help them. 'And we both know that statistically, men often leave it too late to get help. The chances were that he was experiencing some health problems leading up to that moment, but he'd been too scared, or proud, to get treatment.'

If he could get past his guilt and grief to use common sense, Patrick knew she was right, but it was difficult to pull himself out of that villain role when he'd been living in it for so long. It was compounded by his mother putting the blame squarely on his shoulders without ever realising that perhaps her grief was making her lash out irrationally. She'd needed someone to blame, just as he had when Sinead died, and he'd seemed the obvious choice on both occasions.

'Anyway, that's the story of how I killed my father. My mother never forgave me. We had to sell the farm, but I did my best to look after her until she died a couple of years later.'

'It was not your fault, Patrick. You know if it was the other way around, you'd be telling me not to be so silly. To take a step back and try to view what happened objectively. If you could only do that, you'd see it was simply unfortunate timing. Why are you so determined to blame yourself?' Billie was on her feet now, reaching out to him, trying to comfort him, but he didn't deserve it.

'Because it's my fault. It's always my fault. Everyone in my life gets hurt. Why do you think I don't want to let anything happen between us? I can't risk you getting hurt too, Billie.' His voice cracked as he opened up completely to her. He hadn't planned to say anything, to reveal any of his feelings or secrets, but now he'd said it, there was no way of pushing it back in. This time there was nowhere to hide.

Billie stroked his face, and he wanted to bury his face in her hand and forget everything except the softness of her touch. 'Is that what you really think, you silly sod? Is that why you keep backing away?'

Patrick nodded. 'I don't want you to get hurt, too. I don't want to risk what we've got together in case I ruin everything.'

Billie cupped his face in both hands and placed a soft kiss on his lips. A whisper of comfort to soothe his worries. It almost worked.

'I'm not your father, and I'm not Sinead. Don't let misplaced guilt stop you from feeling whatever you're feeling. You have to move on and stop punishing yourself for things that weren't your fault. If you want to be with me, at least try, because it's killing me thinking you don't want me as much as I want you.'

Patrick's eyebrows almost shot into his scalp as she said it. He hadn't expected her to reciprocate his feelings, and he knew what it had taken for her to say it. The fear was there in her eyes that she'd ruined things. He recognised it because it was the one thing he'd been truly afraid of. Losing her.

'What if things don't work out?' His voice was a whisper, as though he was afraid to say it aloud.

Billie smiled. 'I'd like to at least try before we go straight to the catastrophising. Isn't about time we both had some fun at least?'

'Fun, you say?'

'I'm not asking for a lifetime commitment, Patrick. Just that we're honest about our feelings. No more pretending that we don't feel something more than friendship.'

'Oh, what I'm feeling is definitely more than friendship.' Now that he'd got everything off his chest, and he and Billie were opening up to one another, he was definitely feeling more uninhibited.

'Yeah? Why don't you show me what it is you're feeling, Dr James?' This was the first time he'd seen a flirty Billie. She grabbed his shirt and pulled him closer, and he liked it.

Patrick wound his fingers in her hair and kissed her long and hard. Wanting to show her exactly how he felt about her. Billie moaned and moulded her body to his, giving in to the kiss and completely undoing him in the process. Any restraint he'd been trying to hold on to melted away as she wrapped her arms around his neck and kissed him in return.

He'd waited so long, held back from expressing his emotions so long that it was tempting to rush things, but Billie deserved more. She deserved romance and seduction and a million things he would have done differently if he'd known this was going to happen.

'We don't have to do anything tonight if you want to take things slowly.' He broke off the kissing before they got too carried away and ended up regretting it. It was one thing admitting they were attracted to one another, but actually sleeping together was going to change everything between them forever.

'I'm done pretending I don't want this, Patrick. I want you.' She set to work unbuttoning his shirt and letting him know in no uncertain terms that she was ready. It was a big step for both of them, but as much as he wanted to slow things down, passion was already overriding common sense, it would seem.

Billie's heart was hammering in her chest as she portrayed a boldness she wasn't quite feeling. Yes, she wanted Patrick, but it had been a long time since she'd done this. This was a huge step for them both. She just hoped her libido wasn't going to ruin everything between them in the future.

Patrick held her gaze as he slowly undid the belt on her robe. She was holding her breath, waiting for him to see her, to touch her, to love her. When the robe finally fell open, Patrick pushed both sides away, baring her body to him. Even though she was wearing underwear, the way he was looking at her, she might as well have been naked. That undisguised lust in his eyes was enough to give her an ego boost. The new confidence he managed to instil in her drove her to begin undressing him, too. The only sound in the room was the rustle of clothes as they fell to the floor and the hitch in her breath as he stood naked before her.

He moved towards her and kissed her again. There was something sensual about the feel of silk against her skin. More so when Patrick was caressing her through it, touching her intimately without making skin-on-skin contact. He slid the silk against her most sensitive parts until she was cursing the thin barrier between them. He cupped her breasts, tracing his thumbs across the mounds rising from the silk confines. He drove her crazy, making her whimper as he flicked his tongue against hers.

He was taking his sweet time getting her naked, but her body was responding all the same. Wet and wanting.

Now he was sliding his hands under her silk knickers and cupping her buttocks, a possessive move that she had no complaint with. For tonight, she was his. There was no way of knowing what would come next for them, but for now, she was going to enjoy being with him the way she wanted to be. No more pretending this wasn't what she wanted.

Patrick was kissing her neck, nibbling at the sensitive skin behind her ear that made her gasp at his touch. Slowly he pushed her knickers down, and they fluttered to the floor. She was ready to burst with want for him. Who knew that undressing could be foreplay all on its own?

Eventually he unclipped her bra, and Billie's heart was pounding as he let it fall away, her breasts spilling into the palms of his hands. That strong pressure on her soft flesh brought some relief, and she gave a groan of satisfaction when he tugged her taut nipples between his fingers. The sound grew louder when he took those puckered pink buds into his mouth, licking and sucking on them until her legs were threatening to collapse from under her.

That was the moment he backed her onto the bed. She was spreadeagled below him. He had a power over her body she hadn't realised until now, when his every touch brought her closer to ecstasy. His eyes were dark as he looked down on her, sheathing himself with a condom he'd taken from his jacket. Patrick looked sexy as hell.

He lowered himself slowly on top of her, kissing and nuzzling her until she was completely relaxed against him. Then he thrust. That first contact, sharp but satisfying, drew a gasp from her lips. Patrick caught it with his and kissed her until she was moaning and ready for more. He moved slowly inside her, prolonging the pleasure for both of them in the process. That exquisite sensation of being filled completely was something she hadn't realised she'd needed so badly.

She clung to him greedily, wanting all of him all at once. Her hands, her fingers, her legs wrapped around him, holding him as close as possible. If this was the only time they got to have together, she wanted to remember every moment. Relive the feel of him and everything he was making her feel in return.

More than anything, it was the intensity of Patrick's gaze upon her which was the ultimate turn-on. Making her feel like the most beautiful, wanted woman in the world. Leaving her in no doubt about how he felt. This wasn't some casual, convenient hookup. She meant something to him. Only time would tell what that was, and if it was anything they could build on.

Not wishing to start spiralling into the consequences of tonight, Billie focused her attention back on Patrick. Sitting up to kiss him, moving her hips to meet his, she was determined to make him lose control for once. To know what it felt like to give in completely to his emotions. If all that was keeping him from being with her was a misplaced sense of guilt, she was hoping passion might just override that obstacle.

Billie clenched around him, heard him gasp and knew he was as close as she was. She'd never felt this brazen, emboldened by passion. All down to Patrick and the desire he roused inside her. Perhaps if she'd ever felt this way with Thom, he wouldn't have looked elsewhere, but she hadn't realised the strength of passion ready to wake inside her with the right person. Patrick.

They rode the wave together, bodies slick and breath ragged. The pressure was building inside her as she fought that final release, until it became too much for her to bear. The dam broke, and she cried out as her orgasm flooded over both of them. Patrick roared as his climax came hard and fast soon after. He clutched her body to make sure she felt every shudder as it reverberated through his, leaving them both breathless and stunned. They stared at one another as though they'd just been hit by a lightning bolt, both doing their best to recover from the shock.

Patrick lay down beside her, no mean feat when they were sharing a single bed. His chest was rising and falling as quickly as hers. 'Well, that's going to change things, isn't it?'

She knew what he meant. There was no going back now that they knew how good it could be between them. And she wanted more. Even if they couldn't commit to anything serious, she knew she wanted to do this again. It was clear Patrick had enjoyed himself, too, but guilt was holding him back from committing to anyone else. Perhaps the suggestion of a more…casual attitude to being together might just tempt him back into her bed.

CHAPTER SEVEN

'I THINK IT was becoming inevitable, though, wasn't it?' Billie was looking at him with wide eyes, her make-up smudged and her once perfect hair now messy and out of place. She looked thoroughly ravished and more beautiful than ever.

'I guess so.' There was no denying it when that attraction had been growing stronger every day no matter how hard they'd tried to fight it.

'I mean, we spend so much time together, and neither of us has been with anyone else since…' Billie didn't have to finish the sentence for him to know what she was talking about. There hadn't been anyone since they both lost their partners in very different circumstances.

'It's only natural that we're both craving some intimacy. We're still young, and I guess it's unreasonable to think we'll spend the rest of our lives celibate.'

Though he knew the only reason he was even considering sleeping with anyone after Sinead was because the connection he had with Billie was so deep.

It was also the problem he had moving forward. He'd tried to resist the attraction, not wanting to ruin their friendship or start something he knew wouldn't last because of the emotional baggage they were both dragging along with them. Now they'd crossed that line, he wasn't sure where it left their relationship.

'Yes.' Two red spots appeared on her cheeks as she admitted she'd needed this as much as Patrick.

Although he knew this likely muddled things between them even more. They could justify it happening because primal needs had got the better of them, but what if it happened again? Goodness knew he wanted to experience this with Billie, but they needed some sort of boundaries in place first.

'So...what happens now? Do we pretend this never happened and carry on as normal?' Although tonight had been amazing and he wanted to shout about it from the rooftops, he wasn't ready to fully commit to another relationship.

'I don't know. Is that what you want?' The hesitation was there in Billie's voice and the way she was chewing on her bottom lip, and he understood why. This had been a huge step for both of them, and not just because they'd crossed that line from friendship to lovers. Sleeping with someone after being single for so long was a decision neither of them would have taken lightly. It didn't seem fair to pretend it never happened and relegate it to a mere memory never to be spoken of again. As though it was something tawdry that they should be ashamed of. He wasn't. It was simply too much for him to contemplate getting any more involved than he already was with Billie.

The truth was, he didn't know what he wanted, except her. A relationship meant opening himself up again, sharing his life and his heart with someone else. Even though Billie was already a big part of both. There was also going to be the worry that she'd end up getting hurt because of him. She was the most important person in the world to him. If anything happened to her, he'd be devastated. There was a part of him that still wanted to keep a little distance between them in order to protect her. But there was no place he'd rather have been than in bed with her right now.

'I have no idea.' He couldn't help but laugh when they were two adults who'd just slept together, pondering whether or not they were strong enough to admit they wanted more but were scared of the consequences.

That seemed to relax Billie, too, as she cuddled into his side. 'Can't we just do this?'

'Mmm. It is nice…' The soft swell of her breasts pushed against his chest reminded him of what he did want. Sex only got complicated when emotions were involved. They could leave those to deal with another time.

'We could just be friends with benefits, you know.' Billie wrapped her leg around his so their bodies were pressed intimately together.

It was tempting. So very tempting.

'Do you really think that could work? Would that be enough for you?' For him? He didn't want to sound needy, but he wanted it all with Billie. It was taking that risk of going all in, however, which terrified him. Perhaps this was one way of circumnavigating that issue.

It wasn't everything, but it could be something. And who knew? Perhaps it could lead to having it all.

'Neither of us is ready for another serious relationship. Perhaps this will give us both a chance to explore our desires again, but with someone we trust. Surely our friendship has created that safe space for us now we've been open about everything. This would simply be an added extra to our relationship. Why don't we just try it and see?' She tilted her chin up towards him, inviting him for a kiss, and he accepted gratefully.

He wrapped an arm around her and pulled her closer, deepening the kiss and hoping to express his true feelings. Not just the ones he was letting her see. Billie was giving him the chance to be with her the way he wanted without having to commit to anything more. Without having all those fears come rushing back. A friends-with-benefits arrangement meant he could back off if he found himself getting too close, too invested in them as a couple, without feeling guilty about it. Billie was right. It was that safety net which made it all the more attractive a prospect. Something she needed too, he supposed, after everything she'd been through.

Despite a casual physical relationship being a step out of his comfort zone, their naked bodies were more than comfortable together. As if they were made to be together. There were no thoughts of anyone else or worries about the future as they made love for a second time. His body and soul were consumed by Billie alone.

As he drove inside her, every part of him was alive. Wanting her, needing her, and he didn't know how he'd ever live without her. The very opposite of a casual relationship.

It felt to Billie as though she was doing the walk of shame back home, even though she'd showered and changed and no one knew what she'd been up to. Except for Patrick, of course, who'd interrupted her shower to corrupt her once more. Not that she'd had any intention of stopping him. It seemed now that they'd stopped pretending the chemistry didn't exist between them, they couldn't get enough of one another. Probably to make up for lost time.

It was clear the attraction between them was too strong to resist. At least this way they could give in to those impulses without worrying too much about the consequences. If things didn't work out or the chemistry eventually fizzed out, hopefully they could still be friends. They both knew what they were getting into and intended to protect their fragile hearts with this get-out clause. It occurred to her that if they'd done this a long time ago, she could have cut out a lot of the wallowing she'd gone through after Thom. He barely registered in her brain now that it was so full of Patrick and the way he made her feel.

The drive back from the hotel was mostly in a comfortable silence. Likely because they'd worn each other out, but also because there was nothing more to say. They'd agreed to keep things casual, and that would have to do for now. Until either or both of them were ready for more. Or they decided this wasn't what they wanted at all. That negative thought creeping in made her shiver, and it didn't go unnoticed by Patrick.

'Are you cold? I'll put the heater on. I think I've got a sweatshirt in the back if you want to borrow it?' He began to rummage on the back seat behind him with one hand.

Billie rested her hand on his leg. 'It's fine.'

The other elephant in the car with them, of course, was the fact they were going back to real life. A hotel room was a great place to pretend they could have everything, but once they were back in their own environment, they might start to see things differently. Patrick could decide that he didn't want a casual relationship at all and that friendship was enough. She hoped not. She should have been satisfied that they got to spend at least one night free of their issues, curled up together in their love nest. But Billie knew it wouldn't be enough for her. She wanted that every day and night. However, a friends-with-benefits arrangement meant she could have the best of both worlds without risking her heart getting broken. They could still have one another as friends for that emotional support when needed, as well as the physical side which was so enjoyable. It was also reminding her that she was still the attractive, intelligent woman she had been before Thom had taken a sledgehammer to her confidence.

They pulled up outside her place, and Billie gathered her overnight bag containing her stained dress and her award.

'So, what are your plans for the rest of the day?' Patrick asked, eyes trained on the road ahead as though he was trying to put some sort of distance between them again.

'Take Fliss out for a walk first and hope she forgives me for staying out all night. Then I think I'll have to stop by the dry cleaner's and hope they can save my dress. What about you?' She'd already checked the work rota and knew neither of them were on again until midweek. This kind of felt like a make-or-break moment. As though if they didn't carry on with the momentum of last night, it might well just die away, and that would be heartbreaking. Just when she'd been given a taste of what she could have with Patrick, she wasn't ready for it to be taken away.

'I could drop off the dress for you, if you like?'

'Sure. If you don't mind?' She hated that they were back to being polite, almost strangers, and hoped this wasn't a sign of things to come. Not when they physically couldn't have been any closer last night, or this morning. Even if a certain emotional distance still remained.

'No problem.'

Billie handed over the dress, which seemed almost like a symbol of their short-lived romance. It was expensive and had lasted only one night.

She opened the door and put one foot out onto the pavement. 'Well, I guess I'll see you at work, then?'

There was no point in begging for more when she'd given him the opportunity already. If he didn't want even a casual relationship, it would seem desperate to try and make any future arrangements to be together.

'I, er, was wondering…'

Billie waited somewhat impatiently to see where his thoughts were heading when he'd given her no indication since leaving the hospital what he wanted to happen between them next.

'It's Anna's wedding today. You know, the woman we met at the dress shop.'

'I remember,' Billie said with a smile. Who could forget that this white knight had swooped in and saved the day for her and her mother?

'I know we don't really know them that well, but they did invite us. Maybe we could go to the evening reception? I'll understand if it's too much after being out last night, and of course there's Fliss to consider…'

'I'd love to,' Billie jumped in. It wasn't so much that she wanted to go to a virtual stranger's wedding, but Patrick was suggesting a public outing together. Perhaps their first as more than just friends. More than she could have hoped for when she would have settled for a night in front of the telly together.

Patrick smiled, looking almost relieved. She wondered if he'd thought she'd changed her mind about continuing whatever it was they'd embarked on, too. If they ever moved into anything serious, they were definitely going to have to work on their communication skills. It would save a lot of time and anxiety.

'Okay, then, I'll get this to the dry cleaners and pick you up later. Say seven o'clock? Do you have something else to wear?'

'Yes, Patrick, I do have another dress. Though it won't be quite up to last night's standards.' In her mind she was already running through the contents of her wardrobe, trying to pick out something suitable which would also wow Patrick. She wanted to remind him why they should carry on where they'd left off this morning.

'You could wear a sack and you'd still be sexy.' There was that twinkle back in his eye that made her go weak at the knees. She was tempted to drag him into the house and into her bed.

However, she didn't want to appear desperate, no matter how thirsty she was for him.

'I think I might have something a little more sophisticated than a sack.' She gave him a wink and was about to get out of the car when Patrick suddenly grabbed her arm and pulled her to him. He kissed her hard and passionately, seemingly unfazed by doing it so publicly.

Though it left her dazed and wanting more when she did finally make it into the house, Billie hoped it was simply an appetiser ahead of the night's main course.

Patrick took Billie's hand as they got out of the car and headed into the hotel. He almost wished they were staying in the five-star resort in the countryside for the night, but he'd be happy wherever he was, as long as it meant sharing a bed with Billie.

He was uncharacteristically nervous about attending the wedding reception. Not because it felt a bit like gatecrashing when they knew nothing of the families involved. It was more to do with the person accompanying him and the new dynamic their relationship had taken on. He supposed it was a silly notion to get hung up on a date when they'd already slept together, several times, but tonight marked him moving on from Sinead publicly. Even though none of the people here tonight would realise that. Apart from Billie. She would understand the significance, and he supposed that was mainly why he'd suggested coming tonight.

A friends-with-benefits scenario could easily be concealed by hiding away at one another's houses, but Billie deserved more than that. Even if she didn't want anything serious, she was worth more than being anyone's booty call.

'If I haven't said it already, you look beautiful tonight.' It occurred to him that she'd rendered him somewhat speechless when she'd come out to the car. Wearing a pretty floral dress, her hair in loose curls around her shoulders, she'd taken his breath away.

A complete contrast to last night's appearance, but nonetheless impactful. Tonight she looked effortlessly and timelessly beautiful. It was a lesson to him that she didn't need expensive boutique dresses and accessories when she was more than enough the way she was.

Billie smiled bashfully, though he knew she could be anything but shy when the mood took her. 'I think the words you used were "hubba hubba", but I got the gist. Thank you.'

That made him belly-laugh because he didn't think she'd heard him at the time, but the sentiment was true all the same. 'As long as you know you're appreciated. Now, let's go meet the happy couple.'

They followed the signs which had been erected in the hotel lobby to direct them towards the nuptial celebrations, even though they would only have had to follow the noise coming from the main function room. But when they were standing in the doorway surveying the revellers who'd obviously been celebrating hard, Patrick had doubts about attending. He at least was going to have to remain sober for the duration.

Thankfully Anna spotted them and came rushing over, saving them from awkwardly hovering in the doorway too long.

'Thank you so much for coming.' She kissed Patrick on the cheek and hugged Billie.

'You look stunning,' Billie said, handing over a card they'd written from both of them. They'd decided paying for the dresses was more than enough of a wedding gift, so they didn't have to worry about purchasing something off the register.

'I'm sorry we weren't here for the ceremony. I hope you've had a good day.' Patrick thought it would have been imposing too much to be included in the earlier reception, but usually, as proven by the sight before them, the evening was a more casual affair.

'The best, thank you. I'm just glad you're here. Mum! Gavin! This is Patrick. The man who helped with the dresses.' She called over the crowd towards the main table to her mother and the groom, who looked a little worse for wear.

Jacketless, shirtsleeves rolled up and tie loose, he wandered over and shook Patrick's hand. 'Thanks, mate. Anna told me what you did, and we appreciate it. Let me get you a drink.'

'Just a non-alcoholic beer for me. I'm driving.' Patrick was hoping they'd just have a couple of hours here, maybe a slow dance, then head back to Billie's place. In hindsight, a wedding was probably better suited to a fiftieth date rather than a first.

Gavin flagged down a passing waiter and ordered drinks, including a wine for Billie, before pulling a couple of seats over to the nearest table for them to sit down.

'There's a buffet. Just help yourselves. Me and my new husband are going to strut our stuff.' Anna directed them towards the food laid out on banqueting tables at the back of the room before grabbing her partner and disappearing into the crowd.

As people drifted towards the bar and the dance floor, Patrick and Billie were left on their own at the table sipping their drinks. Leaving only to stock up on some finger food. Anna's mother came to greet them too and offer her thanks, then joined the rest of the family on the dance floor.

'It looks as though they're enjoying themselves, anyway.' Billie sipped her wine, watching the others dance, her foot tapping to the music.

'I'm sorry,' Patrick said, regretting the decision to bring her here when they were so obviously out of place.

'What for?'

'I should have taken you out to dinner, or the cinema, or anywhere other than a stranger's wedding. I just thought, well, we were invited, and it would seem like such a big deal to come together here, rather than actually arranging a date.' He felt stupid now. He should have just told her he wanted to do something together tonight instead of making out this was an obligation he thought they should attend.

Billie leaned across and dropped a kiss on his lips. 'I

don't care where we are as long as we're together. Though for future reference, please tell me what it is you want so I don't have to keep guessing. Now, you heard Anna. We can have dinner and a dance and enjoy ourselves.'

She took his hand and led him towards the dance floor, where the DJ was playing a power ballad for all the happy couples to slow dance to together. Although they'd danced together for the first time last night, this felt altogether different. As Billie melted against him and they swayed to the music, they were more relaxed, comfortable together. There had been a certain tension, awareness, the previous evening of what might happen later. Tonight he was sure they were going to end up in bed together, so there was no wondering and worrying about whether or not they should cross that line. There was no going back, even if he wanted to, which he didn't. This felt too right.

He kissed the top of Billie's head, which was resting on his shoulder. Anna's mother caught his eye and gave him a nod of approval. Even complete strangers had seen this coming, and the only reason they'd resisted as long as they had was that they were so scared of getting things wrong. Although that was still a possibility, it was hard to care when they were together like this.

He bent his head down to whisper in her ear. 'Do you think we've passed ourselves yet?'

Billie looked up. 'What do you mean?'

'We've congratulated the happy couple and had something to eat, a drink and a dance. Would it be really bad form to leave?'

'We've hardly been here for an hour, Patrick.'

'I know, but do you think anyone will really miss us? We'll likely never see these people again. Besides, I can think of better ways to spend this evening. Preferably without an audience.' He nuzzled into her neck, into that sensitive part behind her ear he'd recently discovered drove her wild.

She gave a little whimper, and Patrick knew he had her. He let his hands slide down her back to cup her backside and pull her flush against him. Not that he was doing himself any favours now he could feel every intimate inch of her.

Thankfully the slow songs came to an end, and the tempo changed to an upbeat dance tune Patrick had no intention of trying to keep up with. He was saving all of his energy, along with his best moves, for the lady in his arms.

'I think we could safely slip away. The wedding party are having a dance-off over there. It would be a shame to disturb their fun.' Billie was definitely on his wavelength, and they seized the moment to slip away hand in hand.

Not that tonight had been a wasted exercise for Patrick. He'd felt comfortable out as a couple, and at least it had given them some time together socialising before hightailing it to the bedroom.

Perhaps he was learning that moving on wasn't such a bad thing after all when this was the happiest and most content he'd felt in a long time. Not to mention the most horny.

'Come on, then,' he growled. This particular party might be over for them, but there was a new one about to begin.

Thankfully, the drive back to Billie's place wasn't too long when it seemed they were both about to combust with need for one another.

Billie slid her hand over Patrick's thigh. Though she

didn't want to distract when he was driving, she wanted to keep touching him so they didn't lose any of that delicious chemistry bubbling away again between them.

He picked her hand up and kissed it before she travelled too far up his leg, too intimately, on someone trying to keep his focus on the road ahead.

They arrived back at the house just as her neighbour was leaving. She handed Billie the key. 'Fliss has had her dinner and her walk. She's settled for the night in the kitchen.'

'Thank you so much. I'll try not to disturb her in that case. Sorry to impose on you two nights running.'

'It's not a problem. I miss having my wee Jack. It's good to be around another dog. Besides, I'm glad to see you going out and enjoying yourself.' She looked pointedly at Patrick and gave Billie a nudge. No doubt her sign of approval.

Although the woman had always told Billie she was happy to help, Billie didn't usually have much need of her offer to dog-sit, except when she was working a late shift. Mrs Scanlon was a godsend in those circumstances, since Thom's sudden departure had caused her some problems in that area, too. When she'd decided to get Fliss, she hadn't anticipated that she would end up on her own. Though Patrick had always been there to help out, too.

Billie was afraid to wish for more, but tonight had at least shown her Patrick wasn't ashamed to be seen with her. Okay, they might have ended up rushing back to her place anyway, but he'd made the effort. It had been intended as a date of sorts, and that wasn't entirely in keeping with the idea of friends with benefits. That scenario suggested more of a secretive arrangement only the two of them knew about. A salacious affair conducted in private so no one from the outside would know they were anything more than friends. Tonight went against that idea, and although there were no rules, it gave her hope that he saw her as something more than a willing partner.

The sex was incredible, there was no doubt about that. Even if it was about more than the physical compatibility for her. She was falling for him more and more every day. He made her feel wanted for once. Cherished. Whether that was simply part of his usual seduction routine, only time would tell. Though she wanted to believe it was truly how he felt about her. Then they might actually stand a chance of being a couple. The more time she spent with Patrick, the more she was sure that was what she wanted.

Any doubts she had about that had been obliterated last night with their explosive chemistry. She'd never felt about anyone, including Thom, the way she felt about Patrick. Best friend and best lover rolled into one. It was too good to be true because they couldn't have it all. Their pasts meant they felt the need to maintain that last bit of emotional distance. With Patrick still grieving for his loved ones, she knew he couldn't give himself completely to her. That meant she would never feel like his first choice. At least by trying to convince herself this was only a casual arrangement, she might not feel the rejection as strongly if things didn't work out. She might be able to believe this time it wasn't she that was the problem, but circumstance. All she could do was hope that one day his feelings for her might become stronger than those ties to the past, and she might be able to risk her heart on him.

For now, she'd settle for another night in his arms.

'We'll have to be quiet unless we want to wake Fliss,' Billie cautioned as she opened the front door. As much as she loved her dog, she wanted Patrick's attention without having to compete with Fliss for it.

'We wouldn't want to do that when my plans for tonight solely revolve around you.' He was so close to her his breath tickled the small hairs on the back of her neck, bringing goose bumps up all over her skin. This man only had to breathe to make her go weak at the knees.

As they crept into the house and upstairs, it felt very like sneaking a boy into her parents' house. Not that they would have cared. They hadn't paid any more attention to her as a teenager than as a child. She could have been running wild for all they cared, but no, she'd been the model student, the perfect daughter, in a vain attempt to gain their love. At least with Patrick, she felt seen as well as supported. At times, even loved. Certainly when they were in bed together.

Perhaps this was her reliving her youth, acting recklessly and giggling as she led Patrick to her bedroom. She'd spent a lifetime trying to be what everyone else wanted, always to be found lacking in some way. It was different with Patrick. Billie didn't have to try to be anyone but herself with him.

Right now he was kissing her neck and slipping her dress down over her shoulders, seeming enamoured with the woman she was. Perhaps not enough to consider a serious, long-term commitment to, but sufficient for a temporary position. Though she hoped for a permanent promotion further down the line, she was simply glad he'd spotted her potential in the end.

She'd always thought of Patrick as an attractive man, and who wouldn't? He was handsome, successful and thoughtful. The perfect man. But she'd never felt anything romantic towards him until lately as their connection had grown. Now she could see that she never felt a fraction for Thom of what she did for Patrick. Her feelings for him were on a different level. Their intensity scared her at times.

Perhaps that was why her relationship with Thom had been doomed from the start. He'd never elicited the same passion from her, but she'd tried to force it. Moulding herself into the sort of woman she thought he wanted, never really considering what it was *she* wanted or needed from a partner. Apparently that was everything that came in a Patrick-shaped package.

They stumbled onto her bed. He looked right at home there, his magnificent naked form stretched out, taking up that empty space she'd slept beside for too long. Billie straddled his hips, keen to maintain some control when she was at something of a disadvantage in the relationship. Her feelings towards him were anything but casual.

'You're beautiful, Billie.' He always said the right thing, making her feel empowered and appreciated. She hadn't always had that in her life.

'So are you,' she replied with a smile. It was true. He was a beautiful specimen of masculinity as she trailed her hands down his taut torso, taking mental snapshots of every muscle along the way.

The compliment made him laugh, bringing his body intimately into contact with hers and renewing that lust he always seemed to inspire in her.

She let her mouth follow the path her hands had taken, kissing him all over, and hearing his sharp intake of breath as she dipped lower. It emboldened her to know she could turn him on to this degree, seeing the evidence for herself and taking it in hand. There was pleasure in watching Patrick struggle for composure, his eyes closed, his mouth pulled into a tight line as he groaned. She could drive him as crazed with lust as he could her. That knowledge spurred her to coax him towards the very edge of that madness.

Billie dipped her head and took him completely in her mouth, causing him to buck up off the bed. His fingers wound in her hair as she slid her lips along his shaft, every tug as arousing as the power she had over him. When he suddenly flipped their positions so that she was flat on her back, she merely laughed, content that she'd found his breaking point.

'You're playing with fire,' he warned, eyes glittering with desire as he sheathed himself with a condom.

'Who says I was playing? Maybe I want the fire.' She was challenging him to lose control, to close that small distance between them he used like some sort of force field. Then maybe he would see that she was worth taking a chance on.

Her sassy retort seemed to do the trick as Patrick drove inside her with a grunt, his inner caveman apparently unleashed. If she wanted the heat, he was definitely bringing it to her, relentlessly thrusting, unapologetically rushing her straight from arousal to climax. Her head was spinning, her body no longer hers as her orgasm slammed into her.

Patrick's primal roar as he reached that peak too gave her a certain sense of pride that she could elicit such strong feelings within him. Maybe one day he might even be able to admit he loved her. If they weren't so afraid of letting a real relationship flourish between them.

CHAPTER EIGHT

'SOMEBODY HELP ME! Somebody help my son!' A man burst through the doors of A and E carrying an unconscious boy.

'What happened?' Patrick immediately rushed to his side, with Billie following close behind.

'I don't know. His face started to swell up, and he was making this awful wheezing sound like he couldn't breathe. He was clutching at his throat.' The distraught father's voice broke as he described the dreadful sight of his son's suffering.

'In here.' Billie led them into an empty cubicle, where the man laid the child on the bed so Patrick could examine him.

'Does he have any allergies? Did he eat anything he shouldn't?' Patrick observed angry-looking red spots around the pale skin of his throat, suggesting an allergy of some sort.

'No. Nothing that I can think of. Glenn's a very picky eater. Only plain foods, you know?'

The boy's pulse was weak, his blood pressure low, so Patrick needed to know exactly what had happened so they could start treatment immediately. 'Did he complain of any abdominal pain before he passed out?'

'He did vomit, and he complained of feeling dizzy. I just thought it was the heat.' The father was hovering by the bed, understandably concerned by his son's condition.

'If you were outside, was there a chance he could have been stung by something?' It was Billie's suggestion that his condition could have been caused by an allergic reaction to a sting. Something the family might not have been aware of before now.

'It's possible. We were in the park, so there were a lot of bees around.' With the idea further backed by Glenn's father, Patrick looked for a possible sting site and found a tiny puncture wound just below the child's ear.

'Okay, Mr...'

'Flynn.'

'It sounds like your son has had an allergic reaction to a bee sting and gone into anaphylactic shock. We're going to need you to take a seat out in the waiting room while we treat him.' Patrick nodded to Billie, who gently guided the man out of the department.

'He's going to be all right, isn't he?' The man's voice carried down the corridor, followed by Billie's.

'You made the right call by bringing him here so quickly. If you just wait here, we'll update you as soon as we can.' She didn't make any promises, as aware as Patrick was that they couldn't always predict the outcome of these cases.

It wasn't long before she came rushing back to assist Patrick. She hooked Glenn up to the machines so they could monitor his blood pressure and heart rate. Patrick injected him with adrenaline. It would open the airways, reduce the swelling and help maintain heart function and blood pressure.

'Can we get fluids started, and some antihistamines, please?' Patrick asked Billie as he popped an oxygen mask over the boy's mouth to assist his breathing.

'Of course.' She buzzed about, making sure everything was in place. Patrick understood now why the children were so important to her. Although everyone in the department treated them as a priority, Billie had always displayed that extra level of care he was sure harked back to her own childhood.

She made sure all the children who came through the doors experienced top-level care because it was something she'd never had. He hated to think of her as that little girl, unloved, unwanted and likely not listened to. She'd deserved so much more from her parents then. She deserved more from him now.

Although they'd been having fun together these past few days without having to worry about the consequences of serious commitment, he knew it was selfish of him to keep things that way. Despite the casual arrangement being Billie's idea, he wanted more. He was just too afraid of taking the chance things would come to a tragic end. Billie was right. He couldn't keep living in the past forever. He had to stop holding back when it was Billie who'd brought him back to life.

'Are you okay?' he asked, watching as she stroked the boy's hair.

'Yeah. I just hope he'll be okay.' They both knew that the adrenaline could wear off before the allergic reaction. If it did, they'd administer another injection and hope for the best.

'I'm sure at most his father will simply have to carry an autoinjector in case this happens again.' With the prospect of further severe reactions, parents would be advised to carry a shot of adrenaline to inject into the child to save precious time.

'I hope so.' Billie gave him a watery smile, making him want to gather her in his arms and tell her everything was going to be okay. She brought out that side of him, even if he had to rein it in at work. Tonight would be different, though. He intended to pamper her and make her feel as special as she was to him.

'Look, his heart rate and blood pressure are stable. I think you can probably let Mr Flynn come in and see him for a minute. I'll stick around to make sure there are no complications. Then we'll see if there's a bed on the children's ward for the night.' They would keep him in overnight for observation, but hopefully Glenn would recover without any long-lasting after-effects.

On Patrick's advice, Billie went to fetch the boy's father. 'Mr Flynn? You can see Glenn now.'

'He's okay?' The relief on the father's face was so obvious, she found herself welling up, too.

'He's fine. The doctor wants to keep him overnight just so we can keep an eye on him, but you can go in and see him for now.' Billie led him back to the cubicle, letting Patrick explain what had happened and the action that would have to be taken in future. Then they left the father to have a moment with his son.

'Are you due a break?' Patrick asked as they walked out of the cubicle.

'I can take five minutes.' She needed a moment just to gather her thoughts anyway. The kids were always tough for her, and she was glad Patrick was there giving them the best possible treatment in the worst circumstances. He was a very special man.

It was obvious he cared about her, too, in every look, every word, checking in to make sure she was okay. Billie was beginning to realise that was what she'd needed all along. Someone who took care of her. Not someone who simply put up with her whilst she bent herself out of shape trying to please them. Not Thom. Patrick had made her realise she deserved more from a partner. It should be someone supportive, loving, and always there for her. Everything she'd craved growing up, but because of people like her family and Thom, she'd convinced herself she didn't deserve. Patrick had made sure she saw her own worth. If only he could see his, too, and understand that he was worthy of being loved, they might be able to move past these last barriers keeping them from being together properly.

'Why don't we get some fresh air?' With determined strides, he led her out of the department, through the hospital doors and round the back of the building.

'Is everything okay?' she asked, worried that something must be wrong if he needed somewhere so secluded to talk to her.

'Yes. I just needed to do this.' He grabbed her face in his hands and kissed her hard. Until her head was spinning, and the adrenaline was revitalising her work-weary body.

'What was that for?' she asked breathlessly.

'It's just a placeholder for later on.'

'Oh yeah? What do you have in mind?' She loved that he couldn't keep his hands off her. She loved the flirty nature he didn't usually give in to.

'Dinner. Wine. Candles. A bath. Taking you to bed.'

'In that order?' Her body was already responding to the mental picture he was conjuring about the evening ahead.

'Not necessarily…' He kissed her again. This time it was a slow, languid exploration of her mouth that had them both groaning with need.

'You're killing me, you know that, Nurse Wade?'

'I do hope so, Dr James.' She fluttered her eyelashes at him as she walked away, hoping that his last line of defence was beginning to crumble.

'I'll see you later.' Patrick kissed Billie on the cheek just before he left for his shift at the hospital, but it wasn't enough for either of them. Before they knew it, they were locked in a passionate embrace he was sure neither of them wanted to leave. It seemed the more time they spent together, the more they wanted each other. It wasn't a bad thing, except when they had to go to work, of course.

Billie was off today, but she would be on call if any emergencies came in needing the assistance of the search and rescue team.

Although they worked in the same department, they had different positions, different responsibilities and duties. They hadn't consciously made the decision to keep things quiet from their colleagues, but it would probably have complicated things if everyone thought they were an item, given their uncertain relationship status. So they tried to act as normal as possible at work.

It wasn't so bad on days when they had a chance of seeing each other in passing, but days and especially nights when they weren't together were becoming tougher. He was becoming used to waking up with her in his arms, and inevitably making love. They spent most nights at her place, mostly because of Fliss, but he also found he was happier there, too. It made those nights when he was in his own place even lonelier.

Eventually they parted, with the biggest sigh coming from him. He couldn't wait until they could be together again. Definitely a lost cause.

'Okay. You should really get to work.' Billie rested a hand on his chest, apparently not in a hurry for him to leave, either. Patrick couldn't help but wonder if it would always be like this between them. Was it because they were two weeks into a casual fling? The timer was counting down on their relationship until one of them decided it wasn't what they wanted after all and ended things. He didn't even want to contemplate it, not when they were having such a good time together.

It always seemed to be on the tip of his tongue to ask her if she wanted anything more serious between them, but he never found himself quite able to make that jump. He was afraid of upsetting the status quo and losing what they already had together. He was becoming increasingly stressed at the thought this could end at any moment. Patrick realised he wanted more, but the consequences of that were something he just couldn't manage to get past. Opening himself up completely to being with her left him vulnerable to getting hurt again. And by someone who didn't think twice about putting her own life on the line to save someone else's. This one last thread of resistance might be the only thing which could save him if anything happened to Billie.

Although that left the worry that someone else might sweep Billie off her feet.

At some point, he was going to have to find the courage to make that call. All or nothing. Before someone else took that risk instead of him.

When Patrick arrived at the hospital, he made sure to get the rundown from the last shift on the current intake of patients, then set to work on the influx of new patients waiting to be seen.

'Mr Sullivan?' He walked into the cubicle where the triage nurse had put the elderly male, his wife standing tearfully by the bed holding his hand.

'Hello, Doctor.'

'I understand you've been having some chest pain?' He took the man's pulse and sounded the man's heart with his stethoscope, finding nothing untoward.

'Yes. It just came on suddenly this afternoon.'

'What were you doing at the time?' It was important to have some context to understand what could have gone on before he came to any definite conclusion.

'Nothing. Just sitting watching TV.' It was Mrs Sullivan who answered.

'No other pain anywhere else?' A heart attack was sometimes accompanied by sudden shooting pains in the left arm, the jaw and other areas.

The man shook his head. 'I have been a little out of breath and very tired, though.'

'I see from your notes you have no previous heart problems. Is there anything else I should be aware of? Have you been overdoing it, or are you overstressed at the minute.' Patrick wanted to rule out all possibilities which could be contributing factors. Sometimes a simple muscle strain or anxiety could mimic a heart attack.

'Nothing I can think of.'

'Okay, we'll take some bloods, and I'd like to do a heart trace to make sure there's nothing going on there. Nothing to worry about. You're in the best place.' He said it to reassure Mr Sullivan's wife as much as the patient himself. The man's skin was a little clammy, and with some of his other symptoms, it was best to check him out. An ECG would show if there was any problem with the heart's rhythm or electrical activity which he should be concerned about. If so, Mr Sullivan might be moved to cardiac care so they could investigate further. At least he might have some preventative measures put in place in case he was a likely candidate for heart failure. The worst-case scenario would be if he did suffer a cardiac infarction before then, but at least he was in the hospital with the proper equipment and a medical team if it should happen. Here in A and E, it was simply Patrick's job to see what was going on now and treat him accordingly.

'I don't know what I'd do if anything happens to him, Doctor.' Mrs Sullivan was sobbing again, and he understood her fear. Often when partners accompanied the patients, they were just as frightened as the person being treated, because of the unknown. It was horrible seeing the person you loved suffering. Goodness knew he'd had enough experience watching his mother's health decline after his father's death. That helpless feeling was something he'd hoped he would overcome during his medical training, but it didn't work when you were still literally powerless to save a loved one. Sinead was a case in point.

He'd tortured himself, not only with the guilt of driving her out of the house that night but also with the knowledge that perhaps if he'd been there, he could have saved her.

One thing was for sure, though. Mrs Sullivan clearly loved her husband very much. She was so afraid of something happening to him. Of losing him. It made Patrick think of Billie and the feelings for her that seemed to be at the centre of everything. Perhaps the reason he was so scared of something happening to her, the way it had to Sinead and his father, was how deep his feelings went for her. Although he hoped they didn't end up in this particular scenario anytime soon, he did want a close relationship like this one. That wasn't going to happen when he was still pretending that all he was after was a physical relationship. He was in this thing with Billie heart and soul, and it was about time she knew it.

Tonight he was going to broach the subject and take that risk. The payoff he was hoping for, a life with Billie, was worth taking a chance on.

'Give me ten more minutes,' Billie insisted over the walkie-talkie. The others were ready to call off the search, but she just had a feeling they were close. Fliss wasn't ready to stop, either, as she forged ahead, sniffing the air and doing her best to track down the man who'd been reported injured up here in the mountains, near Bloody Bridge.

'Billie, the storm is closing in. We have to shut this down for everyone's safety. We can look again at first light.' The instruction was coming directly from the head of her team, who she knew would inform the police that they were standing down, but the bad weather wasn't just bad news for the team. If someone was stuck out here, lost, injured and perhaps disorientated, there was a real risk of hypothermia for them, or worse. She wouldn't be able to sleep in her own bed knowing that someone was struggling up here. Even Patrick wouldn't be able to distract her tonight, and that was saying something.

These past two weeks together had been amazing. Everything she'd hoped for with Patrick and more. Being with him was a happy mixture of being comfortable together and enjoying a passion which had never been a priority for her, but she now knew she couldn't live without. Anything less would be doing a disservice to her inner wanton, who'd been spectacularly indulged thanks to Patrick.

It hadn't all just been about the sex, though. Since they'd embarked on this journey beyond their friendship, she thought they'd grown closer than ever. Sharing things about their pasts they'd held close for so long, afraid to reveal to anyone. For her, at least, it had felt as though a burden had been lifted by finally opening up. Thom had never shown much interest in her family, never mind why she was estranged from them. In hindsight, he'd only really talked about himself. Their whole relationship had revolved around his wants and needs, and she'd done her best to meet them all. She supposed it had been her attempt to gain his love and attention, acting the same way she'd grown up. Fighting for the love of people who apparently never really wanted her. At least with Patrick, she felt as though she was enough. She didn't have to try so hard because it came naturally with him. Her relationship with Thom hadn't ended because she'd been lacking in some way, but because he was. He wasn't Patrick. She'd simply been with the wrong man.

The difference in how the respective relationships made her feel was like night and day. With Patrick, she didn't have to worry about 'getting things right', because that's how it always felt. Right. For the first time in her life, she was happy. The only blot on the horizon was the idea that it could all be temporary. She'd suggested a casual arrangement thinking it was the only way they could be together, but she was hoping at some point that would change. If Patrick was as content as she was with things between them, then perhaps there might come a time when he was truly ready to move on from Sinead and fully commit to her. After all, they were already spending as many nights as they could at her place as well as working and eating together when they could.

Although there had been times she'd even felt guilty about betraying her friend by falling for her husband, Billie knew he was the one for her. No one else would ever come close to meaning as much to her as he did. The knowledge that their marriage hadn't been quite as rosy as she'd imagined had helped ease her conscience a little. If Sinead hadn't died in such tragic circumstances, perhaps they wouldn't have stayed together anyway. Given the chemistry Billie had discovered between her and Patrick, there was a possibility that they might have explored it. Either way, she hoped her friend would forgive her for falling for Patrick.

The thought of being wrapped up in bed with him tonight was what was spurring her on. The sooner she found who she was looking for, the more she could enjoy the night ahead without guilt or worry weighing her down.

All she needed was a few minutes more and a stroke of luck, and everyone would be happy.

'Billie...' The boss was waiting for her to confirm that she was complying with his order to halt the search for now, but she just couldn't bring herself to do it.

'I'm coming down now. I might just take the long way down.' She turned her walkie-talkie off then, unwilling to listen to whatever lecture he was about to give her. Billie had been doing this long enough to take care of herself up here, and her instincts hadn't failed her yet. Her boss would be thanking her, along with the family of their missing hiker, once she did the job she'd come up here to do.

Although the weather was making it more difficult than usual. The ground was slick underfoot, and the rain was driving against her so hard, it made visibility next to impossible. She was just hoping she would find this man before night closed in, too.

Fliss paced and sniffed before carrying on up the trail worn down by previous hikers, with Billie following. The closer they came to the summit, the more precarious the ground beneath her feet was becoming. Loose stones caused her to slip on several occasions, grazing her shins in the process. Not that such a superficial injury would hamper her search. It was to be expected in these conditions, and a few cuts and bruises would be a small price to pay if it meant saving someone else's life.

The steeper she climbed, the harder it became to get purchase, even though Fliss was able to bound up ahead unimpeded.

By the time she reached the summit, she was exhausted, dirty and bleeding, but it would be worth it to find the man everyone was searching for. Except there was no sign of him. She'd been expecting him to be sitting here waiting for rescue as it would be the most visible place for a drone or helicopter to spot had the weather been better, but there was nothing. On this occasion, it seemed her instincts had let her down. Now, not only had she failed this man and his family, but she was in for a stern telling off from the chief.

Billie paused to give Fliss some water before they made their descent again. 'I guess we'll just have to come back in the morning.'

If she was allowed to join the search again. The rules were there to keep everyone safe, and she'd broken them by ignoring orders. She might have been forgiven if she'd actually found who they were looking for, but instead, all she'd done was ignore the chief and put herself in jeopardy.

'I'm heading back now.' She called in her position and let them know back at the rendezvous point that they could stop worrying. About her, at least.

Every now and then as she made her way down, she called out the missing man's name just in case he might have heard her, but the only sound was of the rain's pitter-patter on her waterproof jacket. It was teeming down, and she had to keep wiping her eyes so she could see in front of her. Thankfully, Fliss was as sure-footed as ever and led her down the trail, which was no longer visible now.

The steep incline was just as daunting on the way down but for different reasons. It wasn't the effort or the toll it took on her muscles making the climb difficult. Instead, it was the momentum which was almost forcing her to run down the rocky face. She was doing her best to stay upright, but it wasn't an easy feat in these conditions. As loose stones eroded underfoot, she was forced to put her hands out to brace herself on the rocks on the way down. Billie tried a different approach, turning sideways and stepping down one foot at a time, but it couldn't stop the loose gravel moving underfoot.

As she faltered, she reached out and tried to grab on to something, but the grass was greasy in her fingers, and she couldn't get hold. It felt as though she was watching herself from above as she fell. A slow-motion scene she couldn't prevent playing out before it all became very real. She felt every bash against the ground, rocks tearing at her skin. All she could do was ignore the pain and find some way of stopping herself from doing any further damage. She put her hands out on either side of her body and fought through the searing burn as she grappled for purchase. Eventually she managed to grab hold of a small thorny bush and saved herself from any further damage.

Fliss barked as she hauled herself back up into a sitting position.

'Hey, it wasn't the way I'd planned coming down either, but I'm still in one piece. Just about.' Billie stared down at her shredded trousers and the raw skin exposed. Okay, so she wasn't exactly unscathed, but she was conscious, and bonus, there wasn't far left for her to get back to the rendezvous point.

She took a moment to breathe, to try and get her heart rate back to normal and recover from the shock of the fall. Fliss bounded over and began to lick her face, clearly concerned.

'I'm okay, Fliss. Let's get back before the sun sets.'

The last thing she wanted was a search party called out for her, too.

Billie pushed herself up, but the second she put any weight on her foot, she screamed. The searing pain seemed to reverberate through her entire body. She bit down hard on her lip, doing her best to fight the tears springing to her eyes. Clearly she'd done some damage in the fall. It could be a fractured ankle, but she didn't want to think about that when she still had a way to walk. The injury made her journey even more arduous. She tried to keep her weight off the right ankle, almost hopping down the rest of the trail. Sometimes she had to sit on her backside and shuffle her way down.

As the light began to fade, she was sweating, in pain and close to breaking down. She had to concede and call it in that she'd had a fall. Thankfully she wasn't too far from the rest of the team, and it wasn't long before several members came rushing up to meet her.

'Billie? What have you done?'

'Are you okay?'

They took an arm each, attempting to help her over towards the cars, but the second she put her foot on the ground and attempted to take a step, indescribable pain shot through her body.

It was the last thing she remembered before everything went dark.

'I'm going to see if we can get a bed for Saoirse tonight so we can keep an eye on her. I don't think those burns are going to need any surgery, but we'll have to administer pain relief through the night.' Patrick was dealing with a young patient who had been sitting too close to an open fire. Her coat had gone up in flames with her inside it. Luckily the parents had acted quickly, but the burns on the child's arms were extensive. There was always the possibility of her going into shock. He'd be happier to have her here being monitored by medical staff in case there were any complications.

The wounds had already been cleaned and dressed, so she was ready to be moved. All he had to do was find a bed for her overnight.

'Thanks, Doctor.' The girl's tearful mother stayed with her daughter as he went out to the nurse's station to put in a call to the children's ward.

It took a few tries, some begging and a lot of logistics involved, to have the young girl admitted for the night. Patrick let the child's mother know what was happening. There would be a wait before her daughter was moved to the ward. It was the best he could do for now.

'Have you seen who has just been brought in?' one of the nurses asked as he passed by.

'No. Who?' He wondered if it was a previous patient he should be aware of, since they were being brought to his attention.

'Billie.'

Patrick didn't hang around to hear a secondhand account of what had happened to her, rushing out to see for himself. The mere mention of Billie having been brought to A and E made his stomach plummet, knowing she wouldn't have come here unless something serious had happened to her. He was also aware she would have been on call today for the search and rescue team, hiking the dangerous terrain she often had to work.

The sight of her being pushed into the department in a wheelchair by her team member made his heart catch.

'What on earth happened, Billie?'

She gave him a wonky smile. 'I slipped.'

Her team member leaned in. 'That's only half of the story. She fell down a rock face, tried to walk on a suspected broken ankle and passed out from the pain.'

'I'm fine,' she insisted, trying to brush away any concern, but the story was there to see in her battered body and torn clothes.

Patrick didn't know whether to hug her or give her a shake, relieved that she was okay but upset that she'd put herself in danger. Again.

'You are not fine if you've broken your ankle and possibly suffered a concussion.' He didn't know how she'd fallen, if she'd hit her head, and whether or not that had caused her to lose consciousness. They were going to need to do some scans to see what damage she'd really done.

'But I'm here and talking, if not walking.' Her attempt at levity didn't make it any better for him. Although he hadn't had time to worry about her out there, now he was facing how he would feel if something worse happened to her in the future. He knew he couldn't go through losing anyone else in his life. Especially not Billie. It would kill him, too.

'We'll have to get you down to X-ray to find out the extent of the damage. Then I want you back here to get fixed up.' He was doing his best to stay composed, but deep inside, he was being torn apart. This was his worst fear for Billie come true. She'd been lucky today, but there was nothing to say the next time she went out on a call she wouldn't suffer more serious injury.

It felt like a warning from the universe. A premonition of worse to come if he got in any deeper with her. Only this morning, he'd been thinking about making a commitment, cementing their relationship and sharing his life with her. Within a few hours, she'd been hurt. She was safer without him in her life, and his heart was probably safer if he kept her at a distance. Things were fine when they'd merely been friends, though he didn't know if they'd ever get back to that. So much had changed, including his feelings. What he did know was that he loved her too much to risk her getting hurt again.

Even the pain it was causing him to see her hurt was sounding alarm bells. A sign of how much he cared for her, and what she meant to him. He had to pull back because losing her would devastate him. Billie deserved more than someone who couldn't give himself completely to her because of the burden of guilt he already carried, too. Some distance from one another would be better for both of them.

Patrick was willing to sacrifice the happiness he'd found with Billie in his life, if it meant saving hers.

Billie knew Patrick was angry with her, though he hadn't said as much. It was there in his scowl and his tight lips, and the lack of hugging. But she was exhausted and sore. All she wanted was to go home and cuddle up in bed next to him. Once she got her foot set in plaster, of course.

'You know you'll have to stay off this for a few weeks,' he said as the plaster set.

'I know.'

'No, I mean it. You'll have to rest it if it has any chance of healing properly.' He fixed her with a stern look which conveyed everything he felt about what had happened. It was more than obvious that he was annoyed she'd put herself in danger. All for the sake of someone who'd apparently walked back in through his front door whilst she'd been up on that mountain.

'Look, I've already had the lecture, Patrick. I think I'm suffering the consequences of not heeding the team's safety concerns. I'll be lucky if they let me back out there with them once I've healed.' Everything was beginning to catch up with her, and she was feeling emotional. One wrong move and she was going to have to take time off work and helping with the search and rescue team. It was going to be difficult not to have those things in her life when that was what had saved her after the breakup with Thom. Apart from Patrick, of course.

'You could have been seriously injured, Billie.' His voice was scarily quiet. She knew he was simply concerned about her. She was sure she'd feel the same if it was the other way around. Perhaps she was going to have to take more care in future. It was possible she took these risks trying to prove herself, but she didn't have to do that anymore. Patrick accepted who she was without her having to risk life and limb.

'I know. I know. I've learned my lesson. That doesn't mean I won't put myself out there again if someone is in need, but I'll be more careful in future.' She wanted to be honest and not make empty promises when they both knew she would always go the extra mile. Next time she'd simply remember to wear boots with a better grip when she was out in the rain. And call for help when it was needed.

'I just… I just can't do this again. I've already lost

Sinead, and now you're taking risks I simply can't live with, Billie.' Patrick's serious face was beginning to scare her more than the prospect of the giant moon boot she was going to have to wear for the foreseeable future.

'What are you saying, Patrick?' There was no way she was going to give up her place on the search and rescue team for anyone, as long as they would still have her back.

Patrick sighed. 'I think we should go end this. I can't spend my days worrying myself sick about what you're doing, if you're okay. I need to keep a bit of emotional distance.'

'So you won't care if I get hurt, then,' she bit back, wounded by the turn of events. At how easily he seemed to be able to end things when it was killing her.

'You know what I mean.' He gave her the lopsided smile that meant she could usually forgive him anything, but she was too hurt to play nice.

'You mean forget anything ever happened between us and pretend we never crossed that line in our friendship.' Easier said than done. How could she forget the best time of her life, or pretend her heart wasn't breaking every time she saw him? She would remember what they'd had together.

'You're a risk-taker, and after everything that has happened with Sinead, I simply can't be with someone like that.'

'I'm not going to change who I am.' No matter who was asking. She'd done that too many times to try and keep people happy, only for them to cast her aside regardless. As much as she cared for Patrick, she couldn't give up being part of the search and rescue team. It was the one thing outside of work that made her feel needed.

'I'm not asking you to. That's the point. I just think it's probably best to call it now before someone really gets hurt.'

Too late, Billie thought, as her heart shattered into a million pieces. Although they'd agreed to keeping things low-key, she'd thought that was simply to protect themselves. Deep down, she'd imagined it meant as much to him as it did to her. Obviously not if something as trivial as her falling was a deciding factor in ending things. He didn't want to worry about her, just sleep with her. That didn't say much for their friendship, either. Not when one person was more invested than the other.

'It's not going to be easy to just forget what happened between us.' She was going to need time to get used to the transition again and put her feelings back in the box they sprang from.

Patrick shifted uneasily. 'That's why I think it's probably best we only see each other at work. I think too much has happened to go back now. I think we should have a clean break. No more takeaways or cosy nights in. We wouldn't want to complicate things any more than we have already.' Patrick's words cut deep. Right to her heart. He knew he wasn't going to be part of her life anymore, a huge void she didn't know how she was going to live with.

These past few weeks, Billie had finally opened her eyes to the feelings she had for Patrick, only to find out they were wasted on him. Unwanted.

'No. I suppose not.'

Despite the suggestion they sever all ties now, there was a part of her still hoping he would change his mind again. Decide that he did want her in his life by any means, after all. But Patrick remained silent, looking as though he'd rather be anywhere else, and Billie swore she could actually hear those last pieces of her heart splintering into tiny, spiky shards stabbing at her chest.

'I guess I'll head home, then. I'll have to sort Fliss out.' Billie struggled to her feet with the cumbersome cast, desperate to get away before she made a fool of herself sobbing and begging him to love her.

'Can I call you a taxi?' Of course Patrick was still being chivalrous, even though he usually drove her home himself. She supposed it was a sign of things to come.

'No, that's okay. The chief is here. He'll give me a lift. I guess I'll see you around.' The smile wouldn't quite form on her lips, wobbling and threatening to give away how cut up she really was that this was the end of any relationship with Patrick.

'Take care, Billie.' It could have been wishful thinking, but she thought she heard a whisper of regret in his voice as she hobbled away. Unfortunately, it did nothing to ease the pain in her heart, which couldn't be patched up with plaster and bandages.

If this romantic interlude had taught her anything, it was that she still wasn't good enough for anyone. Someday she hoped to find someone who could love her for everything she was, and not just a gap filler until someone better came along. Although with those wounds ripped open again, she was beginning to think she was better off with Fliss. At least her dog loved her even if no one else apparently could.

CHAPTER NINE

PATRICK DIDN'T KNOW if it was better or worse that Billie was off work until her ankle healed. On the one hand, it meant he didn't have to see her every day and be reminded of everything he'd lost. On the other, it meant he didn't get to see her at all. Since he was the one who'd told her even friendship was not in the cards, he didn't feel it was appropriate to turn up at her house with grapes and a get-well card, but he was missing her. Life had gone back to simply work and sleep. Back to a house he didn't want to be in, alone every night. It was worse now than when Sinead had died because he'd had Billie to go home to at night, to share dinner with and climb into bed next to. All the things he'd taken for granted in the short time they'd explored life as a couple. He might have fooled her into thinking his feelings for her hadn't gone beyond the bedroom, but he hadn't been able to fool himself. Otherwise he wouldn't be missing the simple things with her like their walks with the dog or chatting late into the night. His worst fears had come true. In giving in to his feelings in the first place, he'd lost his friendship with her, and that was devastating.

Even today when he'd got the call-out as part of the air ambulance crew, he'd half expected to find her waiting with the search and rescue team up on the mountains. Everything in his life these days felt so much duller without her. As though losing her had taken the shine off anything good in his life.

'How's he doing, Doctor?' Terry from the dog search and rescue team approached him in the hospital corridor. Patrick and the rest of the team had worked hard to save the life of the man who'd suffered a cardiac arrest whilst out on a hike, and brought him back to the hospital.

'He's going down for bypass surgery. Thank goodness you were able to find him so quickly. It saved us a lot of precious time.' The man's arteries were so clogged he was a ticking time bomb. It was lucky that the teams had assembled so quickly to find him and get him treatment, or he would certainly have died up there.

'We're all just doing our jobs. I'm glad he's going to be okay though. I might take the new wife out for a drink to celebrate.'

Patrick's eyebrows rose at the mention of a 'new' wife when Terry had to be in his '60s. Not that he was being ageist, but the craggy features of the man didn't lend themselves to the idea of a young groom. 'Congratulations.'

Terry beamed, looking at the shiny gold band on his finger. 'Aye. We didn't tell anyone we were doing it, but we just thought why not. I've been living on my own since May died fifteen years ago. Then I met Linda, and she breathed new life into, well, everything. I never thought I'd meet anyone again, never mind get married, but you only have one life to lead. You have to grab a little bit of happiness where you can, or where's the point of living?'

'You're right.' The words almost caught in Patrick's

throat. They sounded hypocritical when he'd been doing the opposite of everything Terry was saying, and it was obvious which one of them was happiest.

He did have only one life, and he'd thrown away his chance of happiness. It wasn't as if he was content wallowing in his guilt and misery, either. The voice in his head which had been keeping him company over the years, whispering in his ear, telling him it was his fault everyone in his life had died, was quieter these days. He only noticed once Billie was gone. It was down to her, of course. She'd worked so hard trying to get him to believe he wasn't to blame, that he was being irrational, and it must have subconsciously sunk in. Not that it made any difference to his current situation. He'd still lost Billie.

Your fault, that little voice piped up in his ear, reminding him that he'd pushed her away. It was one thing he could blame himself for. For not being brave enough to tell her how he felt about her, or face up to it himself.

'You're a friend of Billie's, aren't you? It's just I have some of her and Fliss's belongings in the car. Once she gets that cast off, she's supposed to be moving to Turkey to train other search and rescue teams about working with dogs. I'm not sure I'll have a chance to see her before then. Could you get them to her?' Terry inadvertently picked up on who Patrick was currently thinking about.

'I, er…' Patrick didn't know what to say in response. They had been friends, but obviously Billie hadn't confided to anyone about what had happened between them. He didn't want to go into the details of her private life with someone he hardly knew anyway, or admit that he'd thrown away the best thing to ever happen to him.

Although that was the least of his worries right now. Billie moving abroad was news to him. Very unwelcome, earth-shattering news. It was one thing not seeing her outside work but quite another never seeing her again. That was a loss he didn't think he could bear. At least not without one last honest conversation with her.

'Sure. I can do that.'

'It's strange not having her around. I miss her. Even if she tests my patience with her daredevil antics at times.' Terry laughed, but Patrick was sure he worried about her safety, too.

'Yeah.' Patrick almost checked out of the conversation, thinking about what it was going to be like without having her around at all. It was bad enough at present.

After days like this when the adrenaline was still coursing through his body after a life-or-death scenario, there was no outlet for it. He had no one to talk to about it and process it with. Now that he'd handed over treatment to the hospital staff, he was going back to his empty home and thoughts of how different life could have been with Billie if he hadn't been so scared of losing her. More fool him when he'd lost her anyway. All he'd done was speed up the process and miss out on anything good they could have had together.

Apart from the mind-blowing sex and the joy of waking up next to her, he was going to miss the companionship most. That feeling of being part of something and knowing he wasn't alone. By letting her go, he was giving in to those feelings of guilt and punishing himself for something he knew deep down wasn't his fault. Even one more moment of happiness with Billie would be better than a lifetime of misery without her.

'Why don't we go to your car now, Terry, and get Billie's things? I'll drop them off on my way home.'

It would give him an excuse to go to her place, and perhaps he might actually find the courage to tell her how he really felt. That he'd been scared of her getting hurt, of losing her, and that was the reason he'd ended things. He'd been afraid of the strength of his feelings for her and the consequences that might arise from them. But losing her without even fighting for her, without ever risking anything for a future with her, seemed like the coward's way out. Billie was never afraid to take a risk, and now it was his turn. Or he would never forgive himself for not even trying.

'At least you'll be packing light,' Billie told a bemused Fliss, who was watching her sort through her wardrobe. She was going to need some light cotton clothes to bear the heat in Turkey.

Although she wouldn't be going for a while, preparing for the trip was at least giving her something to do other than sitting around moping over Patrick. Even if there was plenty of that going on, too. Everything in the house reminded her of him, even Fliss. In the time he'd spent here, he'd imprinted on everything. Not least this room. Hopefully a change of scenery would take her mind off him and maybe even help her move on. At the very least, assisting in the training of search and rescue dogs would keep her busy and make her feel as though she was achieving something. Perhaps if she focused on work, on the thing she was good at, she wouldn't feel like such a failure. When she was out there helping people, she knew she was doing something important. That she was wanted and appreciated. Things she no longer got from Patrick.

Fliss threw herself down on the bed with a sigh. She'd been a bit clingy since Billie's accident, and had also taken to lying at the front door at night. No doubt waiting for Patrick to show up for walks and belly rubs. Unfortunately, neither of them was going to be enjoying his attentions anymore.

'I miss him too, Fliss.' Billie sat down beside her forlorn pup and stroked her fur, wondering if Patrick had thought about either of them these past few weeks. It was the longest time she could remember they'd gone without speaking to one another. She'd been forced to go cold turkey, and she'd do anything for another fix.

Patrick had hurt her deeper than Thom, but that was because she loved him more. She'd realised that because of the ache in her chest and the void in her life, which was greater than she'd ever known. Not that it mattered when he'd made it clear he didn't feel about her that way. It only made the loss greater for her having had that time with him, realising how good they were together, only to find out it hadn't been what he wanted.

The doorbell rang downstairs, sending Fliss down barking excitedly and making Billie hobble down the stairs to answer it. She hadn't expected to see Patrick on the doorstep. Unprepared, her heart tangoed at the sight of him. Fliss, of course, was there to welcome him first, full of licks and tail wags. Billie knew how she felt but managed to restrain herself until she found out why he was there to see her.

'Patrick? What brings you here?' She folded her arms and did her best to look nonchalant about his unexpected appearance. After all, he was the one who'd dumped her. She didn't want to make him think he'd done the right thing by seeing how attached to him she'd become.

'Your, uh, colleague from the search and rescue team asked me to drop a few things over.' He handed her a bag with her personal effects and Fliss's harness inside.

Billie took the bag, that little bit of hope inside her that he might have been missing her, too, suddenly snuffed out. 'Oh, okay. Thanks.'

'I wanted to see how you are. I hope the ankle isn't too painful.' It was more painful making small talk with a man who'd shared her bed for two amazing weeks.

'I'll be glad when I'm out of this thing, but it's not too sore.' She lifted her boot, which was the only thing stopping her from physically moving on from Patrick, even if the emotional journey was going to be longer and more complicated.

'I heard about Turkey.'

'I'm just packing now.' She hoped that would give them both a good excuse to end this excruciating conversation. It was obvious he didn't want to be here, but had felt obliged to come.

'Oh. Could I come in for a minute?' It seemed he was determined to drag this out a little longer when the last thing she needed was Patrick back in her house if she was ever supposed to forget about him.

'I suppose so.' She stood back and opened the door wide for him, before leading him into the living room.

He didn't bother to sit down, and she didn't invite him to, hoping this would be over soon enough. There was no point in dragging this out when seeing him again was simply reminding her of everything she was losing.

'I just wanted to say something before you go. I'm sorry for how things ended between us.'

'I suppose it was inevitable. It was probably best to end it instead of waiting until someone else came along.' That was probably how it would have ended for her. With her madly in love with Patrick, and him dropping her as soon as someone better came along. She supposed she'd been saved that humiliation, at least.

'Do you really think that?'

'Don't you?' She was beginning to wonder what this was all about. Was he trying to ease his conscience or expecting her to forgive him for some closure?

He raked his hands over his scalp the way he did when he was stressed. 'No.'

Her heart leapt as though it had just been given the kiss of life, but Billie didn't trust herself to ask him what he meant. Not without hope evident in her voice. Maybe he hadn't given up on her after all.

'I don't want you to go to Turkey without telling you how I really feel, Billie.'

She swallowed hard. 'And how is that?'

'I'm in love with you. I probably have been for some time, but I was too afraid to admit it even to myself. After my father and Sinead, I was worried that by loving you, something bad would happen to you, too. I couldn't bear to lose you. To be responsible for you getting hurt. Then you had the accident…'

'And it freaked you out. I suppose I can understand that, but as I've told you before, Patrick, none of that was your fault. Accidents happen. You work in A and E. You know that as well as I do. We can't live our lives in fear, and I'm done pretending to be someone I'm not. If I'm not good enough for you the way I am, then I'd rather not be with you at all. I want a real relationship. Not friendship, not just sex. I want it all.' For once, she wasn't just going to go along with what she thought was wanted from her. She was laying out what she needed. If they weren't on the same page when it came to a relationship, then there was no point getting her hopes up that they could still be together.

'You were always good enough for me, Billie.' Patrick smiled as he took her hands in his, and the last vestige of her strength was ebbing away. 'That's why I didn't want to risk you getting hurt, but if you're willing to take a chance on me, I should be brave enough to do the same.'

'How do I know you won't walk out on me every time something happens? I can't go through that again.' As much as she was aching to have him back in her life or how his words were everything she wanted to hear, she had to protect what was left of her poor heart.

'I know. I promise I'll always be there for you, Billie. I've thought carefully about it, and if you'll have me, I'm willing to move abroad with you. I'll prove to you that you're everything I want.'

Billie frowned. 'Move abroad?'

'I heard about Turkey. I'm sure I can get a job there, too. I'll go wherever you want if you give me another chance.'

'You're willing to give up everything you have here? Your job, your house, your friends?' She couldn't believe that he would sacrifice everything for her if he wasn't sure she was worth it.

'Yes. So, how about it, Billie? Is there room for me in your life?'

'Always, but I think you should think again about quitting your job and selling your house.'

'Why?' His face fell, but Billie couldn't help the smile forming on hers.

'Because I'm only going to Turkey for two weeks. You're very welcome to come with us, but I intend to come back.' She was thrilled that he'd been willing to make such a commitment to her. It proved he wanted this to work between them. He wanted to be with her, wherever that might be.

He smiled, and she melted the way she always did. 'That's good to know before I made a fool of myself declaring my undying love for you.'

'Maybe that's something I need to hear.'

Patrick pulled her close. 'I love you, Billie. I want to be with you, and I'm not going to let anything get in the way this time. As long as that's what you want, too.'

'Yes, Patrick. You're all I want.'

He kissed her. In that moment of tender reconnection, Billie knew that she'd finally found her place in the world, and that was right here with Patrick.

EPILOGUE

Six months later

'I NOW PRONOUNCE you husband and wife.' The celebrant smiled, and Billie and Patrick took their cue for their first kiss as a married couple.

Their guests clapped, and barked, to show their approval of the match. They'd decided on a small gathering of friends and colleagues. Including their canine acquaintances, of course. Even Fliss had been part of the wedding as the ring bearer, with flowers and a little pouch containing the wedding rings attached to her harness. She was walking in front of the newlyweds now, tail wagging, as their new family made their way back down the aisle.

Billie had sent invitations to her parents and her brother, and though they'd congratulated her on her upcoming nuptials, they'd made excuses why they couldn't attend. She was strangely okay with it, knowing she'd reached out, but happy she wasn't going to feel under any strain to prove herself. Today she was free to be happy, and marrying Patrick was a dream come true.

He'd proposed during their trip to Turkey when they'd gone to help train other search and rescue teams. Patrick had been a great asset helping teach some basic first aid to the volunteers whilst she'd concentrated on the dog training.

Although it had been quick when they'd only just committed to a serious relationship, they both knew it was right. They'd known one another for years, shared a past, and had an emotional bond some couples never managed to create. Not to mention the passion they already knew they roused in one another.

'Happy?' she asked him as they emerged into the sunshine, guests throwing colourful confetti over them. The photographer captured the moment for posterity.

'Always, when I'm with you.' He kissed her again, already awakening that fire inside her she hoped would get a chance to burn later on when they were alone in the honeymoon suite at the posh hotel they'd booked for the night.

'Can we have the happy couple on their own, please?' the photographer instructed, trying to clear the crowd around them.

'Oh, we want Fliss in the picture, too.' Patrick called her over so she was sitting between them, and Billie adjusted the flower and pearl choker around her neck for the photograph before she decided she was bored playing dress-up.

Billie had decided to wear the dress Patrick had bought her for the awards dinner. Partly because she wanted to get plenty of use out of such an expensive dress, but also because it held happy memories of the night when they'd taken that leap beyond friendship. Following her lead, he'd worn his tuxedo from that night, too. Clothes they looked good in, but they also knew they were comfortable in, and that was what their relationship was all about. Being who they were, without worrying what anyone else thought.

Once they'd finished with the photoshoot, they got into their wedding car to make their way to the reception venue.

'I love you, Mrs James,' Patrick said, kissing her tenderly on the back seat of the limousine. 'Have I told you you look beautiful?'

'I think I heard you whisper "hubba hubba" when I walked in,' Billie said, laughing.

'Exactly. What do you say we skip this reception and go straight to the honeymoon?'

'It's tempting.' They both knew they wouldn't, but now that thought would be in her head for the duration of the evening. The anticipation would inevitably make it a night to remember once they did get to spend some time alone.

At present, they were mainly living at her place, with Patrick spending most nights in her bed. The plan for the future was to sell both houses and move somewhere new together. A fresh start.

As they pulled up outside the country manor, Patrick slipped a box from his jacket pocket. 'It's traditional for the groom to buy his bride a gift on their wedding day.'

He opened the box to reveal an exquisite pearl-and-diamond pendant necklace.

'It's beautiful,' she said, tracing her finger over the single pearl drop.

'Just like my wife.' Patrick took the necklace from the box and fastened it around her neck.

'Thank you.' It was such a beautiful, thoughtful gift, Billie felt herself welling up. Something which happened a lot these days.

'I have something for you, too, although it's not wrapped.' Billie fished in her little clutch bag and produced the positive pregnancy test she'd taken that morning. The result had taken her by surprise, too, but she'd started to realise that there was more than the stress of her wedding day making her tired and emotional.

She watched as Patrick's face changed from shock to absolute joy. 'We're having a baby?'

'We're having a baby.' Although it wasn't something they had planned right away, they had talked about having children. Billie knew this baby would be cherished no matter what.

Patrick pulled her into a hug, that toothy grin firmly back in place. 'Thank you for making my life complete, Billie.'

Although she couldn't get the words out past the ball in her throat, she felt the same. Patrick had given her everything she'd ever dreamed of, and today was the first day of the rest of their new life. Together. A family. More than enough for one another.

* * * * *

If you enjoyed this story, check out these other great reads from Karin Baine

Winter Nights with the Midwife
Spanish Doc to Heal Her
Tempted by Her Off-Limits Boss
Nurse's New Year with the Billionaire

All available now!

MILLS & BOON®

Coming next month

A FAMILY MADE IN THE ER
Alison Roberts

Of course, that kiss shouldn't have happened.

The very last thing either Isla or Jake needed was another complication in their lives.

So, by tacit agreement, it seemed they were both going to choose to ignore it. They'd both been a bit stunned in its wake, so it was no surprise that they just left it hanging a little awkwardly in the air and had gone into their separate bedrooms and shut the doors. Arlo was awake early the next morning so they weren't going to say anything that he might overhear, and Jake got his wish to go and see the driftwood teepee before they drove back to town in time to go and look at houses for sale.

But now it was several days later and still nothing had been said. If Jake was still thinking about that kiss as much as Isla was, he was managing to hide it very well. Their interactions at work since then had been completely professional but now they were heading towards another weekend where Arlo wouldn't be at school, and he apparently wanted to stay with Isla and play on the beach with Ben and that would mean Jake would be there at least some of the time and…

… and maybe that was why Isla was becoming even more obsessed with that damn kiss.

Continue reading

A FAMILY MADE IN THE ER
Alison Roberts

Available next month
millsandboon.co.uk

COMING SOON!

We really hope you enjoyed reading this book.
If you're looking for more romance
be sure to head to the shops when
new books are available on

Thursday 15th January

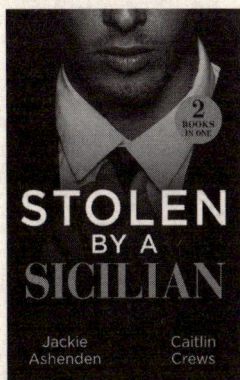

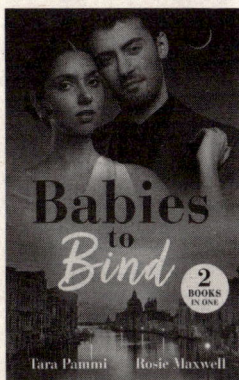

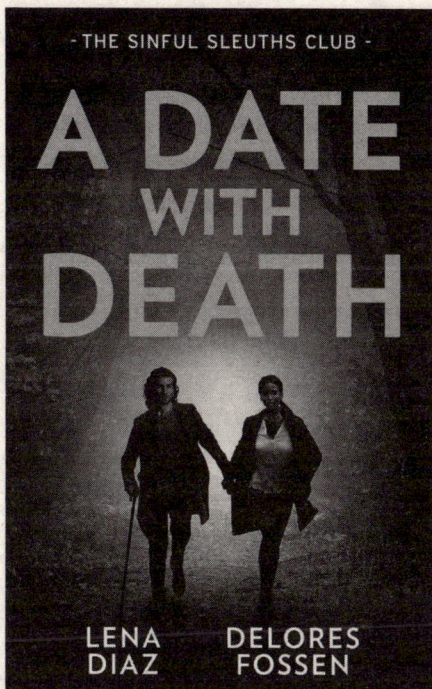